Where

THE NORTH SEA

Touches

ALABAMA

Where
THE NORTH SEA
Touches
ALABAMA

For Dirk, whose work has guided me thru the streets of the capital of the 19th century, the 20th century, and now the now the 21st, the capital of the wide green swamp out of which Patrick appeared and then sank back in.   Nov 2013

Allen Shelton

Allen C. Shelton

Texas

The University of Chicago Press
Chicago and London

Allen Shelton is associate professor of sociology at Buffalo State University. His book *Dreamworlds of Alabama* introduced the melancholic landscape in this work. He lives next to Billy Sunday's first church and an old Italian grocery store, and within a half-mile of an abandoned nineteenth-century asylum. There are no pine trees.

The University of Chicago Press, Chicago 60637
The University of Chicago Press, Ltd., London
© 2013 by The University of Chicago
All rights reserved. Published 2013.
Printed in the United States of America

22 21 20 19 18 17 16 15 14 13   1 2 3 4 5

ISBN-13: 978-0-226-06364-5   (cloth)
ISBN-13: 978-0-226-07322-4   (paper)
ISBN-13: 978-0-226-06378-2   (e-book)

DOI: 10.7208/chicago/9780226063782.001.0001

Library of Congress Cataloging-in-Publication Data

Shelton, Allen (Allen C.)
   Where the North Sea touches Alabama / Allen C. Shelton.
      pages. cm.
   Includes bibliographical references and index.
   ISBN 978-0-226-06364-5 (cloth : alk. paper) — ISBN 978-0-226-07322-4 (paper: alk. paper) — ISBN 978-0-226-06378-2 (e-book)   1. Shelton, Allen (Allen C.)   2. Alabama—Biography.   I. Title.
   F330.3.S53A3 2013
   976.1—dc23
                                                          2013005920

For Anne

CONTENTS

IMAGES

All works are in the collection of the author.

ACKNOWLEDGMENTS

On the back jacket flap of my book *Dreamworlds of Alabama* is a tiny photograph of me taken by my girlfriend Molly Jarboe. It's just larger than four first-class stamps pasted onto an envelope. It's black and white. I'm in a black T-shirt leaning against my desk with one arm sprawled across the front of the desk. The window behind me is filled with white light. My face is barely visible under a mop of hair. It looks like I'm sinking into a dark pool with my white forearm floating like a chunk of meat on the surface. I wanted to be hidden. I got what I wanted. The press pushed the exposure even darker than was intended. Perhaps they were clairvoyant. A reviewer in Mobile, Alabama, described it before reading the book as the worst jacket photo he had ever seen until he read the book and reversed his opinion—the photo was the exquisite complement for the text inside. It was all of a piece of dreamworlds. The English sociologist Graeme Gilloch described the photograph as "not an obscured image but a perfect image of obscurity itself."

The book sold modestly. Molly's name was inexplicably omitted from the credits. I gave some talks. At one I was confused for a dead banjo player from North Carolina who shares my name. The audience still listened politely in their seats. Whether there is an image of me on the cover of this book is unknown as I write this. If there is, Molly took it. I still want to be hidden, which may be an odd sentiment in a memoir. But this book is only partially about me. It's about my friend Patrik Keim. I have the hope that this book will be different. If it is, it is because of others. The name that comes first is Molly Jarboe, who was the closest to me in the production process. The next is Anne Costello, who read every word of the manuscript at least five times and whose eye helped to make sense of the world beneath Alabama.

The first block of this project was a five-hundred-word essay I wrote for *Version* in 2009. It was in this boxlike essay that Patrik had his first starring role in my writing and showed his abilities as a character that could carry a story. Edward Batchelder was the book's Brian Eno, helping to engineer the voice necessary for the project. He described my persona in the text as that of a patient in a mental institution with access to sociology books, Walter Benjamin, and a map of an Alabama valley. I live within a half-mile of an abandoned nineteenth-century insane asylum. It appeared in a piece Patrik did on electroshock treatments in the 1980s. It's not so far-fetched that I would have been infiltrated by a certain influence. A closer examination of my persona would show the writing group I worked with. There is a photograph of us in Buffalo, standing next to a giant grain elevator in the cold. I owe a large debt to Katie Stewart, Donna Haraway, Lauren Berlant, Anna Tsing, Stephen Muecke, Susan Harding, and Lesley Stern and the influence their works had on mine.

The book was put together haphazardly: a piece here, a block there, a stretch of unconnected writing strung across the big graph paper I write on. The project came together because others believed in the book. I thank Howard S. Becker, who showed me the possibilities of new representations in sociology; Jordan Crandall, Susan Lepselter, Laurence Shine, Karen Engle, Arthur Wilke, Staci Newmahr, Kalliopi Nikolopoulou, Charles Mancuso, Sean Pollock, Jonathan Welch, and Lucy Kogler of Talking Leaves Books; Gary Alan Fine, Jon Carter, Anderson Blanton, Derek Sayer, Yoke-Sum Wong, Matthew Dore, Natalie Latchford, Watoii Rabii, Sally Fehskens, Jennifer Ulrich, Justin Armstrong, Jonathan Wynn, and Michael Taussig for their work and support of this project.

By August 2011 I had a thing that looked like a book but no publisher. Jonathan Wynn brokered an introduction with Douglas Mitchell of the University of Chicago Press. Without that, this book would not have happened. I knew Doug's reputation as an editor and that he played drums with Howie Becker. I recognized him by his ZZ Top beard. We sat in a crowded ballroom in straight-back chairs two feet apart. A different editor had described my work as too Sheltonian. I reassured Doug that I had never read Shelton, never intended to read Shelton, and knew nothing of his work. It was an honor to work with Doug Mitchell, his associate Tim McGovern, and the manuscript editor, Ruth Goring. The time I spent with them reminded me how important editors who read and believe in style are for the future of books.

In the fall I flew into Atlanta to talk about the book's future. I was close to having a contract in hand. The next day I traveled by train to Birmingham. I was fixed in my seat by the red sumac leaves in the woods flashing through the window. Redness was soaking into me. My son picked me up at the station and took me for the night to Camp McDowell, where he works. The next day he drove me home. This would be the last time I saw my father alive. The final pieces of the book were falling into place. My memories of Alabama were separating from the place itself to become a hybrid landscape that didn't require flying into Atlanta to reach. I saw a different future for the costs I've paid. My dermatologist told me it was likely I would have died of skin cancer had I stayed in Alabama. My neck, shoulder, and forearms are severely damaged from working in the sun. After all these years, the redness has reached the inside of me. It was at this key moment that Donna Haraway, Graeme Gilloch, Charles McNair, Lesley Stern, and Stephen Muecke threw their weight behind the project. I acknowledge Michael Joyce, who showed me the possibility of a beautiful version of my work and introduced me to Ted's Hot Dogs; and Katie Stewart, who intervened time and time again to help make this possible.

Now that the book is done, something happened I wasn't prepared for. I was now exactly the same as my persona in the book. His life and mine converged in the thin layer of sun-damaged skin. One Allen had paid a cost as a manual laborer in the Alabama sun so the other could write this book. His memories were now mine in Buffalo. In 2007, three cases of whiskey were found buried in the dirt inside the hut Ernest Shackleton used in his 1907 Antarctic expedition. One bottle was missing. That bottle may already be behind the North Wind. The other bottles were frozen but still perfectly preserved. A consortium of scientists and distillers set out to meticulously reconstruct the whiskey at the molecular level. The marketing team nestled the reproduction whiskey in straw in a wooden box that resembled a coffin. I paid an outlandish amount of money for a single bottle. In the presence of Patrik's work, images of Nadja the cat, Andy Blanton and Sally Fehskens, Tyree Shelton, and Molly Jarboe I drank a toast, "to brilliant dirt and whiskey." A shot was saved for Michael Joyce when he returns to Buffalo with the snow thaw.

I would like to thank the Keim family for their support of this project in memory of my friend Patrick Keim.

Between Crooked Mountain and Patrik's

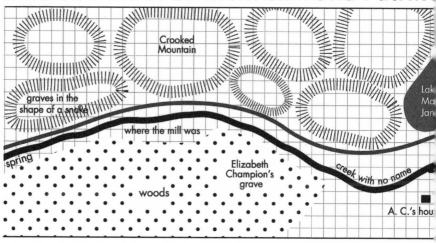

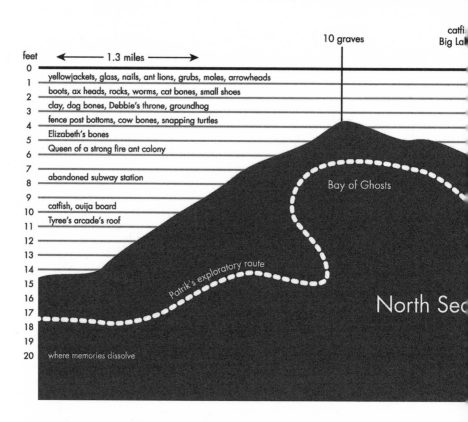

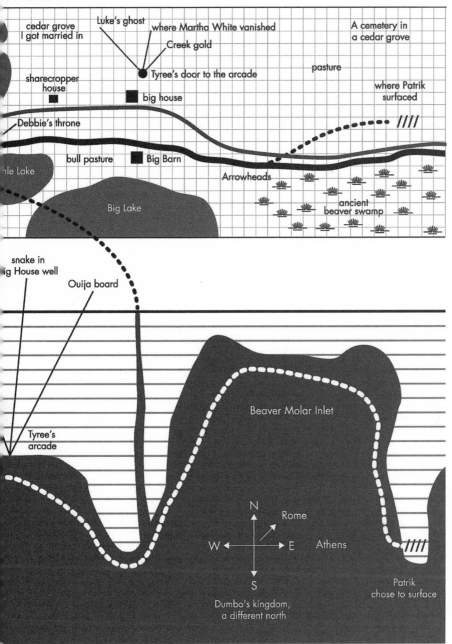

cedar grove
I got married in

Luke's ghost

where Martha White vanished

A cemetery in
a cedar grove

Creek gold

pasture

sharecropper
house

Tyree's door to the arcade

where Patrik
surfaced

big house

Debbie's throne

le Lake

bull pasture

Big Barn

Arrowheads

Big Lake

ancient
beaver swamp

snake in
g House well

Ouija board

Tyree's
arcade

Beaver Molar Inlet

N

Rome

W

E

Athens

S

Patrik
chose to surface

Dumbo's kingdom,
a different north

PREFACE

"It was late evening, when K. arrived. The village lay under deep snow. There was no sign of the Castle hill, fog and darkness surrounded it, not even the faintest glimmer of light suggested the large Castle. K. stood a long time on the wooden bridge that leads from the main road to the village, gazing upward into the seeming emptiness."

This is how Kafka opens his last attempt at a novel. It's also how I opened a short essay I wrote a long time ago about Patrik Keim, the artist who is the subject of this book. Kafka wrote several hundred pages but never found a satisfactory conclusion. The opening is the last moment of even a semblance of clarity. The dark fog that the surveyor K. sees surrounding the Castle seeps into him as well. Throughout the account K. asserts his occupation and his desire to fulfill the contract that drew him here. It's futile. The Castle has other designs. My own part was clear, I thought: I'm a sociologist; this is a book about an artist. I was wrong.

The time I first quoted Kafka in my essay, I thought I knew who K. was and what castle loomed on the hill. The artist Patrik Keim sometimes went by his initials, PK. It wasn't much of an effort to see him as a descendant of K. I was neither the author Kafka nor his mirror image, the character K. I was only someone who knew the artist who is the subject of this book. His work had been stuck on the walls of my apartments since 1983. I met him at an art show on the way to dinner. The art department was on the same side of the street as my office. I didn't even have to cross the street. The buildings were separated by an old cemetery. I was bored. I stepped in. We talked briefly and I left. It was then that this book began. I walked away completely oblivious to the fact that the book had already started.

Two years later I produced several handwritten pages as an introduction to his MFA thesis. He dutifully typed them himself and placed my pages side by side with his own work. They seemed oddly identical. And then I wrote nothing for twenty-something years. The next sentences appeared in a five-hundred-word essay for the online journal *Version*. That block of words became the basis for this book. I had the beginning and the end. "Patrik Keim is dead." "He was where the North Sea touched Alabama." The sentences were simple and direct. I thought I had finally reached solid ground. I hadn't. The book was waiting in a pile to be sent to my editor Doug Mitchell when I got a text message from my sister-in-law Jackie. She didn't say it, but her message indicated that the book wasn't over. "Don't know if U have heard. Your dad was in a one car accident this morning. He is at the hospital now having x-rays." It was becoming clear. I was still taking dictation. My work was still being organized around Patrik. He had opened his MFA thesis with this line: "My childhood allowed no sense of base or roots; our family was transplanted eight times coast-to-coast with my dictatorial father as he climbed the overachieving executive's ladder-of-success to the ultimate climax of the coronary death two years ago." Here I was, repeating his opening in the same way as if I were a character writing a story in someone else's story. I was only just now getting to the beginning of the story about Patrik Keim the artist.

In "Grief and a Headhunter's Rage," the anthropologist Renato Rosaldo is initiated by the his wife's death into the mystery of why headhunters take heads. She falls from a cliff while doing fieldwork in the Philippines. Called to her body, he experiences a revelation like Son House's in "Death Letter"—"I didn't know I loved her till they laid her body down"—only here the revelation isn't love. It's rage. Apparently I needed more dead bodies with which to think. That was sobering. I had thought my original account was straightforward enough. The book opened with the discovery of a seven-foot pine coffin in an old beaver swamp near my home in Alabama. The dozer operator uncovered it while scraping out a lake in front of a new two-story house. He was unnerved. He buried the coffin deeper into the dam. The homeowner wasn't immediately told. I found out several days later. He told me the coffin was over a hundred years old. He noted the hand-cut nails sunk in the heart pine. His estimate placed the coffin in the first stages of settlement in the valley, somewhere between the Creek War and the Civil War. Who was inside didn't concern him. He knew something wasn't right. "It wasn't buried in any cemetery," he told me. This much was hard reportage, like the temperature that day, the location of my home a half-mile up the road, or the presence, on a bluff overlooking the same beaver swamp where the coffin surfaced, of arrowheads dating back two thousand years. What the dozer operator wouldn't see was who was inside or the world underneath Alabama.[1] I knew who was inside the coffin. There, miraculously, was Patrik, who had died a few years earlier. He was real. The coffin was real. Miracles occur in Alabama. Now my father's accident was unexpectedly drawing me back into Patrik's narrative. Was the book becoming why I survived instead of Patrik? Still, the repetition was there and my part was clear. I was the one left to tell the story inside someone else's story.

After an apparently sleepless night, my father A.C. Jr. fell asleep at the wheel of his 2003 Jaguar and drove off the road at approximately forty miles an hour and hit a tree. It was just after seven in the morning. He broke his hip, possibly his wrist, and shattered his knee. He was eighty-three years old. That much was known quickly. The full extent of his injuries wouldn't be known for over a week. The EMTs arrived promptly. He was taken to the local hospital, near where I used to go parking in high school before the hospital existed. He was quickly transferred to Birmingham for surgery. One of my brothers spent the night with him in his room. He complained about the EMTs cutting his leather jacket off him. The surgery the next morning didn't go well. He lost a lot of blood. He was placed on a ventilator and put under sedation to facilitate his breathing. The doctors were still optimistic. Tentative plans were made about his recovery process. He would certainly be in a rehab facility for several months. Would he walk again? Probably, but with difficulty, the doctors said. Other injuries emerged. His back was broken. He was bleeding around his brain. He died two weeks after the accident. In between, there were only brief erratic moments of consciousness in which he came to the surface. My sisters are certain that he heard them tell him good-bye, that they loved him, and that he was going to heaven. That was Friday morning. It was ironic that it would end like this. A.C. Jr.'s last great project was to cut a landing strip into the top of a rise overlooking his house for a personal flying machine. His plan was to fly to his girl-friends' homes and set down in their driveways or in the street in front of their houses. Apparently, the craft needed only thirty to fifty feet to land. He had always wanted a pilot's license but had problems with dizziness. This craft didn't require a license, but it might have actually exacerbated his problem with vertigo. The fear was that he would crash. Was he in the air in his last dreams?[2]

The day was a blur. I taught classes. I had an espresso in the late morning. Friday night I went to the opening of *Love for Sale* at Studio Hart curated by my girlfriend Molly. I had a piece in the show called *The Abduction of Mary Janie*. It was the first art I had produced since the third grade. The piece was handwritten with a Pelikan fountain pen on yellow-green accounting paper that is no longer available. The paper measured seventeen inches across and was completely filled by three densely written columns running up and down the page. Small images, collages, and diagrams were spliced into the paper. Pieces of tape stuck them to the writing. The work described my mother's death. She died after a brain aneurysm. Now my father had joined her on the day of my show. Molly suggested it was too valuable to part with. I priced it at $50,000, an estimate of what it might have taken to change the days around her death and allow me to be with her. The gallery owner affixed a sold sticker on it. That tiny red dot on the title card was like a blood clot about to explode. I flew to Alabama early Saturday morning and rented a Toyota Camry at the airport. I've made this drive down Interstate 20 many times, almost always alone. It was unseasonably warm for February. On Highway 9, I saw men in shirtsleeves and T-shirts on their porches. At my sister's home only the fifteen-year-old Lucky Dog waddled up to greet me. The young dog Eli wasn't around. My sister Mary told me that Eli disappeared the day that my father went into surgery. He was presumed dead. Mary pined, "My friend says he went with Dad to heaven."

At the wake on Sunday afternoon the visitors were confused by my identity. Who was I? Only a few recognized me. I recognized only a handful as well. The funeral director joked with me about an incident from thirty years earlier. "That was the biggest grave I've ever seen." He was referring to the grave I dug for my grandmother Pearl. "I wanted to make sure the coffin fit," I protested. It was my first and only grave. Pearl was a slight woman. She could've been slipped into the ground like a letter through a mail slot. Her grave should've been my father's. He was a big man. His coffin was large and heavy. It was made of oak.

The Monday of the funeral was cloudy. It had turned cold, with the breeze coming out of the northwest. I shivered in a black Hugo Boss suit. I hadn't worn a tie. I walked around the grave before the service. The diggers, two men smoking off to the side, looked bored and mildly concerned about whether it would rain or not. They glanced repeatedly at the western sky. The hole had been dug to specs but without any grace. The mound of dirt to the side wasn't raked smooth and shaped. It was partially covered with a fancy tarp, like the carcass of a small whale. The grass around the grave was clotted with dirt hidden under the green Astroturf carpet. This was nothing like the grave I dug for Pearl. At the edge of the cemetery, crows were perched in the bare trees. The funeral party, dressed in black suits, milled around the granite slabs like fat wingless black angels, a partial sign of the resurrection. The coffin was lowered into the ground: it might be a lifeboat; the crows, a kind of sea bird. Near the entrance to the cemetery was a grave made of hundreds of seashells taken from the gulf. It was dated to around the Civil War. When I dug Pearl's grave, the spade I used left a scallop pattern on the walls just as if I were uncovering a bed of mollusks. Everywhere there was evidence of the sea. I watched the crows take flight like seagulls in a storm slowly blowing into paradise.

My father's house on top of the mountain was likely soon to be the bank's. The two mortgages couldn't be paid off. He had never paid anything on the principal, and the market value of the house had shrunk.

It was built to be a party house for sixty-year-olds. I had stayed in this house on one occasion when Molly and I had come back for a family reunion. We got the guest room. I never saw A.C. Jr.'s bedroom till after his death. I wandered through the room. I picked up his heavy watch from the dresser. Why wasn't he wearing it when he left headed for the accident? The watch was still working. It ran on a battery. The bed was unmade. I recalled certain pieces of furniture from my mother's house: a tall dark wardrobe with a padlocked chain strung through its guts. He stored his guns here. The room was very large and open. It would've been cool in the summer even without the air conditioning. A.C. Jr. preferred the cold. The room where I spent my time with my father was the living room. It had a vaulted ceiling and a monumental stacked-rock fireplace, and looked out onto the eastern valley toward Atlanta. He would sit here reading in a cushioned leather chair. This was his throne room. The Shelton crest was anchored into the rock fireplace. His Audubon collection adorned the walls along with Marine Corps paraphernalia. This was the last outpost of an empire reaching out from my childhood. On the day of the funeral, I sat alone in the house in this room in the leather chair for a half-hour, trying to feel what it was like to be my father interned like a fairy princess in a castle high on the mountain, growing old and alone. The heyday of his girlfriends was over. He was going blind and deaf. It wasn't hard to feel it. I called Molly in Buffalo. For a second I was a teenager again in his house, making a date. From his sitting room I could see over the entire world that surrounded my home in the Big House. I was in a flying machine soaring over the history of the valley. I too suffer from vertigo, no doubt a gift from my father's DNA. On the table in front of me was a map of this region made by a Confederate officer. The view felt like quicksand. I began to sketch the history of this world, putting myself in the third person.

This is the sketch I made the day my father was buried:

The beaver, long leaf pine, flint and quartz, swamp age: 1–1600. The first graves in the shape of a snake at the foot of Crooked Mountain are constructed. Beans and corn arrive from Mexico. De Soto passes by. The final collapse of the mound builders takes place as the blue celt is left behind in the dirt where the Big House will be built.

The mule, corn, cotton, creek, and iron age: 1799–1942. Revolutionary war veteran Tyree Landers arrives. The first Baptist and Methodist churches are established. The Creek Indian War brings Andrew Jackson and Davy Crockett to within miles of my home. The Big House is built with bright interior colors. Elizabeth Champion dies. The Trail of Tears sucks the Creeks out of the area. They leave gold buried in secret places. The Confederate officer John Pelham is killed. The map of this world is drawn by the Confederate officer. The original families that settled the valley go extinct and the exile of the dead begins. The woods overtake the Champion graves. Luke Coppick leaves the Big House. The Big Barn is built. The first telephone is installed in the Big House. The gold is taken out of the ground by an Indian with a metal detector. The long leaf pines are timbered.

The Black Angus, grass pasture, lakes, and steel age: 1947–1981. My grandfather A.C. enters this world from Jacksonville and buys the land that will become the Shelton farm. He builds the first lake and names it the Big Lake. The beaver swamps are drained. Luke Coppick sees a ghost. The subway project is abandoned in the back pasture for lack of funds. Bob Parker goes away. John Parker moves out of the Big House. A.C. III arrives and paints over the buttermilk paint in the Big House. County water is installed. Debbie's throne is cut into the creek bed. The Ouija board is buried in the ditch coming out of the spillway. Martha White goes missing. A.C. III begins his collection of Patrik's art.

The dog, lawn, swimming pool, and plastic age: 1985–2013. The first swimming pool is built. A.C. dies. Tyree finds his door in the sandbox. The chicken houses encroach. Coyotes arrive. Mary Pullen has a stroke in the garden behind her house. Kato the dog is assassinated. The farm is sold off. Mary Pullen and Mary Janie die. The first nondenominational church is erected. A.C. Jr. builds his house on the mountain. Patrik Keim is dead. A.C. III leaves the farm and goes on the road, chasing tenure-track jobs like a dog chasing cars. The Big House is sold to a lawyer. The road to the farm is named Shelton Road. No Shelton lives on it. A.C. Jr. dies in Birmingham. Eli the dog disappears in the woods around

my father's house. The last stronghold of A.C. III's home disappears
underground. A.C. III discovers the North Sea.[3]

Each house I had inhabited in this world, each of my elders, was now
somewhere else. The psychic interiors that had made these spaces my
mother's or my grandmothers' had sunk through the ground into another world. I can see this place. I can feel it. It makes my heart beat
faster. I am interacting there with my relatives in rooms that no longer
exist. My grandfather A.C. always suspected the existence of this other
world. He had wandered the pastures every day, looking for that abandoned subway station in the back pasture that would have allowed him
to go underneath to where the stars fell beneath Alabama. My father
and I are now part of this historical recording and our time here is over.
There is no equivalent to the Lisbon earthquake in this history.[4] The history is parsed out in tiny bits that become monumental only over time,
resembling a layer of sedimentary rock jutting out of a mountain slope
covered in brown leaves and pine straw. In the distance I can hear water
lapping at a shore. Alabama was once underwater according to fossil evidence. The prehistoric is coming back. This new Alabama has a shoreline
bordering a cold sea with no resemblance to the Gulf of Mexico. Kafka
ends *The Castle* in midsentence with the fog even thicker than in the
opening: "She held out her trembling hand to K. and had him sit down
beside her, she spoke with great difficulty, it was difficult to understand
her, but what she said" . . . and then nothing. The rest of this sentence has
vanished into the same fog that opened the book. It's where the North
Sea touches Alabama.

Wüstige See.

Where

THE NORTH SEA

Touches

ALABAMA

36 Etudes

Patrik Keim is dead. I have the obituary. Patrik was a minor southern artist whose career was already in decline when he died over ten years ago. He never sold enough work to support himself. Little of it has survived. Yet he was a strikingly brilliant, if erratic artist. I knew him. He's part of a bestiary that surrounds me that includes my mother, my father, and my grandfather A.C. and his coat; the dogs Red Cloud, Diva, and Ruah; Pearl, who played solitaire as if she were playing the piano;[1] three horses, a ginger-colored pony, and innumerable lizards and frogs; the men I worked with on the farm—the skinny John Parker, Harrison Murray who taught me how to build barbed-wire fences, and Paul Williams the corn crusher; the delicate cat Nadja, who sat on my lap; the enormous rhinoceros beetle I found on the road; the lilac under the pecan tree; the black cat Eli, the gray-haired woman who was my favorite Sunday school teacher, and my son's cat Kudzu who was mangled by dogs; the boy who lived across the street from my grandmother Mary Pullen and the hundreds of bees and fireflies I caught in peanut butter jars around her house; the bobcat who screamed in the back hollow; the red-haired girl who fell out of a truck; the man with a handlebar mustache; and the rattlesnake I killed on the hillside near the Back Barn. The snake felt like velvet in my hands. They're all dead. I owe each of them something.[2]

Patrik would have immediately recognized that he was the only artist on the list. He would've made a joke to cover how flattered he was. He was vain. "Shouldn't I be listed with the dogs?" He had written a short book of poetry called *Dog Eat Dog*, so this wasn't a stretch. He considered himself kind of an expert on dogs. His work was unlike any artist's I'd met till then. I'd only seen beautiful art. His didn't even pretend to be beautiful. Patrik's works of rot, decay, and sharp glass exhilarated me. I remember wondering where you could put such work. It couldn't come into the house. His work was like a mangy hound. The frames were flimsy and secondhand, held together with electrical tape. Violence wasn't restrained. It bloomed ecstatically. It seems he was right after all. He should've been listed with the dogs. I couldn't see how his work could coexist on the same plane as my mother's red Victorian loveseat or even alongside my Mexican surrealist print. I was innocent. The work was a view into a different kind of supernatural. There were no angels singing. His was a dusky world marked with red splashes. Everything was turning into a fine dust. But there was a weird vibrancy and even hints at redemption, that the dryness would be burst by a bubbling spring and the rotting pieces he used in his installations restored. The red splashes that often marked his work could be seen as a hope for a different future. Now it's easy to see how Patrik's works and the red velvet loveseat my mother gave me were entrance points to another world. What world was it? The Victorian writer George MacDonald describes a place where the dead go to wait for Jesus and the resurrection. It's a pleasant place, but often lonely. The dead sometimes climb up into the branches of a huge tree from which they can see those they loved in the land of the living going about their lives. The look is from a long way off. Contact is impossible. For each of us, MacDonald reports, a crowd waits on the other side.

In a rare moment Patrik produced something almost lyrical. It was the first piece I acquired from him. I felt like I'd become an art collector. The piece was a framed eight-by-twelve-inch collage. It had no title. It cost me nothing. Patrik asked me if I would take it. I offered payment. He refused. I think he anticipated that I would be his historian and archivist. In a note he writes: "I have decided to leave Athens again— probably in February. Would you like to have a few small things sent to you? (Otherwise they will be discarded) Sure you'd like to be the official P. K. Archives! If there's anything in particular that you remember and would like to have let me know." The frame is a plain smooth black molding. The first layer is a sheet of off-white paper with black flashes occasionally stabbed across it in broad strokes, particularly in the upper left corner. The second layer of paper, laid in the center of the frame, is a piece of sheet music turned on its side so as to turn the musical lines into

the intricately woven bars of some kind of prison. The title is *36 Etudes*. In the top just off center is a cow's pink stomach turned inside out like a skinned, yawning penis. From its mouth pours a trail of black blocky lines that wind toward the lower right quadrant of the frame and into the right ear of a bald, shirtless man. He has sagging breasts. His arms seem extraordinarily long. His hands are spread like butterflies over the stumps of his legs amputated at the knee. He is blindfolded. He's sitting in a rounded, cushy chair tilted to the front and side that makes it seem he's about to slide like Jell-O into open space. Out of this left ear, the same blocky bars—now red—start up again and march in a regular interval to a tractor with a driver plowing up the bottom left quarter of the frame.[3] A sheet of graph paper is laid on top of the music. The center of the graph paper is cut out so it frames the musical bars, and the hole is colored with what looks like black smoke.

At the very center is a Soviet-era tractor. There is no visible driver. The tractor is stationary, waiting to be turned on. If it could be turned on, what would happen? At the end of the first chapter of *Capital*, Marx imagines a table coming to life, or rather he senses the liveness inside it staring out at him from what he calls a grotesque wooden brain.[4] Seen with discernment, what appears to be an inert commodity is more akin to a prison cocked up on wooden legs waiting for the right moment to "dance." What Marx meant by dance is a sly reference to the popularity of table-shaking during séances. This was an indication for Marx not of specters but of the liveness trapped in the prison house of objects. In Marx's conceptualization, the entire room, with every object in it, could soon be dancing. A dancing table is just one moving castle in a swarming landscape. Turned on, the tractor's relationship with the music would become clearer. Is the music an artifact accidentally uncovered in the turned dirt, or is it the tractor's job to plow it up? Patrik's designs are caught between these two poles. This is what kept him alive as an artist. Toward the end of his life this magnetic field was broken. If he could've started the tractor, he would've plowed the music under. The legless man is a prophecy of his inability to move.[5]

While Patrik grew more locked in space, I zigzagged across the country from job to job for nearly ten years. I became unable to distinguish between certain dreams and memories. I have this memory of driving into a small town in western New York. I parked my Toyota truck on the square. I knocked on a door next to a tavern. A woman came down. I no longer remember anything about her. Upstairs, overlooking the street, I sat down to a dinner party. I didn't know anyone there. Whether I dreamed this or it really happened, I couldn't tell, but I remember Patrik's work. It was faithful. The filmmaker David Lynch (Patrik admired *Blue Velvet*) took an account of two estranged brothers in the Midwest. One brother travels five hundred miles on a riding lawn mower to see the other on his deathbed. Lynch pushes the eeriness into the landscape surrounding the lawn mower. At night the silos hum. A dead possum gets caught in the mower's blades. After Patrik gave me the piece, I'm sure he forgot about it, though the cow's organ, the amputee, the easy chair, and the tractors continued to reappear in his work. He was haunted by these things. What moved to the background was the music. Once the tractor was turned on, it could've been used as an escape vehicle or to push the eeriness away from himself. Either one of us could've traveled a different five hundred miles toward the other. Neither of us did. This piece hung on a nail in the Finger Lakes district of western New York, Walla Walla, Tacoma, Des Moines, Las Vegas, South Bend, and now finally Buffalo. Patrik's piece was a map of my future travels out of Alabama following that same blocky trail that initially drew my grandfather Eli north. He went to school at Columbia. Pearl had gone with him. But their time there was temporary. They returned to Alabama with a mahogany and wicker living room set that now sits in my apartment in Buffalo. How could Patrik have known about Eli?

On the surface it didn't make sense. How could Patrik become an integral part of my world from Alabama? He did. Perhaps that's all there is to it. But there are perplexing continuities. Mary Pullen, my grandmother, was a librarian.[6] Patrik worked as a librarian at the University of Georgia. Like my other grandmother Pearl, he collected stray bits of paper that he had filled with lists and notes. Pearl stowed them away in books, creating unintentional collages. On a blank counter check from the First National Bank, Pearl had copied how each of the apostles had come to his end for a Sunday school lesson and then stored the slip of paper in Xenophon's *Anabasis* along with a note detailing the short history of the Confederate officer John Pelham buried in the city cemetery. This was part of a garden club meeting. The date and the house address were written across the top. She had unintentionally constructed a history of her home and the shifts in the sacred world by adding John Pelham and Xenophon to the list of the apostles. It was a bloody list. Matthew died in Ethiopia. He was killed by the sword. Mark made it to Alexandria to be dragged by horses through the streets. Luke was hanged in Greece. John was boiled in oil but survived. Then he was exiled to the prison island Patmos. Later he was freed and died an old man in Turkey. Peter was crucified upside down outside Rome. James was thrown from the southeast corner of the Temple a hundred feet to the ground. Then he was beaten to death with a fuller's club. James, son of Zebedee, was beheaded at Jerusalem. Bartholomew was whipped to death in Armenia. Jude was shot with arrows. Matthias, who replaced Judas, was stoned and then beheaded. Judas hanged himself from the branches of a redbud tree.[7] Andrew was crucified. Thomas disappeared in India.

Patrik would've read this as if it were a recipe book. The ways he imagined his death can be inferred from his work. In a collage there is a body, face down, arms slightly spread out from the torso. The appendages are chopped into pieces. Another collage shows a list of shock doctors in the United States. Two doctors are in Buffalo just down the street from me. I can easily see a convulsing Patrik strapped into a chair. I'm sure he could, too. The image was probably just under his eyelids. Sharp edges abound in his work. However, the very means he used to exit is never depicted. God, it seems, was torturing Patrik by keeping him alive. His bloody martyrdom was temporarily rescinded. It looked for a time like he would become more like Thomas than Peter and just disappear. Patrik would not have that. His long retreat to his small apartment and death wasn't glorious. He was coming apart toward the end. He became increasingly moody. He abused his medications. He didn't show up for work at The Globe where he bartended and did odds and ends. He was fired from the bar. He was targeted by boys with golf clubs. And then there was always the depressing lack of money. I couldn't send him any. And he wouldn't have taken any anyway. My bills from my divorce and ricocheting from job to job across the country were astronomical. My retreat ended in Buffalo, hardly glorious, but I was more like Xenophon than Patrik.

Xenophon was an Athenian mercenary who led the retreat of ten thousand Greek mercenaries from Mesopotamia to Greece after the defeat of their employer in a dynastic dispute for control of the Persian Empire. He describes this in his book *Anabasis*. Xenophon was a student and a friend of Socrates. He was with him at his death. Exiled from Athens during the Peloponnesian War, he was employed by Sparta and given an estate. I keep the copy in which I found Pearl's slip of paper on my desk. Xenophon survived defeat. He was no martyr. No statues were erected after his death.[8] In his great work there is no visible nostalgia for Athens, where he was born. Instead he conceptualizes himself as a Greek. Around me as I grew up in Jacksonville, Alabama, were statues of dead martyrs. In the town square there was a Confederate soldier staring north. Off to the side was a large rock with an iron plate hammered into its face commemorating the Confederates who died in the hospital set up in the Presbyterian church. In the city cemetery there was a delicate Italian marble statue of John Pelham. Pelham was a local Confederate hero. He showed a genius for artillery and the ladies. He was killed in 1863 in an indecisive skirmish at Kelly's Ford. His body was purportedly shipped home to Jacksonville covered in wisteria cuttings from his admirers. He was twenty-six years old, still boyish and extremely handsome. This was the origin of wisteria in Jacksonville, a thick skeletal prosthesis of vines and blooms that now shares space with the hickories and lilacs and cat briar. The effect was to start the creation of an entirely new dreamworld of Alabama, unimaginable if John Pelham had lived. His death baptized the landscape. His contribution as a living man was his astute use of horse-drawn artillery. Dead, he was as a doorway between this world and the supernatural. I would see him whenever I accompanied my grandmother to the cemetery to tend the grave of her husband, Eli Landers. Pelham changed the shape of haunting in Jacksonville. The purple clusters of blooms entered the local botanical mythology, along with the Christlike dogwood buds and the red flowers of the Judas tree. John Pelham would step up alongside Jesus in this Protestant world to command the dead. I waited for my commands in this world. The Civil War was the great trial. It defined the women of my family from my mother back to my grandmothers. The men seemed untouched.

Patrik worked on the outsides of books as my grandmother Pearl did on their interiors. Titles became parts of new bursts of writing. Their stylized prints were surrounded by Patrik's broader, wetter strokes, and then, to hold everything in place, he bound them in layers of rubber bands. The effect was to make the insides of books a sealed-off world in which the cover was like a door.[9] By themselves these examples are terribly thin, even desperate. Pearl wouldn't have added Patrik to the list of dead men. His books wouldn't have ended up in Mary Pullen's library, but each of these women was preparing me to see Patrik when I first encountered him as a graduate student in Athens, Georgia. I was on my way to supper downtown. There was an art show in a gallery on the way. I stepped in. I'm not sure I even remembered his name the next day. But why would I? He didn't initially resemble either John Pelham or Xenophon. But something was already different. The installation I saw was a tower of glass panels splattered with blood, like an accident on the farm when a small bird would impale itself on barbwire or when I cut my hands on the tin sheets for the barn roof. Patrik was standing by the door to the bathroom bent over, trying to drink from the water fountain with his heavily bandaged hands when I first saw him. I had been fitted for this moment. In Franz Kafka's famous parable of the law with which he sets up the conclusion to *The Trial*, the protagonist Joseph K. listens to the parable alone in a strangely dark church. K. has been involved in a mysterious court case. Increasingly he's alone. The exact nature of the charges is unfathomable. The court system exists outside of the state in the shadowy parts of his city, but its reach and power are astounding. For Joseph K. this parable is an announcement of his guilt and execution. The door to the law is fitted to a particular person and that person alone. In his account the penitent never passes through the door. He memorizes the guard down to the tiniest detail. He recognizes the fleas in his beard. As he's dying he asks the guard why no one has gone through the door. As the guard shuts the door he says, "No one else could gain admittance here, because this entrance was meant solely for you. I'm going to go and shut it now."[10] There isn't the slightest hint that either the guard or the penitent peered through the door left ajar. If they had, wouldn't it be the place the Victorian fairy-tale writer George MacDonald called the land behind the North Wind on the other side?[11] Mary Pullen loved this book. Wouldn't the land on the other side, like the door Kafka imagined, be fitted to the individual outside it and that individual alone? Kafka's account doesn't take up this question. The crowd on the other side waiting for me to cross over is as peculiar and idiosyncratic as Pearl's inadvertent collages or Patrik's intentional ones. No one but me could enter through this particular door where Patrik is the guard. And if anyone else could catch a glimpse through the door, wouldn't the landscape be an empty blank space? While for me it would teem with color and the green ankle-high clover from A.C.'s heifer pasture.

It was an old world. I grew up in the foothills of the Appalachian Mountains, themselves remnants of a former world. I lived in three different houses. My family rented a small new house across the field from the former ruling family of this small college town. A giant bloodhound lived with us. His name was Archibald. My mother's parents Eli and Pearl had built a house in an open field at the edge of town in the 1930s. Now the field was an established neighborhood with spreading trees. A.C. and Mary Pullen lived in a lumbering antebellum mansion surrounded by magnolias. There was an enormous oak tree in the front yard and a corn-field in the back. I moved among all three of these houses. A.C. sold this house in the 1970s, and he and Mary Pullen moved over the mountain to a farm in a small valley in northeastern Alabama, six miles east of Jack-sonville, nine miles south of Piedmont along a corridor running north to south along the southern spur of the Appalachians. There once were great long-leaf pine woods whose remnants are still scattered across the valley and hills, beaver swamps, and muddy creeks with big alligator tur-tles. The largest hill we called Crooked Mountain. It was a steep twenty-to-forty-minute walk up. Someone had built a cross at the very top out of pine slabs, making the whole mountain a grave. A.C. had bundled to-gether a thousand acres of swamp, woods, mountain land, and pasture for a herd of three hundred registered Black Angus cows.[12] Patrik never saw this place alive but he knew me in its last days. He sent postcards to this address. A.C. gave me an old house known as the Big House and two acres as a wedding present and accomplished something he hadn't anticipated. He provided me the last space I would recognize as a home. After A.C.'s death and the cutting up of the farm, I bought thirteen acres from the estate. Patrik's work started to appear like fire-ant mounds on the walls of the Big House. My three-year-old son would lie on my writ-ing desk and look at his work. The house was built in the 1840s. There had been a succession of owners before A.C. acquired it in the 1940s. The huge pine beams holding up my house were alive when Lisbon collapsed in the great earthquake in 1755. Inside the house it was the same. Every-thing was ancient. Church pews from the nineteenth century, unknown relations in mounted black-and-white photographs, a walnut drop-leaf table from the 1840s my wife and I had acquired from an old couple that ran an antique store in town, my grandmother Pearl's mahogany and wicker living room set from the 1930s all worked together to reset the clock in the house itself. Behind the walls were decades-old wasp nests. It wasn't clear even what year it was. I had mule skulls hung on cedar posts along the driveway. A chain of rusted and corroded ax heads was strung on the shed door. Inside the shed were ancient machines, a Little Giant foot hammer, cotton scales, and piles of iron and steel tools in wooden boxes that resembled coffins.

What gave this world age was the nearness of things coming to life and dying. Along the roof joists young wasps crawled through their paper shells and clung to the nest. Inside the toolbox a monkey wrench had turned red, the iron and oxygen meeting on the surface. The cornered timbers were pockmarked with beetle holes. A bumblebee was loudly buzzing while the English spade hung quietly on a nail. The ax heads were breaking back into iron flakes. The corner posts were being chewed into a dry dust inside their own thin skinlike sheathing. I put my finger into a post and wiggled it. To the wood, it must've felt like a beetle grub. It was already a world designed for memory and for forgetting. Now Patrik is there even though he was younger than I. It took three months for me to receive the news of his death, which meant he lingered in a limbo around me as alive as ever. An acquaintance forwarded the obituary from the Athens paper with a short note printed on a Post-it. "I think he was a friend of yours?" He was. He was thirty-seven years old. He used to visit Amsterdam regularly. In high school he toured Europe. Other than these excursions his trips were purely imaginary. If he could've, he would have taken the same trips in a decade other than the 1980s or 1990s. Dead, maybe he can do that. Ideally it would've been the world portrayed in 1930s movies. Patrik was a man out of time. He would've been far more at home in a time of luxury liners and fine leather suitcases. There is a small plaque commemorating him in the art department at the University of Georgia. There is a scholarship in his name. Still, he wasn't well known outside of a particular set of years in Athens, Georgia. He was part of the scene like REM, Pylon, and the Barbecue Killers. He was an integral part of this world and like many of the bands just as ephemeral. Somewhere there must be a photograph and a short write-up of who he was. He died before Facebook. Even with all the sharp edges in his work, both literal and metaphorical, his artistic endeavors seemed indeterminable, as if they were dust particles slowly forming into a rain cloud. Again there is the water. His own death was no less indeterminable. Could Patrik have guessed I would stock a museum of his work in my apartment?

I wouldn't have. His work draws a line through my biography. It wasn't Patrik's death that rearranged my world. It was his appearances. Patrik left early.

The French anthropologist Marc Augé opens his book *In the Metro* with a childhood memory in which a ghostlike figure haunts an entrance to the metro. Augé, too, sees his memories waiting for him across a threshold. The figure guarding the door is a German soldier in a gray cap just emerging from the subway. It's the early years of World War II. The author and his family had fled Paris to the southern countryside but have returned to the city. The Germans were always ahead of them. This soldier was the first materialization of what had been "a diffuse presence." There is the vaguest hint of emotion in his recollection. It's just a fleeting moment. Unlike Marcel Proust, who through the madeleine reclaims or projects a world bursting with color, Augé uses the German soldier to introduce a flickering nonplace, a concept he introduced to describe hypermodern spaces infused with rationality, nonspecificity, and impersonal exchanges. His portrait of the metro is touched with stray bits of the former world and the personal, as if the brightly colored subway map that fascinated him as a child was lit with pieces of himself and others caught in the circuits. The metro provides a spinal column for a vanishing or unseen body of the author's memories. What sentiments there are remain private. What Augé means by the metro becomes allegorical, hinting at another Parisian theorist's allegory, that of the exiled German Walter Benjamin, who lived in Paris amid his famous arcades. How easily and quickly the silhouette of the soldier fades into the gray camouflaged background, indistinguishable from the larger landscape.

Patrik grew up skipping across the country. He lived in Tennessee, Texas, Louisiana, California, Iowa, New Jersey, and Georgia. His father was in business. Like Patrik, I lived on each coast and in between. He escaped the Civil War. I didn't. It didn't figure in his world. He was oriented to Europe and the Holocaust. On the base of the statue of the Confederate soldier in Jacksonville's town square is an inscription: "Men may change but values never do." Surrounding the unnamed soldier are World War I machine guns. The guns are pointed at the soldier. Off to the side is a piece of artillery from the Spanish-American War or the early years of World War I. I played here as a kid. It's a strange mixture of wars and dead as if the unknown designers of this memorial were, like me, trying to reproduce the same whirlpool that draws John Pelham, Patrik, and Xenophon together. Alive, Patrik wasn't part of this. But his escape was only temporary. In his death he moved inexorably into this world. His figure was never mineralized like that of John Pelham. Nevertheless, he stands there in the same landscape, another casualty of the war. His letters are part of a collection of letters I have. The oldest is from a relation who fought under General Lee in Virginia. He was at Gettysburg. There he dreams about fields of wheat. His unit is redeployed south with the assault on Atlanta by General Sherman and the Union Army. He contracts yellow fever. He is twenty-two years old and skinny. He dies in 1863 in a hospital outside Atlanta, twenty-one miles from his home. His sister and mother miss seeing him by a day. Patrik's correspondence is part of this collection. In the letters, postcards, and stray bits of writing I have from him, there are messages that only now cut me as I trace the lines on paper. What was unexceptional at the time is now profound though each is insignificant, a trivial piece of news. In one note Patrik writes: "love, Pat." In another a name appears that touches off a fuse of emotions; I had forgotten Patrik knew of her. He addresses me as "Doc Shelton" on the back of a postcard. Then there are the cracks in his world that I now know reached the point where he took his own life. Reading Patrik, I feel him seeping into me. I can feel his sadness filling my arms, legs, and torso with wet sand. The messages are a siren's song. In my world the figure of Patrik is the gray figure that emerges from the background and then disappears, only to reappear over and over again at other points. He even sent me a postcard to remember this. He is the gray soldier.

Expatriation

I met Patrik in 1983. He was dead by 1998. The coyotes had arrived in northeast Alabama that same year. It's now 2011. I'm approaching the point where I will have known him longer dead than alive. But even in those first fifteen years I was already practicing what it would be like if Patrik were transfigured. He existed then as now in the half-light of memory, in the form of the postcards he sent me. His art hung on my walls. These things have persisted largely unchanged while Patrik aged

considerably before his death. His work was already old. I saw the same representations every day. What is curious though was how Patrik, even when he was alive, was slipping back in time to points before I knew him. He seemed quite at home even in those alien environments, as if he were born to be there. If Patrik had had his wish, he would have met my mother before he died when she was a teenager riding her horse over Crooked Mountain with her dark hair tied up in a red scarf. They died in the same year. My mother had no notion of Patrik. She had looked straight at his works on my walls without comment. And while she never said one thing about them, they were extraordinarily different from anything in her house. But there was some kind of imperceptible effect. She gave me a toad skeleton in a plastic sandwich bag, a perfect Patrik installation, to be added to my bookshelf filled with her father's books, an abacus from Japan, a child's microscope, a pair of seventy-year-old glasses, a locket with velvet lining and a portrait of an ancestor in Confederate uniform, nineteenth-century medical books, my grandfather's pocket knives, and other relics from my childhood. The cabinet with its glass doors formed a miniature city, or what would've been recognized in the Renaissance as a type of memory palace, something like a spatial computer designed to hold memories. Each piece was connected to a network of memories and affects whether I could directly articulate them or not. Together they were a city that was unrecognizable to me except for the feeling it left in me. Patrik was indistinguishable from these memories. He was at ease with my grandparents over lunch in this world. He played with my dogs and got hair on his clothes. He was already the color of my memories.

Patrik's own work had a limited color palette with few exceptions. He favored red, which was almost always blood red, sometimes his own. But the red wasn't permanent. It turned to brown. His work was normally the color of black-and-white TV serials. His de-emphasis of color emphasized a dreamlike setting, almost a theater, where porn, scenes from 1950s physical fitness and military journals, and Renaissance portraits interacted on the same plane. Without color, his work resembled a compost heap of rotting artifacts which he continually turned. Where he utilized color was in his altered postcards, and even these were the smallest number of pieces he produced. I have a postcard rack filled with dingy cardboard postcards with black-and-white collages glued to the surface. Nothing is written on their backs. They were produced to sell for a dollar apiece. They didn't. The postcards with color he purchased. He filled them with writing and sent them through the mail. But the color wasn't his making. One could say he attacked color. But what was he poking at? Often the postcards were deeply personal, as if he thought that out in the open he was hidden. The color was meant as distraction, but his alterations turned even these commercial images into psychic portraits of their sender. I'm not the only one who received these cards. His niece would get them. She saved them as well. What Patrik was attacking was the pristine surface of things. The early twentieth-century French theorist Émile Durkheim would've grasped Patrik's stabbings in primitive Georgia as part of an articulation of the sacred similar to what he found in aboriginal Australia. The churinga was a sacred object made of wood or stone. The markings on it activated the sacred and anchored its place in the totemic landscape. Patrik's alterations were an attempt to score into the sacred, to torture it. He revered the sacred in the aftermath of violence, not before.

The mark Patrik used was a variation of the /.[13] In *36 Etudes* the slash is muscular. It looks like a blocky carpenter ant or the amputated torso of a man. The mark always appears in multiples. In one piece it is a trail of ants. In another it is a jagged foundation for building or a crown placed on the top of a sunken building. The blocks are a force field. They are directions for where knives and scissors will cut. Stood up, the mark is slender but no less violent. It appears as a warning and a countdown. In the installation *Asylum, Asylum* the slashes are long strips of time cards taped together. They hung around Patrik at a desk. It's one of his most overtly violent pieces. At the center of the body-sized maze, where the walls are covered with his writing scrawled around in white paint, is a bed covered in blood. There, where the neck of the sleeper would have been, was a giant cleaver in a pool of dried blood. The slash was an indication for Patrik of both violence and the sacred.

Howard Becker[14] read an early version of this manuscript. Becker was a student of Robert Parks, Louis Wirth, and Everett Hughes, three legendary sociologists in the early part of the twentieth century in Chicago. He has equaled them. He was curious about Patrik Keim's work. He googled him. Nothing immediately popped up. He found the Facebook page of a teenager in Birmingham, Alabama. He was unlikely to be the Patrik I was writing about. Becker then made a pivotal decision. He redefined what sociology could be. It didn't matter if there even was a Patrik. I was there. He vaguely knew me and had read some of my earlier work. He noted the currents in the text that pulled on the reader and the resulting deposits in the deltalike configurations of theory and description within the pages. Patrik had led me to this point years earlier without even realizing it. In a letter dated March 1988, he writes about a detailed map of Coronado's expedition that was recently discovered in a monastery in Mexico. It was an invaluable portrait of the Southwest in the sixteenth century, noting the natural landscape and key Indian settlements that had been previously unknown. The imaginary city El Dorado was also marked on the map. The conquistadors never found anything but pueblos that remotely resembled their city. So why was it on the map? Patrik's account stops here. El Dorado's presence doesn't detract from the map's accurateness. Rather, it adds another dimension to the surface details. The city is the magnetized sacred that drew the conquistadors across the desert. For that alone it should be added. Whether Patrik's return was real or not, he is another version of El Dorado, in another kind of high plains desert. For Becker other things in the text were real enough—the southern landscape, the emotion, the individuals who had previously appeared in earlier ethnographies—which is curious, since the world I'm writing about vanishes the more I look at it. I'm left with an Alabama reorganized by Patrik's haunting. It is a marked-up landscape that acts like Patrik's slashes. It is a warning and, like the scars on Durkheim's churingas, a scored-in sacred that is as real as the wood or rock they are etched on.

Much of Patrik's work lingered on the walls of my house in Alabama even after I moved out. Years went by before we sold the house. My ex-wife never expressed a desire to keep any of his works when we divided up the property. His work dutifully followed those things I had inherited from my family into a storage unit on the highway. His work was imbued with a kind of energy different from the other photographs and paintings in the unit. Almost all my grandfather Eli's books are there in boxes stacked on top of each other, making it virtually impossible to find a particular book. Sometimes I find a Keim stuffed in between the fault lines of a jumble of books like a climber fallen into a crevasse. In this case the cold doesn't preserve. It's an interior cold formed out of the forlornness of abandoned things. There is the slow deterioration of paper touching paper where invisible fingers have smudged the page, rotting the fibers. There won't be an apocalyptic moment when the paper and the print separate and go their disparate ways. The smudges left by previous hands will slowly burrow through the pages, leaving something like dirt kicked out by the tiny feet of some animal going underground. I won't live long enough to see my grandfather's fingerprints and pencil marks vanish underground, dragging my own after them. If these books and Patrik's art make it out of the storage bin and survive a yard sale, they'll persist in piles in the corner of my apartment in Buffalo and watch me grow old.[15]

The storage bin is an actual place. It's located on Highway 21 near the Four-Mile Methodist Church. I pay sixty-five dollars a month for a ten-by-fifteen storage shed.[16] The price is reasonable. My son Tyree has a key. My sister Mary has another in her kitchen drawer. I send the checks every month. In there is almost everything I owned till I was thirty-seven years old. My childhood bed with pineapple-topped posts is stacked in the corner. A brand-new Jotul woodstove lumbers near the sliding entrance doors. It was too heavy to move to the back. My grandmother's hope chest stuffed with old photographs, papers, metals, odds and ends, and a soil-testing kit lies at the intersection of two long tables. The biggest one is made from heavy pine salvaged from a nineteenth-century Methodist church pew, and the other is the table I grew up eating on at my grandmother Mary Pullen's house. A huge mirror, a body-sized oak basket, and boxes of old books keep Mary Pullen's table from flying away. A red velvet Victorian loveseat lounges delicately like a cat near the wood stove. A pine wardrobe the size of Frankenstein's monster's coffin stands rigidly over a wicker-backed rocking chair with framed pieces of art on its seat. In the smaller spaces, like insects hiding in foliage, my tools are stacked and propped. It's a prison space. Penance is being performed. Termites have already destroyed the church pew's legs. I had to give it away to save the other furniture in the shed. I don't know how I'll save these objects that were once beautiful and part of a family. Decisions will have to be made. I returned with my girlfriend Molly last summer. Once I had slid open the metal doors I felt like an English archaeologist stumbling on an Egyptian tomb. It was the first occasion since these objects were interred that anyone other than I had seen them. For a moment the shed could've been a cluttered living room. We had a guest. I touched the loveseat's back. I picked up some books. I found a tiny green tree frog clinging to the blue cover of a 1910 writing manual. I carefully scooped it up in my hands and carried it out to the surrounding trees. The frog was a clue to a newly emerging ecosystem in my shed. The prison phase was drawing to a close and something else was approaching. The space resembled one of Patrik's installations. It was even the same color, though it lacked the smell that was characteristic of his awful logic. Molly and I were looking for Patrik's art pieces. I had started writing about him. I needed to re-see his art. I shipped all of it back to Buffalo except for a small statuelike object which was too delicate to ship. I carried it back with me on the plane in a paper sack.

The statuette was assembled out of several small pieces. Tenderly glued on top with minuscule drops of Super Glue was a dead rhinoceros beetle I'd given to Patrik before the fire ants had gotten to the carcass. He had placed an image of a dung beetle rolling a ball of dung in the frame at the bottom, anchoring the piece. The rhinoceros beetle may be the only instance where I vaguely appear in Patrik's work. Patrik was the dung beetle. On the pedestal was a row of animal and human molars. It was a favorite of Tyree's. He had kept it in his room in the Big House. At airport security, I took the figurine out of the paper sack. The sack was tearing. I carefully laid the figurine on its side in the plastic security box. I watched it pass into the x-ray. The heavy straps slapped the outside of the box. On the other side of the security screen, I put on my boots and belt. The plastic box came through. "My beetle is gone." A security guard came over. He was puzzled. I explained helplessly, "I've lost my beetle. It's art." I picked the figurine up. I was riveted by the absence of the beetle. And then a miracle happened. They stopped the line. Passengers were redirected to another checkpoint. A guard reviewed the tape and watched the beetle go through the scanner. He pointed it out to me on the screen until abruptly it was just gone. Another guard looked inside the scanner. A third guard looked in on the other side. The process was repeated. The search lasted at least ten minutes. No one could figure out what had happened. Without the rhinoceros beetle it was just junk shoddily glued together. It was as if Achilles's heel had been cut off and all the value drained out. My first thought was that the beetle had returned to Patrik. But that was wrong. The beetle had flown back to its home in Alabama. The storage shed was the capital of an empire that stretched out not just miles but years into the woods, pastures, and places I had traveled in that Alabama world. It was preparing a path for my return for those things left behind.

Patrik Travels

On the fifth of June[17] Patrik Keim retired to a small room he used as a studio in his apartment on the west side of Athens. Georgia. The floor and a large table were covered with scraps of images, a pair of large scissors, glue, electrical tape, dentures, a pile of old medical journals, butcher knives, and various small objects. He cleared an open space on the floor. He stood upright and gauged how it would appear when he fell. This was something he couldn't help. Patrik was always an artist. The wall directly behind him was bare. He stuck the pistol into his mouth and shot himself. The bullet penetrated through the brain and out the top of the skull. He fell, however, just off from the open piece of flooring, obscuring various images with his torso and hips, the blood pooling in the slight dip in the floor. Still, the result was surprising and very reminiscent of his early work. His body was found two days later, making it irrelevant that he had showered and shaved minutes before his departure. That Patrik would leave like this I had known for years.[18] It was reflected in the construction of his work, particularly in the adhesives that he used. The rubber bands popped and the glue would come unstuck. There was a built-in decay in his work that crept just beneath the surface. When I met Patrik he was standing next to an installation he'd done splattered with blood. He shook my hand with his own heavily bandaged hand. It was a gracious act in front of all the broken glass. One of the last communications I had from Patrik was a postcard sent to my farm in Alabama. It was a photograph of the North Sea, showing a dark sky and cold, foaming waves with no shore in sight. He had added an image of a bandaged face bobbing in the waves like a buoy that was then outlined in the same black blocks that often characterized his works. They formed a rectangle standing upright like an obelisk. At the top of the rectangle was another empty portal or door saved for me. He was unselfish. All I had to do was cut out the space following the blocks. The postcard announced his coming death as clearly as the cold water rolling in. I'm sure Patrik imagined the bandages in the image not as staunching the blood but as a frozen eruption of his brains that would, like an iceberg, dissolve into the ocean. A few years after his death, Patrik appeared near my farm. A dozer operator scraping a lake out of a swamp uncovered a seven-foot-long pine coffin. He was so unnerved that he quickly buried it back in the dam. Patrik, like Kafka's Hunter Gracchus or the apostle Paul, two other great travelers with whom he had no apparent similarities, is now touring the world in a sea craft, going wherever the North Sea touches the world beneath the world. I didn't have to ask why he surfaced there. He came to see me.

This wasn't the miracle Patrik had waited for, but it was an extraordinary turn of events. He was tantalizingly close to being in the deep water he dreamed of, water so dark it absorbed images. But luck was against him. I would've liked to have been there as the coffin broke the surface in the Alabama sun. From what the dozer-operator Mr. Brown reported, the craft was the color of mud. It must've gleamed. It was a real miracle once it returned underneath the ground. But I'm not sure seeing it would have been enough. The Hunter's visit to the seaside town barely ruffled the surface. Here a kingfisher screamed and flew low over the old beaver swamp. The cows grazing in the nearby pasture didn't raise their heads. Patrik would have to get up and walk with me to the house. Even Kafka acknowledges that walking was difficult for the Hunter, who was carried into town on a bier by his crew. On the solid ground the vertigo of water would have temporarily eased as the Hunter felt his own dead weight underneath his feet. I would've offered Patrik iced tea for the heat and put on a Brian Eno record. He liked Eno. He would have smiled. I would inquire about those he had seen on the other side. Have you met my mother or heard from my old malamute Ruah? In Kafka's telling of "The Hunter Gracchus" no one seems particularly surprised at his arrival or that he's carried in a small procession through town. The Hunter lies still. He doesn't look around. He wakes up and rises to his elbows only in the mayor's presence. His conversation with the mayor is measured, and what emotion there is leans toward the Hunter's nostalgia for the mountains. The mayor is unperturbed in the face of this miracle. Like the dozer-operator Mr. Brown, his life was unaltered by the visitation, and rightly so; there wasn't any faith. He uses the opportunity to ascertain what brought him to this particular limbo, a kind of technical question.

The mayor doesn't ask personal questions of the Hunter. Patrik and I would exchange snide comments on the art scene in Athens. I would be surprised if his sex drive was gone completely. It was such a part of him. Soon I would get anxious. The horses would need to be fed. I needed to repair the fence near the pecan orchard. I would ask Patrik if he would like to help. But he wouldn't, and that is understandable. He had to travel. That it would end like this doesn't alter the miraculous nature of the appearance or the interminable sentence of his traveling. Lazarus is mute after his return from the dead. He gives no report. From a distance, the moist stains left on his gown from the funeral balms couldn't be seen and what Jesus was saying couldn't be heard. The Scriptures are silent about whether the experience changed him at all. It seems neither he nor the other disciples had much to say about that. He was only gone four days, after all.[19] His return, like Patrik's, just was.

Patrik had appeared here following the western movement of his work and its densest concentration in this world. Over the years he'd given me piece after piece that I dutifully hung on the walls of my house or stacked against the bookcases. These marked the furthest point to the west his work had moved in history. Here was a used-up valley that had been my home. It was a place littered with ruins and new homes put together with glue. Patrik's work fit here. Like his work, these homes had an early expiration date inscribed into their construction. This was a place destined for ruin ever since de Soto wound his way north in the sixteenth century. By then the giant mound builders' cities to the south, scarcely sixty miles away, were collapsing under the weight of the viruses originating from the first Spanish contact years before on another part of the continent. The small settlement of Indians who lived at the foot of Crooked Mountain weren't immune. They vanished as well. De Soto and his pigs, horses, and soldiers passed less than two miles to the east. This was the first notable depopulation of the valley. The second occurred in the aftermath of the Creek War and their deportation along the Trail of Tears during Andrew Jackson's presidency. My home was built in that space of time. Next, the Civil War drained the valley of men and mules and sent them to unmarked graves in Virginia, Tennessee, Georgia, Maryland, or Pennsylvania.[20] The last emptying occurred with the sharecroppers put out on the road, starting in the 1920s and ending in the 1940s as the land shifted from cotton to cattle. Then the valley settled into scattered cattle farms before the chicken houses sprang up and the empty landscape started to fill in. A new form of ruins arrived. Houses were built covered in vinyl siding. Patrik's appearance momentarily added to the population.

What may have drawn him to Alabama was his suitcase. It wasn't a matter of a debt. Patrik had left a suitcase with me to hold. He had never said what was inside. I imagined it was filled with various pieces of paper, odd things, and unfinished projects. But he was too late. Patrik had missed me. I'd already left Alabama and carried the suitcase with me. My farm was the only stable address in my mixed-up travels, which was ironic. Alive, Patrik had desired above all things to leave the landlocked South and head back to the city of canals and swamps in the north of Europe, Amsterdam. Now he was trapped in the labyrinth of underground tunnels and rivers undergirding the South where the North Sea is a glimpse, something hinted at in the cold and dark that never arrives. I never wanted to leave Alabama. But I stayed on the road, crisscrossing America for eleven years. The Hunter Gracchus was also condemned to travel in a world he never dreamed of. He fell to his death in the mountains he loved, hunting a chamois. He had never seen the ocean. Now he goes wherever the unnamed body of water touches. In this afterlife it's unclear whether it's a penitential service or a blessing, but he and his crew sail the world in a wooden ship. For Kafka, the original chronicler, why he goes where he goes is determined by the wind. His bark has no rudder. Just as unclear is how he arrived at this fate. It's possible the pilot of his death ship made a critical navigational error or was distracted by how lovely the mountains were. Regardless, the Hunter Gracchus travels with the mountains only a distant view from the water. His visitations in this world are accomplished in the bright sun, completely unlike the fog-shrouded valley into which he fell and bled to death on the rocks looking back up at the mountains. For the German writer W. G. Sebald, the Hunter Gracchus is suspended over a rolling nausea that infects even dry land. Sebald retells the story in his work *Vertigo*. He has the Hunter die for the love of his dog who had slipped out of his arms into the chasm. Gracchus fell, reaching for his dog. Sebald was killed in a car wreck, talking with his daughter. She survived. Patrik's fall to the ground after the shot to his head was, I suppose, to take him into the deep water he dreamed of. Instead he lay in a thin pool of blood before being fitted to his new craft and set loose in the far reaches of the world beneath Alabama. Patrik was a part of the world yet to be, a fossil of the future coming.

The autumn after Patrik departed I considered following him. Objectively, everything was in place. My dog had been murdered and buried in a shallow ditch. Mary Pullen my grandmother was dead. A few months earlier my mother had gone to her grave. The list continues: divorce, separation from the things I loved, and the inevitable effects of a career cutting me to pieces. It is this last fact that is the most difficult to describe. For Patrik this would be easy. He felt abandoned by his father, who died of a heart attack while Patrik was a teenager. What personal relations weighed on Patrik were unknown to me. I knew there were romantic entanglements, but they didn't seem to slow him. Even the number of them seemed light. It was their shrinkage as he grew older and heavier with the slowing of his metabolism that drew the blood and not the tears he sprayed his work with. But this was expected. Art is beautiful. Sociology seems paltry. There was a point early on in the German critic Walter Benjamin's career when it looked like he would take his own life. A makeshift will was drawn up. His career was stalled. There was also the friend's suicide before him holding open the door. Benjamin tarried, the sign of Saturn under which he worked held in check for now by Klee's desperate angel[21] being blown into the future. This was one of Benjamin's favorite pieces. He treasured it. It was in part Patrik's own works that held me in place for now.

Christmas Eve

It's fitting that a history of these occurrences be written by a minor Southern sociologist whose career was so much like and unlike Patrik's. My career flickered on and off while he was alive, and after his death. This is a small and selective history of Patrik and his work. It isn't encyclopedic. It was written in isolation. I didn't contact his family or friends. What need was there? They would've been suspicious. I doubt they would've believed in his return. Instead they would've attributed his return to magical thinking. It could be said that all of this isn't even about Patrik but me. That would be a misreading. Once his coffin breached the surface, the project started. I wasn't consulted about his return or even the timing. None of it was convenient for me. It brought me certain risks. I became a part of one of Patrik's installations, hardly a pleasant thought with its greasiness, death, grime, mourning, and the pull toward suicide. His work was dedicated to the passing of something he couldn't directly articulate, a sensation not unlike having a large snaky body brush against your legs in dark water. His father's early death played into it, but there was far more than just that animating his production. His own death fixated him. There was also a lament for the holy, a gesture that on the surface seems completely alien to Patrik's profanity. And yet he revered the holy. Once Patrik crossed over, he and I were like travelers on either side of a line as thin and hard as a mirror surface, trying to reestablish a connection. Turning away was impossible. What he felt on his side of the world I don't know. For me, there was an undertow sucking me toward where Patrik was now.[22] Why did I write this small history of Patrik and my travels along the divide? The answer is as simple as: He's dead and I survived. He was the more talented and brilliant. I was left behind to take down messages from the dead, a scribe for an ethnographer on the other side. Patrik was a graduate student in cultural anthropology for a year, though his training in methods was suspect. He was more interested in postmodern theory. He liked to quote Baudrillard.[23] That Patrik's last project would take place near my home in Alabama was seductive. It became difficult to distinguish my memories from his reports. I see the logic of his project: I would practice what Walter Benjamin described as psychic materialism on the surface. He would act as a supernatural informant from underneath. The result would be a world investigated from two sides. At some point his script or mine would discreetly cut through the intervening surface. Patrik may have gotten this idea from a book by Vincent Crapanzano titled *Tuhami*. Tuhami was a Moroccan tile maker married to a camel-footed she-demon. He gave Crapanzano regular reports from the other side, though Vincent was unable to verify these accounts. Patrik would rectify this. He was an artist who constructed large and small installations out of salvaged materials. Something of his would come across or could be used to prop open a door so that I could see what was on the other side. It would be our first collaborative project, a two-sided ethnography of memories, landscapes, and the currents sweeping beneath the surface of memory.[24]

I knew there was a correspondence between my world in Alabama and the world Patrik portrayed. In the woods on Crooked Mountain I saw a spirit queen sitting in a brown Naugahyde easy chair surrounded by garbage and dead dogs.[25] The ground around her moved on the backs of beetles while she serenely stared at me. At the beginning of the twentieth century this was the outer reaches of a lynching zone. Three years after I saw her, a dead woman was found by a squirrel hunter thirty paces away in the leaves and undergrowth with a full bright-green can of Sprite next to her. She'd been murdered and dumped here. The rivets on her blue jeans were still bright. The body gave Tyree nightmares. The horror of this was Patrik's subject and it now became mine. At times it was like trying to decode finger taps on the other side of a wall or to decipher the Morse code in the bullfrogs' dark croaks. Nothing about this would be easy. My own training in methods was more stringent than Patrik's, but this was hardly an endorsement of my abilities. Benjamin's own practice of psychic materialism may have contributed to his collapse. This was a risk for me as well. My part in this was unclear. Patrik hadn't made it easy. I didn't witness his possible return. No new postcards arrived with instructions. His art didn't turn into handwriting on my walls. There was no revelation. The coffin couldn't be dug up without emptying the lake. Brown had made sure of that when he reburied it in the dam. It was a test of my faith and my sociological abilities to ascertain why Patrik had chosen the beaver swamp to appear in the sun again and what was driving him in the world beneath this one. I would have to glimpse the other side in short bursts. My reports would have to be written very quickly. In the ancient world, Orpheus turned to look back at his dead wife as she was still emerging from the other side. She was pulled back to Hades. The account describes Orpheus's anguish at his loss for a second time, but Eurydice's subsequent fate is hidden. Orpheus was later torn apart by maenads for his faithfulness to his dead wife. Was the goal of our project for me to see Patrik's face again and send him back a second and final time? If this was my part, what would happen to me in the future?

Patrik would have appreciated the irony of our collaboration on this section of Alabama. I wasn't there. I'd already left for good. Alabama was a shrinking dreamworld for me. It was a decaying set of maps that no doubt attracted Patrik even more, obsessed as he was with rot. I had always imagined I would return to the Big House and A.C.'s farm. I wouldn't. I packed for my travels as an itinerant professor around the country as if I would. Everything I had fit in the back of my Toyota one-ton pickup and the small U-Haul trailer dragged behind it. I took a bed frame, a futon, two matching rocking chairs that I had inherited from Mary Pullen, a wooden table, a ladder-back chair with a seat woven out of baling twine, one lamp, boxes of books, a receiver, CD player, two speakers, a postcard rack and postcards, two Persian rugs rolled up into three-foot bundles, my dissertation notes, my Bridgestone mountain bike, a box of cooking utensils, and four pieces by Patrik. I had no pictures of such size of my son, my then wife, or anyone else—these pictures were in a shoebox hidden like the storybook giant's heart for protection. They were intensely calibrated mnemonic devices that tended slowly to replace the relationships they were supposed to preserve. They became memories of memories in which somewhere lost in a fog in the woods were the original relationships. It's a problem that is not unique to my devices. After the publication of Siegfried Kracauer's *The Mass Ornament*, the German philosopher Theodor Adorno aimed this comment at the book's mercurial author: "To a consciousness that suspects it has been abandoned by human beings, objects are superior."[26] The comment could've just as easily been transposed to another peripheral member of the Frankfurt school, Walter Benjamin, and then to me. Benjamin was just as fascinated by the small things and their jewellike shine and even more committed to the metaphysics of objects than his predecessor Kracauer. With Benjamin, Adorno's one-liner was expanded to a series of letters stringently criticizing his position. Adorno never pointed publicly at the erosion of human relationships around Benjamin. He should have. As he neared the end of his life, Walter was increasingly isolated geographically from what was left of his family and close friends. His exile in Paris accentuated his experience of the great hydraulic achievement of the nineteenth century, the recession of humanness into pools and lakes at the heart of the commodity that Marx described as commodity fetishization. Benjamin was poised to take a more radical approach.[27] New species of *were*-objects were emerging in the hothouses of the arcades. Here Benjamin could have just as easily been describing the Galápagos shoreline as his own disintegration:

"In the arcades, one comes upon types of collar studs for which we no longer know the corresponding collars and shirts. If the shoemaker's shop should be neighbor to a confectioner's, then his festoons of boot-laces will resemble rolls of licorice. Over stamps and letter boxes roll balls of string and of silk. Naked puppet bodies with bald heads wait for hairpieces and attire. Combs swim about, frog green and coral red, as in an aquarium; trumpets turned to conches, ocarinas to umbrella handles; and lying in the fixative pans from a photographer's darkroom is birdseed."[28]

There came a time early in my travels when I came back to Alabama with my things. Patrik was still alive. A.C. had been dead for seven years. Mary Pullen had suffered a stroke. The farm was timbered and then sold off to pay her medical bills. A.C. didn't have a sustainable life insurance policy. My piece of the farm still had a chance to survive. It was temporary. It was a lesson finally coming true. Benjamin was too optimistic about the new landscape and its possibilities. He didn't mark the emergence of new kinds of predators, or how even the old beasts would find new homes. The Pentecostals knew something was coming. They preached it in their services. I applied their warnings to myself in the vaguest way. "Satan is a big hungry lion prowling the streets. You open the door and he'll eat you up." The preacher's mouth worked furiously as if he had a piece of meat stuck between his teeth. "Never go outside without the full armor of God. Remember that," he said. "Ephesians 6:11–17."[29] I couldn't picture what the preacher was saying. As he was talking he kept fingering the top button of his shirt. He was dressed in slacks neatly and permanently pressed and a wide-collared yellow shirt. It didn't make sense. I knew it was metaphorical, but I couldn't picture what the full armor of God looked like. I asked the preacher if Satan had ever bitten him. "That old lion has chased me for years. I hear him roaring outside my bedroom at night. He wants to kill me. And he wants to kill you. Stay in the blood, brother. Stay in the blood." Then it occurred to me why Patrik was obsessed with blood.

The whole thing didn't seem real or practical—that is, until I caught a glimpse of Satan just before Christmas. I was teaching at a Catholic college in Indiana. Ironic, I thought that I would see him here. I thought the pope provided an enormous termite bond that prevented Satan from devouring people. Here nuns fed the ducks on the grounds of the college while dressed in tight pants and galoshes and nothing happened to them. But then it didn't happen by a lake but in an office. It was already dark. Maybe the school hadn't kept up its payments? The department was deserted except for the chair sitting in his office. He had asked me to come by. Within thirty seconds the terms of my employment shrank down to nothing. "Get out," and then an instant later, "Now." I wondered if that line had come to him from a western on TV in which he was the star. The glow of the lamp beside him acted like a spotlight. He was strangely beautiful in his padded Italian suit, brown toupee, and soft shoes. He was squashed into a large leather chair. His hands were folded in front of a thick patterned tie. He was talking. I looked at him hard in the face but his lips barely moved. Our faces were less than two feet apart. "We don't approve of what you're teaching." I almost said, "When you say *we*, do you mean *oui*, like, you know, French?" The instant was already too long. I couldn't distinguish him from the leather. Brown was his color.

I came back to Alabama in the middle of the night popping caffeine pills to stay awake. The sky was dumping snow. The back of the truck was filled with it, and beneath the snow, like sleepy-eyed kids, were seventy-pound bags of sand for traction. It was Nashville before the snow melted away, leaving the bags exposed. At a gas station outside Chattanooga, a local eyed the sandbags. "What's that for?" he asked, edging up in his cowboy boots and cocking his head toward the bed of the truck. "Snow. Coming from up north," I said. "Snow?" he repeated. "God damn. Snow. Get good traction?" "Pretty good," I responded.

"Can you get them sandbags down here?" He put his boot on the bumper. The toe was bright silver like a Christmas tree ornament. "You know we get some pretty good snow sometimes on the mountain." "I've never seen them here." The sandbags began to resemble a ghost hanging around gas stations and hardware stores. "They ought to sell them." He was dreaming of the same white Christmas. "Yeah, they should." I drove off toward Birmingham on Interstate 59. The caffeine was buzzing and mixing with my adrenaline into a cocktail soaking my larger muscles. I had been bitten before. A Rottweiler had once clamped down on my forearm. What was amazing was how much like paper my skin was. There were punch marks through to the muscle. But this bite was different. It worked from the inside out. The bruises floated up to the surface like rose petals broken off from my spine or clouds of ink soaking the paper from underneath.

I couldn't get my armor to fit me. I lacked something like faith. There were too many spaces left unprotected. But the devouring was a perfect fit. I couldn't move without the sticky sensation of blood. Hell fit like a wool sweater boiled to shrink to my exact specifications with me inside it. There's nothing romantic about it. I was apparently naturally gifted. My mother told me I have a chemical imbalance that disposes me toward depression. My wife thought I was crazy and wouldn't talk to me. On Christmas Eve, I cried when she said she was moving out. She helped to shrink away any excess movement that was left. "Stay in the blood, brother. Stay in the blood," I heard the preacher say. It was unfortunately my own. Was Patrik's own obsession with blood about his protection?

There are historical precedents for this. In the first part of the twentieth century in Prague, Franz Kafka imagined a salesman waking up in bed and finding himself changed into a beetle with a hard shiny shell. The salesman has been completely devoured. He still thinks like his human self, but all he can manage is a gurgling sound. He has trouble getting his socks on his dangling feet. It's difficult for him to rise up out of the bed. He is pitifully weak. Kafka restrains his description. He doesn't describe the possible iron bed and the thin mattress that he lay on. The alarm clock that ticked incessantly by his bed is scarcely mentioned. His shaving kit is hidden on the dresser. The big wooden wardrobe that teetered precariously against the wall while watching the change is blended into the background. These additions would've brought into focus the compulsion of the double staring out of the objects in the form of commodity fetishization. The story is *The Metamorphosis*, published in 1912. The character Gregor lives at home with his father, mother, and sister in a modest apartment. He brings home the only income. There are servants to be looked after. There is the penetration of his business concerns into the deepest reaches of his person. Gregor's first thought surrounding his change was his work. Is catching a later train an option? Will the office send someone to check on him? They do. Gregor is obsessed with how with this change he would be able to keep up the proper front for the household.

Earlier in Berlin, social scientists and colleagues Georg Simmel and Max Weber both conceptualized the modern experience as a kind of protective casing secreted from "capitalist" interactional forms. It was a shell more fluid than a suit of clothes and, as Weber put it, "as hard as steel." Here is what I described as the boiled sweater. It was more like a kind of honey had been poured over the person and his belongings and dribbled through the floorboards into the underworld. The secretions that formed on the surface were what Weber recognized as a steel casing, except he was wrong. The steel casing isn't just one layer but a network of infrathin layers,[30] folded like the steel in a Japanese sword on top of one another. An autopsy of Gregor the salesman or Gregor the beetle would've shown the same construction. Why wouldn't the individual enclosures be an approximation of infinity no different from the psychic city of Rome imagined by Freud at the beginning of *Civilization and Its Discontents*? For Freud it was a city of enclosures within enclosures that give nothing up. Simmel's version of the shell appears in his 1903 essay "The Mental Life of the Metropolis." Simmel hides himself in the essay. Whether he is standing off to the side or like a salt pillar in the middle of the sidewalk during business hours, the place from which he chronicles the new world is never fixed. Despite all the style that marks the essay, it is as if Simmel were being absorbed into the crowd. Perhaps he is afraid of the lion prowling the streets. Actual landmarks vanish. A grayness dominates. It's a dream city.

Weber's conceptualization appears two years later at the end of *The Protestant Ethic and the Spirit of Capitalism*. As Weber puts it, "In Baxter's view, concern for outward possessions should sit lightly on the shoulders of his saints 'like a thin cloak which can be thrown off at any time.' But fate decreed that the cloak should become a shell as hard as steel."[31] This poetic prophecy at the end of *The Protestant Ethic* is an abnormality within the larger essay. At no other point does Weber gather his cloak around himself like a prophet standing in the wilderness and intone what amounts to poetry. There's no hint of the heavy desperation in the recorded interviews he did in the United States or his observation of the baptism in rural North Carolina. Further into the mountains he could've witnessed Protestant services where the believers spoke in tongues, drank strychnine, and handled snakes. Whether he attended a black church in his travels in the United States isn't recorded. He talked with a doctor in Cincinnati. He visited a worker's home in Buffalo. The secretion is noted. There is an ordered shell in the smallest white picket fence and the heightened Protestantism in the business acumen that characterizes the physician. In none of his examples is the aridity he saw characterizing the future of these interactions. It's likely that Weber's own nervous breakdown just before his trip to America was triggered by the suicide of a student close to him. This may have provided the cutting edge in his poetry and informed the quiet desperation he predicts across the capitalist future. It is the push of tragedy behind analysis.

In what could have appeared as a footnote in Weber's text,[32] Kafka's Hebrew instructor, a high school teacher named Friedrich Thieberger, describes an encounter with Kafka that must've occurred shortly after *The Metamorphosis* was published:

> One evening, when I happened to be standing with my father in the front of the house when the gate was closed, Kafka came by with my two sisters, whom he was walking home. My father had read "The Metamorphosis" a few days earlier, and although Kafka usually retreated behind an aloof smile when people discussed his writing, he allowed my father to say a few words about this transformation of a human into a bug. Then Kafka took a step back and said with unsettling gravity while shaking his head, as though he were discussing a real occurrence: "That was a dreadful thing."[33]

Neither Weber nor Kafka specifically addressed the "shelling" of the surrounding landscape or what could be called the emergence of the Protestant landscape and then its post-Protestant successor. My trip to Indiana and back to Alabama did.

There had been questions about my reliability and my emotional state from people close to me. "Is all that pain and darkness in Patrik getting to you?" A few, less delicately, have suggested that I may be crazy, but in the best possible way. "Why do you have to be so dark?" Which is then followed by "You admit that your memory is faulty. Where are you telling the truth?" I don't know where to begin. When I was involved in the charismatic movement, I heard stories about faithful men raising the dead around Jacksonville, Alabama, and in the Zulu zones of South Africa. I was skeptical. Women were never involved in any of the accounts I heard. The men wore white shirts and ties. There were no death certificates or tombs. I'm still skeptical. I never saw either the coffin or Patrik inside or outside that box. His return didn't change his appearances in the art that surrounded me. He was like a tiny gas leak in my apartment that didn't make that much of a difference since I kept the windows cracked at night. In my profession of sociology, the narrative voice is unquestionably reliable.[34] It doesn't falter. That is a given. Even in the extreme forms of autoethnography or performative fictocriticism, the narrator is a stable structure. Sometimes this narrator is the last piece of stability as even the grammar around that voice disintegrates. Patrik sent me a postcard with this phrase from Nietzsche: "I fear we do not get rid of God, because we still believe in grammar." I must be an atheist now.

The social and literary theorist Henry Sussman at Yale has suggested the position of the author may be changing.[35] He sees a new kind of sociology emerging. He calls it nomadic sociology after Deleuze and Guattari's philosophical exposition of an antistate, roving, rhizomatic thought process. One consequence of this would be at a certain stage the disintegration of the reliable narrator. I don't pretend that any of this was premeditated. Nothing would've changed even if I had never met Henry or read his book. The same goes with Deleuze and Guattari. I didn't make up Brown or his digging up that coffin. Nor can I alter God's will regardless of my beliefs. Why Patrik and Gracchus are not quite dead or alive is beyond me. I'm just a bystander investigating the possibility of a miracle. That investigation cuts in both directions. The problem reminds me of the ending of Kurosawa's *Rashomon*. A samurai is dead. A thief has been apprehended and charged with murder. A wife has been shamed and sent away. And the one neutral witness, a woodcutter hiding in the bushes, is revealed to be a liar and an accomplice to the crime. Each testifies. The dead samurai tells his story through a medium. Each is shown to be telling the truth. Each is lying. A Buddhist monk hearing this has a crisis of faith. Truth is like the rain on the mountain. There is a torrential rain surrounding the telling of the story. Despair seeps in. And Kurosawa's ending is hardly an answer for sociologists. It's an affirmation of faith. An abandoned baby is found in the temple where they have taken shelter from the rain. A poor farm family takes the child as their own. Kurosawa stops here. He could've shown the repetition of misery reaching through the child's life. He doesn't. He settles on mystery and the affirmation of love. The rain stops and, for an instant, the monk discerns what an Alabama preacher would call God's will. I am just a bystander. I didn't make the North Sea under Alabama. God made that.

Termite Season

Patrik's importance as an artist was limited. He never achieved anything more than a momentary recognition and a meager living from his work. His vita lists exhibitions at several galleries in the Atlanta area and a museum show in Erie, Pennsylvania. This was the furthest reach of his work. In Athens, Georgia, he was a pop celebrity in the specialized ecosystem of the hip. His nickname near the end of his life was St. Patrik, as if his unusual end were already visible. His bicycle hangs solemnly from the ceiling of a bar where he worked, a relic of his violent sainthood.

I crashed on the sofa in Patrik's apartment for nearly a year. I'd show up late at night and spread my sleeping bag out on what I remember as a decrepit Victorian sofa. The telephone was high on the wall. Straight-back chairs protruded upside down from the ceiling and out from the wall. There would be calls occasionally late at night. I would answer, wake Patrik, and lie back down on the sofa with my head spinning slightly. Patrik would appear in a bathrobe with his enormous smile that made him look like a circus clown miming a performance even while he was trying to explain to the unnamed man who I was. He did some album covers for local bands to make money. There was a near appearance in a British documentary about the music scene in Athens. Some of his most stunning pieces like *Utopia: Termite Season* were unsellable. Patrik turned a room in the student union into a gigantic termite mound with stacks of paper, paper tunnels, and scratchlike markings on the wall. These were meant, no doubt, to simulate the gnawing that haunted Patrik. He had

assembled a live model of the superorganism. This piece and others like it were experiences lasting no more than hours before the university would shut them down as hazards. Patrik was a critical articulation point in between the typewriter and the personal computer. He used a manual typewriter. He preferred the dirty side of technologies. He adored sticky scissors, globs of glue, and hot copy machines for how they matched the world he lived in. Patrik was something pieced together from debris.

This may have been what made Patrik a brilliant if decaying artist. His life was in calibration with the materials he used, a costly coordination. Against this decaying world he lay like a chameleon on a rotting picket fence. As his world shrank, Patrik shrank. And Patrik's world was shrinking rapidly. The avant-garde scene in Athens was changing. The bands that utilized Patrik's hard-core graphics were slipping away, changing their sound and audience. The art world was likewise professionalizing. The audiences for rotting installations and big armchairs loaded with pounds of melting butter weren't there. I admired Patrik's emulation of an ax in his approach to delicate craftsmanship. It wasn't precise or digital. Historically, Patrik was at a point similar to Jack the Ripper, who at the scene of one of his murders collected the blood of his victim in a ginger-beer bottle to use as ink for his pen. The blood clotted and was unusable. He had to resort to red ink to write his letter, which was problematic. He got ink all over his hands and on the letter.[36] This was Patrik's world. In the time of e-mails, Jack the Ripper's writing problem makes no sense. Patrik's works were dirty. Clean them and there is no Patrik. Patrik was tied to the archaic. Untied from the dirty world of the past, there was no Patrik. Patrik knew this. But he wouldn't move. Instead, his work retreated from giant installations and performances to the tiny frame of the book. This seems even more ironic and pathetic as the book slides further into the shrinking archaic world. His lines of retreat were limited by funds and his own lack of determination to run. Eastern Europe, Mexico, South America, and South Africa were possible exiles where the archaic could be still be found. But Patrik chose to die in place like a Spartan in the gap. The comparison would have pleased him, if only because of the body that he could imagine was his. But it was also his death sentence. He seemed unadaptable. E-mail was unamenable to his needs of amplification and to the geology of the self he practiced. How could the equivalent of taping and glue be layered into an electronic transmission?

In a note Patrik describes how a car packed with young black men pulled up alongside him riding his bicycle. A youth on the passenger side leveled a pistol at him and spat out, "Fucking skinhead. You're dead." Patrik had shaved his head. He was terrified and rattled to the bone. The car drove off. No shot was fired. Patrik didn't welcome these advances toward his death. It was the wrong finger on the trigger. Patrik took the event as another sign of his inevitable retreat and defeat. In Amsterdam, he was chased by a crazy man with a knife for several blocks late one night. Patrik wasn't suited for running, but he didn't invite the knife to add color to his wardrobe. His move toward his own death was a calculated form of *supplice*.[37] The maximum amount of despair had to be soaked up by his fat. By the time he died he was fixed in place. He was wedged in a tight space. After being hit by a taxi, his musical hero Brian Eno was laid up for a month barely able to move. This occurred in January 1975 in London. Eno was confined to bed. His thin body was still reverberating from the crash, arms and legs stiff and puppetlike. He put on a record of eighteenth-century harp music. From Eno's own description even this was a monumental task. It was only after lying back down that he discovered one channel of the stereo had failed and the volume was set at an extremely low level. Flat in bed, too stiff to get back up, he heard the music, the rain, and the light in the room as one assemblage. In Eno's words, he had discovered "a new way of hearing music as part of the ambience of the environment."[38] Out of his accident Eno generated the beautiful LP *Discreet Music*. Patrik gave me Brian Eno's *Before and After Science*. He was a fan. Patrik's death produced nothing edifying at the time. He purchased a small-caliber pistol to protect himself from his tormentors. This was the pistol he eventually used on himself. I was surprised. I had always assumed he would die of AIDS.

His death was paradoxical. He was freed of Athens, but in my world a subtle oblivion was taking place. Patrik was vanishing in my memories. With Patrik's possible reappearance I went through various scenarios. Of course I would recognize him. Unlike Jesus, he hadn't been transformed. He wasn't that kind of saint. Around my writing table are three different images of him. Admittedly they are from the same period. They form a particular set of windows into his past as well as mine. On the wide window ledge above the table is a small photographic triptych in which the same black-and-white images of Patrik are repeated with his mouth covered in each with printout tape reading "Father, Son, Holy Ghost." By the door Patrik poses with his eyes closed, hands encased in rubber gloves holding a blackbird-sized pair of scissors. On the opposite wall he is sprawled on the ground. His body is cut in half. His legs and hips have been devoured and are completely absent from the photo. With only his head and torso showing, he looks like a bug cut in half. I realized how little I could actually recall about my time with Patrik outside of my time with his images. Patrik was a captive of his work. Other than fleeting flashes of having a beer, meeting him with his hands bandaged, my memories were bound to his works. Patrik, through these windows, has watched my life. He saw my son grow up. He saw my own suicidal crawl. He would know me, but my own world was erasing the soft parts of him. The art is hard and is scattered like an archipelago of volcanic islands in the Pacific. There is no single palace in which the memories are stored. Marc Augé uses the image of the shoreline being built up and washed away by the ocean's currents to capture the dialectics of remembering and forgetting. The oblivion, he writes, is a necessary part of remembering.

Doppelgänger

Patrik placed a fuse in his work. He normally reassembled already decaying pieces into a larger decaying assemblage. In one collage piece, one image is slowly slicing another in half as it falls toward the bottom like the blade of a guillotine. The image recedes into the wall of my apartment. The matting paper is the same color as the wall. I have no idea what title Patrik gave it. The title page of Dr. Otto Rank's book *Doppelgänger* is trapped inside the frame and is the image being cut in half. The publication date is 1925.[39] The page occupies the right half of the frame. Again there is a synchronicity of color among the wall, the matting paper, and the torn page. It flutters on the wall like a moth, almost indistinguishable from the painted wood paneling from the first part of the twentieth century. Patrik's self-portrait is another marking on a cream-colored pool. His head is slightly bowed. His eyes are closed even though in his right hand he holds a large pair of scissors cocked open like a puppet about to move, aimed at a book bound in thick rubber bands. I can hear the scissors slashing and the *thwamp* of the rubber bands being cut as if the act were being played on a tiny radio with a fuzzy speaker. This was the sonic unconscious surrounding Patrik. These sounds were amplified inside his body. He heard the scissors snipping across the surface in the summer heat of Georgia. Outside his studio it would've sounded as if a swarm of insects were massing on the interior walls, the sofa, and whoever was inside.

In November 1989 Patrik ran for mayor of Athens as a write-in candidate. His campaign poster showed a profile of his shaved head against a bleak landscape. The tagline read: "MOVE AGAINST INDISCIPLINE." I always thought Patrik was being ironic. But the evidence to the contrary was in front of me everywhere I looked. Patrik was very particular about his shaving cream. He was adamant about Clinique, which seems strange for a man hovering above poverty. It was the closeness of the shave you could get, he said. Then there was the straight razor in his bathroom, which scared me so much when I found it that I slid cautiously out of the bathroom as if it were alive. I had my own in a box inside a box inside another box in a closet at home. Now I'm surprised this wasn't Patrik's choice for his departure, though he did shave one last time before the bullet. These objects are just the first ring of discipline. In the portrait that opens his MFA thesis, Patrik is captured lounging at an odd angle, filling the frame. What on first glance seems relaxed is muscularly tense. There is something predatory about it, like a praying mantis folded on a branch. It's not the viewer who should be afraid but Patrik himself, as if he were the prey. He's wearing a tightly knotted bowtie with a blazer and a striped shirt. He appears to be an echo of his obsession with slashes, a well-dressed ripper. A pocket square juts out of his pocket. His hair is meticulously cut. He is as well scrubbed as a hospital floor. He appears to be a foreigner in a Western-style suit, much like the Japanese writer Yukio Mishima, another suicide. Even in his own world, Mishima delivered lectures in a three-piece suit that made him appear like a European banker. Patrik looks like Yukio's brother. Patrik was always armored as if he were waiting for 299 other Spartans to join him in the gap. Yukio had his own army and disciplinary regime.

The *Athens Observer* wrote an article on Patrik's run for mayor. He was treated as any fringe write-in candidate might be. There's even a photograph. It's a headshot with him smiling and looking somewhere off-camera. His head is shaved. Athens is hot in September. His head and neck are so long they occupy the entire frame. There is no coat or tie. His issues were all very personal. His chosen issues were bike routes, gang problems, and historic preservation. Patrik was targeted on his bike by gangs. But on this issue he was still progressive. "I'd like to see an increased use of community service as a penalty, instead of flooding our jails. There are so many things they could be doing," he was quoted as saying. His campaign motto, "Move against Indiscipline," was specifically directed at "police officers caught drinking with a minor." "It's time to stop passing the buck and get down to business." I'm not surprised by his concern with historic preservation; even in 1989 Athens still had beautiful buildings from earlier eras. What was revealing was how he talked about it. He used two words that recur in his works: *gluttony* and *cannibalism*. *Cannibalism* in particular he used in regard to his family. In one work titled *A History of Cannibalism*, he reorients a 1930s Soviet-

era family portrait into something sinister and forlorn. Gluttony was not one of Patrik's vices. It was one of his desires, to be eaten like a dog by a dog. His deepest sexual fantasy was to have sex with himself as two Patriks aggressively facing each other. All those cuts with glass and sharp objects may have been an approximation of bone. At the beginning of *The Way by Swann's,* the narrator Marcel is having trouble sleeping. He's passing in and out of the twilight. It's here he feels a hip pressed against him and he curls his body like an oyster around it. It's the hip bone of an unnamed lover in an early hint of the madeleine to come. Patrik's cutting and double fantasies circle around a similar bone. His final comment for the interview expresses his political motivations. "When you swim in a greasy pond, you get a coat of film on you, and politics is a pretty greasy business." Patrik had a thing for fat like his hero Joseph Beuys. On a postcard to me, Patrik has scrolled a line from Beuys: "I do not want to carry art into politics, but make politics into art." In the article Patrik comes across as earnest and naive. He criticizes President Bush's policies for a kinder, gentler nation. He seems like a young John Brown, the abolitionist, one who went to art school rather than becoming immediately embroiled in Bloody Kansas. Kansas and Harper's Ferry are still to come but in a different way in this altered history. In a note written to me during his campaign Patrik captures our future.

> 9/21/89 Well, see what happens—I ask for help and no one responds. Even my psychiatrist told me to wait and come back in January! Now look what I've done—headlong into the public arena, and I *hate* the public arena; yet I live for it, too! It's my lifeblood, mon raison d'être. But if the drug cartel has me assassinated, promise me a retrospective at the Guggenheim. No, better yet the Kröller-Müller in Otterlo, the Netherlands (in 1990 is the hundredth anniversary of old Vincennes hair-trigger accident to the head), *so promise me that one, last request.* Well, the campaign trail calls for me: more dogs to kiss and babies to kick. Bye, P.K.

Patrik received forty-five votes.

Big House

Patrik's appearance near my farm was unexpected but hardly surprising. It was a matter-of-fact occurrence that I had been half expecting since his death. Doubters will point out that I didn't see him or that it can't be authenticated that he was actually inside the coffin. All that is true; I see the points clearly, but they don't deny that a coffin surfaced less than a mile from my home or that there was something profoundly

incomplete about Patrik's art that anticipated a supernatural interven-
tion. It wasn't his death that would complete his work but his half-life. I
made the mistake of not believing my mother's encounters with ghosts
while she was alive. I have rectified that mistake. If anyone could be the
new Hunter Gracchus, it is Patrik, who like the Hunter was completely
unaware of what future awaited at the moment of death. It was the sus-
pension between the living and the dead that would fill in the gaps of
Patrik's work. My own delusions on this point leave me unfazed. I took
it as evidence to the contrary. Patrik did return, if only for an instant.
He wasn't the first from the other side to appear in the valley. Visitors
weren't routine even with the charismatic revivals sweeping through the
local churches. There was talk about appearances of Jesus, miraculous
healings, and demonic infestations. For a time truck drivers on Highway 9 reported seeing Bigfoot lurking along the edges of an old beaver
swamp in the early-morning fog. It turned out to be Eddie Paris wearing a sleeping bag. He pumped gas at the Paris store at the crossroads.[40]
There were even reports of satanic rites in the hills that reached all the
way up to Captain Dothard of the state police, who lived down the road
in the community of Nance's Creek. I never saw anything like that other
than dead animals laid in patterns alongside piles of garbage. But these
sightings tended to be metaphorical. There were no hard firsthand accounts. Rather, the stories wound their way through the valley with no
discernible author or physicality. Patrik's coffin broke the surface like a
prehistoric whale. Brown recoiled in horror.

I talked with Luke Coppick. He had grown up in this valley. He was
here during the first part of the twentieth century. He had seen what
appeared to be a man in overalls standing by the road near the Nance's
Creek intersection, who watched as Luke pitchforked hay into his pickup.
He'd even spoken to him about the quality of grass. Luke's wife, who was
sitting in the cab of the truck, saw nothing, just Luke yammering something, leaning on his pitchfork. This happened right across the road from
my house. My mother inadvertently corroborated Luke's sighting. On
the day she died, she saw her dead mother in a dressing gown playing
solitaire at the kitchen table. Her mother looked up and smiled. She was
really there, my mother told me over the phone. At the time I doubted

her. This was the last conversation I would have with her. My sister says she was there, and she was coming for my mother. Mom saw other things in the direction of Luke's meeting, which was within hollering distance of her front porch. There was a school there, she assured me, though nothing like it appeared on any maps. More routinely, she saw an Indian man with a mohawk in her living room, gazing absentmindedly at portraits and turning the wooden spinning wheel. She claimed he was her guardian angel. If the right moment had occurred, Luke's ghost and my mother's angel could've seen each other, two ghosts from different historical periods, momentarily caught on the same plane like flies in honey. Patrik's coffin had surfaced less than a half-mile down the road. From the roof of my house I could've seen the event.

The sightings were loosely arranged like a wobbly crown around the Big House. The house was a toy by today's standards. There were four main rooms with a narrow extension divided into two small rooms added off the back. Reportedly, the first phone in the valley was installed here. The house was now the oldest in the county, the only survivor from the early nineteenth century. The other houses had burned or been torn down. The house was the capital of the ruins scattered through the valley, the graves, home sites, and abandoned wells that lay just beneath the thin topsoil and the leaf litter in the woods. One hundred yards east of my house, in the pecan orchard, were the remains of a brick chimney. Daylilies burst into small orange heads around what must've been a home. They looked back like a mournful crowd at something I couldn't see. Across the highway, my grandfather A.C., who owned a thousand acres along the eastern foot of Crooked Mountain, had hauled in an old house to use as a barn. A truck dropped it on concrete blocks. It couldn't have come from very far away. A.C. was frugal. He had a shed extension put on, the tin roof painted, and a concrete block propped up against the door for a step. I saw it every day from my front yard. Just before I left Alabama, I salvaged wood from this barn to make a writing table that I could carry easily into apartments. Arthur Rollins built it for forty dollars. He used ripped four-by-four-inch posts for the legs and the internal frame. Just after building this writing table Rollins was cutting an eighteen-inch oak with a chainsaw. He made a clean cut. There was no splintering. The tree got hung up in the branches of another tree. He yanked on it but it wouldn't budge. He cut through the trunk again higher up to drop the tree straight down. The four-foot section rolled off to the side. The tree was still caught on a branch twenty feet up. He grabbed it and yanked. The oak jammed against another limb. He turned to pick up the saw. The branch cracked, sending the butt of the trunk full into his face. It knocked him flat on his back and peeled the skin from his forehead to his chin. His shirt was soaked with blood in seconds. He leaned against a sweet gum tree holding his head in his hands. His head looked like a melon, it had swelled up so much. Yellow jackets were flying around and crawling in the thick pools of blood at his feet. He stood there looking at them buzz. Then he drove home, took a shower, and drove himself to the hospital.

Rollins was careful felling trees. But he was also lucky. He didn't bind the saw in a pinch or leave a widow's seat in the stump. There are always risks cutting into an oak standing in a thicket. Herb Beecham, a pulp woodcutter, was old enough to remember chainsaws weighing close to ninety pounds. He wore penny loafers in the woods. After a thunderstorm blew over a pecan tree in the back pasture, he shaped an ax handle for me from part of the trunk. "Strong as hickory," he told me. Both men were cavalier about what wood could do to the body. A.C. never used a saw. He had no mechanical ability. He hired that out. Another pulp woodcutter named Joe was cutting timber outside Piedmont. His nephew was using a gasoline-powered bow saw so he could cut closer to the ground. The saw kicked back and cut a diagonal slash across his upper torso. He teetered for an instant before his head fell off. At that moment before his body collapsed into a heap he must have looked like a scarecrow without its head affixed. Joe's own hands must have frozen over his head as his nephew stumbled toward him in the pine woods. The anguish is left in the pine knots in the writing table. Occasionally they too fall out. My desk is a limpid clock recording these tragedies. It remembers Rollins. My desk is a part of this network like an obscure part of a Rube Goldberg machine. It ties me to Rollins. The ax handle Beecham made stands in the corner. If this was what Walter Benjamin called a dreamworld,[41] it was a phantasmagoria coated with blood. Benjamin's seemingly simple concept of a dreamworld is immediately more complicated once Rollins, chainsaws, dogwoods, rattlesnakes, loafers, and the Civil War are added to the mix. The hills of Alabama teem with ghosts, insects, hearts, and other organs of darkness. Anthropologist Michael Taussig sees what could be considered the dialectical double to a dreamworld in what he calls a "culture of terror, a space of death" around the rubber plantations in Colombia.[42] Here the magical world of the commodity is placid with the psychedelic root *yage*. The glass and iron structures of the arcade are exchanged for vines, stories, and the woman of the forest. But however misty either world is, stories, commodities, and broken hearts move inside the arcades and what Joseph Conrad called the heart of darkness.

As far as I know Patrik had no such work table. The coffin he surfaced in may be the closest approximation. It allowed him the fantasy that he was a U-boat commander, or at least his lover. What Patrik did was to separate the romance of the U-boat commander from the claustrophobic cold and the underwater eddies, allowing him the fantasy that leather and muscled sweaters operated unimpeded in one facet of the day while the other fantasies prowled beneath the surface. Inevitably his artwork resembled wreckage and his Nazi-officer fantasies turned rancid. Patrik looked at things through a periscope like a U-boat commander. A wooden school desk in a secondhand furniture store floated passively in the corner. Sighted by Patrik, it was heavily laden with memories. Torpedoed, it was studded with protruding nail points hammered up through the seat and the writing surface, a reproduced suicide note pinned to the surface. The desk appears as another successful sinking. My desk is pockmarked with nail holes. If it were a liquid I might be able to see Rollins's face and hands after his accident. There is a mesmerism in the grain of the wood that looks like an undertow in the ocean.

My own apartment is studded with Patrik's images. From his side of the world, it must have been like looking through the porthole of the ship from the seaside as if he were a mermaid, or peeking into my room through something like a knothole in a barn door as Duchamp portrayed in his *Étant donnés*. Each of Patrik's images provided a slightly different view back into me. As a phenomenon Patrik was like a weather system seeping into the various levels of my world. I felt a cold mist blowing into my home. I could feel the seasickness coming from his touch. If only his body were contained in the craft. Inside he must've been slowly turning back into the North Sea as the water steadily eroded the footings under me. How fortunate that he would name the body of water he was to become. How long this would take is incalculable. How long will it take before the tectonic plates undergirding the sea move and leave him stranded on a dry seabed? Is there something like Moby Dick inside the

water with him that will evolve with dryness? I was so acclimated to ruins; I never thought to ask A.C. when he was alive about any of these
houses. Nor did I ever ask Patrik when he was alive what his work meant
or where he would go.

For

Just up the road from where Luke saw the man was a deserted sharecropper's home. Four tiny rooms, tin roof, unpainted pine boards, it was
littered with abandoned pots and pans, limp trusses, colored medicine
bottles, oddly shaped corn whiskey and pop bottles, rifle shells, spent
calendars, newspapers, and magazines with big pictures. There was
nothing big about this house. The house was a post–Civil War relic, built
sometime after the great desert left by that war. The yeoman farmers
were killed off. The man who lived here when I was a kid was named Bob
Parker. His brother John worked for A.C. and lived in the Big House.
I never noticed when Bob left. The house was deserted. No one spoke
about where he went. The house was empty for years until my cousin
Joe tore it down, leaving a heap of boards riddled with nails, providing
a cover for a beetle metropolis. It was houses like this that prepared me
for Patrik's work.

The layout of the farm commemorated the dead. A.C. had named each
pasture after the man (now dead) from whom he had purchased that
acreage. There were the Harper pasture, the Warlick, and the Barnwell.
The descendants of the Harpers still lived on Highway 9. I'd heard stories
about Warlick and his desperate desire to find the Creek Indian gold buried somewhere around the house. He had built a huge mule barn near
the creek down below the Big House. Then there was the concrete cabin
in the back pasture we used as a bee house to extract honey. It was built
by a black dentist in the 1920s. He didn't last long. Then there was the
abandoned house on the hill at the farthest reaches of the back pasture.
There was nothing left here but the foundation swallowed by the dirt.
But then one day, there was. A woman appeared at A.C.'s front door.
A.C. didn't know her by sight or by her initial introduction. She had lived
here on the farm when she was a little girl. Hers was the home on the
hill overlooking the creek in the back pasture. The woman was close to

seventy years old. I knew the house she was talking about. After a hard rain, shards of porcelain plates would come to the surface. A.C. told me that before the family left, the mother and daughter had walked around the house breaking all the china. Why? One afternoon the husband had gone to the hollow next to the tiny stream. There, surrounded by ferns under a hardwood canopy, he shot himself dead with a shotgun. The hollow would have amplified the sound. The wife and children moved away. This woman lived in California. Her car was parked under a water oak next to a dog pen crawling with periwinkle. A.C. asked me to take her to the Back Barn and down into the hollow. No words were spoken. I took her to the head of the hollow. She walked up alone. I sat next to the stream. Where had the body been taken for burial? I knew the top of his head was blown out and depending on the time of year could have been quickly filled with yellow jackets and flies, forming a strange, squirming bloom in the leaf litter against the green ferns. It's been years since I've been to the Back Barn. What was so mysterious about this lonely woman visiting the spot where her father disappeared is now part of who I am. The details have meshed with my fat and become indistinguishable from the butter spread across my muscle. She appears against the woods that are nothing but a whiteness. Then, with her appearance, trees, rocks, and the creek emerge into view.

In my remembrance Patrik's body is likewise a white landscape. It is unmarked. All the cuts are healed. Up close, I might still be able to see the scars as thin slivers strung into a kind of delicate handwriting spread over his hands and forearms. His body was regularly patrolled in life by razors, glass, and knives, but their touch for the moment has been stilled and the blood that seeped out is more like the thin creases of paper cuts forming a lacelike pattern. The critical phenomenon around Patrik is the closing of the wounds. All the memories have sealed themselves off. Bridget of Sweden in a vision enumerated 5,490 wounds on the body of Christ. When Jesus appeared to Thomas, all these were completely healed except the wound in his abdomen where the centurion's spear had been thrust. This is where Thomas's hand was fated to appear. But this miracle was for Thomas alone. The road going down into the center of the farm is now officially called Shelton Road. Its connection to A.C. and me is hidden. The present residents know a few of my cousins, my

uncle, and my father who stayed behind. They had no part in this dream stage of the farm.

Ghost Slip

Inside the Big House on the wall next to the door in the upstairs bedroom, I found an inscription Luke left as a child in 1917. He had written his name and the date on the wall in pencil. It was still there in 1979 when my wife painted over it with a milky latex paint, which meant the interior walls hadn't been painted since before 1917. The note had waited for something that may never have happened, and now it was gone. Luke and his family moved a quarter-mile down the road to a house built from rough pine. The rent was cheaper. They were sharecroppers. Their new house burned up around lunchtime in a chimney fire. Luke's mama was making biscuits. They had just come in from work, and the house caught fire. The chimney was shooting fire into the sky. The pine house turned into a blaze of yellows and oranges with huge clouds of black smoke. The house burned up so quickly they had to leave their shoes on the porch. I found the remains of the chimney slumped in a mound of dirt in what my grandfather A.C. called the Barnwell Pasture. This too was close.

Smithy the backhoe operator who lived down toward Nance's Creek had vanished. His body was found a year later, vibrating with the currents in the muck in a lake at the top of a mountain. But he left no supernatural trace, especially after the power was cut off. A dead pit bull was still tied to his chain. His toolboxes were stuffed with dried-up rattlesnakes. Piles of old photographs, presumably of his family, were dumped in a shoebox in the bedroom. The freezer and refrigerator were moldering with rotting food. What was surprising was why ruptures or slips in the normal like Patrik's, the man in overalls, and my mother's ghost didn't happen more routinely, considering all the ruins in the valley. Here whole worlds had vanished, not once but repeatedly. I knew of no other sightings in the valley. After an extensive interview process with families of the Nancy's Creek Methodist Church and the Hollis Crossroad Baptist Church, I had found no concrete sightings. Fifty-eight percent, a surprisingly high percentage, acknowledged a belief in ghosts though they had never seen one. The idea that there were ghosts in this valley disturbed them. Ghosts were demonic, associated with witches. Jesus ruled this valley, they assured me. That left me with three accounts of the material supernatural. Two informants were dead. The dozer operator refused to discuss the events, though his account may or may not be supernatural. It was a wooden box out of place. Patrik was my supposition that nudged me toward the other three. I was the fourth informant.

No one had noticed these stories in a systematic way. Each of the informants' ghost stories were locked up with them in their own circle of confidants. My mother didn't know Luke. Luke didn't know the dozer operator. Each story faded. Luke's account vanished when he died. The dozer operator clammed up. Only my mother talked openly, but her accounts were densely intertwined with her belief in angels. And the ghosts, if they were there at all, seemed to be an extension of her personality. Certainly she had been disposed to see ghosts her entire life, but only now and in this particular place did she see them regularly. The idea that it was here, in a quarter-mile radius of the Big House, and not just in the psychological structure of the individual, would've alarmed the church families. That would mean it was something about here. My mother was just a divining rod. It was slow coming to me that my mother's ability to see ghosts was a condition linked to a place created over time. It wasn't a genetic or even a special gift; it was a history of nudges, slips, losses, and movements that started when she was a little girl. Her father Eli didn't drive. When my mother was old enough to work the pedals of the car she became his chauffeur. It was a simple push, a tiny displacement, but significant in its proportion. She acted as a prosthetic extension for Eli, his double at the wheel, not unlike a more famous example of Anna Freud's extension of her father as he grew more and more ill with cancer. I was envious when I heard the story as a teenager. But then I quickly recognized what I was envious of didn't exist. Eli wasn't doting toward my mother. There doesn't appear to have been any particular closeness. She hardly spoke of him after his death. His image hung silently in my grandmother's house. A photograph of Eli solemnly posed in our living room without comment. My mother had to wait in the car like an arm asleep until Eli returned, except the sleep that touched at her was more pervasive than the surface of the catnaps she took waiting for him in the car. She was the youngest of three children and was slotted to be the practical one. She was in a life where ghosts watched her and waited for the right moment to appear.[43]

Neither Luke nor the dozer operator saw a ghost before or afterward. It was only in this loose crown pointing north and east from the Big House that the supernatural slipped through. Inside this crown there must have been a constant humming, a kind of singing in the grass and in the dirt that my mother heard, like air being forced through tiny holes. I never heard the sound. My mother must have. It wasn't her imagination. According to the historian Elias Canetti, the dead often appear first behind the living as a singing or humming. In his book *Crowds and Power* Canetti retells a story about the South African Xhosa in 1856. A little girl goes to the river to draw water. There she encounters strange beings. She hears something like the water singing. They are emissaries of the dead. Behind them are thousands waiting to spill into this world. She tells her father, who tells a powerful chief. The dead have a message. They want to return and rid the land of the English. But sacrifices have to be made first. The prize cattle have to be slaughtered. Their blood is to soak the ground. The cattle are killed by the thousands as the day approaches for the dead to slip across the threshold. With so much protein now consumed by the dead, the living are pulled across the same threshold. There is widespread starvation and death. The day arrives. Nothing occurs. The dead never appear. Out of a population of 124,000, some 68,000 die of starvation. The survivors are weak skeletons and are now totally dependent on the English. The chief, who initiated the uprising, survives. He is more powerful than he was before.[44] Canetti makes the point that the dead stare as a crowd across the invisible line separating them from the living. Their voices, their songs, are more melodic and stronger, and in that moment were more seductive. In the world of the dead, the cattle are fat; the millet fields are thick and spread across the hills. There are no British. The dead appear here in Alabama as isolated lonely ghosts, survivors of some holocaust on the other side where even the dead are no longer safe.[45]

Geological Slip

The congruence of sightings around the Big House hinted at a fault line, a geological Freudian slip. From Patrik's side of the world, the valley must have appeared as a landscape dotted with soft spots where a coffin could emerge amid the long strips of rock and hard pack that formed broad planes where it would be virtually impossible for even a supernatural craft to surface. I could see the heads of these soft spots on the surface: fire-ant mounds, hand-dug wells, graves, deep mud, and beaver swamps. But these were omnipresent in the valley, however critical they were as emergence points. What made the Big House special was its very survival. It was what Canetti refers to as the survivor, the last one standing in a field of corpses. The house was the last standing structure from the first settlement wave. It was singular, like a mangled word in a perfectly disciplined line, a standing wooden version of what Freud noted as a slip point into a floral unconscious, a place where the ghosts of animals, wisteria, and cornstalks mingle with the human in a supernatural landscape.

On the mountains west of A.C.'s pastures the big timber companies had hired crews to poison the hardwoods. Another crew would follow planting pine seedlings once the hardwoods had died, in the now-open understory. Some of the dead oaks and hickories were large enough to be seen from the pasture below. They looked like the pale hands of drowning men sinking into a green sea. I had a dream that beneath these trees were tunnels running through the mountains back to a moonlit ocean. I had a compass. I could feel the water's current. These dead trees were temporary doors. Once the roots rotted and the dirt settled, the doors would be closed. What was beyond these tunnels and the moonlit sea that I couldn't guess then? This was before the first of my grandparents died and decades before Patrik. In my dream, I caught a fleeting glance of the moon's sheen on the water, which seemed to be physically a part of the moon as if it were a giant tadpole squirming on the surface. Now I would say with certainty this was Patrik's North Sea. The dream is another sign from my past, another piece of history preparing me to step across the threshold.

The material surface underlying the dream wasn't pretty. Gangs of skinny, sunburned men and teenage boys—my brother worked on a crew like this—lugging bush axes, high-powered aerosol cans of bug spray for yellow jackets, and a mechanical syringe filled with poison, methodically crisscrossing the woods, killing trees. The axes were used to slash big gaping hunks from the trunks to administer the poison. Yellow jackets and rattlesnakes were constant hazards. I stepped on a rattlesnake in these hills once. Only strange luck prevented me from being bit. The cuts left in the tree trunk weren't what Freud meant by slips, though like one, a world was unintentionally released in the reordering of the ecosystem and in my dreams. The bite the bush ax left formed an open mouth. A slip is like a mouth appearing on the surface of an interaction. One of the great slips in Freud's life occurred when his father was accosted by ruffians. His hat was knocked to the ground. His father left and walked off. Freud was humiliated by his father's passivity.

In his own work on slips Freud barely acknowledges the setting except as a silent backdrop for the conversation. There is the vaguest contextualization in which the slip occurs. One of his most sustained examples occurred around 1900. A middle-aged Freud is on vacation. He is on a train running between Vienna, his home, and an unnamed Italian destination. In the compartment he starts up a conversation with a young Austrian Jew who is familiar with his work. Already Freud is a minor celebrity. The conversation turns to the position of Jews in the Austro-Hungarian empire, a subject that touches Freud deeply. (To attain his coveted professorate, several valuable art pieces were moved from the household of one of his clients to an official's home.) The young man is passionate. Ambitious, capable Jewish careers are stunted. There have already been anti-Jewish riots in the empire. Discrimination is routine. The Holocaust is scarcely a generation ahead. The young man concludes his speech with a line from Virgil's *Aeneid* where Dido, the queen of Carthage, curses Aeneas, the legendary founder of Rome. He presents the quote in Latin: "From my bones let an avenger arise." Freud would've immediately known this reference to Hannibal's invasion of the Italian peninsula in the Second Punic War. Here's where Freud's account takes a decisive turn. The young man has rearranged the quote, omitting a pronoun. The line is actually stronger with the omission. Freud knows the correct line and politely supplies it. Ruffled, the young man challenges Freud. He knows that Freud maintains that no mistake, however small, is accidental but is rather connected to an unconscious drive. Freud accepts the young man's proposition with one condition, that he answer each question as honestly and without reservation as possible. What follows is a loose network of seemingly disparate images—vials of dried blood, old men who look like vultures, the French occupation of Italian cities, the accusations of child murders against the Jews, images of saints. The pieces come together quickly for Freud. The young man is awaiting news of whether his lover, who is probably gentile, is pregnant. Freud goes further. He begins to point to the connections back to Dido.

The young man is reliving Dido's curse on the gentiles. Horrified, the young man stops Freud and falls back into silence.[46]

Freud doesn't record whether anyone overheard his conversation with the young man. It's likely that if they were there, they wouldn't have noticed anything unusual other than the young man's passionate expressions, and then the ensuing silence. They wouldn't have noticed the slip, even if they were listening carefully. The ensuing conversation moves so quickly through the young man's associations that it would have been difficult to follow. Not to mention the historical and literary demands made upon the eavesdropper. The conversation needs to be slowed down to see its gaps and its mazelike structure. It's not enough to see Freud's attendance to the young man's slip as a slip in and of itself. Certainly it is that, but as a slip it reaches back through Freud to some of his deepest memories. Slowed down, the surface of Freud's account shows fissures that reach toward other worlds. The discreet dryness of the scene comes to life. In the Freud account, the young student's slip is a single word, an omitted pronoun. Freud argues for a strong monogamous bond between this word and the repressed thought. But any word in the disputed line from Virgil could have and would have arrived at the same conclusion—some sooner, some slower. The entire line is active, not just the omitted word. But what if the recognized slip in the quoted line was just the tip of a pyramid buried in sand? And what if as the pyramid was excavated, the hole became larger and larger as the surrounding conversation, the other actors, the actual leather, wood, and steel constituting the setting in the railcar, the body postures spread across the seats, and the network of commodities interlacing the participants into a giant corset, were dug up and brought into view? The tip Freud sees turns out to be the smallest part of a pharaoh's labyrinthine pyramid.

One of Patrik's installations was titled *Translucent Lid*. You entered a room with rows of folding chairs. A record player was playing the New Christy Minstrels. The walls were empty. The record was scratchy and saccharine. At front, functioning as an altar, was a kitschy coffee table covered in broken glass. Laid on top was an enormous beef tongue. Almost immediately the tongue began to disintegrate so that it could lie more tenderly on the shards. The rot created a network of invisible frames that emanated out in widening circles. The show was closed that night. The Pentecostal tongue was removed, the pieces folded up. The record player and records were taken back to the apartment. Patrik's own tongue was no doubt imagined on the glass and then in the garbage, licking stickiness. What Freud imagined as a slip of the tongue had slipped out of the mouth and into the world.

Toolkit

When I was five years old I tried to uncover an underground river. Grandmother Pearl had told me stories about underground rivers and how sinkholes could open up and swallow a house. On the way to school at the corner of Pelham Road and Mountain Avenue was a gray, bleached-wood two-story house. The house appeared deserted, but different objects would appear in the street-level windows as if they were actors on narrow stages with the curtains drawn behind them. A glass jar with a sweet potato balanced with toothpicks, an empty vase, a red-headed hammer, a cigar box, and a metal pot appeared. I imagined the inside of the house had already disappeared down the river. I didn't tell anyone about my plans to find the river. I waited. The extended family was at the farm for Sunday lunch at the concrete cabin. We did this every week. I knew Indians could hear things before they could be seen by putting their ears to the ground. I bent down and put my ear to the dirt. I wanted to hear the water. The ground around the tulip poplar was bare. Cows slumbered here to stay cool. I heard it. I hammered at the ground with a hoe. I could barely scratch the surface, the ground was so hard. Sometimes before I fell asleep I had nightmares about turning over and over as if I were caught in one of those underground river currents in a tight space that created the horrible sense of a dark claustrophobia. I needed sky in which to drown. I was terrified of that water. Why was I trying to find it?

My attempted excavation was a failure. I didn't know how to use a hoe or a shovel. I was too weak to shoulder a pick. That changed. In front of the Big House was a hand-dug well. Its depth is almost unfathomable in my memory. It was probably no more than fifteen feet deep. I could see my own face looking into its bottom. For a while a king snake lived on the dirt shelf framing the water. The water table was easily accessible, but I keep feeling that the well was an inverted Tower of Babel. Its depths were as mysterious and unreachable as a photograph of Pearl as a young woman. She was a beautiful woman. I could've dug the well. I'm taller and stronger than the man or men who dug it in the 1840s. My shovel is sharper and its head more tightly socketed than those dead men's. But the difficulty for me is different. It's a hole I can't dig because these holes are now narrow shafts drilled in darkness by a mechanical apparatus. The deepest hole I ever dug was four feet. It was my grandmother Pearl's grave. I'd never dug a human's grave. I was born too late to learn that skill. I had buried animals, dug ditches, and planted trees. These were related skills, but a grave required a new set of abilities. I'd never gone that deep.

In Alabama, the legal requirement is eight feet long by two feet wide by four feet deep. That is a sizable amount of dirt. The space in the cemetery was constricted. To the right of Pearl's grave was my grandfather Eli's crypt. There was a relatively small space for the thrown-up dirt. The rest would have to be hauled off in the back of my pickup and dumped along the edges of the cemetery. The grass around the dig needed to be kept clean. No dirt could be ground into the grass blades. The dug-up dirt would have to be shaped and smoothed into a form resembling a beached whale for the funeral. A perplexing problem was how to keep the sides straight going down. I had a tendency to widen the hole as I dug deeper. The English spade left a scalloplike pattern on the sides. I laid out the grave with four spikes, string, a carpenter's rule, and a roofing square. I laid the pattern in the ground parallel to Eli's grave and square with the Landers headstone. I sharpened the spade with a bastard file. Then I cut the grass into long rolls and carefully placed them to the side. I spread a dull green tarp on the ground alongside to catch the dirt. I drew the wheelbarrow along the side to catch the dirt to be hauled off. I cut a shallow trench with the spade at the top. I scooped out the loose dirt that was left in the square space at the end. I used the spade to push a row of dirt forward. I then stepped back in sequential steps, until there was a soft bed of dirt. I pulled the long-handled shovel out of the truck and removed the loose dirt in long sweeps. The result was an eight-inch imprint of a grave, like the top spread of a bed pulled back. The ground was hard packed. I used alternately a railroad pick and a grubbing mattock to open up a step at the end so I could repeat the process of pushing blade cuts of dirt into the open trench. I could have reached the mythic six-foot mark under different circumstances. I would have gotten more dirt in my hair throwing the dirt out. It would have been a bit more difficult to keep the sides straight. Even at four feet I had a tendency to curve out the bottom. My grandmother's grave I stole from a backhoe. It was my mother's gift to me.

The ends of this act were unexpected. The spade was stolen. The shovel handle broke. The rake disappeared. The framing square may be the one I still have in my car. The carpenter's rule rusted at the hinges. The wheelbarrow ended up in the landfill after slowly disintegrating in the weather. I sold the truck and bought a Datsun three-quarter ton. An old woman turned her giant Chevy like a missile into the broadside of the truck. The truck was totaled. I bought the Toyota one-ton that I traveled the country in. After 230,000 miles it was stolen while I was in Thailand. A snake-skinny white guy squeezed through the sliding rear window after jimmying the lock on the camper shell. He was incompetent. It took him forty minutes to hotwire the truck. A neighbor watched the whole thing from her balcony in the dark. The police took an hour to arrive.

For Patrik the surfaces of things were membranes to be violated. He looked for tiny cracks and fissures where something could be inserted. But his object was to move across the surface not like a rock climber but like a deep-sea diver, looking for an entrance to the tunnels beneath the ocean. He didn't have any special skills to go to the floor of the ocean. He could barely swim. He couldn't hold his breath for thirty seconds, but it wasn't about physical talents or even concrete possibilities. He wanted to materialize where it could only be imagined. He wanted entry into the world where the rock plates thrust and erupt in long horizontal folds. He thrived on the friction and the floating vertigo in the world beneath the world. Patrik left behind a representation of his toolkit. He took an antique manicure set and clumsily attached printout labels to most of the instruments. The effect was an immediate tension between the slender and slightly sinister-appearing tools and the cranked-out gas station–like labels stuck on them. The set had simulated ivory handles and was carried in a leather case with a soft, towel-like interior. In Patrik's hands it looked like a cut-up organ in a hospital display case. Patrik's undergraduate degree was in economics, and here pieces of that past reappear. The tools reads left to right like this: Top left, "individualism" is tagged to a slender hook. Next to it, "classical ideas" is a flat narrow blade. Then there is a piece missing. Completing the row is "the philosophy of history" on a nail clipper. The second row starts with "economic doctrines." It's a tiny blade. A long file is named "progress of society." An emery board appears with no name. It's just a board. Underneath, a pick stars as "the laws of production." No name is given to the most delicate and sharpest tool in the kit. The next tool after that looks like a tear stretched out at 180 miles an hour. It isn't made of metal. It's "modern science." "Of money" is a blunt tip. A small pair of pointed scissors lies there like a dead ibis. Patrik has given it no name. The last tool looks like a dog bone stood upright. It's the "role of government."

Patrik's toolkit was different from the one Sampson used in the execution of Damien, the regicide in 1746 in the book *Discipline and Punish*. Michel Foucault uses this event to crack open the door to his history of the French penal system. He, too, spent time in Buffalo, in the early 1970s. Patrik's work vibrates on my walls less than three-quarters of a mile from where Foucault lived. This would have pleased Patrik. His tools are metaphors here. His deadly body-biting tools are out of sight. Butcher knives and leather belts were part of this list. Electricity in chairs and shock treatments would have to be included. Poor Damien was tortured, then drawn and quartered. What was left was thrown into a pile of wood and burned to ashes. A stray dog was drawn to the warm spot left by the fire. The tools the executioner Samson used were an iron ladle to pour boiling lead over Damien's hand, a large iron pincher designed to pull the plug of flesh from the body, various ropes, a small jackknife he used to cut Damien's shoulder tendons, an unmentioned leather whip for the horses, and six small, undernourished draft horses. Foucault noted that the execution followed a logic designed to produce the maximum experience of pain and the production of a sign coded into the tortured body. Singularly, each tool was insignificant in the production of this sign. Whether each tool had larger metaphorical implications isn't revealed by Foucault. Patrik took this step in his manicure kit. And by doing so, he moved the directions of the individual tools in the manicure set to society itself. For once, blood is absent. It approaches a kind of political statement. The violence is deferred.

In the few paintings I have by Patrik—he painted rarely—he has taken the next step and revealed the violence again. Across the portraits of contorted bodies with erect penises the size of baseball bats, he has written the same kind of political terminology. Reconciling these two different pieces isn't necessary but it may be as simple, if that word is ever applicable to Patrik, as his fantasy to shave me. It remained his fantasy. It was never mine. The idea terrified me. Patrik was fascinated by a large surgical scar over my lower back just above my butt. It was in the shape of a bull's head, and the horns reached around my waist. The top of the bull's head looked over my jeans in the space between my belt and T-shirt. The scar was the product of a skin graft after the removal of a cancerous birthmark. The head replaced the birthmark. It was a sign that the new labyrinth that the Minotaur dreamed of was already there and was the same as the person.

Wet Stench

The idea that the Big House was haunted never occurred to me when I lived there. A middle-aged woman who visited my home as part of a historical tour of homes told me she sensed a supernatural presence in what was once a small bedroom on the first floor. It was now the bathroom. I no longer remember who told me that an elderly woman had died in her bed here before 1940. The room was very small. Her bed must've been big enough just for her. I never sensed her.[47] That I no longer know who told me the story is my haunting. It's as if both of them are hiding from me. The claw-foot bathtub in my house lay back in a stoic iron silence, completely dead but benign. The large mirror over the mantle threw back distorted, wavy reflections as the silvering came loose unevenly across its surface, but it comforted rather than startled me. My wife Debbie interrupted a foot-long king snake stretched out on the bathroom floor in the sunlight. Chimney swifts fluttered in the chimney. A redheaded woodpecker hammering on the window frame inside the bedroom woke me up from a nap. None of these things disturbed me. The house became haunted when I no longer lived there. Then it became difficult to come into the Big House. My ex-wife had changed it. My things moldered in the corner or gathered dust in heaps on the floor. She had added new pieces. Everything was transformed. I could barely stand up when I came into the house. Memories pounded me. The threshold from the kitchen to the living room was insurmountable. I had to be pulled across by the force of Debbie's voice. "Your things are in the next room."

Walter Benjamin described a similar phenomenon. In an early essay on Kafka he noticed the difficulty of movement in his stories and then compared this with an excerpt from a physics textbook.[48] Characters like Gregor Samsa seemed fixed in place, while Kafka's own sentences seem to take off in a swirling musical movement like a Johann Sebastian Bach cantata that shifts, ever so slightly, in theme. The physics text describes the turbulent molecular construction of the floor and the difficulties inherent in taking a step across it moving seventy thousand miles an hour and landing on solid ground. I wanted to go back in time and atone for my involvement in pain. I wanted to hold what had slipped away from me. What I thought was the past ached to spill out of my arms and legs. It wasn't. It was the shock of seeing myself trapped like Luke in the Big House, another name on the wall, being buried alive. A ghost would've given me hope that I wouldn't be erased from my own home. Dirt might have poured from my shoulder socket if it were wrenched free, just as if I had been buried.

This was a different kind of haunting from the one that opened itself to Luke and my mother. It was closer to what Freud described in his essay "The Uncanny." Freud didn't believe in ghosts, but hauntings were a different matter. Like me, he was seemingly unfazed by the possibility of a ghost. The uncanny was different. Freud describes a series of events that momentarily disturbed, even frightened him. The first is his reaction to the E. T. A. Hoffmann story "The Sandman." The story was published in 1819, exactly one hundred years before his own published essay. Freud uses the story as his template for the uncanny without ever articulating what drew him to the account or his own reactions while reading it. It could be that what was most disturbing to Freud was just how close his own preoccupations and themes were to Hoffmann's. It was as if he and Hoffmann were interchangeable actors in a preordained script playing a repeating role. It was the horror of realizing, as Borges puts it, that you are a character in someone else's story.[49]

Offhandedly, Freud then notes other examples. A medium's advertisement caught his eye as he was passing by on the street. Freud avoids telling the reader what specifically ruffled him. He doesn't mention whether he saw the Sandman at some point. The Sandman is the most disturbing incident of the uncanny Freud trots out even if it is inside a short story. The story must have had diminishing effects with his repeated readings and its demystification on his library shelf. Other examples are likewise ephemeral, like the coincidence of a birthday with a hat-check number. The omnipresence of the panoptic grid in Vienna, in which addresses, hats, and seats are numbered, provided a spinning roulette wheel for psychic coincidences. Freud was relatively unfazed by these occurrences.[50] They were regular and, by their very nature, short in duration. What Freud described as the uncanny wasn't like stepping into an anthill in the half-light and having fire ants crawling up your leg—the anthill could have been seen and avoided, and its effects are predictable. But the next example is the only incident that specifically took place inside his home. It was during the war. His sons were serving on the Eastern Front. Their safety was not assured. The British embargo had created severe shortages in Vienna. Unmentioned is whether Freud's caseload had declined. He's reading the British magazine *The Strand*. One particular story pricks his interest. A young couple moves into an apartment. The furniture is adorned with animal feet. In the dark at night they feel something moving around the room. There is a wet stench. Freud is momentarily unnerved as the room in the story changes into a swamp crawling with crocodiles. What doesn't disturb Freud? H.D., the writer/patient/ friend, recounts Freud fondling his collection of statues and figures from the ancient world.[51] These objects seem like Patrik's work, perpetually uncanny like the constant movement of the sea.

Early in his essay, Freud comes to a singular point while trying to articulate what exactly the uncanny is. The first section of the essay is devoted to an archaeology of the word. Freud rummages through a series of Greek, Hebrew, Latin, English, and German dictionaries he probably pulled from his bookshelf to arrive at his operative definition of the uncanny as the un-homely. It is a curious act of prestidigitation that leaves one extension of the meaning of the uncanny unexplained, virtually un-noticed even by Freud, who includes it in his encyclopedic zeal. It comes near the end of this section. It isn't highlighted or particularly noted, but the passage prefigures what is to come in the next sections, "The Sandman," the crocodile passage, and two of Freud's revealing footnotes about repeatedly returning to the red light district in a foreign city and about encountering his double in a bathroom mirror on a train. The passage describes a dry lake bottom becoming wet.[52] The full passage reads thus:

> "What do you mean by 'mysterious'?" "Well, I have the same impression with them as I have with a buried spring or a dried-up pond. You can't walk over them without constantly feeling that water might reappear." "We call that uncanny; you call it mysterious. So, what makes you think there's something hidden and unreliable about the family?"[53]

Freud's imagination is not normally geological but archaeological. But here he conceptualized the uncanny as an underground network of riv-ers and streams looking to come through the surface at soft spots, form-ing a liquid Rome. Patrik was adrift in these waters.

The vertigo of the uncanny occurs when the seemingly solid gives way to liquid—what Benjamin described as seasickness on dry land. Benja-min's phrase refers to what he considered the unstable quality of Kafka's prose and its effect on the reader. Whether he felt it or not away from the book is unclear. Freud identified this sensation, the imminent overpow-ering wetness and the loss of footing, as the dead coming back to life. This was the foundation for the uncanny. But neither he nor Benjamin could quite face it. An important part of Freud's essay is his control over the disturbed moments. He cuts off the transformation. He reestablishes the seal over the dry lakebed to prevent the repressed from bubbling up. There was nothing about even those objects and moments described in his essay "The Uncanny" that approached a critical threshold of trans-formation into something incarnational. Freud's essay is instead haunted by the Sandman and dryness, dry eyes, dry vaginas, dry swamps, and sawdust-stuffed dicks. Sand pours into everything.

There was a dryness in Patrik's work that expanded even to his wit.

His work aimed at becoming a dead lakebed with the evidence of its former life bleached on the cracked mud. If the school hadn't closed his exhibit on the very night it opened, Patrik would have allowed the beef tongue to split and come apart with rot, and then harden into something like the glass shards it lay on. Water would have destroyed *Utopia: Termite Season*, but Patrik imagined fire. The uncanny as Freud imagined it is wet, even if it is haunted by sand. But that's evidence that a larger body of water is or has been nearby, something like a river or an ocean. Patrik wants the aftermath of wetness. He wants a dead lake.

The Sandman

Kafka was familiar with Freud's work, though he dismissed it. The Austrian Freud was probably completely unaware of his Czech countryman Kafka, although they were both subjects of the Austro-Hungarian empire till its breakup in the aftermath of World War I. Benjamin read both and was influenced by each. He was the youngest of the three and, unlike them, born in Germany. He was the son of bourgeois Jewish parents. He attended lectures by Georg Simmel and early on formed the ambition to become Germany's greatest literary critic. His academic career was troubled. He never received his terminal degree or a coveted academic position. Instead he traveled, wrote pieces for magazines and journals, and for a time produced a radio show for children. Instability seemed to follow him. His marriage broke up. He was increasingly identified as a Marxist. Finances were a continual concern. He translated Proust into German, and almost imperceptibly he became a virtual exile. He went to Moscow, Naples, Paris, Capri, and later Denmark, but never home. By the 1930s, Benjamin couldn't safely return to Berlin. His own worsening economic situation and the deteriorating political situation made such a move extremely costly. It wasn't only the money and the Nazis, it was something Benjamin described as an illness, against which he had to be inoculated. It was homesickness. This homesickness wasn't ordinary. Benjamin rarely surfaces in his own work or appears to be the least bit sentimental about family members or friends who might have remained in Berlin. So what is the feeling that resembled an illness? Is Benjamin homesick for the future of Berlin? It could be the same feeling of vertigo that characterizes the uncanny. The nausea is part of something falling out of the self. This may be the heart of what Freud called the uncanny. It's not just the spring bubbling up through a dead lake bottom. It is the feeling of dust dissolving into the mud as the water's head pushes through.

In 1932 Walter Benjamin started work on his record of home, *A Berlin Childhood around 1900*. In retrospect, the book acts as an introduction to the enormous memory palace Benjamin excavated in *The Arcades Project*. Here Benjamin attempted to reproduce in his version of nineteenth-century Paris the same moving equilibrium as that of the storm that blows his famous angel of history in the debris in his recovered mosaic of bits, quotes, and rubbish. The project was begun in the same decade but never finished. Its end was unreachable. The small book about his childhood was produced as an inoculation against homesickness. It, too, was never finished. Benjamin never returned home. The only way to stop the *Arcades* project was for Benjamin to become part of his paper city. He had to slip across the threshold into the land behind the North Wind. There is nothing like the iron scaffolding that Benjamin chronicles in his history of Paris holding up *The Arcades Project*. There are instead thousands of tiny passages threatening to bubble up, though that miracle seems indefinitely postponed. The vertigo never happens.

Benjamin's *Arcades Project* is an enormous memory palace with empty streets touched by shadows. The Sandman has come and gone, leaving a dry world. In that massive voice collage, there are three Americans who appear. The easiest to see is Edgar Allan Poe, who through Baudelaire exercised a mesmerizing influence on Benjamin's readings of Marx. Poe's influence could be added alongside Proust's and Kafka's. The second is a man known as Count Rumford, a chemist who immigrated to Prussia and obtained rank there for his work. The last is Ambrose Bierce, the writer noted for his harrowing accounts of the Civil War. He disappeared into either the Colorado mountains or Mexico, likely another suicide. He appears in *Konvolut K* in *The Arcades Project*, "Dream City and Dream House," in a passage on magnetopathic experience. This was a door to Patrik's North Sea. In the Bierce short story Benjamin refers to, a condemned man is pushed from a bridge over Owl Creek. The rope catches. His body jerks, swings back against the railing. The rope shreds. He falls into the water. The soldiers fire their breech-loaded rifles and miss. The current grabs him. Miraculously, he's able to get his hands untied. Almost a mile downstream, he climbs out of the muddy water. His clothes stick to his body. His boots are sodden. He trudges through the woods headed for home. It's near the end of the war. In the distance across the field, he sees his wife come out of the house headed for the well. She is winding the bucket down into the water. He's out of the woods. Only the field separates him from her. He's just starting to call, when he feels the rope around his neck snatching him back. His wife vanishes. The dream is in the instant, in the space as he falls off the bridge. Bierce stops the story here. But what if the rope breaks only after the fantasy is blacked out? He falls into the water again. He's recaptured. He's rehanged. This time he knows he can't trudge through the woods. He has to race. He has to strain even harder to get his wife to look up, so that when the rope catches he will see her face. Maybe she'll call his name before he blacks out. He is practicing the last microseconds, straining to get home. Each time the memory is repeated, a blackness encroaches along the edges, turning the wide woods into a tunnel, then a trail, to a line the size of a paper cut, leading back home. He is a different kind of Marco Polo, aimed at a home he can never reach, even as the tunnels in his memory palace are collapsing. There is no dry land. Everywhere is water. The dreamer skims across the surface like Peter going toward Jesus on the Sea of Galilee before he collapses into the rolling water.

Ivory Soap

The horses that my ex-wife Debbie loved had scratched a trail in the pasture with their hooves as they ambled up to be fed. There was a wider and deeper path left by the young bulls that curled around the slight slope toward where there had been a salt lick. The last path was unrecognizable to me. It wasn't left by animals. It was left by me. It was barely there in the grass and dirt, hardly a trail at all. For years I've walked across the pasture toward the creek where it was easy to cross, then up the slope through the ash trees, hickories, and giant wild grape vines into the red barn, and then the final hill with its white chert[54] driveway to A.C. and Mary Pullen's house. What I was seeing was something like a photograph in reverse, the resubmerging of the image into the solution. My footsteps were the lightest, shallowest scratches and the first to vanish. The stability of the Big House was an illusion. Even it doesn't stay still. It moved on thousands of tiny mouse, beetle, and toad legs. The house scurried. It had heartbeats. For an instant I saw the Big House rear up on its haunches. I had a house jack, a strangely small contraption with some heavy oak blocks. With it I could raise quadrants of the house off the brick pillars it rested on. It wasn't hard. Once it was jacked up, I slipped in shims ostensibly to level the floors, but there was no calculation or level used. It was more an act of trying to wake the house up by getting it off the ground it had heavily settled into. From underneath, the house's muscles could be seen in the huge long timbers that carried the weight. Now freed of me, it moved at will, a castle with legs. In my world I didn't change into a beetle. The Big House became a hive that moved.

I couldn't enter the house freely. I had to knock to be admitted. No dog barked for me. The pasture looked different. It was noticeably smaller. The creek bank was overwhelmed by alders and willows. Years earlier, I had planted a weeping willow for Debbie, near the creek in view of our bedroom window. I nailed together an enclosure around the tree to keep the young bulls from belly-rubbing the skinny trunk and eating the tender leaves. The creek bank was clean then. Young saplings were ruthlessly grazed by the bulls. This was the first willow to die as a seven-foot tree. The bulls' weight pushed over the posts. They squeezed against the open spaces between the boards. Now the ground was dry and hard. There were more fire-ant colonies. A neighbor's mixed-breed cows had overgrazed the pasture. A large branch had fallen to the ground, splitting the trunk of the Princess tree. The longleaf pines slumbered along the edges. New Chinese barbed wire was strung across the rusty scraps of the old wire.

Inside the house I can't recall the proper sizes of objects in their spatial frames. Things loom. Others shrink and skitter away like mice. The room changes dramatically like a giant lung, expanding and contracting around the imagined space of my person dropped like a deep-sea diver into the dark sea.[55] I rely on my obsessive figuring and the measurements taken when I lived in the space. The blue room was seventeen paces times fourteen. The stove room was broken into quadrants of different sizes. But even these decay and mutate. The numbers in my measurements take on animal bodies and masks. They smell as if my mother, a mathematician, had handled them. The stability of the frame itself is momentary. Each room becomes a door to another room, sometimes far, far removed in time and space. When I came back through the door into the house, everything was alive.[56] The first to speak were the Kenmore refrigerator and the ancient pop bottles collected on top. Together they said my name over and over. The Kenmore was like the sound of the sea rushing, and the pop bottles screamed like skinny seabirds. The pie safe by the door, older and coming unglued at the joints, said, "I know your mother." The table under the window remarked that it would follow me. "I'll wait for you in your apartment in Buffalo," and then it slipped out that it has had many owners and I'm not the last. I was called into the blue room through the open door. I wanted the sofa to remember the night Debbie lay stretched out in a pink camisole. As I crossed the threshold, the room was turning, with the cast-iron ceiling fan acting as a winch. The fireplace was roaring. I'd only seen a glimpse of a fire in it years ago when an artist used the house as a studio. But that was a small domestic fire. This was a furnace. The threat of a chimney fire was imminent. Bricks were missing in the chimney above the roof from previous near-catastrophic fires. Behind me, the voices changed. No longer was it my name. The bookcase murmured something incoherent. The individual volumes were a bundle of different voices whispering different names and their original value on the market. It struck me—it was all in English. I put my ear to the collection of arrowheads in the mahogany case. The arrowheads sounded like beetles trying to scuttle underground. The seashells sang; it sounded like my mother drowning. The frog skeleton hummed as my grandmother told me, "Ivory Soap, it floats, Ivory Soap, it floats." Beneath the floor I could hear a strange crying—the buried sonic effects of a thousand years ago when the mound builders lived here. With the frog skeleton and the arrowheads was an artifact I'd had since I was six years old. It was a knight from a castle that my mother got me for Christmas. He was the last survivor. I remember how fascinated I was that he came from Germany. I couldn't bear to hear what the knight was saying. Marx argued the knight would utter only the statement "Our use value may interest men, but it does not belong to us as objects. What does belong to us as objects, however, is our value. Our own intercourse as commodities proves it. We relate to each other merely as exchange values." Whether this would be in German or English is unspecified by Marx. The knight spoke in German to me but I understood him. The meaning would be the same in Marx's superorganism of capital. Our relationship would be superfluous. The commodities calling out my name were descendants of the sirens luring me onto a dark sea.[57] I thought I could see a coffin bobbing on the water.

I wait for the dead I loved to return in dreams. I wish for them hard. I want to step outside my own body and call them in from the pasture. This would be better, but the ghosts I've inherited from my mother aren't the same kind she lived with. Hers had bodies. I have things through which the dead watch. Patrik is part of a memory system now, along with A.C., Mary Pullen, Pearl, my mother, the malamute Ruah, the dog Red Cloud I befriended when I was six, and the stories of my ancestors in the Civil War. Dead, Patrik became another feature in my apartment. His art hangs alongside pictures of my family. His body drips blood and forms in the air like a fine foglike mist that penetrates my grandmother's sofa, my son's baseball glove, and whatever I'm working on. He isn't just here; he is part of a network of water and ruins surrounding my farm. It had been years since Patrik appeared in my dreams. But there he was, shorter and frailer than I remembered him, as if he'd just returned from an ordeal on the tundra. Wherever he had been, there had been a cost. We talked in what was my mother's front yard. The ambulance that carried her away would have parked right about where we were. The resemblance between him and the Indian man with a mohawk whom my mother considered her guardian angel was very close. All of the ghosts here are frail. They've paid in fat to appear on this side of the world. They've squeezed through the holes like solitary ants from a dying superorganism behind the living. The ghosts seem lonely, isolated, and able to sustain themselves aboveground only for minimal bits of time, as if the doors here hung precariously and could shut suddenly, leaving them stranded. Lazarus came back from the dead only when Jesus called his name. There's no mention in the Gospel of his reaction to what happened to him after his return. Perhaps he, like Jesus himself after his own resurrection, returned to the other world. What else could Lazarus do? What evidence could be procured for those who doubted him? There was no miraculous hole in his abdomen. Did Patrik have a soft spot that fit my finger in the back of his head where the bullet exited? There was no mark left by the coffin submarine when it made an appearance in the old beaver swamp. Mr. Brown made sure of that. You can never tell the owners what happened, he told me. A coffin would have necessitated an investigation. That couldn't happen.

In the 1955 Mexican novel *Pedro Páramo*, the narrator comes to his mother's village. He has never been there, though he has heard her talk about it his entire life. He has never seen his father. He has no interest in the man. On her deathbed, his mother extracts the promise that he'll return and get what is due from his father. This is the last moment in the novel in which the boundaries between this world and the world of the dead are clear. The first person the son encounters on the road leading toward the village seems alive. But that's all. There are only shells of the living in this village. A shell is fitted like honey poured over the narrator. He is covered in a thick second skin. This is only temporary. The honey moves with an inexorable force, pulling him deeper into the other world. The novel, by Juan Rulfo, was a favorite of Gabriel García Márquez, who could recite the book by heart. It would turn out to be the author's final work. The imminent follow-up that played on the edges never materialized. The author finally destroyed what pieces there were in 1986, just before his own death. There are certain biographical convergences between the author and Patrik. In Mexico it was a dry ghostworld, a hollowed-out superorganism. In Alabama it's a green world of frogs, red ants, and pine trees that draws Patrik to the surface. There is no mother's wish.

His father was dead and buried in Tennessee. It was something about me and my world that was magnetized, that drew Patrik back into a world that, like Juan Rulfo's narrator, he had never seen. And now even my own world was beyond my memory. There was no recognizable path. But there was never a moment reminiscent of the crocodiles in the English apartment of the young couple described in Freud's essay on the uncanny, though his appearance in broad daylight at the old beaver swamp is comparable. If that could happen, there might come a time when I would sense Patrik in my apartment.

Dumbo's Kingdom

The first time I encountered Patrik was in 1960. He hadn't even been born yet. But there he is when I think back. I was five years old. There was a Christmas party at my school in the early evening. I can't remember the presence of anyone other than my mother, though I'm sure my whole family was there. In the back near the door I see someone I know is Patrik. He's wearing a bowtie with a striped shirt and a blazer. I got a windup bird toy. Thirty-five years later I bought my son the same toy. We went down to the edge of the creek to fly the bird. Immediately the bird flew into a hole in the darkness. Tyree has no memory of the toy. Leonardo da Vinci designed it. After the Christmas party we went to the drive-in theater to see Jules Verne's *Journey to the Center of the Earth*. James Mason played the visionary geologist. I was already obsessed with the world underground. I thought Dumbo the elephant ruled Limbo, which was suspended between the surface of the earth and hell. I came to conceptualize quicksand as the doorway to Dumbo's kingdom. But once one passed through that door, Limbo was dry and was an underground theater of enormous dimensions. It would take days to fly from end to end. There is a similar underground in the movie. The characters descend through a passageway in a dormant volcano in Iceland, following the map left behind hundreds of years earlier by a Norwegian alchemist who had been to the center of the earth and back. At the center the explorers find a luminous interior lit from within, an ocean, and dinosaurs. Pterodactyls soar overhead. I knew even at five this was a movie, but still I believed in Dumbo's kingdom, a world pieced together from Disney, Tarzan films, Sunday school, and this movie. If I had let my bird toy loose it would fly back here. This kind of childhood bedazzlement fascinated Walter Benjamin. He studiously collected children's books and toys. It could be said that his attraction to the Paris arcades, a miniature city housed in iron and glass structures, was inspired by a child's snow globe, and like a snow globe, the arcades seemed to be eerily lit from inside. The underworld was what Benjamin might have described as an inverted arcade, a world beneath a world. For Benjamin, the arcades were the breeding swamps for commodity fetishization and provided one of the first habitats for the emergence of half-human objects and half-object humans. Dumbo's world was an inverted arcade sunk back into my psyche and memory. Patrik reached back and turned the key in an old box lock and opened the door to a network of swarming memories. Now I see Patrik at the Christmas party and at the center of the earth flying with Dumbo.

My mother regularly encountered spirits. I thought I'd never seen them before Patrik. I was wrong. I was very young and staying with my grandmother Mary Pullen in the house in town when the ghost appeared. The ghost never moved. It stood in the corner and stared at me next to a half-opened closet door. The ghost was very tall and wore a hat. I was convinced it was Abraham Lincoln come for me since I was a rebel. The visitation happened in the upstairs bedroom known as the blue room. The blue room was at the front of the house overlooking a red light on Pelham Road. Late at night the room was infiltrated by the sounds of the big trucks gearing down and then rumbling through the intersection. When I was older, I moved into the bedroom across the hall. There you could hear drunken men yelling out the jailhouse windows. I never saw anything in this room or ever again in the house that was built for haunting. It was built by slaves in the 1850s. For a time it must've been grand, but by the 1930s, when A.C. and Mary Pullen moved in, it was in decline. The white picket fence that surrounded the house was overgrown with privet. The world around it had evaporated. The nineteenth-century Baptist church behind the house had been demolished. Widows and spinsters lived in the houses across the street. There was a service station across the street. A car lot and a Western Auto store nudged up close to the edge of the yard. The house was a big slumbering pile of brick and wood. Mary Pullen and A.C. lived there by themselves, except for grandkids on Saturday night. I lived with them for nearly a year when my family moved away to North Carolina. It was then that I saw Abraham Lincoln. At the time I didn't appreciate the honor. Nor did I suspect this would be the first visit from the other side to prepare me for the future.

I played in the ruins of the Baptist church behind the house. My grandfather Eli had attended this church. It had been the largest church in Jacksonville. Hundreds of bodies had congregated in these ruins. The structure had been hauled away except for the basement, which was sunk deep in the ground. It looked like the abandoned swimming pool at the elementary school, except here were the psychic remains of an invisible crowd in the piles of brick and torn-up hymnals in the corner. For me the church was a castle that had been overrun and demolished. An older neighbor girl with dark hair named Bernice guided me through the underground rooms. I thought she was Joan of Arc. I had a crush on her, though it's likely her name is wrong—a residue of Dante's narrator's guide through the *Inferno*. I've never forgotten this screen memory even though the screen was as thick as the wall. The plaster and brick walls of the basement were one stratum. There were no layers, no cutaways in which history could be read. It was like the mud walls of the spillway behind the Big Lake. The dark-haired girl was held like a ghost's fossil in the plaster.

The stories I told Tyree growing up were about the hidden worlds like the church basement that quivered next to ours like angels or prehistoric dragonflies. Neither he nor I ever tried to fly out the second-story window or saw those dragonflies. Their origin was in my own childhood, which meant that things from my past were still looking for me. Behind the Big House I built Tyree a sandbox under the shade of a pecan tree. I laid in treated timbers in a square and dug out the interior box so Tyree could dig deep into the sand. I wheeled in loads of sand and filled it to the top. Our dogs liked to belly sprawl on the sand to stay cool. Tyree would sit on our Rottweiler and pretend he was riding a wolf. Just under the first ten inches of sand was a locked door. I didn't have the key. A faraway sound could occasionally be heard on the other side. When I knocked, the sound receded. The door remained locked. Tyree knocked one day. We heard footsteps slowly coming up the stairs. After a moment the door opened, though no one was there. Tyree and I went down the stairs. At the bottom was a very long corridor lit from within. We walked south for a quarter of a mile. The air was pleasant. We came to a large open space streaming with a greenish light. There were no light bulbs or gas lamps. Above us like a sky was the Big Lake. I could see the catfishes' white bellies, the torpedo-shaped grass carps, sunbathing bullfrogs, murderous bass, snapping turtles in the mud, and a muskrat. At the end of the lake, there were stairs that went to the surface. We came out behind the spillway. The spillway behind the Big Lake slid through the woods like a fat copperhead. The water coming out of the dam was an oily muck in the deep shade. The branches formed an arcadelike roof over the ditch. The ditch wasn't pretty. There had been no attempt to naturalize the cut. It was brutally dug. Smithy did it with a backhoe. The ditch petered out several hundred yards from the lake. In places it might have been ten feet deep. One of his deepest sections became the landfill for the farm. Here the bottom couldn't be seen. The surface was littered with debris that had been deported here in the back of my truck.

Map

James Joyce constructed *Ulysses* to be an architectural blueprint for Dublin. His objective was to compose a map so detailed that if some catastrophe were to wipe it off the map, Dublin could be rebuilt exactly as it was in the first decade of the twentieth century. Measurements were needed. Numbers helped to keep the distortion of memory under control. Joyce kept in touch with friends in Dublin and used them to provide the figures.

I have few contacts where Patrik appeared. What I do have are maps. The first is a topographic map of the valley. The map isn't very useful for my purposes. You can find the Big House on it. A.C.'s lakes are listed. But the scale is wrong. I can figure the mileage, an important parameter, but it doesn't record the psychic eruptions in the designation of family names, deserted houses, or the owner's occupation in the square blocks drawn into the simulated holograph of the topographic map. The second map was produced by the Confederate Army sometime near the end of the Civil War in 1865—Lee would surrender at Appomattox on April 9, 1865. Why the Confederate Army commissioned a map of the valley surrounding the Big House isn't apparent. There appears to be no strategic significance. Sherman had blazed a sixty-mile-wide swath through Georgia and was already pointed north toward the Army of Virginia. Mobile was sealed off from the sea, and Federal troops began their assault on March 27. Tuscaloosa, Montgomery, and West Point in Georgia were gone by early April. Chattanooga to the north had been in Union hands for over a year. Deserters were already limping home. The field office in Macon Georgia, from which the map originated, would be in Union

PART OF NORTHEAST AREA OF RABBIT COUNTRY CALHOUN COUNTY ALA.
COPY OF MAP MADE IN 1865 BY CHARLES F. BAKER, TOPOGRAPHICAL CORPS, CONFEDERATE STATES ARMY AT MACON, GA.
SCALE 1" = ½ MILE   INCHES = 1 MILE

hands by April 21. But before that, it was a sequestered island in an archipelago soon to be submerged under Federal control. The map may have
been a leftover of a ghost order finally being processed like the mysterious work order that K, the surveyor, gets in Kafka's *The Castle*. It is the
aftermath of a military campaign.

A local druggist who collected historical documents came into pos-
session of the map in the 1960s. I'd heard rumors of the map, but I had
never seen it until my father acquired a copy of it around 2005 and hired
an artist to produce a print of it. By this time my mother was dead and
my father had moved to the top of a mountain overlooking the valley.
From his porch the valley was easy to scan. He'd even kept a pair of binoculars nearby, though ostensibly they were used to zero in on birds and
jets landing in Atlanta ninety miles away. My father, A.C. Junior, had
moved on top of the mountain to escape the new houses. He'd chosen
the highest point. Even Crooked Mountain gave up its top to his eyes.
A.C. Junior's mountain is listed without special note on the map. There's
no indication of its elevation. At almost the exact center of the map is
the Big House, bearing the name of its first owner and described here as
the Wid. Burton house. The three letters are what are left once "widow"
is cut in half. A third of a mile to the west is the Widow Champion's,
which is curious. I've seen her grave and she was dead by 1852, or at least
Elizabeth Champion was. Her tombstone still exists in the woods near
the creek. Before her descendants repaired the gravesite in the 1980s,
her marble tombstone lay on the ground split across the middle with
a jagged lightning flash as if the stone's heart were broken. Around her
were at least ten graves, recognizable only by the small piles of rock at
the heads and feet and the slight sag in the ground where each grave had
collapsed. Middle-aged hardwoods had sprung up through the softer
ground. I'd cut a walking stick from a young dogwood here. There was
no evidence of a homesite. The chimney and the stone footings might've
been poached or simply wandered off by themselves. Here on the map
another Widow Champion, with the same name as the one dead in 1852
and likely now in one of the unmarked graves, clutches the door to her
house. Just farther west on the road to Jacksonville are two more widows. The Widow Cannon's house is at the foot of the mountain my father
built his house on. There is no visible evidence of the Cannon house now,

though a surveyor my father hired found a single brick hiding under the leaf litter. He thought he'd stumbled onto a farm nestled onto a small flat plateau next to a wide gentle cleft in the hill. There were long piles of rock edging up the hill, further evidence of a farm. A field had been cleared, cut out of the woods, and the rocks piled along the edges. What he couldn't see was that it was in the shape of a snake encircling an egg. The university archaeologist immediately saw otherwise. The surveyor had stumbled onto a two-thousand-year-old Indian burial ground.

In the days before the giant longleaf pines were timbered and the secondary growth crawled over the hill, the snake would have been easy to see. The altar rock at its center would've been prominent. The Widow Cannon's memory would have registered that she was the first white settler. Her kin hadn't moved these rocks. Wouldn't the moment finally occur when she would have seen the giant snake coiling around the rock egg? It must have happened before her house was built. And yet she probably never saw it. Native sites were routinely and ruthlessly destroyed in the creation of a Protestant landscape. She didn't see a burial ground with a sacrificial altar. She saw a piece of ground cleared of rocks for farming. But something must have stayed her and her family's hand. The grave rocks weren't used in the construction of her home. There was the single, bread loaf–sized handmade brick the surveyor found. It was all that remained of her chimney in the upper reaches of the soil. What supernatural power was accorded to those graves? The road, as it started over the mountain on the Jacksonville side, was named Ladiga after the Creek leader who sold the land to settlers and was a prominent citizen. Rabbittown was named for another Creek leader. But the memories of the violence of the Creek Wars and the Trail of Tears still must've colored the imagination of the widow. Today the widow's residence is insignificant. What happened to the bricks or the widow is irrelevant. It's the pre-Creek burial ground, of a people who saw the rise of the mound builders and vanished likely with the same plagues that are now remembered. One night, or likely over a series of nights, the snake must've swallowed the widow's house and buried the widow inside its own graves.

There are only two graveyards shown on the map, and both existed on the farthest edges to the west in Jacksonville, where John Pelham was buried, and to the east, backed up against the mountains in Rabbittown. I've seen this small church's burial ground. The church is Baptist now. No denomination is marked on the 1865 map, just a square with a cross sticking out. Across the road from the Widow Cannon's is the Widow Wright's. Her house was next to a road that today exists only as a deer trail through the woods. The woods have closed it off. Even on the 1865 map there is evidence that the woods were already closing in. The road fades into a dotted line, and at the end is the Widow Wright's. The small block that represents the house is dwarfed by her name; the widows seem to loom. I count thirteen on the map. Each is dutifully marked. Their dead men were likely Confederate soldiers. Their bodies would have been dumped down wells in Maryland or left to rot in the leaf litter of the Virginia woods. It was too costly to send them home by rail. In the Jacksonville city cemetery there are marked Confederate infantrymen's graves, probably the aftermath of the wounded shipped west by rail out of the Atlanta campaign. The designation of widows stands out on the map like soft granite markers for those who were buried in unmarked graves on Civil War battlefields far from home.

Where Patrik Appeared

On the map, the creek near where Patrik surfaced is indistinguishable from the road. Known as Cottaquilla Creek, it runs almost the entire length of the north-south axis, narrowing at the northern tip into a thin single line winding through the space between two mountains. To the eastern margin is Choccollocco Creek. At the northwestern tip Calvary Walnut Springs is noted with a broken line pushing toward an unnamed mountain. Someone has written "unidentified line" on the map above it. There are no other bodies of water recorded. No lakes, no springs, no beaver swamps are drawn. The lakes would arrive in the mid-twentieth century and then stop with the arrival of the county water system. Swimming pools supplanted them. Wells must have been so prominent in 1865 that there was no need to show them. Each house would've had a well and been connected to a different kind of capillary system from the plastic water lines the county installed in the late 1970s. Across the roadway from Crooked Mountain was the headwater of a creek less than two hundred yards from the burial grounds. I've seen this spring. The creek ran parallel with the highway. This was the creek that powered a small mill. Near the Big House, the mill shown in 1865 is already ancient. It's known as the old mill. But the creek that powered it, and a hundred years in the future filled up the four lakes A.C. built, isn't traced. Only creeks of a certain size are noted. A mile downstream the creek broke out of the narrows formed by the hills and opened into a floodplain. My farmhouse stood on the north side on a slow rise out of the creek. The hillsides on the south were littered with quartz arrowheads. The creek ran another three-quarters of a mile before emptying into Cottaquilla Creek. It was large enough in a big rain to spill over its eight-foot banks. The next site for arrowheads overlooked this intersection from the cleft of a hill above a spreading beaver swamp. The highway cut the swamp into two pieces. My grandfather drained the southern half and cut the timber. Now it was turning back into a swamp. Just above the spring were the arrowheads. Across the highway, a rich lawyer had built an imitation Southern Federal–style mansion with a small lake in front that looked like a dark swimming pool. This is where Patrik would appear.

Debbie's Throne

In the northern fringes of what's represented is a cotton gin house, though on the map it just says "gin house." On the same wavelength across the mountain spine to the west is White's Tanyard. There are no slave holdings or even large farms noted on the map, much less plantations. It was an area of yeoman farmers. Because of the gin house there must've been cotton, though no fields of any kind are represented. There is a poorhouse near Jacksonville. Two doctors are represented. Stephenson's Mill is listed, which is near where the dozer-operator Mr. Brown's house is now. There are no rail lines. It's difficult to distinguish between creeks and roads. Both are drawn in parallel running lines. Just off the center, running north to south, is the largest highway, the Talladega-to-Rome road. It's large enough to hint at being the reason the map was commissioned, except the scale is wrong. The east–west movement of the map is the largest. The Talladega–Rome road is just another detail, and yet there is an odd brilliance to the map. There is a profound sense of proportion. Grief and loss gently dominate the woods, fields, and mountains that flow around the widows' houses like a warm sea, so innocuous and omnipresent that they need no representation. As a war map, it is about the costs of war more than a new campaign. In "A Berlin Chronicle" Walter Benjamin imagined putting together a map of his childhood in Berlin,[58] He wrote: "I have long, indeed for years, played with the idea of setting out the sphere of life—bios—graphically on a map. First I envisioned an ordinary map, but now I would incline to a general staff's map of the landscape around my house, if such a thing existed."[59] What Benjamin couldn't quite imagine when he wrote this in 1932 was that the invading Soviet Army in 1945 would have assembled just this sort of map in its building-by-building destruction of the city.

I've drawn a map. There is no invading army,[60] though in a photograph I have of my son and me, he stares across the landscape like Napoleon on the Russian steppes. What I see in my recollection is that across the pasture, broom straw has taken hold. It is a sign of how poor the soil is. Black bears have returned to the area. There are increasingly frequent painter (a local term for panther) sightings in the mountains. Armadillos scurry across the roads. Bobcats are still scarce. Coyotes thrive. Wild turkeys strut along the roadsides, having lost the shyness that hid them when I was running through these woods. Fire ants dominate the margins of the pasture. It's a different kind of invasion from what took Berlin. The ecology of my memory world is changing. The mill on the creek was evidence of how dominant corn was here prior to the Civil War. It would have been primarily a subsistence crop. Cotton was grown for cash. On the south side of the Big House, overlooking the creek on the rise, was evidence of a cotton field. Coppick's family sharecropped this land in the first part of the twentieth century. The grass here was good. The land sloped off toward the beaver swamp. When this was a cotton field, terraces were edged in to slow erosion. There were still stump holes from longleaf pines that crooked down sometimes two feet or more where the taproots had finally decayed. A.C. would fill the holes with rocks. A cow could break its leg in these holes. What was now a cow pasture had been cotton fields after the longleaf pines had been cut down. When these trees had been here, the understory would have been open. It would have been easy for the original Indian population to walk from the burial grounds to this spot.

The unnamed creek that cut behind the Big House is the spinal column for my mapping. It figures in some way in almost every recollection I have. When Debbie and I moved into the Big House, she would walk up and down the creek looking for snakes. The bank was completely clear then. There were no alders and willows. The young bulls grazed the pasture clean. Close to the road to A.C.'s house the water had cut a narrow chute through the rock, making a small waterfall. There were three large cedar trees nearby in the center of the pasture. Debbie used the smooth shelf in the chute as a chair in the cool water in the summer. The water poured around her shoulders and chest. The image is just another unhinged memory I have of my home. I'm not sure what she's wearing. I think one of our dogs is with her. But the image is inexplicably lovely and dear to me. Now Debbie looks up and says my name. The water is coursing around her as if she were a queen. In the pool below are rock bass that dart like lightning in the water. The bulls are resting in the shade on the banks of the spillway. This moment appears only on my map. The throne in the creek is still there. The cedars have been cut down. The water is shaded now, overgrown with small trees. There are more snakes. The water runs very fast in the narrows and then slows as it broadens out in the softer ground. It was here, just below the Big House, that I crossed the creek every day to go to A.C. and Mary Pullen's house. My feet and arms still recall the motion and steps to get across without getting wet. My cattle stick was used to pivot me from one flat rock to the shore in a quick move. It was on this rise that a team of archaeologists found sackfuls of points from the prehistoric period, relics from the Woodland Indians who built the burial complex in the hillside. In the soft dirt under the Big House I found a blue celt, a ceremonial stone according to a local anthropologist, in the shape of an ax head or heart. It could be stone planchette. Along the length of the creek, there were only two points where arrowheads were ever found. The other was three-quarters of a mile down toward the ancient beaver swamp, on a bluff overlooking a spring emerging from underneath a giant poplar tree. Tyree and I would walk there every day after school to look for arrowheads, and at the fox skeleton in the woods. As a memory system, the creek wasn't like French anthropologist Marc Augé's metro line in Paris. The subway held his memories stable. Augé's map is a brightly colored image of crisscrossing lines anchored by family and loved ones. Historical figures, landmarks, and big events expand the map temporally and spatially. The stops on the line were both historical and personal markers for a man who spent his whole life there. The creek erased memories. Its waters dissolved everything but the hardest recollections, which it shaped to its flow. Even the stone from the old mill was winched out of the creek and hauled off.

The unnamed creek was too shallow for baptism. The creek it emptied into would have been the only water for miles where this would've been possible, except that the beaver swamp surrounding their intersection along the road made it impossible to access. I don't know how the original Baptist congregations handled this in the ninetieth century. Now each church has its own baptismal font, a small part of what could be called the interiorization of the sacred. Before the baptism moved indoors, the congregation must have traveled. In the baptism Max Weber witnessed in North Carolina, some of the participants traveled up to forty miles to a particular sacred location on a creek. There were no such places on this stretch of water. The Champion graves that overlooked the creek settled back into the hardwoods. A.C.'s cattle strolled over them. The sacred zones here weren't Protestant. There was a roughly assembled pine-slab cross on top of a mountain overlooking the Indian burial ground, but there were no crosses evident around the Champion graves or any acknowledgment of Jesus on the one tombstone. There were just head- and footstones. Cow pies were laid in the leaves around them like land mines. What dominated was a more primitive totemic landscape that superseded the Protestant. Giant longleaf pines left over from the loggers, piles of rocks, hundred-year-old barbed wire strung through the hearts of hardwood trees that had grown around it, A.C.'s lakes that were big reservoirs of creatures and dreams,[61] chestnut posts left over from the blight, rocks left behind in the pastures from where the creek had shifted with floods, and fire-ant mounds in the full sun created a sacred landscape of traces, a different form of writing scripted into the ground. A.C. was aware of it but couldn't express it in words. He walked for hours a day checking the cattle, the ditches, the spread of yellow tops in the pasture, and the movement of fire-ant mounds. His work on the surface was very Protestant. He had a definite work ethic. Profit was calculated. Records were kept. But inside of this was an acknowledgment of an alternative memory of the sacred. Again, there are no crosses or Jesus. There are water, grass, cattle, and the marks they left behind in the ground. A.C. was a man obsessed with the stars beneath Alabama.

It's just under the surface and on top of the red clay that the old world still existed. In some places this is scarcely two inches deep. The topsoil is thin in Alabama. Behind the Big House I put in a garden by hand. The main part of the garden had once been a woodpile and rubbish heap. I dug up a bedspring, squashed boots in the shapes of pancakes, ax heads, glass, nails, thin rubber tires, medicine bottles, whiskey bottles, Clorox bottles, and pop bottles. Then there were hundreds of creamy white grubs the size of thumbs, earthworms, and predatory moles. At ten inches I hit clay. Then it was a dead world, rocks and no insects. There were rocks the size of fists, a giant's heart, and squash. At the edge of the pecan tree, roots thick as a girl's arm pushed this deep but no further. The part that had been a pasture had to be chiseled. The ground was hard packed and the first inches matted with Bermuda rhizomes. There were no grubs or earthworms. There were no artifacts, just rocks. I buried the cats under a foot of dirt. The dogs were interred under two or more feet of dirt. Around the shed in the fine soil, ant lions had spiraled pyramids into the ground. The Big House was built on brick pillars. A strong fire-ant colony can reach down as far as five feet, which is the equivalent in human scale of an eleven-story building sunk underground. The fifteen-foot hand-dug well in the front of the Big House isn't much of an achievement by ant standards, barely one story deep. The well was dug with one man in the hole with a pick, a shovel, and a bucket attached to a winch at the top. Another man would wind the bucket of dirt out. A third might be hanging around with a wheelbarrow. Hand- and footholds were carved into the side. I admire the skill that produced the smooth round walls. In the Bierce account of the twice-hanged man, the victim sees the door to the other world in the distance. It's the well his wife is standing next to. If only he could have gotten across the field to his wife. She would have touched his hands, kissed him, and ushered him down the well to the surface of the water. There in the dark the rope would have missed him. The bucket would be substituted. It would be hanged. At the mouth on the surface he could've seen the stars, the well acting like a dark telescope, and his wife's face peering over the edge. The man would fall back into the water like he was being baptized. There he would've found others. Bodies were often dumped down wells during the war. In my world I have tied up watermelons with rope and sunk them into the water past the king snake that lived on the thin rim at the bottom to get them cool. The well was a door to the North Sea.

Benjamin's last project was an attempt to articulate the ceiling of dreams in the iron and glass roofs of the Paris arcades. In Benjamin's portrayal it was a bright, sunny world during the day. At night with the gas lamps, it was a ghostly city. Apparently it was always dusky even in the bright sun. The glass leaked. There was no way to clean the smudgy panes. The arcades were ruins from the beginning. The longleaf pines and sycamores didn't function in this way in Alabama woods. Their canopy of needles and leaves didn't foster commodity fetishization. The arcades were enormous ornate greenhouses with leaky roofs and dingy glass. Benjamin's emphasis on them as key dream structures in nineteenth-century capitalism was overplayed. Department stores quickly supplanted the arcades in the formation of dreamworlds. They were left behind like abandoned locust shells. Actual physical dimensions weren't Benjamin's strong suit. He never cites how high the ceilings were or how many square feet were contained. Rather, his conceptualization of the iron and glass ceiling was spread across the sky, encasing the city, so that it resembled a toy city inside a snow globe. Nor was his attention directed at the arcade's floor and foundation, though there are notable sections on the road surfaces. Memories and dreams are sunk in Alabama into the thin topsoil and the red clay. There inside an inverted arcade roof of fire-ant colonies, graves, wells, animal burrows, taproots, and postholes, memories vibrate. Benjamin's *Arcades Project* portrayed a city on the edge of war. The boulevards were about to split open with the German occupation. It also portrayed a man falling backwards into the future like his own angel or a man being baptized. The work is the act of a man named Benjamin even though the memories produced aren't his own. They are the other Benjamin's, a man whose looks are identical, whose past is the same but whose future is different.

Zeno's Waterfall

What drew Patrik to me initially was more than the suitcase that existed only in the future of our relationship. He had no obvious gifts for prophecy. He saw me as a banker of his work. I would save it. He wouldn't. It wasn't likely he was clairvoyant. I certainly didn't see myself as an archivist. I talked about his work, which was unusual. There was a muteness around it. There were certainly those who liked it—he was hired to do CD cover art, he was in the elite hip scene, and with his membership came the compulsion to acknowledge his work and its artistic value, but the work itself was just out there, something ugly and violent with few if any deft craft moves. His work was, for all its texture, smooth to the eye. I wrote an art review[62] and with Patrik's help posted it around town and on bulletin boards in the art department. It was promptly torn down. Patrik was a controversial character. And then he was intrigued by my own clean-cut qualities that he himself abhorred. I must have seemed like a perfect gentleman descended from Kafka's friend and biographer, the proper Max Brod. I wasn't a part of the elite hip ecosystem. I had no artistic or literary credentials. I was his friend and his banker in the world that would eventually pull him under.

My mother bought me a scroll of maps of the Bible on a four-foot wooden spool. She had acquired it in the dispersal of property of an acquaintance of my grandmother. The dead woman had been a Sunday school teacher at the First Methodist Church. My favorite map was Paul's travels through the Mediterranean world, ending when he was beheaded. It wasn't an ordered excursion but instead resembled a man lost in the labyrinth, first in Palestine, then in Asia Minor, Greece, back to Asia Minor, circular loops that looked like the tracings left by a fly in a morgue flitting from body to body. I was drawn to this. I had it mounted and hung it in my small office in Athens. Patrik would've seen it. It was a map showing how a man's life ended. The colors on the map were soft and soothing. Rome, where his head and body would be separated, looked just like Athens, where he gave his sermon to the unknown God. I had grown up on stories like this. My grandmother Pearl told me two stories about the Civil War. One of my ancestors served as a doctor with General Sherman and was part of his march through Georgia. He was a Georgian and lived outside of Atlanta. When the Union Army came through his home city, they burned everything except his house—the last survivor. This was the only detail of this man's life my grandmother knew. Presumably he returned home after the war. When she told the story there was no condemnation or judgment; instead there was pride. He was an officer and he was there during the great trial that continued to define my grandmother's life. She was in the Daughters of the Confederacy and was a member of the Daughters of the American Revolution. The second story was about a Confederate enlisted man. There was no survivor. There was no coming home in this world. My relation froze to death at night in Virginia under a thin wool blanket and a wet snow. He had survived other storms. There was a trick to staying warm. If one stayed perfectly still underneath the blanket, the snow acted as a white quilt. But if the snow was cracked, the cold would reach in. He must've been dreaming of home. His thighs twitched. His arms unfolded and he froze to death. Pearl described the cracks in the snow as if they were an imprint of his last dreams, a kind of secret hieroglyphics inscribed from below. Now I can add a story of my own to Pearl's accounts.

Near Christmas my son Tyree took me off-roading in his Toyota FJ Cruiser. We broke off Crooked Mountain Road onto an old logging trail through the scrub hardwoods and pines. At some point the county had attempted to block vehicle access into these woods with berms at the entrance. There were bullet-ridden refrigerators tentatively poking their large white carcasses out of the brown leaves, a couple of sodden mattresses, and big plastic bags spilling their guts in an oily ooze. The berms had been flattened out by four-wheelers. Tyree's and other large trucks had gone next. At a couple of points Tyree had the Toyota on three wheels to negotiate the ruts and berms. Small branches scratched the vehicle. We were headed for a waterfall I used to go to before I was married. My brothers Jeff and Jake had discovered it riding horses. They would take their Appaloosa and quarter horse far out into the mountains on these old logging roads. The fall was thirty or forty feet tall, which made it the giant in this part of the county. Just before the creek the trail became impassable for us to drive. A sweet gum tree had fallen across the road. This is where thirty years ago I found a group of Navajo Indians who worked for the Forest Service sitting in a canvas tent around a fire in the middle of the day. It was eighty-five degrees outside. They had been planting pine saplings for the government. I was invited in to sit by the fire. The recollection seems unreal. I used to come here after that and build sand castles next to the creek that even when I was eighteen years old were designed to re-create a time from my childhood when I lived on an island off the North Carolina coast. It was getting dark. It was easily twenty years since I had walked this trail. The waterfall was another half-mile up the slope and around the top and then down back toward Nance's Creek Road to the east. A different creek coming off the mountain powered the fall, though each was headed toward the same larger creek, the same one Patrik's coffin popped up next to. It was after four-thirty. The dusk was encroaching even faster now that Tyree and I were under a thick tree canopy and stumbling down the eastern face of the mountain. We dropped off the trail where I thought the water was. The fall wasn't there. I followed the creek and walked down until the ground flattened. Tyree was getting anxious. There was no trace of a waterfall. "You know where we are?" "Yeah, yeah. It's got to be right here." It was almost completely dark when we stumbled into a small clearing ringed by hardwoods. There, standing alone like an obelisk, was a stone chimney, and around it broken pieces of a foundation from the nineteenth century. The house must've been overcome by fire and then the woods. I'd seen it before, but its effects had been mediated by the certainty I had about where I was and who I was. I was lost now. I didn't know where the falls were. I kept remembering the last time I saw them. The rocks at the top looking down into the small dark pool were covered in white shit—a raptor or vulture, I was told by a wildlife painter. I saw those white-shit-splattered rocks clearly in the twilight. We pitched back onto a deer trail headed up the slope. Tyree was certain we were lost. We were. This was at the beginning of a new experience for both of us. In the Toyota, Tyree didn't feel lost. The insides were crammed with his stuff—Frisbees, stickers on the window, bottle openers, a cooler, various pieces of backpacking gear, old wrappers, CDs, my book *Dreamworlds of Alabama*.[63] How could you be lost in a truck littered with your belongings that smelled like you? In the woods here in the dark, Tyree had no bearings. What had once been familiar to me was utterly strange. I was a foreigner in a foreign land. The senses that had supported me hunting for lost goat kids in the dark along the mountains bordering the far pastures years before were gone. I wanted to show Tyree how much I was like him when I was his age. The waterfalls were to be a gift. Now the ruins meant something else—a beautiful, lonely prophecy of me here in Alabama. I understood better Mr. Brown's reaction to the coffin. The future had to be reburied, if only temporarily. Near the top I found the main trail. We hurried down the narrow logging trail clotted with branches, jumped the creek, crawled into the Toyota, and drove out of the woods. "We should come back in the daylight. I know I can find the falls." "Sure, Dad, next time you're here." The moments for that are narrowing. I missed Patrik's return. I missed the falls. There were good reasons for both. It wasn't in either case entirely my fault.

I did go back and try to find the waterfall. I took my original miscalculations into consideration.[64] The first time, the dark had overtaken us. This time we would start in the morning. But immediately things went wrong. The entrance to Crooked Mountain was closed off with zigzagging ditches. Tyree couldn't get his Toyota cruiser across the obstacles. We had to park much farther away and hike in. In the intervening five years the woods had grown even more dense and unfamiliar. Even the creeks had seemingly altered their courses. I found what was left of the old logging road, and we trudged up the slope. At the top the question that overwhelmed me the first time repeated itself: where on the road do we drop off into the woods to find the waterfall? I remembered the drop was steep and rocky. I had stepped on a young rattlesnake here thirty years ago. I left Tyree and his friend Zack on the logging road. I dropped down to the creek at the bottom of the slope off to my right, imagining I would walk down the creek to the falls. The creek bed was rocky and almost dry. Alabama had been suffering from a drought. The banks were thick with briars and low-lying branches. I bulled my way a quarter of a mile without finding the falls. At two different points I intersected with two other creeks running in different directions. I hollered for Tyree and Zack. They followed my voice and joined me. I walked back up the log-

ging road. I would follow the other creek. They would wait for me. They called up birds. I pushed down the ravine following the creek. I could find no waterfall. It had already been two hours since we left. I rejoined Tyree and Zack. There were three small birds within feet of their outstretched arms. We headed out. It wasn't the right way out. The chimney Tyree and I had found here was nowhere in sight. We were completely lost. I decided we should head east over the mountains to intersect with Nance's Creek Road. The climb and the descent were difficult. We came out at Gaddis's horse farm. Tyree no longer believed in the falls. "No, it was there," Gaddis told him. "Y'all must've just missed it."

For the second time I couldn't find the waterfall. When I was young and lived on the farm, it was easy to find. I never failed. Even then it couldn't be seen from the trail, nor could it be heard. But I was never lost. I found it. Now it seems unreachable and even my memory of it is in question. I remember it being at least thirty feet from where it fell through an opening of large rocks to the small pool at the base. My sister and brother disagree. "Ten foot tops" is their assessment. At the time I was a far better judge of distance. Attached to my memory of the water is that I knew it to be the tallest waterfall in the area. I remember this tag like it was a name on a map. It acted as a placeholder in my recollection. All of it could easily be a screen memory. Or more likely, something like a thorn stuck in my thumb, a torment that has to be cut out. At times like these I better understand Patrik's fascination with cutting. The scars, however thin and delicate, are the marks left behind by the edge, a certainty of memory in the flesh of the past. After my last attempt to find the falls, my calves were cut up by the briars. It was a painful reminder of my failure to show Tyree I was once like him. The cuts were like fragments of the territory left behind on my skin. The world itself was hostile. It closed on me like the dirt in my own grave. Benjamin compares the excavation of memory to a man digging. It's unlikely he ever used a shovel or a pick. However beautiful his image is, it has no physicality, what Benjamin would have described as tactility. His description doesn't sweat. Calluses don't appear on his hands like stigmata. Roots aren't severed. Muscles aren't torn. Even in digging there is an art and skill. Strategies have to be employed. The hole is a live space teeming with the ghosts of the memories from former worlds.

I returned to the woods to find the waterfall. The woods were denser than I remembered. I heard something in the leaves. I stopped. It stopped moving. I stared into the brush separating us. It must be a deer. I came closer. I heard a whisper, "Come closer." I came closer. Through the brush I saw an outline hunched over. Then it stood up to its full height on two legs. I ran. The woods were dark. My feet were heavy. It was chasing me and was very fast. I could hear its feet rustling in the leaves behind me. I saw an ax protruding from the trunk of a tree. I grabbed the handle with my right hand. The ax was locked solidly in the tree. My hand stuck to the handle. In a moment whatever it was would reach me. I took my pocketknife and sawed through the tendons of my right hand. My hand cut just like it was made of fat.[65] I left it there dangling from the handle. I escaped. At a café, with cups of espresso, the talk turned to evil. What is evil? I took my right arm out of my coat pocket and pointed to the empty space protruding past the stump. "This is evil," I said.[66] What crime had my right hand committed that my left hadn't contemplated or touched already? In my living room I have a heavy Swedish ax leaning against the wall; next to it is a hand-forged maul, an English spade, a pecan ax handle, and a walking stick used to run cows. The tools stare across the room at pieces by Patrik and the writing table Rollins made. On it is a blackened fence tool used to cut barbed wire and to hammer and to yank. It looks like a prehistoric bird. On the same table are a stack of Eli Lander's and Mary Pullen's books. There is A.C.'s magnifying glass. A transparent German fountain pen lies on top of French graph paper. A French pocketknife points east toward the sun. Sulking in a metal block is an 1898 Underwood typewriter. Above it is a forged letter from the Soviet Union granting Patrik asylum. A record is playing on a stripped-down turntable. The motor and pulley are exposed. The record is *Murmur* by REM. Like the tree in the woods with the ax in its gut, in the corner is a postcard stand filled with correspondences and handmade postcards turned out by Patrik. He would've stumbled in the forest[67] and then cut and cut at himself. Patrik's great trial was Patrik, despite his military fantasies.

Martha White's Disappearance

If Patrik's coffin ever surfaced again, I never knew of it. Like its first appearance, any others remain a secret miracle. I was the only one that saw through Mr. Brown's report into the coffin itself. It must have been excruciating to be buried again, though probably it was only in the underground water that Patrik's weight might have been buoyant. Why he never came back is undoubtedly related to why he left in the first place. He had one departure. He had an appearance in my world. There is symmetry. I was absent for both and haunted by both. And while disproportional, Patrik reminded me of another disappearance. Martha White was a delicate white cat. She appears in several photographs I took around the Big House. She liked to follow Debbie on her walks up the creek. One moment she was there, Debbie reported, and then she was gone. The most probable explanation was a hawk—Martha White was a small cat—but it was near the place where the ghosts had appeared to Luke and my mother. There was no sound. Did Martha White cross to the other side? A year or so later I thought I saw her crouching along the fence line under the wild roses, hiding from mockingbirds. I called her. There was nothing there. If she or Patrik had been there, could I have endured losing them twice?

Patrik made one visit. But as quickly as he appeared, he was gone again, the coffin buried back into the same mud. I hadn't considered that time was even a factor. Is it like the locusts and Patrik can appear only once a cycle is completed? Why would I suppose he had any control? His art clings to my walls like the split exoskeleton of a locust. At night underneath my anxieties I see what appear to be photographs of my farm in Alabama. It's been twenty years since I've lived there. But the images are still there in quick glimpses stuffed in between other concerns as I lie awake. Some of them are mine—I remember these and I recall them like they were a collection of heavy hieroglyphics. Others I can't recall. Nor do these share the same viewpoint or framing devices as the ones I know. It's as if Patrik's coffin were a camera transmitting images to me from underneath my memories of Alabama. They keep me up. I wait for the next image to appear in the sky formed by my eyelids. Like the lightning Benjamin promised, they illuminate the landscape for a second before turning dark again.[68]

A reasonable person wouldn't suppose Patrik was inside the box. There wasn't any concrete evidence or indication in his work that would have suggested this eventuality. The dozer operator wouldn't have recognized him even if he'd momentarily stepped out of the box into the sun. If he had seen him come up out of the coffin, he likely would have cut him in half with the dozer blade, inadvertently fulfilling one of Patrik's fantasies. Kafka wisely avoids this problem. An announcement comes to the mayor detailing the Hunter's arrival. He portrays the Hunter Gracchus as visible on a bier carried into town, and the Hunter is able to talk with the mayor. There isn't at first glance any indication in Patrik's work that might predict this afterlife. Likely there was nothing in Lazarus's life up to the point of his death that would predict his return. Lazarus and the Hunter represent two different kinds of resurrection. The Hunter is dead but suspended in this world, a victim of the supernatural accident. Lazarus was alive again and would die again presumably, though how his second death would unfold is still impossible to decipher. An absolute zero of biographical details is recorded in the Scriptures. Would his second death be more composed since he had glimpsed the other side, like falling asleep or more like freezing to death or drowning, shivering and gulping? On top of Crooked Mountain, from which Patrik's return could have been glimpsed through ten-by-fifty binoculars but as if through a microscope scanning a virus cell, a rough-cut pine cross is sinking into the mountain like a splinter into a fat thumb. It isn't necessary to see the resurrected Jesus. That's why the Holy Ghost was sent—to be a comforter and an inspiration. Of the twelve disciples only Thomas immediately recognized the risen Christ, and then only when he was instructed to place his hand in the wound.[69] The others, who loved him, knew him, couldn't or didn't see him until he developed in front of their eyes like a photographic negative.

The Hard Facts

Whether it was even Patrik in the craft is questionable since he never showed himself, and it hides the question whether Patrik could appear and be in multiple places at the same time. If his grave were dug up, an embalmed body would be inside the coffin that would be identified as Patrik. But the coffin in the mud itself was a hard fact. Mr. Brown, the bulldozer operator, was still shaking days later when he told me the story. "Shelton, it was the damnedest thing I've ever seen. Who'd bury somebody in a swamp?" He pointed to the dam. "I put it back in the ground. It's in deep now. It isn't coming up again." I'd never seen the dozer operator like this before. His voice was stretched. He was fidgeting. He was a short, heavy plug of a man and a Baptist. He wasn't superstitious. He was sweating under his beige Caterpillar hat. "I'd of quit right there if I didn't need the money." Brown's insistence on the permanence of the second burial was probably not well founded. His knowledge of water was limited. He dug black dirt out of drained lake bottoms. Hydraulics were another matter entirely. In this he was like Patrik. Though he often dressed like a German sailor from the Weimar Republic on shore leave, Patrik had no experience with the sea. He was from a small town in Tennessee. I'm not sure he could even swim. It's ironic, then, that he, like the Hunter Gracchus, would spend eternity on water. He had been practicing for the sea in his work, which is filled with images of water and liquids—

the North Sea, giant slabs of butter melting in fat chair bottoms, images from medical journals of men training underwater in concrete pools, a tongue turning into a greasy slime on glass shards, a man dangling from a ship in shark-infested waters, and the ocean—a ring of blackness made from electrical tape encircling the Gutenberg Bible.[70] At the center of a wooden oval is a medieval portrait of a sailing vessel on a stylized sea. The waves are oscillating lines composed of small V shapes strung across the surface to mimic the water. A man is either being pulled feet first from the gaping mouth of a sea monster or being fed into it headfirst by the crew. Either way a torrent of red blood has spilled out on the frame and has soaked the bare wood and spilled further onto a cluster of snail shells grouped together in a colony. The blood stops here, but something like a canvas deck or a giant, hard, flattened worm extends into space. The effect is an upside-down man's penis. Once his hand is in the sea monster's mouth, the piece has turned into an icon in a church.

One of his key signatures was his own blood splattered on objects as a residue of himself left behind like a cum stain. Here Patrik drew a line. However replete his work is with strapped, erect penises and asparagus spears nudging toward the Virgin, there is no semen. Instead, bleeding is cuming. Patrik's last gesture was to spray the bare wall behind his head with blood. The small pool that formed on the floor parted like the Red Sea for Moses when his body was moved. The installation Patrik constructed around his death shows two overlapping tendencies in his work and life. The first is the desire to turn solids into liquids, and the second is the all-important stain left behind as a marker for the person. It would be more apt to say that Patrik looked for the ocean wherever he was, craning his neck like an ibis in the desert, opening up springs with his scissors. The beginning of the world happened for Patrik when salt water mixed with blood. In each spill he made a tiny reflection of the sea.

A smaller mystery was the coffin Patrik appeared in. It wasn't the one he was buried in. That choice was made by his family. Whether this choice was his or someone else's is uncertain. Kafka never deals with the previous owner of the craft the Hunter Gracchus sails. Similarly, his ship isn't contemporary. As an aesthetic choice, the older coffin was more like Joseph Beuys's fighter plane that went down in the Crimean tundra during World War II. Beuys was rescued by Tartar tribesmen and encased in reindeer fat to keep warm. This may have inspired Patrik and his knife's hatred of fat. His was the superior aesthetic choice. But that the coffin wasn't his isn't surprising. It's part of the miracle, although a small part. Patrik, or at least one Patrik, may still be in his burial coffin in his original grave. It must be pointed out that this is not the transformed Patrik. The choice of the seven-foot pine coffin was probably based on its ability to negotiate the cloudy underworld networks of Alabama. It had been cut from wood indigenous to the valley.

Brown dug dirt out of drained lake bottoms for topsoil. He also dug graves at the Four-Mile United Methodist Church. In the lot next to his house were dump loads of dirt and gravel arranged in long lines like bodies laid out to be buried. Patrik springing up out of the ground threatened this separation. Mr. Brown dug the lake like a grave, and a grave was no different from the soft bottom of the drained lakebed. It was, after all, dirt, nothing more. Patrik's appearance was unacceptable, even for Patrik, since it meant God could be real. The lake was dug in the shape of a bulging circle in the bare dirt. There was no attempt to naturalize the lake into the landscape. It might as well have been a quarter-mile-round swimming pool. There were no shallow edges. The bottom dropped off quickly. The lake was built on top of the springs. There was some concern the weight of the lake itself would shut the spring down. Mr. Brown was certain that the seven-foot box was a coffin. There is a big man in there, he assured me. His opinion was credible given that he dug graves. His estimate of the size was likewise reasonable. He made his living estimating feet and inches. This is how he got paid. He was used to sinking coffins into the ground. This one popped up from the mud buoyant as a boat. This lake was the last one built in the valley before swimming pools took over. Buried inside Weber's essay "'Churches' and 'Sects' in North America" is his account of the baptism of a banker in a muddy river in North Carolina. For Weber, the baptism was crucial to the thesis he advanced that publicly acknowledged church membership functioned as a protective coating for business and facilitated, even intensified, the spirit of capitalism. As an ethnographer, Weber wasn't interested in the water and didn't acknowledge the shift that was happening around him in the Protestant cities he visited in the United States. Baptism was moving from rivers—its original frame in the Baptist denominations—to baptismal fonts, sacred swimming pools inside the church, an unavoidable consequence of urbanization and the consequent shift in the shape of the sacred. In the valley around my house, the shift was part of the hyper-development of the same values Weber chronicled in the first part of the twentieth century in a new storage system of capital and display.

Buried, the coffin left no trace apart from Mr. Brown's insistence. The coffin was well concealed. What Mr. Brown didn't know was that the average weight and height of a man during the Civil War was only five foot six and 140 pounds, which would have made the man inside the seven-foot coffin almost monstrous if he was from that time. Brown himself was no taller, but he weighed 237-plus pounds. He was certain, though, that the coffin dated that far back. I found how certain he was on this point several months later. He had dumped a load of river gravel in my driveway. We were standing in the oily shade of a large mulberry tree next to my tool shed. He bent down and picked up a handmade nail from the dirt, a short square-headed nail: "Same thing in that coffin." He then looked at my house. "Heart pine?" "Yeah," I replied. "Same wood as the coffin. I clipped the edge of that box with the dozer blade. You could smell the turpentine through all that mud." These seemingly insignificant details dated my house to a period before the Civil War. Brown immediately saw the connection. It was a link between my house and the box. Brown's insistence that what he dug up was a coffin forces a whole network of disturbing stories to the surface. He finds the coffin in a cut-off piece of an old beaver swamp. The coffin was sunk in mud to rot the body. The muddy springs still pumped and oozed around this site, which was less than a hundred yards from the road. The road dates back to at least the 1840s. A body was dumped in the box in an unmarked grave near a road. There isn't the slightest indication that anything is there. The closest graveyard, unmarked on the map, is at least a quarter-mile away on higher ground, anchored now by thick cedars. It's a small family plot with stone markers dating back to the 1840s. To get the box in the ground would have required serious work even in soft mud. It's as if Brown imagined a communal murder of a very tall individual. He draws back from saying this.

The old men in the valley were small.[71] A coffin the size Brown saw would've swallowed any of them like a prehistoric whale. John Parker, who worked with me and lived for free in the Big House on A.C.'s farm, was typical. Small in stature, wiry, he was approximately the same size as the average Civil War soldier. He had worked his whole life. His meals were cooked in a cast-iron skillet. He hunkered while we took a break in the shade during roundups. I was flat on my backside. He had seen the murder of other short men. One happened just down the road. A tall man of his age was a rarity because of the protein infrastructure in this world of yeoman and tenant farmers. Such a big coffin would've stressed rooms and doors in the older homes. Once upon a time, if it wasn't Patrik in that coffin, there was a great murder here, a Goliath of an event. I dug a hole in the beaver swamp, so I knew how much effort it would take. A.C. had taken me to where a small cow had died and had to be put underground. He speculated on what had happened and then walked with his arms folded over his stomach to his Buick and drove off. The ground was soft. Big clumps of grass sucked at the mud. I used a long-handled shovel to cut up the muck. On the rise above me I would have been using a pick to chisel out small shovelfuls of dirt. Here the problem was the opposite. The mud pulled on the heart-shaped blade. Occasionally there would be a big rock. It made sucking sounds coming out of the mud. The cow's legs were already stiff and wouldn't bend. I didn't have what it took to break them. Getting that animal into the hole was difficult. I tried pulling the animal with baling twine tied on its legs. The twine was too thin to get a good grip, and I ended up ripping part of the leg off the body like I was yanking a turkey leg off the carcass. I didn't want to touch the animal with my hands. It was too wet to get a truck and chain down here. A.C. didn't own a tractor. I took a large iron bar used for dislodging rocks and camping posts and pried her into the hole. The hole was broader than it was deep because of her outstretched legs. There was water in the bottom of the hole as if I had poured it to cool her in the hot sun. It was a messy grave with the heavy clumps of mud and grass piled on top. In a few weeks, it had sunk level and the grass had reknitted itself across the surface. I couldn't tell where the grave was. A.C. knew its location longer.

This was just across the road from where the coffin was dug up. It was part of the same ancient beaver swamp. I marveled at the difficulty in burying a seven-foot coffin in the muck. If it wasn't Patrik come back—a prospect that mortified many—there was something more horrible buried there. Patrik was at least a redemptive hope. The other was a crime. That Patrik would be connected to a crime and horror is regular. Everything about him and his work points to this kind of convergence. It's the redemptive hope that is surprising. I can't get my head around the particulars. The coffin was there. Brown dug it up. It was pre-Civil War. It was in an unmarked grave in a swamp next to an insignificant rural road. Did Patrik in his supernatural coffin choose to surface here in this network of springs for the first time, or was it that the original grave was like a door to the underworld left open, and Patrik and its occupant had changed positions in God's plan? The first body had been there for over a hundred years. Surely he was convicted by the Holy Ghost by now. The Hunter Gracchus's funeral ship must've had previous passengers. Patrik was a passenger headed toward redemption. I couldn't guess how many years he would travel before God's plan would tire of him.

The possibility of Patrik's appearance generated my own set of questions that overlapped with Mr. Brown's concerns. It seems there was an invisible network of tunnels and passageways undergirding the surface world. I knew stories of underground rivers. I know Brown knew them as well, but before the coffin's arrival they seemed benign. I saw sinkholes in the pastures. I knew there were sedimentary crusts that pointed to a particular geological past and pressure. I was more familiar with miraculous appearances coming through the atmosphere—ghosts, angels, visions of Jesus, and demons: things that squeezed through the oxygen to show themselves. This ghost had come from underneath, covered in mud. My mother regularly saw ghosts. The Pentecostal church I attended was thick with spirit manifestations, but none of these sightings ever became physical or incarnational. Patrik had emerged from this world that is at once behind and beneath mine. He was a new kind of haunting in the Alabama hills, something at the intersection of geological formations and commodity fetishization. What "new" means here may be misleading. My mother's ghosts no doubt came from this intersection that turns like a Möbius strip between the two dimensions, leaving momentary appearances as the only clues to that which rises and falls between the surfaces. Walter Benjamin saw commodities forming a geological plate composed of a swarm of hard-shelled pieces working together like ants in his *Arcades Project*. This didn't preclude ghosts. In his notes for the project, Benjamin describes following a ghost through the walls of houses. The poet Baudelaire may have seen the ghosts Benjamin was looking for to act as his guide to nineteenth-century Paris. *The Arcades Project* seems ready-made for ghosts, but there is no haunting. The uncanny never materializes. The issue is the lack of movement. The hard-shelled pieces are still. It resembles one of Atget's photographs of Paris, in which the streets are emptied of the living. There are buildings and streets but no people. It's a dead colony. Marx's own molecular vision of commodities isn't static but a shifting mosaic of individual commodities bound together in a continually expanding world empire.[72] Marx conceived capitalism to be a kind of superorganism drawing the interior worlds of commodities, the rat tunnels inside walls, memories, desk drawers and suitcases, mining networks, and sewers, into a set of sets reaching out indefinitely toward the land behind the North Wind.

At the end of *Capital*, it's clear that Marx isn't interested in how capital accumulates into grand estates, breathtaking displays of objects, or even gleaming machines. Factories loom in the text like Kafka's castle, foreboding, but are left undescribed. The great metropolises like London and Manchester are unarticulated. Instead, Marx worked on the elaboration of deteriorations at the edges of accumulation—the body, education, food, family, and the home.[73] The text details the formations of new wastelands at the peripheries like Ireland, the psychic interiors of humans, and the rural zones in England. His pawned coat reappears as his lament for his double in the land behind the North Wind.

Soft Spots

For Patrik's submarine coffin, it seemed a more practical matter of hard and soft spots where he could emerge. But scattered near me for miles in either direction were soft spots that other visitors could pass through. Patrik's coffin had surfaced in an old beaver swamp that in 1810 had stretched for nearly a mile. A man named Pinky Burns had trapped the beavers to near extinction, and my grandfather A.C. had drained the swamp, but the water table was still so high the ground floated. It was soft here. Farther north into the stand of pines and hardwoods the ground was hard. A grave would've been chiseled with pick and shovel and the bites measured in inches. Hardness was the regular condition. The humus was a thin layer strewn over red clay and rocks. It's doubtful if even a supernatural coffin could have surfaced there. Regardless, it didn't. For some reason, Patrik missed the well in my front yard and the nearby network of old wells hidden beneath blackberry vines and sodden oak planks. The coffin was like a submarine trapped under the polar ice cap. Patrik had to make a series of both dramatic and navigational decisions to break the surface. He had to locate the soft spots from underneath. I find it difficult to conceptualize what his map looked like except at the points where it intersected with my own, traced out on the surface.

Where he broke the surface was one of several springs within a mile of my address. This was the eastern extreme of a one-mile radius from my home, where the springs were clustered together, making a large, soft opening perfect for a craft to breach. Directly to the south in the body of the old beaver swamp was another large spring that bubbled up from beneath a giant sycamore tree. This spring had been there since before de Soto, based on the archaeological evidence. On the rise directly above it were quartz and flint points. A.C. had built a network of radiating ditches to control this spring. Once A.C. died, the ditches filled up with silt and the beavers came back. But something unprecedented happened. After a decade-long drought the spring dried out. There were more springs farther south in the farthest pasture, a good twenty-minute walk from here, placing them outside the possible surface zone. West was dry to the foot of Crooked Mountain. Here was the spring[74] that fed the creek that emptied into the larger Cottaquilla Creek, just east of where Patrik had arrived. Near this spring was the two-thousand-year-old Indian burial ground with hundreds of bodies laid in snakelike rock piles crawling up the mountain. This would've been a perfect place for Patrik's appearance, except it was out of sight in time and wouldn't be discovered until years later. Patrik was an artist who needed his work to be seen.

He emerged in one of a handful of soft spots in the valley. There was another kind of emergent point that showed up in the recently cleared pastures. These were deep holes that could swallow a leg up to the hip.

The holes were left by the disintegration of tree roots after the trunks had been cut, bulldozed, and burned. A.C. filled the holes with ham-sized rocks as if he suspected something was coming. Besides the beaver swamp or the wells, Patrik would have had to squeeze through one of the fire-ant hills scattered across the pastures around my house. A powerful colony can reach the depth of five feet, a foot deeper than the legal requirement for a grave in Alabama. This choice would've paralleled the scene in *The Way by Swann's* where the past of Proust's narrator Marcel pushes through the madeleine soaked in tea. The cookie is the soft membrane separating the two worlds. In the half-light of the novel's account, the madeleine inside Marcel's mouth is alive. Almost fleshy, the cookie turns into a new species of scallop on the edge of an ocean that is contained in a teacup. Nothing else in the scene is transformed. The bank of pillows on the sofa stays inert rather than bursting into brightly colored coral. The cravat around Marcel's neck doesn't squeeze tighter. This is the world Benjamin[75] points to in *The Arcades Project*, spilling out into the parlor now in the first part of the twentieth century when Proust detailed the deep ecology of capitalism. The arcades were an aquarium with newly emerging life forms. Benjamin was a historical naturalist tracing the evolutionary transformation of the commodity into its modern form. The iron and glass arcades created a conducive environment for the proliferation of commodity fetishization. Pushing through a fire-ant mound, Patrik would have arrived covered in ants, his coffin no different from a cookie.

Gasoline Werewolves

Patrik had steered his craft to within a half-mile of my house; another half-mile and the small mountains of the Appalachian foothills began. Back to the east the relatively flat valley turned into a larger spinal column of higher ridges and pines stretching south to Mount Cheaha, the highest point in Alabama. It was a narrow gap. This part of the valley was still lonely. Patrik had landed in front of a new house going up and halfway between my house (built in the 1840s) and a farmhouse (from the 1920s). Across from it was a tiny house from the 1940s at the edge of a poor pasture. Patrik arrived in the same temporal window as the

coyotes. In addition to the tight geographical squeeze there was a temporal window. Once the lake was built this opening would be closed.
In a few years more houses would be built around the opening Patrik
chose, limiting further the possibility of soft spots in the valley where
a craft could surface and leaving Patrik even fewer choices. The spectral geography had shifted to a different terrain, like my grandmother's
hope chest, like certain pages of books marked by my grandfather, Eli's
dried-up fountain pens, a frog skeleton my mother found in her garage
stored in a plastic baggie, a 1920s 7-Up bottle I found under the house,
a wooden planchette from a 1930s Ouija board, or the fire-ant hills that
were undeterred by the new homes. These pieces were saturated with
the auras of those I loved. At the same instant, they were portals into the
underworld that Marx saw in commodity fetishization. A simple shift in
development didn't necessarily preclude Patrik's reappearance. It wasn't
just the density of houses, the shift from mud-bottom lakes to concrete
swimming pools, but a change in the type of fetish that moved across
the landscape. McCulloch chain saws replaced axes. Gasoline-powered
werewolves patrolled the woods. And then there was the final introduction of hypermodern technology into the home world. Could Patrik pass
through the digital pool of a big-screen TV? The interiorization of the
sacred was in full bloom. The beginnings of the shift were already apparent in Paris on Saturday, January 8, 1938. Michel Leiris, a sometime
participant in the surrealist Durkheimian experiment initiated by Roger
Caillois and George Bataille called the College of Sociology, marked the
shift when he delivered a lecture titled "The Sacred in Everyday Life." He
defined the sacred like this:

> If I compare these various things—top hat, as sign of the father's author-
> ity; small-barreled Smith & Wesson, as sign of his courage and strength;
> moneybox, as sign of the wealth I attributed to him as financial support
> of the house; stove that can burn even though, in principle, it is the
> protective spirit of the hearth; the parents' bedroom that is the epitome
> of the night; the bathroom, in whose secrecy we traded mythological
> accounts and hypotheses on the nature of sexual things; the dangerous
> area stretching out beyond the fortifications; the racecourse, where
> huge sums of money were staked on the luck or skill of important

persons, prestigious through their costumes and deeds; the windows opened by certain elements of language, onto a world where one loses one's footing—if I gather all these facts taken from what was my everyday life as a child, I see forming bit by bit an image of what, for me, is the *sacred*.[76]

Leiris doesn't explain the origins of this new order of the sacred or even acknowledge the oedipal structure inside his own description. Leiris takes it for granted that the father is imbued with the sacred, though what he means by the oedipal father is different from Freud and closer to Patrik. Here there are a literal pistol and gold coins. For Leiris, the new sacred already existed. But his exposition[77] masks a significant revision of Durkheim's work in *The Elementary Forms of the Religious Life* that loomed in the background. Published in 1912, Durkheim's investigation into the underpinnings of society took him into the fieldwork and reports coming out of contacts with the Australian Aborigines, the American Indians, and the islanders of the South Pacific. At the minimum, Leiris takes Durkheim into the psychic worlds of children in Paris and finds them as mysterious and potentially as bloody a world as elementary Australia. In between Durkheim's ancient forms and Leiris's surrealist portrait is the normalized order of things that wrapped around the public spaces of Paris. The objects consolidated the passing of the sacred from the public monument to the interiors of houses, where the sofa becomes an obelisk in the living room. From there, in the decades after Leiris, the sacred drifted like a fog to the interiors of people and things. The world in which Patrik's craft appeared was at the end of an ecological phase when the longleaf pines lost their dominance, hills were being developed, and the logging roads and trails from the 1940s were patrolled by new Japanese four-wheelers. The woods didn't vanish entirely. They passed into another phase, a different kind of spectral wilderness inside the home, like the pages of books, where a craft like Patrik's could emerge.

One consequence of the shift was how Patrik could appear at almost any place or time I held dear—even in the past before his death and now in his death's future. And if Patrik could, my mother was right about the netherworld: entities could momentarily pass through to this world.

It has not happened to me in the way my mother experienced it. She saw the dead. I see what amounts to whitecaps on the ocean horizon. Each break of a wave into foam in the distance mimics something like Moby Dick breaching the surface. In Melville's novel, the whale himself is barely seen. He appears in pieces, in the gold coin nailed to the mast, sailors' stories, the empty space below Ahab's knee, the sound of his artificial leg on the deck at night, the exegesis on color the narrator performs—hinting that there is a larger, more formidable mind at work than that of the nominal narrator, who functions as a double to Moby Dick. These two presences weigh on the account from the beginning. Each whitecap on the horizon could be Moby Dick breaking the surface. Added together, the slips of the ocean are larger and more monstrous than the whale. Each one is a door opening and shutting quickly on the underworld. I've been waiting for Patrik's return in a hallway of doors cut out of relics from Alabama. Even the ants are part of this world. Behind our rented house on Church Street, I had a garden. There's a snapshot showing me in a Marine cap on my knees holding a sixty-pound watermelon. In the afternoons, a young black woman looked after us. I was killing fire ants when she asked me if I knew the Ten Commandments. I looked up and said yes. Then why are you killing ants? I was perplexed. I remember she was very pretty, and after she had left, my mother told me ominously that she was the mistress of the man who owned our house and the antebellum mansion surrounded by magnolias on Pelham Road. I had no idea what this meant. Only that it was part of the world of partially lit tunnels burrowed into spaces beneath our house and around me.

Like Patrik, ants arrived by ship. The ants came to Mobile in the 1930s from Argentina and then fanned out across the Southeast. Fire ants are an invasive species. Their structures reach three to five feet underground. The mounds can rise as much as ten inches off the ground in a fine powder. When my son Tyree was three, he fell onto a fire-ant hill. His arms and legs were covered with bites. A swarm can kill a ninety-pound calf. The ants use their jaws to seize and hold the host and then draw their abdomen up to deliver a sting. Eradication is difficult. The ant queen is encased inside an empire like a throbbing heart. At my mother's funeral I was compulsively rubbing Tyree's crew cut. I see my own arm reaching for my son's head. Off to the side is a fire-ant hill. Someone has kicked it over, and for an instant in my memory there is red boiling against a sandy scab in the green grass.

Patrik's Genealogy

I have Patrik's bound copy of his MFA thesis in my bookshelf. The requisite signature is there in red ink from his major professor. He passed. The title was curiously simple in the light of his normal titles: "11 Installations 09.1983–06.1985." There is a small artist's statement at the beginning[78] and a fake genealogy I produced as part of an essay about Patrik. He was born in 1957 in Sweetwater, Tennessee. His father died of a heart attack in 1983 during what Patrik described as the climb of an overachieving executive on the ladder of success. When he wrote this, his mother was sixty-two, his sister thirty-two, and his brother age thirty. Patrik listed himself first as twenty-six, then he put a slash through it and noted twenty-seven. The slash is like a prophecy of his death. These details are discreetly separated from my genealogy. Patrik appears as a product of a series of unlikely encounters and relationships.

Genealogy

Kurt Schwitters	Gertrude Stein over at Bauhaus
Walt Disney, installationist extraordinaire	Anne Frank
Duchamp's sister who only remembered his boots floating in the corner by the bed	an S.S. Officer
Grandfather Marshall[79] hit by a train while reading algebraic gossip	Florence Nightingale
A woman known only as Lilith	K.
An Amish farm girl who misunderstood his intentions and use of space	This is not Magritte
A Trappist monk	Lizzie Borden, a woman who placed art over feeling

P. K., the artist

The genealogy is a diagram of a speeded-up evolution. Patrik asked me to write something for his MFA thesis. My essay appears next to a short piece written by a former psychiatric nurse who was in love with Patrik. Her name was Linda. My stretch of writing occupies the largest part of Patrik's thesis in script. There is a Polaroid of Linda and me sitting around laughing and smiling. Patrik must've taken the picture. What is strange, looking at it now, is how in that single moment frozen on Polaroid Patrik has forced his way in and eclipsed Linda and me. We're just minor characters in the scene. I was absolutely sure he was in the photograph with us. He wasn't. But there he is, broadly smiling in any recollection I have of that moment. It wasn't the masklike smile I saw as the tragic clown's in his performances but just a guy having a beer. That kind of smiling was something that happened when he was away from being Patrik the artist, drinking beer in the corner at the old 40 Watt Club. The more successful he became, the more he was forced to be Patrik the grinning artist. The costs of such a mask were tremendous and difficult. That mask even appears in his obituary. Patrik's friend John Seawright said, "He just had this very refined sense of the ridiculous and of the comic. If he got angry or upset, he couldn't keep his stern look for long." His coffin was a giant wooden mask that engulfed his body. His brief appearance was his last great art performance.

The primary space of his thesis was occupied by the photographic documentation of his installations between 1983 and 1985. Patrik's installations are difficult to describe in a coherent, straightforward way.[80] His own documentation even in his thesis is virtually nonexistent. There aren't any diagrams, narrative notes, inventories of objects, or overviews. Most of the individual pieces that were assembled into his giant installations returned to the dump. Other pieces that appeared in more than one installation, like the record players, were stored in his apartment. The only documentations Patrik supplied of his work were some barely passable three-by-five photographs. He shot his own work without pretension or skill. He lazily hacked at his installations with the camera as if it were an ax. But even this description is too much. He photographed his own work like he was a bored tourist or a serial killer too empty even to care about killing his victims. I saw many of the installations, but they have slid like trash down the slope into a pit. They were like trying to recall a pile of garbage that moved like a Portuguese man-of-war on the water. The garbage, like the man-of-war, is actually a colonial organism made up of multiple species. I can't separate the lines the artist has laid into the work from the natural collapse and spread of decay.[81] The infrastructure is impossible to see except as a psychological phenomenon. The colors blur and shift like a jellyfish in a warm current. I'm certain there were distinct patterns in the garbage extending out from it like tentacles. But it was dangerous to touch even with a stick. There was a current in the work, something electric and horrible that hit my spine when I saw it. My recollections of Patrik's installations are reduced to feelings, boiled down over the years. I can recall feelings, wonderment, and astonishment at how his body could've moved so much material across those spaces. The man-hours in the installations had to be astronomical. The workmanship was calculated but brutal, if not also childlike. My own squeamishness would've stopped me from sorting through the garbage. Patrik's vision had its own kind of hands and hours. The photographs Patrik took for his thesis have replaced what images I might have had otherwise. Horrible shots, they capture something of the horror that was his work.

Patrik shared studio space with another artist, near the art department. This gave me the opportunity to see Patrik's and another artist's work in progress. The student shared Patrik's vision. He was an installationist as well. He was also southern in a way Patrik never was. Patrik's most visible Southernism was reading Flannery O'Connor. Otherwise he appeared far more like a poor student in the 1930s German gay scene. The student wore Liberty overalls and white T-shirts. One afternoon Patrik showed me his studio mate's final project. It was an old pie safe stocked with murky mason jars filled with pickles, small dirty medicine bottles that he'd dug up or bought at a secondhand store, blue Clorox bottles, and out-of-time pop bottles with now-strange emblems. Behind them were images from *Life* and *Look* magazines, faded postcards, and a thin wooden church fan with a funeral home advertisement. The safe was painted white and tottered on its thin legs. It was very close to the pie safe in the Big House. It was almost identical to the cabinet in the Bull Barn where A.C. stored cattle medicine and a spare tattoo kit for registering the cattle. There were musty farm manuals on the barn shelves. A pile of burlap bags was off to the side. A broken ax was propped jaggedly near the door. Only the half with the dull head remained. The difference between this and the artist's work seemed minimal. If he could have, Patrik's colleague would have framed his piece inside a barn or sharecropper shack just like this.[82] Patrik's studio was a helter-skelter of pieces. Unlike his colleague's work, what he assembled in the gallery was always beyond what I could see around the Big House. There were stained mattresses on Crooked Mountain Road. But Patrik pushed beyond this. A mattress in his installation was transformed into a bloody cake. This confirmed for me my inclusion of Lizzie Borden in his genealogy.

In the genealogy, historical figures from different times and worlds find each other, on what for Patrik must have been bloody, desperate beds. Each link in the genealogy crawls out of the soiled white sheets like a frog squirming out of the swamp. Whether the genealogy can be psychologically verified or not is irrelevant. It's obviously a forgery and a deliberate conceit that, like his work, requires the viewer to weigh each of the images, to turn the images over and over as Patrik assuredly did the garbage in the dumpster while retrieving pieces for his installations. The artist Patrik Keim was a set of elaborate masks[83] represented here in the genealogy. His own face changes imperceptibly in my memory. What few changes took place are probably an illusion caused by how they are lit in my head. While his body aged, his face in my recollections didn't seem to. It got puffier in the photographs as the masks hardened, but I notice this only in retrospect. The faces in his genealogy resemble the shells of ancient erections or a pack of gaunt dogs nailed to a barn wall or something like the painted skeleton of a rhinoceros beetle in which another beetle appears on the back of another beetle on top of another beetle.[84] When I see him smiling in my memory, I feel my own mouth pulled and stuck with pins to hold it in place. In his portraits there is a similar coercion, but this time the face is frozen in a different pose. The imminent moment of a smile has vanished. The corners of the mouth, which were raised like the two forearms of a praying mantis, are refolded into a body stretched out on the floor. Whether it's a look of determination, resignation, or the long, flat neck of a letter awaiting a thin blade to be slipped in to open, I can't tell. These faces swarm in the background of his mediums of self-immobilization. Even the writing in which Patrik obsessively wrapped himself has the smell of gasoline. He has tied up each of these characters in his genealogy. At some point they'll be stacked like cordwood and set afire. Patrik sent me a color copy of a photo of a house on fire. He had fixed in black tape this paragraph on the sheet: "Ever since he saw his father burned to death in a house fire, the smallest whiff of smoke makes his blood run cold and the hair on the back of his neck stand on end."

Did it work? No, Patrik replied flatly. It didn't work for them, he said, referring to his thesis committee. The no wasn't just about the genealogy. The no reached across the body of his work.[85] They didn't get it. Still, they all liked Patrik. He passed. They did connect him to a more conventional genealogy.

In his journal describing the events, Patrik writes:

Ron silent much of the time with a couple of most relevant remarks— can compare with the older established circuit of artists—(like Accone, Connor, Kienhuffe, Borofsky) each piece different time to call it quits fellas. Andy with his offense of directly opening up towards me with his questions if you then—do they like or dislike my work; why? And what criteria do they use to evaluate it with? Mike says yes he likes it but doesn't know if it's good. He feels he can formally defended [sic] if needed, but what makes it good? Or bad? And he feels it's average compared to "art world" but potential for loads more later. Bill rudely read his *Art News* and then chimed in on tonality at the end, prettiness and beauty and market greatness . . . self-destruction, decay, recycle, is a sickness lacks clarity—more specific; Bill says not too articulate. I feel the more ambiguous the better.

I found his work breathtaking and nerve splintering.[86] The genealogy worked for me.[87] The genealogy was a playful and an awful continuance of his artist's statement, awful in that it was prophetic. One figure recedes into the paper, disappearing entirely except for its initial. It is K., who functions as Kafka's voice in *The Castle* and a figure that bears an uncanny resemblance to Patrik. For both, the urge to communicate with the castle is their desperation and their undoing. In this sense, the sins of the father are visited on the son. Patrik Keim was represented by the initials *P* and *K*, separated like twins. Alone, the *K* looks like Franz Kafka's solution for the principal character's name in the novel *The Castle*. On the other side the *P* stands like a dead brother, alone in a mirror. It was the artist's choice. The brother stretches ahead like a shadow. He can be described. Kafka doesn't bother to describe K. beyond a few particulars. He was a surveyor who stumbled into an installation waiting for him.

Several years after Patrik's death, I met a man where I live now who knew him. He had been one of the part owners of The Globe, where Patrik had worked. He'd even hired him. They talked about books, art, and movies. Now he too was in Buffalo. Patrik never knew I'd moved so close to the kind of water he dreamed of. My Athens identity was completely hidden to the bar owner, which isn't surprising. I was more like one of Patrik's characters—a thin man lost in the woods rather than someone who would've been remembered.[88] He, on the other hand, was a man in the broad Athens sun, and while I couldn't recall him, I knew each of the spaces he hung out in and all the Athens celebrities that he moved with. I, no doubt, saw him at The Globe. He probably poured me a Guinness. His name is Laurence Shine. He's an Irishman. He referred to Patrik as St. Patrik. One of Laurence's friends was the local writer/historian John Seawright, who appeared prominently in Patrik's obituary. I vaguely recalled his name and recognized him from his appearance in the Athens music-scene documentary. Laurence tells me he is dead now as well. The woman who fronted the Barbecue Killers is dead, I tell Laurence. I knew her. Laurence knew the band. It was a spectacular time. There were possibilities that bands could follow the B-52s and REM into the national scene. Pylon famously declined to open for U2 and then disbanded. Patrik had his moments, but he couldn't adjust his obsessions with the rapidly evolving scene. His installations look like beached and rotting whales. His color reproductions with phrases superimposed over images looked like knockoff Barbara Krugers. If Patrik was a Spartan hoplite in the gap, the gap itself was becoming larger and larger, leaving him like a solitary man in the middle of Interstate 85 around Atlanta in the twilight.[89] At this moment, Patrik's work itself turned smaller as if he were attempting to escape through the tiny doors left by mice into the back of the North Wind. That escape would come later and other than he imagined.

In a postcard Patrik described his farthest trip north. He had flown into New York City and stayed in New Haven overnight. New York was for Patrik a lonely, sexual place. Then he moved north to Burlington, Vermont, through four inches of snow in the dark. He stays in what he describes as a "dark graying half-mast village on the edges of Lake Champlain—inhaling animal crackers and anxiously watching for the 12 inch to 24 inch storm expected here Friday. Thought I might settle here a bit, but after a couple of days of breaking off two frozen toes. I realize I only have eight more to give." Here again is the countdown that dominated Patrik. He ends the note affectionately, and even innocently, "Call you soon, love, Pat." I was the closest of my family to the land behind the North Wind. The relation serving in the Confederate Army was part of the invasion that reached Gettysburg. A.C. once traveled as far as Cincinnati. Eli and Pearl lived in New York City for a time. My father and brothers have gone much farther, but I am the only one to be aware of the world Herodotus described to the far north. Patrik had been here.[90]

The Unusable Image

Patrik passed on an image to me that he couldn't use. Perhaps I could? The image was a Polaroid taken of the lynching of a fourteen-year-old boy in Mobile, Alabama.[91] The boy is cuffed with his hands behind his back and strung up against the trunk of a tree. For some reason I'm convinced it's an elm, but there is no reason to presume that. It's probably a water oak. His feet are barely ten inches off the ground, as if he was too heavy to hoist or the lynchers too weak and frail—either option ratchets up the monstrousness of the event. The Converse sneakers point helplessly toward the ground just barely out of reach. They're black. His torso is wrapped in a zipped-up windbreaker and it looks like he's wearing khakis. Both details seemed wildly incongruent with his death and emphasize that I can't see the boy himself—only the things he's encased in. In the background you can see the outlines of a modest brick house with a white concrete sidewalk leading up to the front door. Everything seems out of place. It isn't a remote dark zone but right in front of his house. The rope is so short. The knots are clumsily tied. The worst is that the scene isn't imprisoned in the past in a horrific black-and-white photograph with the Klan standing solemnly in front of the dead. The photo was taken with a point-and-shoot Polaroid from the same time and place that frames me. No one else materializes in the photograph. No one is standing by the boy. No one peers out of the window. The boy is alone. Only his Converse sneakers, the only recognizable brand name, have stayed behind to tend the body, the modern counterparts to Mary and Elizabeth, who washed and wrapped the dead Jesus. This photo captures the dead at a moment similar to Peter's vision of Jesus. The cock has crowed three times. Peter realizes the fulfillment of the prophecy. He has turned from Christ three times. In the photo it is as if the sneakers had come off the boy's feet and walked away. It's a different point in time. The shoes stayed. At the funeral home they are finally slipped off, but with his resurrection they will return. The reason Patrik passed on this image wasn't its monstrousness. He dealt routinely with this side of the world. It was because of the historical moment. It was too close.

Much of Patrik's work veered into the darkest places. The high school desk studded with nails and the reproduced suicide note pinned to the desk were hardly delicate. He wrote obsessively about being lost in the anal tract with such graphic detail that it couldn't be read as metaphorical. His later work included gay porn. His portrayals of domestic scenes were unsparingly grotesque. In his installation *Asylum, Asylum*, Patrik placed two mattresses stacked on top of each other at the heart of a tiny maze. Suspended from the ceiling above the bed was a thicket of sticks. A bloody meat cleaver is buried in the mattress. There is no romance here for his parents' conjugal bed. Patrik imagined he crawled out of a stinking swamp and wrote repeatedly about returning to that greasy mud. In another piece he juxtaposed a childhood portrait of his father playing in his yard to bodies thrown into a pile against the building of a concentration camp in Czechoslovakia. Looking for the beautiful in Patrik's work was like poking in shit for a lost gold tooth. His retinal attack had moved to the lyrical. In a Christmas letter Patrik wrote me, all this horror comes out.

One night we were going through a big box of really old photos, some from 1860s–70s. And all of a sudden, mixed in with the ancient photos of my grandmother Frida and her ancient grandparents at family reunions (a la horse and carriage), there were a stack of photos from uncle Bernie's "trip" to a Czechoslovakia concentration camp when he was in the Army during WWII. My lungs gushed empty. The mildew smell of curiosities and memories instantly turned into the rotting odor of stacks of carcasses, burned skeletal hands reaching out of the ovens, stacks of human firewood alongside outside Spartan barracks decorated for Christmas. Gruesome beyond belief. Pictures of my father as a child, chewing on a chicken leg or rib-bone, stacked on top of this other death. New meaning? No sense and nonsense for me. But none of it helped to explain the festering strangeness I felt at my mother's house during the holidays, filled with too many family members. And that strangeness is here in Athens too. Am I in that much of a daze? Is there a mist in my head? Maybe I'm being paranoid, but these continual zigzag, disconnected thoughts and actions make me feel more and more distant from these familiar people and places—they look at me like I'm a primate in the zoo, Tom foolery in a glass cage. They seem to want to communicate, but it's just like with the monkeys in the zoo, the languages don't mesh, so the Observer walks away partially entertained for the moment, usually forgetting the encounter as soon as they turn on their heels, so where do I go from here?! Nice chatting to you. Love, Patrik

It wasn't the horrific violence in the Polaroid set against the suburban stability surrounding the boy in the tree. It was the historical period and its isolation from his own psychic dramas. It was outside Patrik's gaze, not bloody enough. The body is too intact and not in the right setting. It doesn't resemble his or his father's neighborhood. Patrik wasn't faltering before the sacred. It was a technical question about whether it could be turned on himself. And the answer was no. It had no connection to the time of his father's childhood. There wasn't a totalizing logic in his work. The porn was contemporary enough. His musical taste included the German electronic band Kraftwerk. But his portraits of contemporary suburban life were dated, just out of time by decades as if they were re-creations of his childhood. During *Asylum, Asylum*, Patrik wrote in the work journal that was part of the performance, "Thoughts of my mother

and past several years—remember lethargic childhood on couch in front of TV with Mike Douglas." Even he too momentarily remembered and pointed backward.

The world Patrik's work slid up against was primeval. But it was always on the other side of green things in ruin and decay. It was a dusty, grimy world. Historically, it was the aftermath of the psychic terrain Max Weber chronicled in "The Protestant Ethic and the Spirit of Capitalism" that is now crowded into secondhand stores and landfills.[92] It formed its own tangled bank and perverse ecosystem. Patrik was only vaguely interested in these kinds of historical trajectories and commentaries, which made him a limited historian. He wasn't interested in ancient America. He could have taken sample images from Matthew Brady and the Civil War and the long documented history of lynching, but he didn't. Instead he drew from images of America in popular science magazines, lifted quotes from a Salvation Army store where he shopped, incorporated pieces salvaged from secondhand stores, to anchor a world just off from now, the just past, or the storm chasing the present.

Why I Am a Christian

It was nearly thirty years ago when an evangelist from Bastrop, Louisiana, cast a demon out of me. Her name was Clarice Fluid. She is a bishop now. She's dyed her hair blonde to match the gold streets of heaven. She favors faux animal prints. On a website she's wearing an endangered-snow-leopard print. I still recognize her even though our time together was brief. I'd already met Patrik. His work was poised along the edges of my world, maybe like a snow leopard about to jump onto the walls of my home and become part of that system of objects. That moment was imminent. Neither Clarice nor her husband George was aware of Patrik as a person, though they glimpsed him as a ghostly outline in my exorcism and predictably misidentified him. I met Clarice formally. Five men came to the back of a Pentecostal church where I was sitting taking notes on the service. I knew all of them. They surrounded me. The leader, the largest man, bearlike with his thick beard and tweed jacket, said, "The Lord wants to deal with you." The other men were slight, almost feminine in their Sunday pants. Two of them slipped their arms under my shoulders and walked me down the aisle. From a distance it must've resembled a gay wedding. There was already a crowd of hopeful congregants strung across the front of the church. The line quivered like a single strand of barbed wire being stretched across the pasture.[93] Clarice went down the line punching each person on the forehead with the flat of her hand. "God," she said, "has super blessed me." It must've been true. Whoever she touched fell backward in a swoon. This is called being slain in the Spirit. I wish Patrik could've seen me. He would have recognized me even from the back of the church. My trousers were thick cotton duck made by the outfitter Patagonia. My skinny hundred-percent-cotton outline was singular in this space. Even my blue Oxford button-down was thick. Around me were polyester blends, a mark of the new Protestant ethic. When Clarice faced me, it was a confrontation of different histories and assemblages. When she touched me, she had to be aware of our completely different materiality. Three times she tried to slay me in the Spirit. I was a problem now. I was the only body still standing in a line of individuals simulating the dead. It was then that she cast the demon of unbelief out of me. It's only now that I realize the exorcism went the wrong way. She wasn't casting out a demon from my past but introducing a demon into me. She named the demon as unbelief. It was after the exorcism that I didn't believe, not before. Clarice disappeared into the crowd as the service ended. No one spoke to me.

The next day I went back to see Clarice and talk to her about our encounter. Before I arrived I stopped at the Christian bookstore. My copy of the book *Does God Exist?* by the German theologian Hans Küng had arrived. Clarice would not have approved. He was Catholic. The book was a hardback. And then she might say, "Isn't the Bible enough?" by which she meant, "Aren't I enough?" I never had that conversation. Clarice was resting. Her husband and the prayer director were available. Neither remembered me from the night before. Neither of them could recall that Clarice had cast the demon out of me. She had said it loud enough for 160 people on their feet clumsily swaying to hear and shout back "Praise God!" It was odd they didn't hear or remember. "Why are you here?" they asked. I explained that Clarice had cast the demon of unbelief out of me. "Praise God," they intoned. If only I had only left it at that. Then neither they nor I would've glimpsed Patrik. "Clarice cast the demon out of me," I said hesitatingly, then, "I didn't have a demon." The phrase hit them like a hammer. "I want to know what happened." Another hammer hit. The inevitable occurred. They cast another demon out of me, which again I refused to admit to. Then I was taken before the preacher and the elders of the church loafing on the preacher's front porch and was declared apostate and cast out of the church. What evidence did the husband and the song director need to proceed? After failing to find confessions of drug use and heavy metal, they shifted their investigation under the guidance of the Holy Ghost to see images. "I saw a man screaming," intoned the song director. I was perplexed. My answer to them at that moment was wrong. "I have an album by King Crimson with a man screaming on the cover." It was as wrong as their question, which was too narrowly focused on music. Now I see that the screaming man might be Patrik.

With that acknowledgment the exorcism started all over again. Their musical knowledge was limited. They had never heard of REM or the B-52s. Their scrutiny shifted to the books I owned. "You must burn all your books." And then, once it popped out that I was a sociology graduate student, I had to immediately drop out of the program. "Sociology is the devil's." If only, I thought. I gravely argued that all knowledge is the Lord's. I quoted Paul at the altar for the unknown God in Athens.[94] My resistance only tightened the screws. Clarice's husband showed a weird brilliance. "What kind of furniture do you have in your house?" "Antiques, primitive pine pieces, some church pews." I said. His answer was quick and unequivocal. "They have to go. They're possessed by spirits." And then he was helpful. "Sears has good furniture and you can charge it." The husband's plan was sound. Exchange furniture soaked with history and complicated networks of exchange and memory for the well-upholstered, empty pieces from Sears, whose lifespan was limited. I could have pointed out that my furniture was heavy and often uncomfortable. What he didn't know was that this was the same furniture Patrik activated in his installations and was, if bland, also the framework for the perversities he portrayed. The Fluids and Patrik had grown up with the same furniture and now stared across it uneasily. Here the new Protestant ethic at the end of the twentieth century was passing judgment on the Protestant landscape from the nineteenth and early twentieth centuries. The broad pine church pews from the time of Reconstruction were to be exiled to the landfill. What was destroyed was the community of saints that have been for two thousand years the invisible crowd behind the visible church. The apostles and the Nicene Creed were abolished. The Fluids have a commitment to a one-dimensional world. Any vestiges of former worlds, like my antiques and books, were threatening. The Fluids ruthlessly sought to touch the past and destroy it. Any memory was suspect. The preacher, the deacons, the men I had eaten with, preached with, worked with, forgot me. Patrik did not.

Red Cloud

Before she died, my mother put together a photo album for me out of the family archives, which consisted of drawers of photographs piled on top of one another in the form of a tornado laid flat in a box. Each image was moving at incredible speed with Christmas ribbons, greeting cards, comments, diplomas, and old letters inside the wooden space of the drawer. She sorted through the mix and drew out an impressionistic history, fitted to me from scraps of myself. She did this for each of my brothers and sisters. To my sister Mary this is another bit of evidence that Mom knew when she was leaving. Mary points to several prophetic occurrences identifying May 9 as the date. Mom missed it slightly. On May 12 she had a massive aneurysm. She never regained consciousness. By the 15th she was officially dead. It was several years later that I got the album. After her death the house was in turmoil. The album was in a cardboard box with some of my grandfather's books, art I did as a kid in school, various diplomas, and report cards. The photographs looked as if they had been soaked in a mild bleach to remove stains. They weren't black and white but gray, overexposed, ghostworlds. Only a few were in color—hazy, square Polaroids and garish drugstore prints. One of the Polaroids shows me on the night of my high school prom. I'm sitting on the red velvet Victorian loveseat with my date Patsy Lou, gazing uneasily back at the camera. Patsy Lou exudes confidence. Her makeup and dress make her look like she has just stepped out of a plush burgundy coffin. My father has chosen my polyester blue suit and white shirt. Behind this moment was a threat. This is the same loveseat where my mother saw the Indian with a mohawk sprawled out, lounging lazily in the afternoon. He was her guardian angel. I inherited this loveseat. The Indian hasn't directly appeared to me. His appearance was always along the margins and in different guises. When I was six I named my dog Red Cloud after the Sioux chief. My sister Janie found him in the neighborhood. My father was stationed on Okinawa. My mother, two brothers, two sisters, and

I lived in a red brick rental near Grandmother Pearl's house. Red Cloud was a mutt with two big red splashes on his back against the white. I had a book about Red Cloud with small black-and-white drawings.[95]

My father was transferred to Camp Lejeune, North Carolina. He found a house on an island and moved everyone there but me. I stayed behind to finish second grade. For a year I lived with my grandparents, floating back and forth between houses. The night I came home to my family, Red Cloud jumped into my arms, barking and licking me. He lived for twenty years. Kafka imagined being a Red Indian on a horse approaching a speed at which the stirrups, the saddle, and then the rider and the horse turn the same color as the prairie under their feet. I imagined a different kind of speed at which the dog, the house, and I aren't obliterated but are enchanted. In that world Red Cloud speaks. He is a Sioux chief. I'm alone but not deserted. This must be similar to what my mother saw in her guardian angel. The album recorded the existence of an exoskeleton in the repetition of the tiny antlike segments of the images. I have the same look on my face when I was six that I do when I'm seventeen. The lips are closed. The eyes are soft. The head is raised in submissive attention like I've been summoned. My spine is straight. The family dramas nudge up through the surface of the repetitive gestures in the photographs. Exposed to air, they turn into a hard insect shell. Since I was a kid, I've seen myself as another kind of solitary insect, a praying mantis hiding in tender green foliage.

Patrik was a different kind of insect. He was a variant of the social insect. He created hives around himself as if he were a queen. In the giant installation *Utopia: Termite Season* an entire room was remade into a paper hive. The walls were paper. Paper was wrapped into oblong, hound dog–sized eggs. Stacks of paper were scattered through the tunnels like garbage or piles of dirt. But the teeming hive was up for less than an hour and then deserted again except for Patrik's projection once the fire department closed the show. How is it only the firemen could see what a match or a lighter would do? Patrik imagined a paper hive ablaze, the fire running through the tunnels like workers or termites devouring everything, leaving him as he imagined, alone in the holocaust, another name for a vanishing crowd. He wasn't exactly what Elias Canetti conceptualized as a survivor. Patrik didn't want to survive the crowd but to be alone in the rubble and corpses before finally succumbing himself in the deserted corridors of a superorganism.

The photographic record stretches in an uneven line from when I was a newborn to my early thirties. Because my dad took most of the pictures, there were almost none of us together past the age of four. Then there was the year I lived with my grandparents. There are none. It's like I died and dropped out of the photographic record. Neither my grandmother nor my grandfather used a camera. From the age of nineteen I appear sporadically in the family photographs. Those images are stored in my ex-wife's garage in a box. But the biggest gap isn't temporal, it's spatial. There are only a handful of photographs from my grandfather A.C.'s farm. Most are blank shots of the pasture with black angus cows scattered like pennies. In one of the few with people, I'm sitting on a pony on the other side of a barbed-wire fence. I'm around seven years old. I have a crew cut. I remember the pony's name was Ginger. I'm imagining I'm Geronimo or Crazy Horse. They were my heroes. My grandfather's arm sticks out of the edge of the frame—he's wearing a plain-colored long-sleeved shirt and holding the reins of another pony beside me. These gaps in the photographic line are another kind of soft spot in the landscape. They are the thin membrane in the photographic exoskeleton. Patrik might have surfaced here if he could've maneuvered his seven-foot craft in these tight spaces.

Gutenberg Bible

Patrik sent me a postcard from Amsterdam. The picture was completely altered except for the very center of the card, which showed a Gutenberg Bible open on a reading table. Patrik had surrounded the Bible with black electrical tape and then scratched the word *void* in the tape. The word itself is barely discernible. There is nothing lyrical about the image. There's no muscularity. The scratch is thin and imprecise. It wasn't done with a straight razor or sharp knife. The black tape resisted and in the aftermath seems ready to swallow the word back into its emptiness, a point made even stronger by what Patrik surrounded himself with— dulled knives, giant scissors from secondhand stores, and broken plate glass. Behind the masking electrical tape was a field of bright color. A deep scratch would have released color, and Patrik had no intention of doing that. The thinness of the black tape couldn't resist a sharp blade. It reminds me of how delicately the soft topsoil is strung across the pasture. There is in places only an inch or so before the hardpan. The red clay is the equivalent of the color field behind the tape. I had always thought that the blackness was the void. Now I see it with the sign scratched into the surface as a warning of what's lurking underneath. The blackness is like dark water filling in the space around a drowning man. But for Patrik it was something alive, like grasses moving into a scar in the ground. I received this card while I was still in the Big House. I worked on the farm. I didn't need to remember. Photographs of what I saw every day were unnecessary. Now the Big House is that Bible in my memory—something blacking out.

Instead of photographs of the farm, I have a cassette tape my cousin made just as the farm was being cut up and sold off. A.C. will die soon. Mary Pullen will be knocked down by a stroke next to the compost pile in her garden. My marriage was slipping away, and though I didn't realize it then, the world of my childhood was turning into a ghostworld out of reach except for those already dead. Even more since the reproduction technology is dead also. Listening to the cassette is like being in a séance. A.C. is there, Mary Pullen, and I, but different. My girlfriend Molly barely recognizes me. "You have a southern accent." For a moment I sound like I have a home. The tape was produced in 1983, when my cousin Matt visited me. He lived ninety miles away in Atlanta. He was a musician. I lived in the Big House with my wife and three big dogs. The Norwegian woodstove at full tilt could keep the inside twenty degrees warmer than the outside. My wife hated the house. It leaked dirt from the ceilings. In the fall, hundreds of wasps and dirt daubers slipped through the clapboard and down the chimneys into the living room, creating a wasp arboretum. It wasn't romantic. The farm was done. My grandfather A.C. had called it quits. The cattle had been sold to a cowboy from south Alabama. A chicken house was built on one of the back pastures. The sharp ammonia smell moved lazily with the breeze for a half-mile or so before fading. Matt's arrival was an occasion. Visitors were scarce now. Matt had come with a purpose. He had a portable cassette recorder in his coat pocket. His plan was to capture as if he were an anthropologist the last days of what we the grandkids called the farm.

The Superorganism

Walter Benjamin worked on a similar project in his *Berlin Childhood around 1900* until the very end. He opens the book with a desire to inoculate himself against homesickness. Matt[96] had come back to the farm with a similar desire. By the end Walter and Matt had succeeded to the point where they had almost scratched themselves out of the memory altogether. Even before he died, Benjamin's Berlin was already gone. The Nazis were in control. The spaces he remembered were still there, but the faces were different. Benjamin's project was akin to Odysseus tightening his own knots against the sirens. Inside his writing was an itch or desire to vanish into a maze of something like ant bites, or through the gaping wounds left by the rope cutting into flesh. This was most clear in his celebration of his ability to get lost in the city as if it were a wilderness, so lost even Walter himself starts to disappear. The best passages in *Berlin Childhood* teeter on the dizzy moment before being slain in the Spirit. For Benjamin this would not have been falling backward into outstretched arms, but into the void that Patrik scratched into his postcard.

Much of the material for *Berlin Childhood* was drawn from an earlier essay called "A Berlin Chronicle." He would rewrite and reframe this essay for a more general audience. *Berlin Childhood* was sold to a newspaper in serial form. At one of the few emotional junctures in "A Berlin Chronicle," Benjamin describes the suicide of a friend. The friend never directly resurfaces in Benjamin's work, but he is one of the writer's guides to Berlin and to the larger project of charting the superorganism-like structure in *The Arcades Project*. Whatever color there is in Benjamin's descriptions[97] is swallowed by a gray fog that is the same color as Kafka's world. It is the same half-light that illuminates Marx's *Capital*, where the furnaces are surrounded by a world in which it is neither night nor day. For me this is the same color as my memories. Once the name Berlin is stripped from his work, Benjamin's account of the city looks different. Since there are no crowds in his portrait, the imaginary crowds that are part of the Berlin scene vanish as well. What is left is hardly a conventional portrait of the city but a series of strategic personal close-ups. But here even the word *personal* is suspect. Take the scene "News of a Death." Benjamin is five years old. He's in bed. His father sits beside him on the edge of the bed and tells him his cousin is dead. At first glance it is an intensely emotional scene. But Benjamin himself is barely there, hardly more than a ghost. The scene is an atmosphere where the architectural features and the human are secondary—the sadness generated is more like a smoky gas than a tear. It's a gray world in the tunnels of the superorganism.[98]

In Georg Simmel's 1903 essay "The Mental Life of the Metropolis,"[99] the German sociologist described the graying of the modern world without commenting on the actual atmosphere. For him the grayness was associated with the exhaustion of the sacred through rational calculation.[100] The brightly colored money circulating beneath isn't even mentioned. It's a curious essay. Simmel provides a psychological x-ray of the city without any specific city materializing. He ignores specific buildings, streets, or locations, and no individual or interaction is glimpsed. At one critical moment he imagines what would happen if all the watches in Berlin suddenly went wrong in different ways, even by only as little as an hour. It's a singular occurrence as a specific commodity pushes through the surface to be seen. Noted, the essay fades back and concentrates on mapping the affective currents and how they are wired into sex, money, and rational calculation coursing through the metropolitan spaces. It's a radical move. He conceives a public psychology virtually independent of any individual, as if psychology were an enormous electrical grid. Simmel was an idiosyncratic thinker straddling the nineteenth and twentieth centuries, and he shied away from the emerging ultramodern that would erupt in World War I. His own use of electrical shock was closer to parlor games than to the new electrical infrastructure. He was pushing toward a view of the city as a colony that behaves as a unit, shows idiosyncrasies in behavior and structure, and undergoes a cycle of growth and reproduction that is adaptive. Add the phrase "and is differentiated into queens, males and workers," and American zoologist William Morton Wheeler's 1911 essay "The Ant Colony as an Organism" is reproduced. By 1928 Wheeler called the social insect colony a superorganism: a living whole bent on preserving its moving equilibrium and integrity. Simmel is very close in his conceptualization of the metropolis as a depthless electrical system spread through mental and physical space.

Matt's Recording

The recording opens abruptly. Matt must've clicked it on at an opportune moment. I am putting on the new Talking Heads album to play a song about home. I don't know I'm being recorded. Matt has hidden the recorder in his jacket pocket. I probably have my back to him. Matt is next to the bookshelves. He's asking me about a book. I'm standing, first, in the doorway between the living room and where Matt is. I am eight feet from the front door to my right. Immediately below my left leg in the room is a small closet built under the scaffolding of the stairs. To my left are two doorways. The first, sheared of its door, stands as a passageway to the kitchen, the upstairs staircase, and the door to the outside.

In Kafka's first novel *Amerika*, his young hero Karl steps back into the ship to retrieve his umbrella left in his cabin. He entrusts his suitcase to a stranger and then immediately loses his way. But already it's no longer exactly a ship. It's a floating superorganism with oscillating tunnels and passageways that open into a tribunal. Through the portals Karl sees the ocean and the Statue of Liberty with her sword (Kafka writes it not with a torch but with a sword) raised over her head in judgment.[101] Inside the hull, space and time are distorted.

Facing me like an enormous animal at the center of the room was the woodstove with a double-steel pipe poking from its rear into the chimney three feet back.[102] On its side was a relief of a moose facing a man felling a spruce tree with a crosscut saw. The Norwegian cast-iron stove was the only heat in the house. Above it was a wooden ceiling fan to move the heat. On the mantle was an enormous wavy mirror that weighed at least sixty pounds. The stove's four legs stood on a steel sheet on top of an asbestos pad. The floor around the stove was a different color, pieced together out of yellow pine, evidence of a near-catastrophic fire years ago. The surrounding floor was a saturated red, twelve-inch-wide hand-planed boards. Next to the fireplace was a board-and-batten door to the outside. There were three windows—one to the west and two to the north. My writing desk was six feet long and three feet wide. It was made from a 125-year-old church pew. A ladder-back chair with a twine seat was scooted up against the desk. Sheets of paper and books were scattered across the surface. Another ten-foot church pew, a twin to the one slaughtered to make my desk, lined the north wall. In the bookshelf were streams of books that belonged to my grandfather Eli, dingy paperbacks, sociology books, and gardening books. The room was large by contemporary standards, fifteen by eighteen with eight-foot ceilings. A huge stack of records and stereo equipment was stashed inside a reproduction of a nineteenth-century pine cabinet. Off to the side of the room was a smaller room, which Debbie and I had turned into a bathroom. The room had southern exposure. This is where an old woman had supposedly died in bed years before. She never appeared even to my mother. The door to this room was painted to resemble a panel door more delicately assembled than its board-and-batten construction. But as a counterfeit it was unbelievable. The door was a part of the collage of different historical periods and styles coexisting in the room called the study. The woodstove and the reproduction ceiling fan were critical machines the functioning of the house. There was a severity to the room—Protestant pews, a stark desk, straight-back chairs, a stepladder with a saddle resting on top. The room was what Freud might have described as a material screen memory, put together out of pieces whose individual careers had for various reasons intersected with me and fit the hard look I needed. Over my desk a group of Patrik's works were tied together with cord to look like a climbing team traversing a glacier. They had already escaped from a larger installation. The other parts ended up in the landfill.

Each addition to my memory destabilizes another piece of the map.[103] What I can't find in my memory is my grandmother's hope chest, which stored different photographic collections. Inside the box in which Debbie's Jerusalem Bible came were hundreds of slides I'd taken of our life in this house. And then, piled on top, was a netherworld of photographs I had inherited from Pearl, my grandmother. Without Pearl the photographs were unreachable. They were just strangers posing in front of the camera decades ago. The chest itself was large enough to have been Pearl's coffin. She could have been folded up and tucked inside like a magician's assistant in a stage show. The chest now moved on the surface of my anxieties. The vertigo I imagined inside that hope chest was based

on the certainty that my image would become eventually as unrecognizable even to my son as Pearl's collection was to me. It would even be more so.

Tangled Bank

Pushed beneath the surface of my account there is another pulsating world that is not recorded but threatens to burst through at any moment. The surrounding grounds of my house are overrun with weeds. Imported exotics are spreading across the lawn. The man who formerly lived in this house is old and arthritic. He now lives two miles to the east in a tiny prefabricated house. He sits on the porch in a straight-back chair just as he did at the Big House when he lived here. He wears faded overalls that hang on his thin shoulders. On the grounds there are moles, groundhogs, bottle flies, mosquitoes, and ant colonies. Beyond the grounds feral tomcats prowl the edges of the farm, and in the lake giant carp bask in the sun like unexploded torpedoes. The faraway rose hedges are woven around barbed wire, and the resulting assemblage is stuffed with birds and foxes. Mice prowl the kitchen counters at night. The cat Kudzu pees on the fireplace floor whenever she gets in. Then there are the objects that fill the rooms: chairs with graceful calves, plump sofas, paintings, beds eaten up by bird mites, army jackets hung in pine wardrobes, brushes, Persian rugs, bacon, roast beef, stale bread, oats, rotting potatoes, tea in ceramic canisters, Wedgwood plates, silver forks, leather boots, and fountain pens that look like German U-boats. Outside in the cold are the muddy spades, the axes, a dulled bill-hook, a rusty scythe, a heart-shaped shovel, moldy leather harnesses, and an anvil. Staring through this haze of things are two ghosts that only my mother sees. All together the pieces form a more complicated version of what Darwin describes as "the tangled bank."[104] Darwin didn't include the supermaterial side of the ecosystem, even though he must have continued to see his dead daughter around the grounds of his house after her death. She doesn't appear in *On the Origin of the Species* directly. Reportedly, spiritualists at the time read Darwin's chapter on seeds in the wind and water currents and their long travels as a metaphor for the soul after death. Darwin was an adamant materialist, though he did position mirrors in his studies so that he could see the surrounding grounds and the entrance to his house without being seen, a convenient means to spot his own double or a ghost in the garden. Darwin likewise had a fascination with mud from his pond. He famously counted how many different seeds were in a single spoonful. Viscous mud was the foundation for the tangled bank. How many of those different plants with their associations led back to his daughter?

This may be the clue to why Patrik imagined blood mixed with seawater at the origin of the world. He was approaching a different level of viscosity between the poles of honey and water. Here was the absent cum in his work, concocted out of its constituent elements of blood and water. The viscosity of memory is what Proust and Benjamin rubbed between their fingers. It is the stickiness that holds the scene together. There is a density. A scent trail leads back to the metropolis. Simmel defined the metropolis in a peculiar way. There are no demographic dimensions. Rather he articulated a psychological definition. He conceived of the metropolis as extending in concentric circles into the person. Walter Benjamin reproduced Simmel's work in his representations of early twentieth-century cities. The city itself barely appears at all except in close-ups and offhand descriptions—a vague sense of the traffic, the rooftops, and the effects of snow, for example. If Benjamin had been writing of New York City, the Empire State Building might not have appeared. Robert Park's classic definition of the city[105] produced in Chicago in 1925 emphasizes the fluid, soft interactive streams and the electrical impulses of the moment and not the concrete and steel structures. By 1941, the carpet-bombing of cities would theoretically reassert the centrality of concrete even though cities continued to function in the rubble. When he committed suicide in bed in a small inn overlooking the Mediterranean on the Spanish-French border, Benjamin was still deep inside the superorganism, encased in a dense network of objects, sentiments, and residual shocks, the far-reaching gravity of the metropolis. The city for Simmel is a psychological density. The room, the photo albums, and the furniture are marked depths in a memory well that was dug all the way through me into the water Patrik's craft traveled to arrive down the road.

Land behind the North Wind

The tape captures the entirety of the Talking Heads song. No one says a word for three minutes as the record plays. There are small breaks in the recording that mask transitions where Matt has turned off the recording. Then we're outside walking through the high pasture under pecan trees. The grass crackles and whispers on the tape. Around us are six-foot-tall white beehives and a collapsed shed that had been a blacksmith shop a hundred years ago. I point out the ruined foundations of a disappeared house. Orange daylilies have spread through the scattered mud-red bricks. We head down the hollow and across the creek. The creek is recorded strongly. We are headed toward the mule barn built in the 1920s by a man named Warlick. A giant barn owl roosts in the loft. The ground around the barn is choked with dockweed. It's biblical desolation. As we walk up, a groundhog scurries off. In the background of the recording, Diva, a sixty-five-pound Kuvasz, a white Hungarian guard dog, is barking at something, maybe Matt, even at this distance. Diva will die that summer of cancer. The morning she died, she woke me up whining. I got up to check on her. She was sprawled on the ground. I lay down beside her white body in the gray dirt next to a pale green fig tree and held her. She quit whining. That was in the early morning. Only after she died did Debbie and I know. "Cancer," Dr. Braum said.

I make a comparison that is slow to materialize. I'm not in control on the tape. The comparison is too much for me. At the time I couldn't see around it, but it's clear now as piece by piece, story by story, the comparison is assembled. Matt doesn't ask me a question. I choose to tell him about what I described desperately as the most painful moment of my life. It was Ruah's death.[106] He was a long-legged malamute that looked like a wolf. Debbie had found the dog and fallen in love with him. We named him after the breath of God. Ruah would run with me around the mountain. We had to put him down. Lupus. The vet injected him as I held him. It's the right thing. "The dog will suffer unnecessarily if you don't. He'll be in constant pain." His fur was falling out. He moaned in my arms. His back was covered with bald, ulcerated patches. Debbie and I had assumed it was an allergic reaction to fleas. The veterinarian was so certain. He was a salesman dressed in a white smock. Ruah died instantaneously with a jerk as I held him. "No, I don't want him wrapped in black plastic." I carried him out of the clinic in my arms. I was covered in his hair. It was in my mouth. I cradled him in my arms in the bed of the truck, leaning against the cab. At home I dug Ruah's grave in sight of the back porch under a large pecan tree next to a winter honeysuckle bush. I wanted to see it as a reminder of my faith in an afterlife. My feelings about what happens to animals after death had changed. I prepared Ruah's grave with the same care as my grandmother's. He was the same size as a man. On his hind legs, he stood over six feet tall and weighed 120 pounds. The ground at the grave site was hard packed. It took a pick and mattock to make headway, and the grave had to be wide to accommodate his long, stiffening legs. The grave took several hours. I had cried on the ride home in the back of the truck. Now I would sob. Ruah's death was like having my thigh muscles cut from the bone. The local preachers were certain he wouldn't be a part of the afterlife. This wasn't a new idea for me, but one that reaches back to my earliest memories. At four years old, I was convinced that the big-eared elephant Dumbo ruled a kingdom called Limbo suspended between earth and hell. If you died in quicksand, you became a denizen of this realm. I had given up certain childish things for a time. Now I knew better. In *At the Back of the North Wind*, George MacDonald deals with the question of whether animals will be in heaven. The principal character is a little boy named Diamond. He's named after his father's horse. Diamond the boy sleeps in the loft over old Diamond. He hears old Diamond talking one night to an angel horse. On another occasion while with the North Wind, Diamond sees the wind gently aid a honeybee in distress. This is God's work. For Mac-Donald, animals are included in God's plan and will be in heaven. No scriptural verses are cited. He doesn't appeal to the land before the fall or to the temporarily reprieved world inside Noah's ark—no blood was spilled during the ordeal. MacDonald sees an equality between humans and animals that reaches back through the Victorian or contemporary sentimentality toward what the feminist theorist Donna Haraway describes in her new book *When Species Meet* as knotted together.[107] These knots are a hybrid of affect and that weird place where animal blood, human blood, and Christ's blood are first substitutions for each other, then combine in the Eucharist. These knots are more than a figure of speech; they are an attempt to articulate the twitch in the thigh, the shudder in the body, that animals and humans share in relationship. I felt in my heart and muscles the jerk that ran through Ruah as the veterinarian callously injected him. The feelings that knotted me are the evidence of those ties. If Patrik could be saved in the future, Ruah would be in the land behind the North Wind and then in heaven.

There was no ceremony. Debbie had gone into the house. She couldn't bear to see. I fitted Ruah into the grave looking north and placed my straw hat over his eyes. It was hot. The dirt was clotted. I broke the clots into a finer ground with a hoe. I carefully shoveled dirt around his face. The effect was as if Ruah were diving headfirst into another world as his head and then his body was submerged. I stacked rocks from the creek on top. Unexpectedly, I was constructing a habitat for black-widow spiders that hid in the dark creases between the large rocks. This was different from when I buried my grandmother. I was in the room when she died, standing in the back behind my mother's brother. I saw the heart monitor go flat. I remember no sounds, no emotions. I drove home. That night I decided I would dig the grave. I persuaded my mother. I dug

the grave. I buried her. My dog Ruah's death was more painful than my grandmother's departure. Matt knew her. He played harmonica next to her grave after I had finished burying her and smoothing the dirt. Matt, Debbie, and I were alone after the funeral. My grief was not foreign. On the mountain, a man had built an altar to his hound dog, but it was solitary, just as he undoubtedly was.

Matt never comments. I keep talking. The next piece of the comparison goes on tape. I tell Matt about the farm vet Dr. Boozer's death and what it felt like to me. The week before his death he was at my house talking to me about strawberries. He was a great man, I tell Matt. Then I mention Harrison Murray, who had worked on the farm for years. Matt knows Harrison. He couldn't work anymore, too old and ill. "Do you know Paul Williams?" He doesn't. "You should meet Paul. Your brother Joe knows him. He ground the feed for the bulls." I then absentmindedly point out how the pine boards are popping free from the barn. The boards have worked free of the nails at the top near the roof and have twisted backward into a line of old men poised in a slow fall. The comparison is in place. It's taken twenty minutes to get from how Diva died to the last of these old men. They were what held the farm together. They kept it nailed down. And by implication, my dog looking north was one of them. I had put together an apostolic succession of the dead waiting to reach out and hold A.C. and—though I didn't imagine this in my early thirties—me.

The pain around Ruah's death seemed proportional. He was a big dog. But now years later in Buffalo, a seven-pound cat named Nadja has died. She was sixteen. We lived together for a brief time. She was so delicate and lovely. In my lap she was hardly there, a heavier part of the blanket spread across my thighs. But her death was large enough to swallow me whole. It didn't feel like my thighbone was cut out when she died. It felt like my lungs were beating against my rib cage, trying to fly away after her. This is a familiar feeling for me. I want to reach across that space that divides us and hold her one more time, not unlike the dead wanting to reach across that same space and touch me. I'm not disturbed by this. It isn't even about clinging to memories. What Marc Augé so gently described as the oblivion that is the other side of remembering, with his lovely metaphor of the eroding shore, must've grown into a storm at some point in my life. I remember very little. Instead I feel like I'm easing myself into those waters. Borges tells a story about a man who remembers everything. Each detail pricks him. Memory is torture for him. There's no room for anything else. I remember a world more like the floral wallpaper in my grandmother's house. It's fading and I can see another layer behind it. I remember the swirl in the wood grain of my ax handle and Nadja fetching her blue ball. These memories don't feel like briars in my hand. In the summer, I would dive through the warm surface water to the muddy bottom of the Big Lake and lie in the cold until I had to come up for air. This is what remembering feels like.

The recording shifts to Mary Pullen's kitchen. Matt had never worked on the farm. He didn't know how to string wire or work a bull down the squeeze. But Matt was an integral part of the kitchen. He'd show up and my grandmother would stoke up the kitchen. Breakfast was toast or biscuits, hoe cakes, bacon or sausage, grits, poached eggs, and hot Postum with honey. Fig preserves, mason jars of applesauce, and a pitcher of honey were on the table. What for Marcel was a cookie was here a feast. Specific techniques of eating were part of the memory. The poached egg was mashed into the grits. Honey was poured on the hoe cakes. Matt was unparalleled as an eater. The table was seven and a half feet long. It was without any history, just a plain pine table painted white. The chairs had been painted white, but the color was beginning to chip. I'd seen the same chairs smashed to pieces in abandoned tenant farmers' houses along the edge of the farm. Directly behind where A.C. sat was a short bedside dresser with a mirror that had been pulled from the bedroom. You could see A.C.'s back as he ate. One drawer was filled with red rubber bands from the newspapers. A rotary phone sat on top.[108]

At the end of the tape Matt is talking to A.C. A.C. says flatly, "I have no desire to keep on living."[109] In the background my grandmother is getting dinner on the table. A chair is scooted across the linoleum. Glass plates clap against the pine table. Matt can hear Grandmother calling them to dinner. Matt interrupts A.C.: "Granddad, it's time to eat. Grandma's calling us." A.C. replies in what seems to be a drastically different tone, almost a chuckle, "Well. I just come when I'm called. Let's go in." Matt never comments. The tape cuts off. Back on, Matt is leaving. He is talking to my grandmother Mary Pullen. It's still light outside. "I want to get home before dark." "It's good to see you." You can hear her hugging Matt in the words squeezing together after that, silence. The humming of the tape sounds like the murmur of incoherent animals deep underground. A.C. would not have heard the same sound. He would've heard the whisper of an ocean sunk in his large ears. It's the same ocean Patrik's craft would cruise in the future.

Benjamin's Memory

Benjamin hoped his scratching at his past would act as an inoculation, but against what? Benjamin describes it as homesickness, but the nostalgia in *Berlin Childhood around 1900* is muted and the world he describes is closer to Kafka than to Proust. The flat gray world is punctuated by occasional bursts of color in agony, more like wounds, like the burst of red that erupts on Kafka's last page of *The Trial*, where Joseph K. is stabbed.[110] This may be precisely Benjamin's point. His childhood Berlin is a city poised on an apocalyptic age. Berlin had grown into an international capital in the late nineteenth century but was now creeping toward a new primeval stage of development. An early section titled "Victory Column" recounts the military parades after the Battle of Sedan in the Boer War. The colors here are "golden cannon," "red-letter date," "a dim light reflected off the gold," and "against the sky they appeared to me outlined in black." The colors vibrate ominously. This heroic militarism would be smashed into the mud in the trenches and buried alive by artillery shells with the new war coming. World War I is within fourteen years of Benjamin's childhood memory. The city is untouched by the war except for the squeeze marks left behind by the blockade and the enormity of the casualties. And just outside the text's margins are the Nazis marching through Berlin in the 1930s as Benjamin constructs this passage.

By 1938 Benjamin's name is on the Gestapo's list. His book, slyly titled *German Men and Women*, escaped the censors' notice at first and sold well until it was banned. Berlin is closed off. At the beginning of the summer of 1945, Benjamin's childhood city was in rubble. The Allied air strikes and the Soviet invasion scratched it entirely off the surface of the earth, leaving only a name on a map. But the wide boulevards and the brick buildings with their deep foundations had withstood the initial Allied bombing raids. Only 25 percent of the city had been severely damaged by the spring of 1945. The fire bombings that had consumed Dresden were impossible here. Electric service continued with minor interruptions. Berlin would be Hitler's final stop. In 1944 an enormous underground capital was completed fifty-five feet beneath the gardens with its own independent water, electric, and air-conditioning service.

Hitler entered the bunker in January. He left only twice before his death. The Soviets arrived at the outskirts of the city. They had nearly three million men massed for the final attack. Opposing the Soviets were 320,000 men. Block by block the city was destroyed, first by artillery, then by tanks and flame throwers. The zoo that Benjamin loved as a child was hideously destroyed with its otters.[III] Hitler committed suicide. His body was burned in gasoline and scraped up and buried. Berlin surrendered unconditionally days later. The city resembles Benjamin's description of the 1755 Lisbon earthquake, but beyond even Benjamin's imagination. In the end Benjamin's Berlin is nothing but rubble. In its death, Benjamin was temporarily inoculated. After the war Adorno returned to Germany from his exile in New York and Los Angeles. He collected the final version of *Berlin Childhood around 1900* and arranged its publication. The money that Benjamin so desperately needed in those last years now went into the air or a trust fund for his son or to the rebuilding of Berlin. No street is named after him. But his sainthood is assured. Benjamin, like the city around 1900, is a messianic hope that materialized in ways no one could have imagined. He is now regarded as one of Germany's greatest critics, his youthful ambition.

The Hoped-for Sign

I have one photograph of Patrik and me together in the same frame. He has cut most of the image off. The result is a slender photographic column. I'm stretched out on the sidewalk reading a paperback. Patrik is on his haunches against the wall. We don't look like we go together. I'm in a button-down shirt and jeans, wire rim glasses, mustache, and a bowl of longish hair on my head. Patrik is in shorts and a ratty T-shirt. His head is shaved. I seem quite comfortable. Whoever Patrik removed from the image doesn't disturb me in the photograph. In all likelihood it's a woman. Women fell in love with Patrik regularly and tragically. He had no interest. We were an unlikely set of friends. It was an unequal friendship. Patrik's work inspired me. I had no work to show him. I just talked. I wasn't part of the scene. "Who is that with Patrik?" No one knew. That might be one reason we were close. I was an escape from the scene. The other was Patrik was attracted to J. Crew–like men. In a letter, Patrik described stumbling on a fraternity boy on his knees outside The Globe, being baptized by a preacher. It's in the broad daylight. Patrik is wracked by an erection. He's fixated by the event and staring at the young man's crotch. Will God show him a sign and his dick get hard? God moves no blood. No sign materializes. Patrik commits it to writing and sends his conversion fantasy to me. The only sign that materializes is I occasionally wear the cowboy boots Patrik admires, hardly a sign from God, much more like a distant siren. I tell him a phrase I learned from an itinerant Baptist preacher I worked with that describes his conversion fantasy. The preacher worked bees in his spare time for money. I would help out on big jobs with the robbing and the extraction. During the extraction process, the honeycomb is cut with a hot electric knife. Hot honey would dribble on your hand. When he'd get burned, he'd say, "Hot as a preacher's dick." I told him Patrik the story. He smiled. Patrik and I never hugged. We shook hands rarely. It was often assumed I was his lover. He did nothing to discourage the rumor. I didn't care. For a year I lived on his sofa during the school week. I went home on weekends to work and see my wife. I was poorer than Patrik then.

Behind Patrik's conversion fantasy was his fascination with the Protestant landscape. Weber never mentioned this except indirectly in passages from smaller essays such as "'Churches' and 'Sects' in North America," included with a later American publication of "The Protestant Ethic." He has a conversation with a tombstone salesman on a train.[112] At the baptism of the banker in North Carolina he barely mentions the creek.[113] The surrounding woods are left out entirely. And Weber describes without knowing it the proliferation of what Augé will call non-places in the American landscape. At the beginning of the twentieth century suburbanization was already occurring. Weber describes the real estate developers anchoring their newly created neighborhoods with boxlike churches with steeples that looked to Weber like toys. These churches were nondenominational. New seminarians were hired to fill them. Theology was less relevant than how the churches stabilized real estate value.[114] There are glimpses of the landscape in Weber's work on the spirit of capitalism. It just never materializes. In Patrik's work, the Protestant landscape is connected to his father the salesman and the suburban world he grew up in. It's a stand-in for the Protestant landscape, though Patrik acknowledges they aren't identical. Patrik despised the suburbs. He was drawn to the earlier world behind them in the old values and the wilder denominations like the Baptist preacher on the street. By no means was Patrik a Protestant or a believer. One of his most beautiful works was a simple collage of Michelangelo's sculpture showing Mary holding the dead Jesus in her arms—hardly a Protestant image except in its sentimental dispersal of mother and son into the card rack in a drugstore.

One trail leading back to Patrik's Protestantism starts in an alternative poster he produced for his campaign for mayor. "Move Against Indiscipline" appears one word at a time over what appears to be an antique electric chair with nail points protruding through the seat and back in tight sequential rows. "Write in PK, for mayor of Athens" runs across the bottom. Electric shock appears repeatedly in Patrik's work, as do its accomplices, leather straps and convulsing immobility. Inside an old brown wooden frame, Patrik placed at the center, like a heart with a bull's-eye on it, this Protestant exhortation by John Henry Jowett inside another small brown frame. "When you and I are tempted to sell the Lord, when we are tempted to make a dirty bargain at any time, when we are tempted to prefer money to integrity, or unholy ease to stern duty, or soft flattery to rugged truth, let us have swords in our hands—'the sword of the Spirit which is the word of God'—and let us slay the suggestion at its very birth." Around it in alphabetical order is a list of shock doctors. The doctors are stacked like cordwood with their credentials and the hospital they practiced in. It's a somber piece. Patrik was under the care of at least one psychiatrist. Whether he received electroshock is never mentioned in his work or correspondence, though he often acted as if he were a sanatorium patient who had been hooked up. He played this role for a week in a shaved head and purple pajamas in *Asylum, Asylum*. What is curious is that here God or at least his distillation into a certain kind of Protestant landscape is his lost protector. At other places in his work God mocks suffering or is part of Patrik's anal fantasies. He quotes Martin Luther on the back of a postcard he sent to me: "I am like a ripe shit, and the world is a gigantic ass-hole. We probably will let go of each other soon." Scouting for pieces in a Salvation Army store, he salvages another quote he finds on a piece of yellowed paper in a corner by itself:

"And I said to the man who stood at the gate of the year: give me a light that I may tread safely into the unknown! And he replied: go out into the darkness and put thy hand into the hand of God. That shall be to thee better than light and safer than a known way." Again, he sent it to me. In this case the lines weren't merged with other parts into a larger piece. For Patrik, this era of secular Protestantism in late nineteenth- and early twentieth-century America epitomized a continuation of what the Civil War historian Drew Faust described as "the republic of suffering."

During the entire length of our relationship Patrik kept a studied distance from my travails. He knew I was being ricocheted around the country, trying to score a permanent position. He knew I was losing my marriage and farm. He may have even known my dog was killed. My pain wasn't part of our relationship. Patrik never talked about his pain. It was written or performed in his work. Sympathy wasn't something he expected. He never referred to it. He never expressed any condolences even when my mother died. He wanted a kind of artistic appreciation for his suffering. Patrik's tears didn't turn into precious jewels as in a fairy tale. They were salty drops that stained the page. He had a calculated heart like a clown in makeup. He hated the nickname Emmett I gave him. I found an exception to his confessions in a letter he sent me. He describes a weekend in Amsterdam. He met a sociologist named Paul from Belgium. He actually wrote out, "I opened up my heart to him." Paul invited Patrik to come back with him to Belgium. Patrik refused, then regretted his decision. It was too late. In The Globe where he had worked, I heard another tragic love story about Patrik. He was in love with a much younger man named Michael. Patrik never mentioned this to me, though Michael occasionally appeared in our correspondence as a minor figure. Michael was in love with an older man dying of AIDS. Patrik moved in to help Michael care for his lover. After his death, Patrik imagined they would be finally together. The older man died. Michael moved on, leaving Patrik. I was told Patrik never recovered from this. More likely it was the configuration of themes in Patrik's work coming together all at the same time—the blood, the Pietà scenario of the death, the won/lost column, the rejection, and the impotence of his artwork to restore his own body's vitality. By this time, I was laid up in the Finger

Lakes district, recuperating with a thirteen-inch incision up my abdomen. I'd nearly died. Patrik's stomach was unscarred.

Alexander's Empire

In the pastures a metamorphosis was occurring that neither I nor A.C. suspected. Patrik may have seen it from beneath. A.C. waged an interminable war against fire ants in his pastures. He'd jam his walking stick a foot deep into the mounds and then ream a large hole into which he would delicately sprinkle poison crystals. His technique went specifically against the directions for the poison. The phrase "Do not disturb the mound" was clearly printed on the label. Regardless, his technique seemed to work; the ants went away for a time before new colonies would erupt on the surface several yards from the original mound. Then A.C. would return with his can of poison under his arm. His Buick was parked a half-mile back at the barn. These ants hadn't existed in the landscape A.C. had grown up in. They weren't part of his childhood as they were part of mine. The ants were immigrants, arriving in Mobile in the 1920s and then sweeping into northern Alabama. Their arrival was part of a stage in the lives of A.C. and this valley—part of another kind of development in which cattle, broad pastures, and man-made lakes were set on top of old cotton fields. Unknown to A.C., a slight but significant genetic mutation was happening in the fire-ant colonies. The gene that centered individual colony defense on a specific queen was mutating to allow the emergence of super-colonies with multiple queens working in concert. A fire-ant empire larger than Alexander the Great's was developing in the subsoil and across the surface of Alabama. It was what E. O. Wilson, drawing on Wheeler's work, describes as a superorganism. A.C. was obliterated in the new empire.[115]

The week A.C. died I collected Osage orange seed balls from Paul Williams's farm. The tree trunks made excellent fence posts split into rails with their yellow hearts. I walked through the small lot north of the Big Barn and used my boots to push the seed balls into the mud. After a couple years there were three-foot-tall saplings. I moved to Iowa to teach. Most of the saplings ended up being bush-hogged. A few survived.

They were the ones edged closest to the big rocks and the barbed-wire fence. The grass and the faster-growing privet crippled the seedlings. If I had been there these would've been cleared. The land didn't acknowledge my presence. A.C. had warned me of this. "Allen, you can pour your life into a piece of land and it won't ever be finished." He told me this as I struggled to straighten the sagging fence posts, now held up by the shiny new wire strung over the rusty snags of wire and blackberry vines and briars. Years later, as I approached the tangle of wire, I saw what I thought was the spade I used to cut the edges of my grandmother's grave. The tool had been stolen years before while I was in Iowa teaching. But here it was. Like a loyal hound it had found its way back home and lingered around the property waiting for me to return. My heart was pounding. I was trembling. My shoulders felt its weight. At ten feet it was clear it was an illusion. It was a cheap plastic-handled spade, the plastic stained with enough grime to resemble wood. It was propped against an ancient cedar post studded with nails and rusty snags of barbed wire like a decrepit angel at the mouth of the tomb, too tired to praise God continually but set there as a reminder, however pathetic, that the tomb was empty. A year later I had a chance to see my old farm again. The spade was still there with a hint of corrosion creeping across the edges of the blade, splattered in mud, the plastic now dull colored. The testimony of emptiness is still projected.[116] Across the creek is the space where the Big Barn stood, still framed by the oaks and the cut in the hillside. A few rotten boards slumber under a thin covering of leaves. If I thought hard, I could see A.C. with a steel bucket under his arm, his cattle stick hooked on his arm, big black rubber boots, straw hat, slide through the dockweed, headed toward the ancient cedar post that anchored the gap to the cattle squeeze.

However hard I try to remember, I can't re-create the feeling of the heat wrapping around me like a rat snake. There is an absence of life. There is a coolness as if my body's temperature has dropped beneath a threshold. It's a simple difference that signals that the memories are from a place underneath and have the same temperature as the bottom of the well, the insulated air swirling around the base of a fire-ant mound, or the world Patrik travels in his coffin craft. There came a moment when I doubted whether Patrik had appeared. It wasn't the evidence I suspected but rather the visitor. Was it Patrik or me? Had he come back or was it I who had dropped into his world where my own memories blended with the dead? Last summer Molly and I walked around the Big House and the pastures. Tyree was in his mother's yard playing with his dog. My ex-wife was on vacation. Her new home was impenetrable. I can imagine the interior. There would be pieces from our time together mixed into this new world.[117] Outside, it was only the heat that remembered me at 14.7 pounds per square inch. I wasn't from here anymore. The ground was baked hard. But under my feet it felt like an ocean. I could barely stand. I wanted to fall into the rolling vertigo and disappear into the ground. The undertow was powerful. It was as if I had been slain in the Spirit and propped up by sticks and hooks. The cross stood still while the earth rolled. At the very western edge of Tyree's mother's property was a holding lot. It was approximately 2,925 square yards. Years ago when I lived here, I had given this small pasture over to oats. There was a nice stand. My Uncle Henry pocketknife had slipped out of a hole in my jean pocket. It was somewhere in the lot. I walked to the center of the field and turned in a circle with my eyes to the ground, and then I added a wider circle to the first and so on and so on until I found the knife. It's possible I would've found it sweeping the lot back and forth in long lines. But the spiral from the snail shell is the better plan. It's the labyrinth hunting a monster.[118] Now I was lost in that same small pasture. There were no oats. The grass was burnt up. But what was looking for me?

Olga's Letter

Under my TV is a child's writing desk. It's something left behind from a failed relationship. She's a dean now. At the time I was an itinerant professor. In the hallway of my apartment is a wooden high school desk covered with initials separated by the + sign in a kind of hopeful mathematics. It's from an even earlier failure. Under the child's desk is a blocky suitcase with a DVD player on its top. This is the suitcase given to me by my friend, the artist Patrik, to keep for him indefinitely. He was divesting himself as if he were a heavily laden ship on its way to Amsterdam.

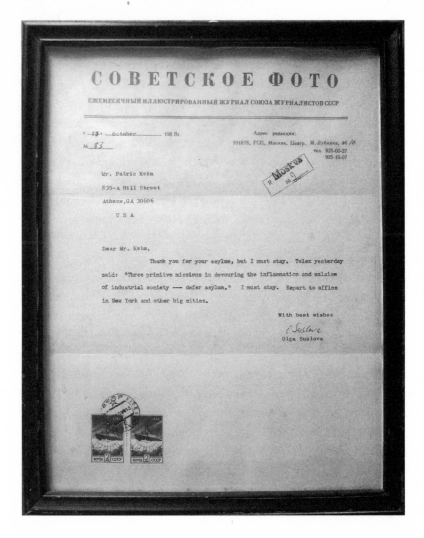

He would retrieve it soon enough, he assured me. I've had it for twenty-two years. He's been dead ten. He used the suitcase as a storage unit for pieces in various stages of completion. I treated the suitcase like it was a safety deposit box and I was a banker. It moved with me undisturbed around the country as I followed teaching jobs until it came to rest under the child's writing desk in Buffalo, New York. Patrik had never expressed any interest in the suitcase.[119] It was too much weight for him to carry while he was alive.

Near the ten-year anniversary of Patrik's departure, I pulled the suitcase out. Molly, my girlfriend, was convinced that it was a centipede metropolis and if it were opened thousands of skeletal soldiers on tiny feet would pour out of a hole in the landscape. I opened the suitcase. I wanted to hold him in this world a bit longer. Inside was a dingy leather catcher's mask, his MFA thesis, various papers, posters on his work, butcher knives bound together with electrical tape, a ceramic bust of Jesus, a dirty drinking glass with dentures at the bottom, cutouts of hardcore gay porn, a military compass, and a straight razor. It didn't occur to me then to wonder why he had left these pieces with me. I fitted the catcher's mask on Jesus's sad, dropped face and hung him over the writing desk that Arthur Rollins had made for me from wood salvaged out of the barn across the road from the Big House. The top was scarred with nail holes and cracks—another convergence with Patrik's work. Patrik was another surface in my apartment, another relic.

I pulled out all the pieces and placed them in order around the suitcase. I reread the thesis. I paid particular attention to Patrik's artist's statement, looking for clues to what happened. I went through the loose papers carefully. One was a page torn out of a German edition of Marx's *Capital*. It was clearly from an old edition. Patrik had worked at the university library and occasionally pages like this would turn up in his work. He knew I admired Marx. On it, in tiny print across the top, was "for Allen, a blue-eyed Marx." It had been over ten years since I'd heard from Patrik. He would have been fifty-one years old. This was a love letter from the dead. For an instant he was there in the room dressed in a German sailor's uniform, his bald head beaded with salt, his muscles and fat seal-like from years underwater in the world beneath the world. Patrik couldn't have guessed when I would have found this gift or that he would reappear. He never mentioned its existence. The effect was dizzying. I could smell the ocean. In that moment, I felt like a man suspended over the side of a ship with dark bodies sliding in the water beneath me. My blue eyes were another ocean, a mutant space in Patrik's work.[120]

He had done this kind of thing before. On the wall over my writing table I have an official letter from a bureaucrat in the Soviet Union that Patrik had altered. His typewriter matched the other typewriter's strokes. But this was different. I was folded into the installation. He had produced a portrait of Marx with blue eyes, my eyes, he said. Patrik, even dead, couldn't have guessed when I would find this gift. It should've happened years before while he was still alive. Now the association of the color blue with the ocean was disturbing. It reminded me of a view of the sea from a long way off that was narrowing. While Patrik was still here I was a teacher at a vacation Bible school at the Church of the Messiah, a small Episcopal church looking over a small lake in Heflin, Alabama. I performed a skit about Jesus for a group of kids. I wore flippers, a Hawaiian shirt, a flight helmet, and goggles. I flopped down the center of the church like a giant frog blowing a horn. The kids were screaming. I sat down on the rise to the altar and told a story about Jesus. In front of me, a chubby kid with curly hair was tearing a piece of paper into scraps. His mother sat next to him. They were partially hidden by the pew. After the sermon, I found my Bible face down on the floor where the kid was sitting. There were tiny pieces of paper scattered across the floor. The torn paper was the memento from my grandmother—the Sunday school lesson she had written on the back of a check listing how all the apostles had met their ends. John was exiled. The others were martyred. Thomas the doubter walked into India spreading the gospel and was never heard of again. Now that check too met its end in Christ's presence. My grandmother was dead. By the afternoon, I had imagined driving my truck off the mountain into the gorge choked with kudzu and sinking into an ocean that wasn't there. The mystery was still, even now, how by engineering my own death I could be floating in that ocean Patrik swam in. Patrik couldn't answer the question. He reminded me that the vertigo that swept over me and nailed me to the floor was part of that ocean.[121] On the wall, Jesus's head looked at me with no change in expression.

One night I followed Patrik through the portal he had left open for me. But it wasn't the North Sea or even the Netherlands he loved that was on the other side, it was my farm in Alabama. The sky was overcast, so much so I couldn't see the sun. I couldn't guess what time of day or night it was. Adding to the overcast was smoke trailing from the gigantic chimney of my house. Debbie must have put some green hickory into the Jotul woodstove. The pecan trees around the house hung like heavy sails. The leaves were barely moving. The only explanation was that the hog-wire fence separating the house and yard from the orchard had kept the winter inside. I wondered when my dogs would start barking. The willows and alders that at the end of my time there had clogged the creek bank were gone. The bank was the same as it was when the young two-year-old bulls grazed here. This meant A.C. and Mary Pullen were still here. I was married. I could see the arrowheads along the hillside glistening like fireflies in the leaf mulch and mud churned up by the bulls. The urge to see A.C. and Mary Pullen was overwhelming. I wanted to run into the house and hold Debbie. I was cautious. There was a strong chance that if I saw anyone I would be jerked back out of this world like the man at the end of the rope. The grass around the pines had been recently mowed with a scythe. There was a hitch in my hip as if I had done the work. No one else used the scythe. But that was twenty-five years ago. Everything here was already dead, but in a place just out of the reach of an arm or a breeze. It was George MacDonald's land behind the North Wind. If I could see the sky, I would see my own apartment as through a film of water and myself sitting in the same chair that was my grandmother's that is in this space in what Debbie and I called the blue room because of the ancient color left behind from the original owners in the 1840s. My house is surrounded by mulberry and pecan trees.

Once inside Patrik's world, my memories in Alabama were edged up against each other.[122] I could pass from a moment on the farm when I was seven to twenty-six without difficulty. My grandmother's house in Jacksonville over the mountain was right there, just beyond the longleaf pines on the hillside. Other spaces were available instantly. This might be the capital of my dreams, but the empire reached out in widening circles as if I had been dropped like a corpse or a rock in a lake. Marc Augé describes modernity's new spaces as nowhere. It's like the world of dreams has been breached by another kind of landscape and turned on its side. I loved Patrik. But everything I could have said would have changed nothing. I couldn't materialize myself in that world. There is nothing there other than another half-dark labyrinth. I can't squeeze through the opening. Only my voice can be strained into the land of the North Wind whistling through the breach.

Benjamin's Death

When Walter Benjamin finally left Paris in 1940, it was as if he were rehearsing a scene from the movie *Casablanca*, still two years in the future. In the movie, Humphrey Bogart's character and Elsa, played by Ingrid Bergman, are drinking champagne in a café when they are interrupted by the sounds of heavy artillery in the distance. They have plans to meet at the train station—the last train out. It's raining at the moment the train departs. The luggage gets wet. Elsa doesn't come. Instead there is a note from her that disintegrates in the rain as Bogart reads it. Bogart and his companion, the black musician Sam, escape to Casablanca, where he establishes Rick's Café Americain. There must have been some operating capital in their bags. Walter's escape is far less dramatic and lucky. There is no beautiful woman. There is no friend. Instead, Walter is concerned with what to do with his papers and a print by Paul Klee. He's been working for ten years on a history of nineteenth-century Paris. It's a curious history made up of quotes and samples with almost no narrative strands. The print is titled *Angelus Novus*. His friend described it as looking like a waiter hovering in space. It's one of the few things that remain of Walter's collection of books and toys and relationships. It's been his constant companion since around the time of his own suicide attempt. Now it's unframed and rolled up into a tube. No tears are recorded. Does one cry saying good-bye to a picture? The image doesn't appear in his Paris history but gets a cameo in the smaller essay drawn from the larger—"Theses on the Philosophy of History"—and makes the most of it. It's the most famous single passage Benjamin wrote. It's called the Angel of History.

This must have been how Benjamin himself felt, a chubby angel of a man blown backward into the future gazing at the debris of his life. He was soon detained. He was interned at a camp outside Marseille. But luck was still with him. He was discharged. He made his way to Marseille, where he hired a guide to smuggle him over the Pyrenees, where the possibility of making Lisbon and then New York was very real. But for a man with nothing, he had a heavy suitcase.

On the morning Walter Benjamin was heading over the border into

Spain, he met his guide and the others in the party of refugees in an open field outside of Marseille. In an attempt to conserve his strength, he'd spent the night in an open field near the climb across the Pyrenees. He must have slept on his back with his glasses on, looking straight up into the sky. When he met his companions, it looked as if he was bleeding from his eyes. Benjamin was completely unaware of his wounds, which turned out to be the red dye in his eyeglasses soaked with the morning dew running down his cheeks. The effect was startling and eerily prophetic.[123] Benjamin would be dead in three days from a morphine overdose, lying in a small bed in a tiny inn on the border overlooking the Mediterranean. I picture him again on his back like some kind of old turtle, eyeglasses on, the redness bleached out, looking up at the darkness in the room, replacing the possibility of gazing out at the water emptied of light. The climb over the mountains was difficult, and Benjamin had been in poor health, though he never complained. Benjamin was again the problem: this time like a bureaucratic form being passed back and forth between officers or the very form he describes in his own introduction to Kafka's work. At issue was how and where Benjamin would be buried. More relevant was the disappearance of his famous suitcase.[124] Benjamin described what was in it as "more important than my own life." His guide described him lugging it over the mountains, crushed under its weight. At the inquest the suitcase was found to be nothing more than a briefcase. Not like iron, but light as the proverbial feather. The contents are listed as six passport photographs, an x-ray and medical note, a pipe with an amber stem, glasses and a dilapidated case, a pocket watch of gold with a worn nickel chain, an identity card issued in Paris, a passport with a Spanish visa, and letters, magazines, and papers—some of which may have been a manuscript, contents unknown. Many have mused that what was so valuable to Benjamin was a more finished version of *The Arcades Project*. Others have settled for the more modest-sized "Theses on the Philosophy of History." There in his own writing is Benjamin's motive for suicide. Unable to finish the *Arcades* in this life and afraid that the fascists were already winning on the other side, Benjamin entered the afterlife to save the dead. Because even the dead won't be safe if the fascists win, and his Paris was always a dead Paris; in his own work it was already emptied of crowds. Perhaps the other side is alive with ghosts.[125]

What his last thoughts were is discreetly passed over by most commentators. A clue could be ascertained by how he was dressed or the indentation his body left in the mattress. These details are ignored. In the future an autopsy—if his body could be found, the grave is not likely his—might be able to recover the last image on his retina and where his eyes were directed in the room. Could that piece of the room be traced back to his home in Berlin, or Paris, or his last great love Asja? The image would be his final gesture pointing to the entrance to the subterranean tunnels of the superorganism.[126]

Patrik's Transformation

Debbie produced this portrait of me before I met Patrik. She copied the technique I would use in his MFA thesis.

King David—Rapunzel
a Brother Grimm—Mary, Queen of Scots
Jack Orion—Savoy
Errol Flynn—Jeanne D'Arc
Mr. Rogers—Victoria with a secret
T. S. Garp—a water nymph
Allen, Khan of the rabbits, kingfishers, and field mice

Few would recognize me. Most would see more resemblance to me in Patrik's genealogy. They would be wrong. I'm still there in Debbie's portrait. Think of Dorian Gray. His portrait is painted when he is a young man. The painting ages, Dorian doesn't. The painting is hidden in a locked room. It does something Patrik dreamed of. A grotesqueness spreads across the surface of the canvas that mimics the degeneration of the person. Debbie's portrait of me is in a drawer. It was written on bright blue paper that has faded slightly. There is a crease in the center of the paper where it has been folded, hiding the portrait. Dorian inadvertently discovers a method by which the original image can be restored.

He kills the painting, and in so doing he dies. The painting returns to its original image. I can't destroy Debbie's portrait. Patrik has seeped into it. It's infected with nostalgia.[127]

I left Alabama a long time ago. I carried Patrik with me. His work and his story were known by strangers. He never had to open his mouth. Alabama was the mystery to most. I couldn't be from there. The Big House and Debbie were things I'd made up. Patrik became a kind of geography, the place I came from. Occasionally I called him at work at The Globe. We'd talk. No, I didn't know where I'd be next year. How are you? Where are you living now? And then I lost touch completely with Patrik as a voice. He worked erratically. There was talk of him going back to Amsterdam. On my side of the dead phone I was surrounded by Patrik's work. His pieces hung on the wall. The postcards were stacked in a revolving display rack from a drugstore. There was no angel like the one in Klee's print that hovered over me. Patrik's work floundered on my wall like an old horse in a broken-down pasture. Except on the anniversary of his death, Patrik's pictures didn't come alive at night. I never heard him padding around in bare feet and a bathrobe, tapping his cane as he photographed himself for his last great work *Asylum, Asylum*. This is how Patrik dressed late at night and early in the morning in his apartment in Athens. He was so civilized. He wore a terrycloth bathrobe. He even had slippers. At the end he appeared prematurely aged and broken like the crippled psychiatric patient he emulated.

The years haven't been kind to Patrick's work. Besides their own decay and the slump of the often-shoddy materials he used, the decade's fashions in which they were produced have become more prominent. His performances now look like a kind of baroque ornamentation or the curved animal legs on a Victorian loveseat. His works bear the imprint of their times as if they were fossils rather than art. At the very least, what "brilliant" meant in 1986 hasn't persisted. *Brilliant* may not be the word to describe his work at all. It was powerful, gripping, and resembled a car wreck twisted into a bank of wild roses along the road or a marble pattern in melting butter projected onto an entire room. The brilliant in his work touched on the glass edges that often occurred, but these were like lightning flashes across a wide expanse of moldy gray sky. Maybe he was a brilliant naturalist disguised as an artist. That may have been part of his work's attraction for me. These fossils allowed me to slow time, to always be the man in Debbie's portrait and hold at bay the inscription at the base of the Confederate Memorial in Jacksonville: "Men may change but values never do." Patrik showed me a way to translate my life into my work and reach back to my dead mother and grandmother and their kingdom underneath Alabama. There was a chance I could still be Khan of the rabbits, kingfishers, and field mice.

One of my favorite postcards from Patrik was a collage constructed around Michelangelo's *Pietà*. At the top of the card, Mary is holding the outstretched body of Jesus.[128] He is dead. His body is limp. There's no color to the stone. Directly beneath it Patrik has spliced in young, tender asparagus spears nudging upward into the image. One layer further and there is a bed of yellow popcorn kernels in full bloom. Patrik has typed the single word "for" and glued it to the card. Patrik wasn't raised Catholic. Nor was he particularly close to his mother. Unlike images dealing with his father, whom he detested, there doesn't seem to be any biographical reference behind the image. It's a memory of a desire that isn't part of his past. He's scratched himself in. Almost pornographic, the image captures Patrik's desire to be borne up in death by the supernatural. His Mary is a marble scaffolding and then just rock, with no more Mary. The third part of the image reproduces an asparagus bed planted in the soft dirt of a grave made of popcorn and cut radishes.

In 1606 a Jesuit missionary in China unintentionally assembled a similar image for a Chinese book.[129] His name was Matteo Ricci. He was from a small town in Italy near where the Virgin Mary's last home in Palestine had been moved across the Mediterranean by a pack of angels. Pilgrims to the Holy Land had confirmed the authenticity of the event. The foundations of the house in Palestine perfectly matched the location of her new dwelling in Italy. Matteo Ricci was a frequent visitor to this holy site near his home. Matteo was a practitioner of the memory arts, especially the construction of memory palaces. In this he was particularly skilled. For the book he chose an image of the Virgin and the infant Jesus. What he failed to recognize was that to the Chinese this image suggested a dragon's body hidden beneath the gown with a human's head. What he also failed to appreciate is how deeply the image was cut into his own

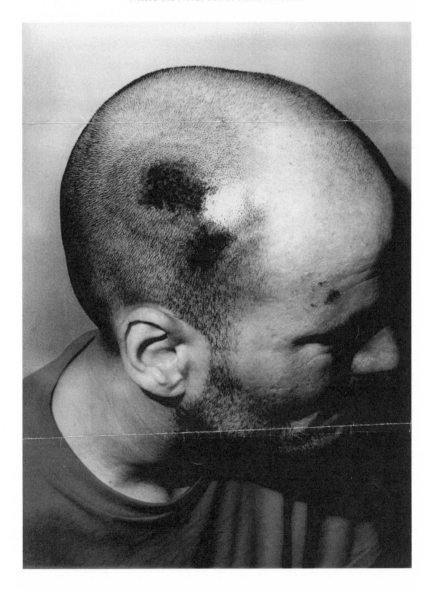

psyche, his homesickness, and his own childhood. The image worked then as a network of layers that moved progressively through his missionary motives and his cultural and biographical scripts into a Chinese cosmos before finally vanishing into the nonhuman. Proust's madeleine had evolved backward into a scallop without any recollection of Marcel or a home. There were the tides and sand.[130] For Patrik, this was glory. He was where the North Sea touched Alabama.

"Shall I trash the dentures or slip them to you in a box?" Patrik has crossed this line out with a red pen and then written: "(or in a casket is where they belong) Where many of us end up anyway."

NOTES

Preface

1. Freud was involved in a similar set of adventures, which he recorded in his 1919 essay "The Uncanny." There is even a small supernatural dimension. Freud is startled to see a medium's advertisement on the street. And while the moment never develops, he senses a soft spot in the landscape, a porousness through which the dead could pass through. They don't. Freud dispenses with ghost encounters in the essay. Instead he substitutes dread for the dead, which for him is the half-buried image of bloody genitals after castration and the horror of the mother's wet vagina in the unconscious. The genital dread is later consolidated in another image in the essay, the muck and stench of a crocodile swamp that emerges out of the floor at night in a young couple's apartment.

During the isolation of the Great War, I came across a number of the English *Strand Magazine*. In it, among a number of fairly pointless contributions, I read a story about a young couple who move into a furnished flat in which there is a curiously shaped table with crocodiles carved in the wood. Towards evening, the flat is regularly pervaded by an unbearable and highly character- istic smell, and in the dark the tenants stumble over things and fancy they see something undefinable gliding over the stairs. In short, one is led to surmise that, owing to the presence of this table, the house is haunted by ghostly croc- odiles or that the wooden monsters come to life in the dark, or something of the sort. It was quite a naïve story, but its effect was extraordinarily uncanny. (Freud, "The Uncanny," 151)

Patrik emerged in swamp muck. There was nothing uncanny about it for me. The dozer operator had a different experience. Together, our reactions are a subtle gloss on Freud's mapping, adding a situational relativism. I wanted to see the dead come back. For me, it is a question of what Walter Benjamin called porosity in his essay "Naples." Where could the miraculous occur in the Alabama landscape? In Naples Benjamin noticed that the walls separating the living room and the street facilitated percolation. They were porous. Things and experiences commingled into new patterns and arrangements. Benjamin, like Freud, doesn't add the supernatural. But he does observe something that, once his level of detail is increased, becomes monstrous. In apartments, the pasture, the street, and the living room pour into each other. "Even the banal beasts of dry land become fantastic. In the fourth or fifth stories of these tenement blocks, cows are kept. The animals never walk on the street, and their hooves becomes so long that they can no longer stand" (Benjamin, 175). Benjamin's image is discreet except for the monstrous hooves. But what about the shit and urine, the hay and grain, the water, the flies that are part of this new ecosystem? At the animal's death do the owners slaughter it in the living room? How else do you move a several-hundred-pound corpse down five flights of stairs? Unexpectedly in his relatively dry essay on porosity, his porous living rooms start to resemble the swamplike living room Freud described in "The Uncanny." Perhaps the uncanny is linked to wetness or is a specific instance of porosity where the wetness suddenly bursts through a thin dry surface. Back in Alabama, I had a clue now as to why Patrik appeared where he did and where others might pass through. Wherever muck and dread appeared together, there was the possibility of the miraculous.

2. My father would not have appeared as he does in my work if he were alive. This was to spare his feelings and the inevitable aftermath. He was a Republican. He wouldn't have approved of my project. In the first book he had a cameo appearance that he was proud of. He pointed it out to his girlfriends even though he didn't understand the book. In the scheme of things, this is a small point. At least he bought the book. He gets this work only after his death. It's an important job for me. I need an entrance point back into the landscape. Then again, a lot of my working capital is invested in my family and adventures on the old farm. It's almost psychoanalytic except the patient is the ground underfoot. It's a digging. Family members have worked a long time in this archaeology. Not all of them are dead. My son Tyree has dutifully labored without pay since he was a child. Occasionally one of my brothers or sisters appears. Quite by accident I realized I could substitute family members for theoretical concepts and achieve a similar kind of canonical authority with an entirely different effect on the material. My grandfather A.C. could stand in for Marx. The cat Nadia's scratches across the surface of my writing were as rhizomatic as the scratchings of any of Deleuze and Guattari's mad pack of theorists. The two acquaintances, Walter Benjamin and Michel

Leiris, utilized their own family, friends, and selves strategically in the construction of certain works. Leiris's work in *Manhood* is swollen with relationships. Benjamin opens "A Berlin Chronicle" with a dedication to his son, who never appears but nevertheless performs an important function. The account is an arid recollection of architectural formations in Benjamin's youth. Other family members and friends barely materialize except as ghosts or vapors, perhaps as odors in the room. It is relentlessly anti-Proustian in its recollection. The son acts like a blue silk scarf draped over an empty chair in an empty room. There was someone here at one point. I can smell another blue silk scarf. Someone else has left it behind. It's a sign that only now am I an orphan. A friend tells me this after my father's death. His name is Laurence Shine. He knew Patrik. He lived in Athens, Georgia, Patrik's last home. It's also near where James Joyce's novel *Finnegans Wake* begins: "by the stream Oconee exaggerated themselves to Laurens County's gorgios while they went doubling their mumper all the time" (3). He didn't know me then. He never met my father. His own father was an Irish army mapmaker. I'm not sure this is meant to console me or point me toward something else. All the other desertions were temporary. Only now, he points out, can I really write about home. Laurence is a believer in exile. He is a Joycean scholar. He doesn't live in his home country. He lives now near the largest repository of Joyce's work, in Buffalo, New York. I'm not convinced it's an even trade. My home may be the world inside the frame created by Patrik's work hanging on the walls of my apartment. And he has been dead a long time. His return is not seeable.

3. Now I find myself the only survivor on this side of the divide between the living and the dead on a map that I have drawn. It's a very personal map. Others still on this side are omitted. But then the map was never meant to be complete. It details the particular turns of the screws that cut my vertigo into me. I have been thinking about it a long time. I had picked up facts here and there. At my father's funeral, an archaeologist told me stories about the prehistory of the valley before the Spanish arrived. There were lots of Indians here. The woods were like a supermarket, he tells me. But then, ominously, he notes the evidence of defensive fortifications around villages and the endemic violence before this culture's disappearance. I look through the sketch, as if it were a pane of glass, at past faces. Some of them, like my family and Patrik, I recognize; the other faces could be wildflowers blooming out of torsos and shoulders. If I strain my eyes, I can see Patrik still writing postcards to me. They are delivered at night in my sleep. The question of whether I'm the author or the secretary of this account brings a certain amount of disquiet.

In his essay "Partial Enchantments of the *Quixote*" the Argentinean writer Jorge Luis Borges asks the question "Why does it disquiet us to know Don Quixote is a reader of the *Quixote*, and Hamlet is a spectator of *Hamlet*?" (48). He quotes a passage from the Victorian philosopher Josiah Royce's work *The World and the Individual.* The work is from the year 1899, a score away from Freud's essay "The Uncanny."

> Let us suppose, if you please, that a portion of the surface of England is very perfectly levelled, then smoothed, and is then devoted to the production of our precise map of England. . . . But now suppose that this our resemblance is to be made absolutely exact, and in the sense previously defined. A map of England, contained within England, is to represent, down to the minutest detail, every contour and marking, natural or artificial, that occurs upon the surface of England. . . . For the map, in order to be complete, according to the rule given, will have to contain, as a part of itself, a representation of its own contour and contents. In order that this representation should be constructed, the representation itself will have to contain once more, as a part of itself, a representation of its own contour and contents; and this representation, in order to be exact, will have once more to contain an image of itself; and so on without limit. (Borges, "Partial Enchantments of the Quixote," 46)

Royce's map isn't drawn on paper but inscribed into the very ground it's mapping, as if the terrain were a criminal being marked with the sign of his crime. Presumably the philosopher himself would be found on the map, overseeing the inscription of the map into the ground by a worker with a spade, hoe, and rake, and then again, writing the very passage that describes the map on the portion of England that has been perfectly leveled and smoothed. If he were like me, the map would start to creep across his own body. My meaty calves find analogues in the landscape. My scars are signs linked to the sketch.

I am playing my part in the history. My handwriting looks vaguely like my mother's crumbling under the weight of fire ants. My sketch is a mirror with no world on the other side. It's a pool of water in which the images skitter like minnows and come together in fleeting composites of images showing possible futures. Royce's map reminds me of my grandmother pulling a heavy quilt up from the foot of the bed to bury me. Once she turned out the light, it was so dark. My sketch is light. It's punctured with holes. The landscape is marked with cuts and wounds, like Jesus was. Whether the wounds will turn miraculous in my lifetime is uncertain, despite the claims of Jesus's imminent return. In the conventional histories of Jesus, the attention is focused on Jesus. The post he is nailed to is omitted. He is the axial point on the map on which everything turns. How deeply the post he is nailed to is screwed into the ground isn't mentioned. The vultures lazily soaring overhead against the blue sky escape notice. The flies in the wounds aren't colored in or counted. Various other human actors are noted. The name of the hill is given. But details on the map are scarce. Jesus was a superorganism, not a single entity. A tree was cut down, split with wedges and hammers, shaped with an ax, stuffed into a gaping hole, and then packed with iron rods with rock and dirt to hold it up right. Some commentators see the pole as a descendant from the Tree of Knowledge in Eden. A beetle was crushed underfoot. Sparrows scattered into the air. A mole's head was splintered. Jesus is the head of one big screw that turns deep into the landscape. The whole valley aches with the map's vibrations on it.

4. The Lisbon earthquake of 1755 killed eighty thousand people on the first day. More would die in the ensuing weeks from other complications created by the quake. Its destruction was equivalent to losing Chicago or London, reported Walter Benjamin on a radio broadcast for children in 1933. He had been writing and performing radio scripts for three years. This was his last broadcast. He starts the show by comparing himself to a chemist weighing the powders needed for medicine, gram by gram, with a finely calibrated set of weights. His weights are minutes that he has to measure out carefully if the show is to come out right. It's a curious and antiseptic opening to the introduction of an apocalypse. He offers a long firsthand account of the quake from an Englishman on the scene:

> When evening settled on the desolate city, the landscape seemed to turn into a sea of fire; the brightness was such you could have read a letter by it. At a hundred different points, at least, the flames rose to the sky, and they blazed for six days. What the earthquake had spared, they now consumed. As if petrified by fear, thousands gazed at the flames, while women and children prayed to the saints and angels for help. The ground continues to tremble more or less violently, often for a quarter of an hour on end. (Benjamin, "The Lisbon Earthquake," 540)

Benjamin then concludes the broadcast with the same antiseptic quality with which he opened it:

> So much for that day of misfortune, November 1, 1755. The catastrophe it brought in its wake is one of the very few that can render men as impotent now as they were 170 years ago. But here, too, technology will find ways to combat it, even if in a roundabout way: by prediction. For the moment, however, the senses of some animals are still superior to our most sensitive instruments. Dogs, especially, are said to display unmistakable signs of agitation days before the eruption of an earthquake, so that people keep them as helpers in the lookout posts in earthquake-prone regions. This brings me to the end of my twenty minutes, and I hope they have not passed too slowly for you. (540)

The radio broadcasts were to be Benjamin's last steady source of income until his death seven years later. His last sonic image is that of a sensitive dog on the watch for earthquakes and other calamities. Eli the dog and Lucky Dog are found dead in the woods. They had been murdered by three pit bulls. There are no dogs on watch now.

Where the North Sea Touches Alabama

1. My grandmother Pearl Landers loved to play solitaire. No, she was obsessed with solitaire. She played it while she was alone. She played it in company on any available surface. It made no difference to her whether it was the kitchen table, a sofa cushion, or her own lap as she sat in a chair. She played like a pianist trying to recover a forgotten melody. Winning wasn't her object. She won often enough. She was, I think, looking for a certain sequence of cards. What would happen if this sequence turned up I can't say. Hell might fall in. The Messiah might briefly appear. Patrik might come back from the dead. Even after Pearl's death my mother saw her ghost playing solitaire. If she had kept a systematic notebook of her games it might have looked like Walter Benjamin's *Arcades Project*, which at his death totaled nearly a thousand pages of notes arranged to look like innumerable reproduced games of solitaire or tarot readings laid out on the page.

2. Two days after I buried Pearl in the city cemetery I dreamed about her. She wasn't playing solitaire. Instead she led me down the hall of her house to the locked door to the attic, unlocked it, and then disappeared. I reached inside and pulled out Xenophon. A blank check with a Sunday school lesson written on it was stuck in the book as a marker. The next morning I drove over to her house and loaded her library into my truck. Benjamin carried his history of nineteenth-century Paris from country to country for the last thirteen years of his life. It was supposed to be his masterpiece. The work was continually interrupted. There were the incessant financial demands. Benjamin had no steady income. The rise of the fascists in Germany turned him into an exile. And then there was the creeping melancholia that settled on him like a heavy mist. Benjamin described himself as writing under the sign of Saturn. The project was never finished. It probably could never have been finished by one man in one lifetime.

3. While the *Arcades* was never completed, Benjamin used the work to generate several essays over the same time period. Perhaps it was already finished insofar as it was a machine generating other texts. Susan Buck-Morss has shown how the *Arcades* produced all of the material for Benjamin's writings in the last decade of his life. An early essay drawn out of the *Arcades* was "A Berlin Chronicle," a memory piece about mapping the city. Benjamin reworked the essay into a series of smaller pieces under the title *Berlin Childhood around 1900*, a small book he tried unsuccessfully to publish. In its first iteration Benjamin describes the suicide of a friend. It's deleted from the book. "You will find me lying in the Meeting House" ("Berlin Chronicle," 605).

4. What Benjamin was attempting to do in *The Arcades Project* is likely related to his earlier work *One-Way Street*. Both are collage texts that are grabbing for a concrete materialism in which things speak in their own voices. *One-Way Street* is a series of short passages inspired by street signs, public writing, and dreams, but

there is a residual narrative. Benjamin's own sentences dominate. It's still a book. The text doesn't become what Henry Sussman called "the thing that *The Arcades Project* is." It's a thing, a blueprint, a presence, but the *Arcades* isn't a book. There are visible relationships configuring *One-Way Street*. Benjamin dedicates the book like this:

> One-Way Street
> This street is named
> Asja Lacis Street
> after her who
> as an engineer
> cut it through the author

The weight of the beloved is named in the text. No dedication is given in the *Arcades*. Whose weight lies on the text is unclear. This was undoubtedly one of Benjamin's points and one of the tragedies of his life. But does one dedicate a thing or a machine that simulates on pages an entire city? If Asja was able to punch a single long street through the author, Benjamin engineered through himself an entire network of boulevards. How it would have looked completed is a mystery. Instead of chapters, the text is arranged in files organized around themes like iron, the interior, shop girls, and Marx. There is no narrative. Each file or *Konvolut* is a network of movable pieces—small gemlike quotes mined from other texts that were placed in a particular order but were designed by Benjamin to be moved, reconfigured into different sequences with a different musicality and meaning. Benjamin's own voice is the tiniest part of the text, a servant of his organizational designs. Each file resembles a long hallway with multiple doors opening to just as many different background texts and stories. Benjamin here is content with portraying the doors. There is no readily apparent individual behind any of the doors. It is as if he had constructed a city of closed doors, a city completely asleep waiting to be awakened or turned on, since there are no actors, just voices stuck on the page as doors.

5. The weight suspended over Benjamin's head like the sword of Damocles was his revolutionary politics. But there were other weights that pressed on him. The dead friend was one. I wouldn't add any from his family in his lifetime. His father had a leg amputated in 1925 and died soon afterward. They were estranged. His death hardly seemed to ruffle the surface of Benjamin's world. It was deaths in the future that burdened Benjamin. For me it was in the past. This list is my own arcades, though a bestiary is a warmer configuration, with its animal fur and blood. They are dreams I can't wake up from. I killed the rattlesnake on the hillside overlooking the Back Barn. I was bringing twenty young heifers in from the pasture for grain. I saw several of them bolt toward the barn, kicking and snorting. Another group pooled around something on the hill. A large rattlesnake was trying to cross the open space between the banks of trees on either side of

the broad swath of grass. The snake was as thick as my forearm. I hesitated. I didn't want to kill it. But what if it bit A.C.? The snake was coiled. I crushed its head with a rock. Once it quit moving I cut the rattle off. As I held its body in my hands, it felt like velvet and I was convicted of my crime. I flung the carcass into the trees. I should've let the snake crawl into the woods, the same woods where the farmer had shot himself in the 1930s. I kept the rattle in my grandmother's hope chest. Now I can't find it. Benjamin wrote under the sign of Saturn; I write under the sound of the snake's rattles coming from different corners of the room.

6. In *The Castle of Crossed Destinies*, the Italian writer Italo Calvino describes how a group of travelers come together in an inn and, having inexplicably lost their ability to talk, each tells a story using tarot cards placed in sequences. The first card is a high priestess reading a red book. Mary Pullen kept a small library of her favorite books on the shelf in the living room. There was an edition of Grimm's fairy tales, *1001 Arabian Nights*, *At the Back of the North Wind*, *Anne of Green Gables*, and *The Prophet*. These are the only ones I can remember. Each was salvaged from the public library. The books faced pieces of her porcelain Madonna collection on the piano. Above the piano was a giant photograph of a family posing in front of their house. One young man stood with a dinosaur-looking bicycle. The wheels were huge on a thick skeletal frame. A vine crawled up a trellis on the porch. The house looked reminiscent of Mary Pullen's house off the town square. It wasn't. The people weren't any relations of mine at all. It was art. I just didn't know it. Mary Pullen didn't play the piano either. The books, the Madonnas, the piano, and the photograph were assembled quotes slipped out of their original contexts to project an alternative history, a truer history if that is possible, of who Mary Pullen was. And who was she? She was the daughter of a hardware store owner in Boaz, Alabama, on Sand Mountain. She wasn't beautiful. She married A.C. Shelton. They had three children. She was the town librarian. She loved *As the World Turns*. She tended a wild, crazy garden. When she swam she resembled a seal.

7. This card is followed by two lovers. The story shifts to a train trip. It's reminiscent of an old movie starring Spencer Tracy and Katharine Hepburn, but it isn't those actors. The lovers are kissing in a sleeping compartment. The woman has reddish hair. She smells like cinnamon. I recognize the woman. I vaguely knew her when she was just a girl. We went to different high schools. I only saw her at church camps. We flirted. She was tall and skinny with long red hair. Her skin was translucent. It was as if you could see the future coming through her skin. In church she was always well covered. It was a freak accident. Her grandfather was teaching her to drive his pickup, a Chevy with three on the column. They had driven to a creek through the pasture. She went wading. On the way back she was riding on the edge of the truck bed when she just dropped into a headfirst dive and hit the ground. She never regained consciousness. I didn't know her well enough to go to the funeral. I heard about the accident at the Farm Supply. Alan

Baines told me. She must have looked like Sleeping Beauty with only her face
and hands uncovered in her coffin at the funeral home. I remembered her when I
taught my cousin Julie to drive a pickup near the Big Lake and whenever I drove
by the grandfather's farm on Highway 78, which ran parallel to Interstate 20 and
the Birmingham train. Now it's when I find a red hair on my jacket.

    8. The next card is an upside-down Seven of Cups. The woman with reddish
hair is suspended from the train compartment ceiling over the top bunk as if she
were a tilted wineglass about to be poured onto the floor. Her muscles are tense.
It's a strange acrobatic feat. Her lover is stupefied. He stares up at her. She could
be a red honeybee about to fly away. The girl is still going to fall, but now it's as a
woman from the ceiling and not from the truck. The train tracks in the distance in
the first account become even more important. For a second time, I won't be at
the funeral. I wanted my mother to meet her. How does one introduce a phantom
to the dead? My mother was enamored of the occult. Maybe it would not be difficult? She saw angels. Why couldn't she see a phantom? She believed in fate. As
a young woman she visited a fortune-teller. She told the story of the encounter
over and over. What the fortune-teller told my mother was a world coming into
focus. It would all be true. She would just have to wait patiently. Whether I inherited my mother's ability is questionable. My sister points out that like my mother
I am bipolar. I see the North Sea as part of that. I've never seen the ghosts. But
I feel hauntings in the landscape. My mother saw individuals: an Indian with a
mohawk, her mother, and others. She didn't see crowds. She didn't see the land
or rooms as haunted places. These were stages. She was a star in high school and
college plays. Ghosts appeared with her as actors. For me the world around the
Big House was always haunted. I may have been an actor on a stage, the world
around the Big House a theater, but my audience was ghosts. My relationships
in the here and now were the bit players. Mom believed in reincarnation. Her
remembrances were never systematic like those of certain Buddhists who in
meditation trace each thought back to the previous one, eventually arriving at the
moment of their birth before passing across the threshold into another life before
the remembering one. Mom's speculations and remembrances were more theatri-
cal. They jumped across time to key junctures where she was a different person in
another time on another stage. But like her ghost sightings, these remembrances
were monuments in our own museum. Last night I dreamed I was back on A.C.'s
farm. In the dream I tried to evaluate the dream landscape against my memories.
Even in the dream I couldn't escape the anxiety that they didn't correspond,
though I couldn't point to any definite distinguishing features. Awake, I felt the
same unease. What I saw in the dream isn't there, but the spectacle's roots in me
were so entrenched that I couldn't discount this ghost landscape. Not all regions
of my memory are accessible without special organization. Memories unfold into
other memories. Benjamin described it as a fan opening up. He could have been

imagining at the same moment a deck of cards fanned out before solitaire or a tarot reading. Benjamin's comparison is beautiful but unproductive. I link one memory to another until there are eight distinct memories in line. Then I stack them four deep to form a block of memories acting as a single unit. The formation, like a phalanx, protects my tender parts and allows me to move forward. Unfortunately, it shares the trajectory problem that beset the phalanx. The linkage causes the formation to swerve slightly to the right under duress, and the terrain of memory is duress at every step. I see the object of my desire off to the left as I keep swerving away.

9. In Calvino's telling, each segment of the account is tentative. Each image has to be carefully evaluated and its linkage to the next image double-checked. This could have been what Benjamin was attempting with his collage of rubbish, quotes, and concrete bits of history, what Freud may have recognized as a serial dream interpretation. The *Arcades* was an automaton that generated texts. It wasn't a book to be read. It was not the book in the high priestess's lap. For the *Arcades* to turn warm, it needs the weight of the beloved restored. In a fairy-tale version of Benjamin's life, his son Stefan lives with his father. Dora, the mother, has gone to England. Walter works every day in the library constructing this book. There is a fire. Walter is killed. Stefan lives clandestinely behind the walls of the arcades. He works on finishing his father's work. Walter's favorite print of the angel looks on from the wall in the boy's hidden apartment. Stefan grows old. The book is thousands of pages long. He can't figure out how to turn it on. And what sense would that make? How can a book be turned on? The answer comes by accident. He reads a certain sequence of quotes out loud. The angel blows his horn. The mirror surface pulls back like a curtain and there is Paris a hundred years ago with Walter, happy, waving at his son to join him. This may have been what Pearl dreamed of. It is what I dream of.

10. Kafka, *Trial*, 217.

11.

When he came to himself after he fell, he found himself at the back of the north wind. North Wind herself was nowhere to be seen. Neither was there a vestige of snow or of ice within sight. The sun too had vanished; but that was no matter, for there was plenty of a certain still rayless light. Where it came from he never found out; he thought it belonged to the country itself. Sometimes he thought it came out of the flowers, which were very bright, but had no strong color. He said the river—for all agree that there is a river there—flowed not only through, but over grass: its channel, instead of being rock, stones, pebbles, sand, or anything else, was of pure meadow grass, not overlong. He insisted that if it did not sing tunes in people's ears, it sang tunes in their heads, in proof of which I may mention, that in the troubles which followed, Diamond was often heard singing; and when asked what he was singing, would answer, "One of the tunes the river at the back of the north wind sung." (MacDonald, *North Wind*, 103)

12. It's a misconception that the three hundred Spartans stood alone at Thermopylae. Besides the elite Spartan hoplites, there were one thousand men from Tegea and Mantineia, over one hundred from Orchomenos in Arcadia, one thousand from the rest of Arcadia, four hundred hoplites from Corinth, two hundred from Phleious, and then there were eighty Mycenaeans. Joining them were seven hundred Thespians, four hundred Thebans, and one thousand Phocians. It was a Hellenic force. Facing them, according to Herodotus, were 1.7 million infantry and eighty thousand cavalry, divided into twenty-nine national contingents under the command of six generals. Modern historians have revised the numbers closer to between seventy-five and one hundred thousand men. The Spartan-led force confronted the Persian army at Thermopylae, which was a very narrow pass between a spur of Mount Oeta and the sea. It was less than fifty feet across. The core of the Hellene force was the hoplites or armored spearmen. Each carried a three-foot-in-diameter wooden shield faced with bronze. It weighed between twelve and sixteen pounds. It was supported on the left arm in a double grip. They wore bronze helmets, shin guards, and bronze breastplates of a composite armor formed from layers of linen, leather, and bronze. The complete panoply would have weighed up to sixty pounds, though fit soldiers could move nimbly and run. Each soldier carried a thrusting spear, seven to eight feet long, fitted with a bronze end spike. A short, straight iron sword was carried for close combat. Each soldier supplied his own weapons and armor. The Spartans were the elite Hellenic hoplites. Their standard battle formation was the phalanx. The formation deployed eight men across and was between four and eight men deep. The front line was a face of interlocked shields and spears, backed by calf, thigh, and abdominal muscles. It was a mass shock combat formation. The second line used the cover of the front shields and spears to thrust their own spears over the top and down at the bellies and chests of the attacking soldiers. The light armor of the Persians was no match. What defeated the Hellenes at Thermopylae was a successful flanking maneuver by the Persians around the narrow pass. A contingent of the Persian army came around the mountain under the cover of oak trees. Herodotus tells us that the thousand Phocian hoplites that were guarding the pass were alerted by the sound of the approaching soldiers' feet in the leaves. They were caught undressed for battle and were quickly swept aside. Once the flanking maneuver was complete, the Hellenic expeditionary force's fate was sealed. The Spartans were slaughtered like registered purebred cows.

13. On the outside of Patrik's work, the sign ////, or sometimes only ///, often appears. It is omnipresent in his works *Crawfish* and *Oleo*. It also figures prominently in *Utopia* and *3 Selections (Wise Blood)*. What does it mean—how does it relate, if at all, to the crime Patrik inherited from his father that animated

his production, or to the castlelike mystery lurking in the background, or for that matter to his art at all? Its repetition may be indicative of something other than the simple pleasure of stroking the slash marks. Its aim is antistructure, breaking apart the traditional relationship between signified and signifier. The technique is also applied to the artist himself, who, for whatever motives, tries to break apart the connections among memories, images, and emotions. The slash marks indicate a construction, or rather a deconstruction, project in which all structure is violated. It acts as a warning to the viewer. It also acts as an account of the artist's personal life. Like one cut to the wrist /, two slashes on the forearm //, three hacks with a cleaver ///, four deep gouges ////, and five you are dead //// with the fifth mark running through the body from the throat on the right to a bleeding foot on the left. As in *Oleo*, where Patrik has scrawled "W32 L33" (won 32 lost 33), there is always an account being kept. This theme is picked up again in *Asylum* in the precommunion examination and *3 Selections (Wise Blood by Flannery O'Connor)*. In this deconstruction process, Patrik acts as a heteroto-piaist. Objects, memories, experiences are cut open, sewn back together, made to fit within his conceptual framework that asserts the primacy of mind over matter. By dismembering himself, he attempts to float through the spaces between the stones and escape altogether from the audience.

14. Howard Becker plays piano. He prefers a certain style of jazz. I'm not capable of saying which with any certainty even though I've heard him perform a concert with an upright bassist in a modern art museum. What I can say is, it was marked by craftsmanship, a certain nostalgia, and melodiousness. It wasn't discordant. I know that it wasn't Dixieland. I could imagine hearing him playing on Marian McPartland's NPR show *Piano Jazz* or in a speakeasy with Walter Benjamin listening, clumsily tapping his feet. Benjamin confesses in his hashish essay to doing this in a café in Marseille while listening to jazz, which brings him closer to Becker. Becker's attitude toward the piano was calculated and relaxed. He didn't flail about or pound the keys, though I suppose that's more reminiscent of Jerry Lee Lewis than a jazz piano player. I was impressed. I'd never seen live jazz before. There was an intelligence about his playing that extends to his written work as well. On paper Becker works like a locksmith carefully describing the lock, the door, and the pertinent details in the surrounding room. This description occupies the largest part of his writing. It's only as the essay is winding down that Becker introduces the obvious sociological concept. It's only then that the finished key is placed in the lock. It is at this moment that the sociology of the essay is recognized. It is when the key turns the lock, and that click races back through the room, changing and organizing the description, that the sociological revelation occurs and something like music happens. The piano player has found the right note, the right rhythm for that particular moment, in that particular telling.

15. My storage shed is filled with cold, inert commodities that are too heavy to lift back into the market. I paid top dollar for the Austrian scythe and the English-speaking fork. Several pieces of furniture had once lived in grand houses. The desk with the foldout writing surface must've had lineage. Its legs are delicate and fine. Their market value now is tied up in a very specialized ecosystem that I can't quite access. My cousin Joseph is an artist. He knows their value in the Atlanta market. Their destinies are flea markets or the landfill. I used to stand among them as equals. Now they are dead portraits of Allen taken years ago. I've been convinced that Marx's volatile commodity was the basic unit of that thing called me. A commodity is there in the foreground or lurking in the background of any memory I conjure up. But what I had ignored, and what Marx had neglected as well, is that commodities cool off, come out of the market, get stranded in space and time, virtually die, become gifts, and are collected into memory palaces surrounded with a different kind of liquid from that which floats active commodities. The French anthropologist Marcel Mauss had to resort to words and concepts outside of the contemporary European frame to approximate this world. He employs a variety of interrelated concepts drawn from the Pacific Islands to get at what animates the "gift" and strings individuals and whole societies together like an archipelago of islands. Mauss observed the gift in precommodity worlds, but he was also describing the cooling off and the reheating of commodity fetishization in his world and our own. His acquaintance André Breton projected the story of a young woman against the flea markets and the community commodity networks of Paris. Her name is Nadja. She is the tragic gift that is heated and cooled into a surrealist bloom. She appears and then disappears into an arid sanatorium as if she were secondhand furniture from an estate sale. Benjamin drew from this book in *The Arcades Project*.

16. Prior to the Civil War and the commercialization of embalming techniques, premature burial was a threat met with a certain degree of ingenuity and old-fashioned vigilance. Sextons were on duty. Alarm systems were rigged inside crypts. A bell could be rung. I get a notice that my rental payment for storage is overdue. Memories are a kind of premature burial. Poe's House of Usher is a memory palace breaking up.

17. This date is wrong. Patrik committed suicide on August 30. It was likely a hot day in Athens. Patrik hated the heat and panted like a dog. I've kept the mistake on the surface because it announces what for me was D-Day, an invasion of occupied territory. In that way, it isn't a mistake. The day Patrik died happened twice for me. He died the day I got the news and then again as I tried to reconstruct what I was doing on the day he shot himself. The details were unrecoverable. My partner had just dumped me on the drive across country to her hometown. I took a $20,000 pay cut to keep working as a sociologist. I'm sure I walked aimlessly to a café for an espresso. I cried. My life was a shambles. Sleep

was difficult. The power in my apartment wasn't turned on yet. I called Tyree and pretended I was okay. If only Patrik had waited. I was slipping across the threshold. I gained twenty pounds. I looked like a cop. I become a version of his twin fantasy on this side of the North Sea.

18.

There is an ancient story that King Midas hunted in the forest a long time for the wise Silenus, the companion of Dionysius, without capturing him. When Silenus at last fell into his hands, the king asked what was the best and most desirable of all things for man. Fixed and immovable, the demigod said not a word, till at last, urged by the king, he gave a shrill laugh and broke into these words: "Oh wretched ephemeral race, children of chance and misery, why do you compel me to tell you what it would be most expedient for you not to hear? What is best of all is utterly beyond your reach: not to be born, not to *be*, to be *nothing*. But the second best for you is—to die soon." (Nietzsche, *Birth*, 42)

19. John 11:1–45.

20.

The Trojans have that glory which is loveliest:
they died for their own country. So the bodies of all
who took the spears were carried home in loving hands,
brought, in the land of their fathers, to the embrace of earth
and buried becomingly as the rite fell due. The rest,
those Phrygians who escaped death in battle, day by day
came home to happiness the Achaeans could not know;
their wives, their children.
(Euripides, *Trojan Women*, 261)

21. "His face is turned towards the past. [*Behind Patrik a languid angel stands with his wings outstretched and one arm weakly wrapped around his waist and the other cupped over his mouth.*] Where we perceive a chain of events, he sees one single catastrophe which keeps piling wreckage upon wreckage and hurls it in front of his feet. The angel would like to stay, awaken the dead and make whole what has been smashed. But, a storm is blowing from paradise" (Benjamin, "Theses," 257).

22. This is the gravitational pull inside the *Doppelgänger*'s compulsion and why Freud, in a dressing gown, recoiled in horror from his own reflection in the bathroom mirror in half-light on a train. He saw himself in the mirror as a disagreeable old man. Nevertheless he reached across the space to confront his own reflection. It could also be what fascinated Walter Benjamin, who looked longingly into the eyes of his Angel being blown backward into the future while he himself was being dragged face-first across the threshold in the same storm of debris.

23. Patrik produced this passage as part of a larger piece on performance:

Then in the new lexicon of contemporary art criticism, based on French social theorist Jean Baudrillard's "simulacrum," that review was intended to serve as a "fake." Better yet, it goes one step further, operating as a "fake" upon a "fake," a circle turning in on itself. The dizzying spin of this centrifugal force, playing on the critical community's narcissism, falls not out, but into a centripetal spin by way of its connection to the lack of a critic and the lack of original performance, disrupting comprehension with confusion. The substitute (the semi-fictitious "review") works toward rendering the existing "traditional" critical apparatus and process transparent. This whole experience for me as a performer and as an antiperformer (including artist, writer, and critic) exists in a societal state where imitation blueberry flavoring tastes more "real" than real blueberries and where the historical facades and enclosed outdoors simulated at a local mall are more "real" than either history or nature. In a more wide-angled view of "performance art" as life, the pinknosed, Disneyland-like "blissful naivete" of the U.S. is more "real" than homelessness, hunger, and poverty; and the surface image of life, forced down our throats via contemporary criticism in the media, appears more important and more acceptable than the reality of constant deceit. This is "performance art" at its grandest, exposing its worst (and real) potential, because it's everyday, "real" life: a staged sham of truth, justice, and the American way. It is a corrupt perfection of illusion that is ultimately only conquerable through new assaults by art and its criticism. Strangely enough, most of these new assaults have yet to be realized. (Keim, "Manifesto")

24.

When I had prayed sufficiently to the dead, I cut the throats of the two sheep and let the blood run into the trench, whereon the ghosts came trooping up from Erebus—brides, young bachelors, old men worn out with toil, maids who had been crossed in love, and brave men who had been killed in battle, with their armor still smirched with blood; they came from every quarter and flitted round the trench with a strange kind of screaming sound that made me turn pale with fear. When I saw them coming I told the men to be quick and flay the carcasses of the two dead sheep and make burnt offerings of them, and at the same time to repeat prayers to Hades and to Proserpine; but I sat where I was with my sword drawn and would not let the poor feckless ghosts come near the blood till Teiresias should have answered my questions. (Homer, *Odyssey*, 115–16)

25. I've told the story hundreds of time. The remembrances hardened and the surrounding landscape is narrowed into a tiny track that barely accommodates me. I remember the assertions. It was very hot. It was early afternoon in August.

I was wearing a white Hanes T-shirt, black bicycling shorts, cushioned gloves, helmet, and mountain biking shoes strapped tightly into the pedals. I was riding a Bridgestone MB1, the last model made in Japan. Tyree was a baby. Pearl was dead. I lived in the Big House. I had just come over Crooked Mountain. My water bottles were empty. The road was deeply rutted and I had to be careful about burying my front wheel and flipping over it. Near the foot of the mountain, on a curve in the road hidden from the highway, I saw her. She was sitting in a brown Naugahyde chair. The scene was like a huge Cornell box without walls. It was spilling out. The woman was intricately constructed. Her head was a hound's skull topped with a red wig stuck on a rusty tailpipe that led down into a white terrycloth bathrobe, which was pulled ajar exposing the metal chest. Her torso was a rusted-out Datsun muffler. The robe ran down the bone to three-quarters length, too heavy to move. Two broomsticks were stuck into a pair of dirty white high-top Nikes. The brooms' straw fans filled her hips. The hands were from two different worlds. One was a clear Miller beer bottle; the other was a brown cotton work glove. Phone wire was strung from the muffler to her hands. At her feet were dead animals laid out as if they were worshiping her. On one of the dead hounds, a steel choke collar gleamed. Around them were piles of garbage. But she herself seemed at the edge of movement, as if her legs and arms and head and torso were about to come alive.

26. Quoted in Osborne, review.

27. There is a series of technical problems in this transformation that neither Marx nor Benjamin fully resolves. The first is the porosity of the human and the commodity. Another is the variation across commodities. Does lace or iron melt more quickly into the skin? Then there is the stability of the holding pools and the effect on the ecosystem within each as rain forests become deserts and vice versa. There are the particular limits of the hosts in the transformation into *were*-object or *were*-person. The pumps or processes to make the transformation are never articulated. And then how stable is the process? Is commodity fetishization a historical construction that will cool off or fade out? One significant feature of Benjamin's passage is the absence of anything carnivorous or any of the dread that Freud consolidated in his usage of the uncanny. There is none of this dread in Benjamin's writing on toys or on another source of exteriorized humanness, books. Instead, Benjamin was an avid collector.

28. Benjamin, *Arcades*, 872

29. The full passage from the Scriptures is as follows:

Lastly, strengthen yourselves in the Lord and in the supremacy of his might. Put on the full armor of God so that you can stand against the treacherous attacks of the devil; because ours is no struggle against flesh and blood, but against the realms, against the authorities, against the world rulers of this darkness, against the spirits of evil in heaven. Therefore assume the full armor of God so that you can oppose them on this evil day, and, overcoming all, stand firm. Take your stand then, belted around the waist with truth, wearing the breastplate of righteousness, and your feet shod with the boots of the gospel of peace, over all holding up the shield of faith, with which you will be able to put out all the burning arrows of the Evil One. And take the helmet of salvation, and the sword of the Spirit, which is the word of God. Do all this prayer and entreaty, praying in the spirit on every occasion. (Ephesians 6:10–13, Richmond Lattimore's translation)

This was an often-quoted passage at church. For the congregation everyday life was war. Backed-up toilets, financial problems, illness—all were the result of the devil's attacks.

30.

It is with this in mind and for want of a better term, that I have come to think of society as a "set of sets," the sum of all the things that historians encounter in the various branches of our research. I am borrowing from mathematics a concept so convenient that mathematicians themselves distrust it; and I am perhaps using rather a grand word (in French the word for set is ensemble, which also means whole) to underline the obvious truth that everything under the sun is, and cannot escape being, social. But the point of a definition is to provide an approach to a problem, to lay down some guidelines for preliminary observation. If it makes that observation easier, both at the beginning and in later stages, if it helps to produce an acceptable classification of the material and to develop the logic of the argument, then the definition is useful and has justified itself. If we use the expression "set of sets" or in French, "ensemble des ensembles," does this not usefully remind us that any given social reality we may observe in isolation is in itself contained in some greater set; that as a collection of variables, it requires and implies the existence of other collections of variables outside itself? (Braudel, *Wheels*, 459)

31. Weber, "Protestant Ethic," 121.

32. Weber's essay is about the transformation of a set of extraordinary affects around work, discipline, desire, and the self into ordinary affects, with certain strands of Protestantism acting as the catalyst in the event. But by the beginning of the twentieth century, even he saw that the Protestant ethic was no longer necessary as the casing or the preliminary stage for the capitalist work ethic. Capitalism was triumphant even as he had acknowledged the pockets of the traditional work ethic still scattered across Western and Eastern Europe. In the United States, Frederick Taylor was reshaping work and the laborer based on close readings of the watch and the profit margins. He pointed toward a new kind of desire and set of ordinary affects outside of Protestantism. Weber's associate Simmel was already chronicling the vaporization of the Protestant ethic in the first part

of the twentieth century. His metropolis isn't Protestant. It's something entirely different with its new rationality and gray light. The anthropologist Katherine Stewart traces the still-lingering residues of this old world in the first part of the twenty-first century in the suburbs, airports, motels, and trailer parks. The old world still lingers in the spaces on the periphery of the metropolis. Now Simmel's gray fog is condensation on the surface of things, a residue of a perpetual twilight. What was extraordinary is now what Stewart describes as ordinary affects, a kind of everyday flat line punctured by occasional emotional spikes in a world where Patrik exits and returns so matter-of-factly.

33. Stach, *Kafka*, 201.

34. One of the greatest narrators in American letters is Herman Melville's Ishmael in *Moby-Dick*. The work begins with Ishmael contemplating suicide and ends with him as the only surviving witness of the whaling ship *Pequod*'s destruction. It's not an auspicious beginning or end. But what gives Ishmael stability is that he is a front for an omniscient intelligence, as if the whale Moby Dick were communicating through him. Ishmael knows things he couldn't possibly know. He acts as a medium transmitting the messages Ahab's ivory leg might feel but can't communicate. Melville's contemporary Edgar Allan Poe depended upon his "unreliable" narrators to reproduce the texture of weirdness woven into the ostensibly young but haunted America. Even the rational detective Dupin, who solves the purloined letter and the murders in the Rue Morgue, is vampirelike. He sits in the dark in his study, brooding. There is more than a touch of darkness about him. In the early twentieth century, Franz Kafka deployed a series of doubles of himself—Karl, Joseph K., and K.—in his novels to reveal a disturbing musical harmony with the larger landscapes surrounding the characters. All that ambient noise in the landscape was touched with the same hyperrationality and weird noises inside Kafka's doubles. Sociology has no equivalent Poe, Melville, or Kafka. Professionals in the field would say, "Why should we? That kind of voice would dismantle the entire project." In conventional sociology, C. Wright Mills's famous concept of "the sociological imagination" articulates the domestication of a Kafka-like narrator:

> Nowadays men often feel that their private lives are a series of traps. They sense that within their everyday worlds, they cannot overcome their troubles, and in this feeling, they are often quite correct: what ordinary men are directly aware of and what they try to do are bounded by the private orbits in which they live; their visions and their powers are limited to the close-up scenes of job, family, neighborhood; in other milieus, they move vicariously and remain spectators. And the more aware they become, however vaguely, of ambitions and threats, which transcend their immediate locales, the more trapped they seem to feel. Underlying this sense of being trapped are seemingly impersonal changes in the very structure of continent-wide societies.

The facts of contemporary history are also facts about the success and the failure of individual men and women. When a society is industrialized, a peasant becomes a worker; a feudal lord is liquidated or becomes a business-man. When classes rise or fall, a man is employed or unemployed; when the rate of investment goes up or down, a man takes new heart or goes broke. When wars happen, an insurance salesman becomes a rocket launcher; a store clerk, a radar man; a wife lives alone; a child grows up without a father. (Mills, *Sociological Imagination*, 3)

For an instant he sounds like Poe in one of his stories dealing with claustro-phobia and premature burial, or Kafka's character lamenting the endless series of hallways and doors separating him from the Law. It's just for a second.

35. In 1872 Phileas Fogg traveled around the world in eighty days. He wasn't known as a reader. The anthropologist Claude Lévi-Strauss took twenty years to accomplish the same task with a trunk of books. Professor Henry Sussman spent forty-six years on the trip. It wasn't geographic space he traveled but, by a con-servative estimate, 1,241,664 pages that, pieced together, form a dominion the size of Alexander's when he and his horse looked back west from India toward where Henry would appear. His travels are chronicled on his university webpage. He was educated in Waltham and then Baltimore, just a short trip. He spent time reading in the European capitals, the classic sentimental journey. How-ever, no mention is made that he has unruly hair and that he, like Gregor Samsa, underwent an insectous transformation. In Henry's case it wasn't debilitating. Instead he became a voracious reader, a solitary wood beetle working inside the library. He was at Buffalo for thirty years, reading and producing books at regular intervals. What is remarkable isn't a single book's appearance, even as Henry's travels turn like a screw into wood, but the network of books encapsulated inside the work. On a single page Henry might arrange seventeen different authors into a brightly colored bouquet that threatens to turn the page back into a field of savage wildflowers. Henry has read a floral empire, a prodigious feat, but like those of his ancestors, his world is waning. The anguish of the tropics has passed to the page, turning writing into another archaic form of tattooing. There is little evidence of this in his house in the suburbs. There are paintings, a comfortable couch, an out-of-date computer the size of a compact refrigerator. An IKEA chair and stool lurk at the edges. Beneath the basement, though, is Henry's library. It measures 212 by 210 feet. The roof at one point soars into a cathedral ceiling, uncomfortably close to a neighbor's swimming pool. The industrial shelves are seldom dusted. The lights flicker. The Victorian wingback chair he used to read Proust still sits in the corner, near a radiator. A large cat often sleeps on the cush-ion. Henry still has the vital body of the reader, what Foucault described as an "alert manner, an erect head, a taut stomach, broad shoulders, long arms, strong fingers, a small belly, thick thighs, slender legs and dry feet" (*Discipline*, 135). But

the world has changed. Now it takes the determination and genius of Phileas to travel a single page, much less the distance between his house and his office. It's here that Henry's guise as a tenured professor who teaches survey courses with a Buddhist's dedication and dutifully fulfills his service obligations turns on a pivot point into a historic transformation. Henry is at the end of the idyllic reader. His biography on the university webpage doesn't acknowledge this; instead it glows on the screen with a luminosity that the page can't reproduce.

36.

25 Sept. 1888

Dear Boss,

I keep on hearing the police have caught me but they won't fix me just yet. I have laughed when they look so clever and talk about being on the *right* track. The joke about Leather Apron gave me real fits. I am down on whores and I shant quit ripping them till I do get buckled. Grand work the last job was. I gave the lady no time to squeal. How can they catch me now. I love my work and want to start again. You will soon hear of me with my funny little games. I saved some of the proper *red* stuff in a ginger beer bottle over the last job to write with but it went thick like glue and I cant use it. Red ink is fit enough I hope *ha. ha.* The next job I do I shall clip the ladys ears off and send to the police officers just for jolly wouldn't you. Keep this letter back till I do a bit more work, then give it out straight. My knife's so nice and sharp I want to get to work right away if I get a chance. Good luck.

Yours truly

Jack the Ripper

Don't mind me giving the trade name

Wasn't good enough to post this before I got all the red ink off my hands curse it. No luck yet. They say I'm a doctor now. *ha ha*

(Ripper, "Letters")

37. It was a calculated punishment that was conceptualized to move in sequential stages and symbolic wounds to the greatest possible intensity of pain such as drawing and quartering. This was called *supplice* and was meant in its performance to produce a clear sign, a kind of forward memory broadcast to the viewers, that could be read unequivocally.

38. Eno, notes to *Discreet Music*.

39. Sometime in the early 1940s in Jacksonville, Alabama, a small mill town in the foothills of Appalachia, my grandfather stepped off his front porch, walked to the edge of the lawn where it met a large field, and posed for a photograph of himself in front of his new white house. His stomach stretched his black suit jacket, and his hair stood up in a thick, wavy crop like a hat on top of his head. Between him and the house the grass could be an ocean. His name was Eli Landers.

He was an education professor at a small teachers college. He never published any work. He rarely traveled even short distances. He preferred to play croquet. I don't even think he could drive a car. But he fantasized about a certain kind of traveling. In his library were several copies of Xenophon's *Anabasis* in both Greek and English editions. He read James Frazer's *The Golden Bough*. He was in a long retreat from the poor white farming district in Clay County where he was born. He just didn't get very far in space. His childhood home was less than an hour's drive away. This time in my family's history is blank. Whether my grandfather suspected the Holocaust or was swayed by the American hero Charles Lindbergh prior to Pearl Harbor was not one of the stories my grandmother told me. The stories came from the Civil War and the Revolutionary War. She was a member of the Daughters of the Confederacy and the Daughters of the American Revolution. My father enlisted at seventeen and served for a short time in China as part of the expeditionary force. The lawn on which my grandfather stood was mowed weekly by a hired hand named Henry and opened into the surrounding fields that teemed with whippoorwills. Eli died in 1955, the year I was born. His death was hastened by being stung by his own honeybees on the same lawn where the photograph was taken. When he died his library was moved from his office to inside the door to the attic. The books were stacked on the ladder steps. The door was locked. A photograph and a painting of him sitting in his desk chair hung in the living room. He never got his PhD. The beehives in the backyard were destroyed. A contemporary of my grandfather in Europe, Walter Benjamin, was conceptualizing a similar kind of traveling in keeping with Eli, who shared the same mop of hair. Benjamin believed in the archaic and the power of angels to haunt the present. He never left Europe. He spent time in Naples, Moscow, Denmark, Paris, and eventually the Pyrenees Mountains. There are no Brazilian rain forests in his texts. America was an imaginary vista he never visited. Benjamin saw the new mimetic technologies, and especially the camera's ability to see what previously could not be seen, as the door to the discovery of a new geography. Benjamin added the camera to Freud's exploration of the unconscious. The addition expands the unconscious landscape. Time as the shutter speed is recorded against Freud's oedipal grid. In a frozen photograph, new geographies are discovered that make possible new Marco Polos, new kinds of anthropologists; a Brazil inside Brazil is discovered or, in Benjamin's case, an indefinite number of Parises are found in Paris that have to be transversed. The optical unconscious scores deeper into the moment instead of spreading outward into the geography. Like Zeno's paradox in which the traveler moves continually half of the distance, forever postponing arrival, time and not space is the dimension to be crossed. Here time is as thick as honeyed napalm. There is a collapse of distance and what movement means. Movement is like the vertigo of having your feet in the sand at the beach and the undertow sucking you across the surface for an instant without your body moving. The undertow analogy is strong for another reason. What Benjamin found in the optical unconscious was a new experience of terror. His own writings do not forcibly express this discovery. It took his life to do that.

40. Ahab's store was a one-story concrete block building on a small rise overlooking Highway 9. He sold nails, bread and milk, pop, air fresheners, potatoes, cheap stereos, and antiquated eight-track tapes. The store was directly across from White's Gap Baptist Church. There were two gas pumps. Eddie Paris, the boy who dressed up as Bigfoot, pumped the gas. His grandfather was Ahab. His grandmother Mrs. Paris worked the cash register. Sometimes her granddaughter who was known as Woman ran the store and pumped the gas. I had come in from the pastures to get a Coca-Cola. An unknown woman was at the register. She was reading a tiny green Gideon New Testament. She had greasy brown hair pulled into a hunk, a tight sweaty T-shirt—there was no air conditioning—and she was fat. She looked like a bowl of gravy with lumps. At the register I looked at her hands holding the Gideon. Her nails were bitten. They were awkwardly small like sparrows. I asked what she was reading. "Corinthians," she said. "I love reading about the gifts of the Spirit. Are you a Christian?" I was afraid of her spit getting on me. She was so excited. "Can I sing you a song I wrote about Jesus?" She was out from behind the counter before I could answer. We were almost touching. I felt like there was no choice but to say yes. Then she sang the most beautiful song I'd ever heard. I was ashamed. How could this be happening? It was a gift and a lesson from God. We became friends though I never knew her name. A few months later she offered her seventeen-year-old daughter to me. "Marry her, she's pretty isn't she? She'll make you a good wife." She must have looked like this at one time. Eddie and Woman were her children as well. She had one more daughter who was profoundly handicapped. She was rope-tied to a chair in the store. She was maybe ten years old and in diapers. She couldn't speak. She moaned and rocked back and forth sucking on pop bottles from the cooler. All of these kids lived with Ahab and Mrs. Paris in a double-wide trailer just above the store on a hill. The woman sang so beautifully. After her daughter's wedding to a skinny local boy, I never saw her again. The daughter I would see riding in the back of a pickup truck leaning against the cab holding a baby. She wasn't smiling.

41. Elizabeth Hubbard was born to a respected family in Alabama. She heard Freud's lecture at Clark University, which prompted a lifetime of study. She married a wealthy man of some prominence. She was a member of the Daughters of the Confederacy and was convinced she was the reincarnation of the Confederate officer John Pelham. She proposed a radical reformation for the treatment of the mentally ill in Alabama. Her plan was briefly considered because of her husband. Little of it ever happened. She was partially responsible for the statute of John Pelham. She imagined parks with Confederate memorials, dogwood trees

and flowers blooming near benches that would act as a floral prosthetic for the disturbed. For Walter Benjamin, whose life overlapped with Elizabeth Hubbard's, a dreamworld was the phantasmagoria that sprang up in the shopping arcades of the ninetieth century, where dream fetishes and commodity fetishes were so intertwined as to be indistinguishable. The effect was bedazzlement in the face of a new kind of heavenly city or an intensely luxuriant ecosystem with strange new creatures like combs that swam in aquariumlike display cases, corsets that stood like statues among stacks of pressed cotton shirts, air rifles that were named for the goddess of the hunt, and faces on billboards that steadily grew into gigantic smiles. Mythic creatures populated the ur-forest of the modern city. Benjamin's dreamworld was a hybrid space made from dreams, commodities, and memory compressed together under pressure. The dreamworld was the luxuriant space that developed alongside the arid worlds Marx describes in *Capital*. Compared to Elizabeth Hubbard's world, Benjamin's is less arabesque and more enthralled by the new ecosystem of magical commodities flourishing in the arcade's beds and undergrowth. But in Benjamin's public writings there are no animals, no vines, nor the personal grief and scars that can mar the page. Hubbard wasn't enamored of the shine on things or the new phantasmagoric world, as was Benjamin. Out of Elizabeth Hubbard's obsession with Pelham something terrible, beautiful, and at times humane developed from the pain that can be felt in her diary. She never divulged her own psychoanalytic material directly, preferring, like Walter Benjamin, to write in an allegorical style about her personal grief. But what if Benjamin's and Hubbard's landscapes were overlaid like transparent maps on the same terrain? Then the mysteries of capital reaching into memory and the ecosystem around John Pelham could be seen.

42. Taussig, *Shamanism*.

43. A feral cat had wandered into the yard and the dogs had caught sight of the animal. One of the dogs was a hound called Smoky. He was a large blue tick. His bark was a low booming roar. There were at least two other dogs. Mom and I were outside. We saw the cat streaking across the grass with the dogs right behind it. How my mother was able to catch the cat is a miracle. She picked the animal up in her arms to save it from being torn apart. The cat bit her, leaving a deep cut on her forearm. She dropped it and the dogs were on it. In desperation, the cat jumped into the lake and tried to swim away. This lake had a hole in its deepest part through which all the water drained away every summer. The dogs jumped in and the cat was done for. They tore it to pieces. The barking stopped. The cat's carcass half sank into the muddy water. My mother was treated for rabies. The shots were extremely painful. I have been terrified of these shots since I was a small child and read about Louis Pasteur in my child's encyclopedia. My mother stepped in front of fate and she bore it.

44. Canetti, *Crowds*, 193–200.

45. More than once the dead have vanished in the world behind the Big House. The discovery of an ancient burial site on my father's property opened up for me a lost world. It was an invisible world. I'd never heard of it until I read John Sullivan's essay in *Pulphead*. North in Tennessee is the largest concentration of cave paintings east of the Mississippi River. Some of them date as far back as 4000 BC. There were three distinct cultural periods in the prehistory of the Southeast, culminating in the collapse of the mound builders. The three periods were the Adena, and the Woodland, and the Mississippian. All were mound-building cultures with the great mound cities the early Europeans encountered coming from the last stage. The mound builders didn't vanish entirely from the scene until 1731, when the Great Sun, chief of the Natchez, was sold into slavery by the French. The site next to Crooked Mountain was Woodland. The cave paintings indicate the emergence of a death cult in the South just prior to the arrival of the Europeans. The image of a round, pumpkinlike human head that has been severed with gore spilling out of the neck appears more and more frequently. It has weeping eyes. Other paintings show human faces with crested topknots like mohawks. Maybe my mother's ghost was a local and not from the Buffalo area. These crested men are drawn similar to woodpeckers. The Trail of Tears that emptied the Southeast of the Civilized Tribes touched the Big House. The local population of Creek Indians was expelled. Directly across from the Big House near where Luke encountered the ghost, an Indian with a metal detector found a box of gold buried in the pasture. He made his living retracing the Trail of Tears. He dug it up in the middle of the night and left the hole as a monument. This happened before A.C. bought the property. Warlick, who lived in the Big House, didn't hear a thing. He'd been looking for that gold for years. Now he had an empty hole to look at from his front porch.

46. Freud, *Psychopathology of Everyday Life*, 12–13.

47. In a note in *The Arcades Project* Benjamin imagined following a ghost through the walls of apartments. Unacknowledged is that to do so he would have to be a ghost himself. It's an intriguing alternative map to the invisible Paris that lies inside his own project. Does Benjamin have any idea what is behind walls? Rats are not part of his documentation. Insect colonies proliferate without his reportage. He knows nothing of construction. Marx chronicles something similar in his account of workers' apartments. He cites the cubic feet and the amount of available oxygen in the apartments as if they were perverse iron lungs squeezing their occupants to death. His workers were interned in windowless cell-like rooms. Light would have been something that marked the edges of things, like a tiny hole in an outside wall, the bar of light beneath a door, or the after-light in the hallways like a ghostly afterlife floating through the buildings: exactly what Benjamin hoped to follow.

48. Walter Benjamin captured the moment in his sample of a physicist's text:

I am standing on the threshold about to enter a room. It is a complicated business. In the first place I must shove against an atmosphere pressing with a force of fourteen pounds on every square inch of my body. I must make sure of landing on a plank traveling at twenty miles a second round the sun—a fraction of a second too early or too late, the plank would be miles away. I must do this whilst hanging from a round planet headed outward into space, and with a wind of ether blowing at no one knows how many miles a second through every interstice of my body. The plank has no solidity of substance. To step on it is like stepping on a swarm of flies. Shall I not slip through? No, if I make the venture one of the flies hits me and gives a boost up again; I fall again and am knocked upwards by another fly; and so on. I may hope that the net result will be that I remain about steady; but if unfortunately I should slip through the floor or be boosted too violently up to the ceiling, the occurrence would be, not a violation of the laws of Nature, but a rare coincidence. (Benjamin, "Some Reflections," 141–42)

49.

Why does it make us uneasy to know that the map is within the map and the thousand and one nights are within the book of *A Thousand and One Nights*? Why does it disquiet us to know that Don Quixote is a reader of the *Quixote*, and Hamlet is a spectator of *Hamlet*? I believe I have found the answer: those inversions suggest that if the characters in the story can be readers or spectators, then we, their readers or spectators, can be fictitious. In 1833 Carlyle observed that universal history is an infinite sacred book that all men write and read and try to understand, and in which they too are written. (Borges, "Partial Enchantments," 46)

50. Freud was spared coming home to his old apartment in Vienna after the war. He died before he could feel the uncanny loss inside what had been his home.

51.

It was a smallish object, judging by the place left empty, my end of the semi-circle, made by the symmetrical arrangement of the Gods (or the Goods) on his table. "*This* is my favorite," he said. He held the object toward me. I took it in my hand. It was a little bronze statue, helmeted, clothed to the foot in carved robe with the upper incised chiton or peplum. One hand was extended as if holding a staff or rod. "She is perfect," he said, "*only she has lost her spear.*" I did not say anything. He knew that I loved Greece. He knew that I loved Hellas. I stood looking at Pallas Athene, she whose winged attribute was Nike, victory, or she stood wing less, Nike A-pteros in the old days, in the little temple to your right as you climb the steps to the Propylaea on the Acropolis at Athens. He too had climbed the steps once, he had told me, for the brief-

est survey of the glory that was Greece. Nike A-pteros, she was called, the
Wingless Victory, for victory could never, would never fly away from Athens.
(H.D., *Tribute*, 68–69)

52. Freud, "Uncanny," 129. I was not consciously aware of this passage. I doubt
if I ever would've found it, even in this small essay, without meeting Anderson
Blanton. Anderson is another southerner. He's from the hills of North Carolina,
but he's been to West Africa and France. He's cosmopolitan. He drives a Toyota
truck and has hung out with the Slovenian philosopher Slavoj Žižek. His French
is passable. His French motorcycle jacket is canvas and sublime. He is an anthropologist trained at Columbia and resembles a taller Marcel Mauss. He wears log-
ger's boots. Anderson was in Buffalo with a group of scholars who were devotees
of Freud's essay. It was late. We were at a bar talking. Anderson made a comment
about an early draft of this manuscript and how I had incorporated Freud's definition of the uncanny as a repressed spring coming back to life into the work. I was
astonished. Yes, that's exactly right about the springs. They are the dead coming
back to life, another manifestation of the North Sea underneath Alabama. But
Freud never said anything like that. I said this with a great deal of conviction. I'd
taken a special class just on this essay with an acknowledged expert on Freud. He
never mentioned this. And what does Freud know about springs? I appealed to
the other scholars there. Did Freud write this? Absolutely not, they agreed. But
Anderson was convinced. He mentioned three other related passages to support
his contention. They were cobbled-together assemblages of Freud's text and
outside additions. They weren't righteously remembered. But what, I thought, if
he is right? Anderson bet me a $130 hand-forged, Dutch-made, American-pattern
rake, which he now owns. It is a beautiful rake. Where does Freud write this in
the essay? In what part does it appear? Anderson was unsure but convinced it
was there. I took the bet. That night at home I scoured the essay. More and more
I was convinced that my teachers and colleagues were right. There is no spring
in this essay. But then it was there, hidden in a list of dictionary definitions as if
they were leaves scattered across the small mouth of the spring in the woods. I
bought Anderson the rake. How did he notice this passage? He attributed it to
two of his professors at Columbia, John Pemberton and Marilyn Ivy. When I told
them about the incident, they had no recollection of any emphasis on springs in
the essay. No doubt Anderson was guided by the Holy Ghost. It was a word of
knowledge. For more of Anderson Blanton's work and adventures, read *Until the
Stones Cry Out*.

53. Though there is a specific family under discussion here, Freud makes clear
that the uncanny is attached to the family in general.

54. Chert is a chalky white sedimentary rock. In this area of Alabama it is
cheap and readily available.

55. The distortion of space isn't limited to my memory. It seems to be built

directly into my person. And here it takes a particular shape. For me the weight of objects can become buoyant. I can't appreciate their weight. Underneath the Big House with a house jack, I had no idea what was safe and proper. The brick pillars were in need of repointing. Many of the bricks were crumbling. But I thought I was completely safe. I had faith. On another occasion I was knocking down a small shed that had a metal sheet roof nailed on pine boards over a broken trough. How I got under that roof I've no idea, but I remember thinking it was where I should be when I knocked out the last post. I would hold it up and then push it over. How much could it weigh? My legs were strong. Immediately the roof pushed me to the ground till I was flat on my back. All around me were sixteen-penny nails protruding through the roof. I could've been killed easily enough—my heart, lungs, and liver punctured. No one was around. I crawled out from under the roof. This wasn't simply a misjudgment. The ancient Greeks would have called it hubris. Whatever it was, it was an integral part of me. I thought that I could've borne Patrik's weight. I could've stood. I wouldn't have oozed my blood through the floorboards. If Patrik had been there with me on that day tearing down the shed, we would have easily held the roof up. Patrik wasn't strong. It was about balance and distribution. Would I be wrong to assume this might have been one of his motives for returning?

56. In *Capital* there are no recurring characters. Authors are quoted. Aristotle is named as someone who came very close to unlocking the secrets of the commodity. Marx had read the early church fathers. Then there were the screen projections of the working class, like the nine-year-old laborer William Wood, or the young girl who was worked to death on a lace collar. These individuals are a kind of vapor or smoke generated by the system Marx records. Almost indistinguishable as well are the government officials who produced the earnest reports on working conditions throughout England that Marx drew on. The dominant character in Marx's work is the commodity. It appears in a multitude of forms as a coat, iron, bread, a lace collar, cotton, and labor itself. It's not that any individual commodity is robustly portrayed. They are one-dimensional as well. It isn't a red coat or Engel's coat; it's simply a linen coat. Marx has assiduously cut away any traces of the personal. As his text is written, it's impossible to detect the personal aura of any given commodity. The most profound effects of commodity fetishism are visible only once the personal and the setting are restored. Marx kept this part hidden.

57.

The bourgeois interior of the 1860s to the 1890s, with its gigantic sideboards distended with carvings, the sunless corners where palms stand, the balcony embattled behind its balustrade, and the long corridors with their singing gas flames, fittingly houses only the corpse. "On this sofa the aunt cannot but be murdered." The soulless luxurance of the furnishings becomes true

comfort only in the presence of a dead body. Far more interesting than the
Oriental landscapes in detective novels is that rank Oriental inhabiting their
interiors: the Persian carpet and the ottoman, the hanging lamp and the genu-
ine Caucasian dagger. Behind the heavy, gathered Kilian tapestries, the master
of the house has orgies with his share certificates, feels himself the Eastern
merchant, the indolent pasha in the caravanserai of otiose enchantment, until
that dagger in its silver sling above the divan puts an end, one fine afternoon,
to his siesta and himself. This character of the bourgeois apartment, tremu-
lously awaiting the nameless murderer like a lascivious old lady her gallant.
(Benjamin, "Manorially Furnished," 446–47)

58. This represents a different kind of detailing from what was included in
Benjamin's mapmaking in "A Berlin Chronicle." He imagines a colorful map
borrowed from the military in which he would locate his world. But it's in *The
Arcades Project* where his mapmaking skills turn rabid. Benjamin copied passage
after passage from books and laid them like tiny stones in a mounting avalanche
of patterns that spread across the page into a labyrinth. He blew up Edgar Allan
Poe's "The Man of the Crowd" into a weird, relentless inventory of qualities
without any single person appearing in the ecosystem. His map approached the
level of completeness that might cover Paris. Individuals were spectralized into a
constellation of details that foreshadowed his own disappearance. His materialist history of nineteenth-century Paris is an unintentional psychosocial map of
his own world in an endless repetition toward infinity. His end-time essay "The
Storyteller" unintentionally retells his demise as stories vanish from the world.
He was transforming from a singular man to a pack of objects. He was left as
words held in a specific gravity.

59. The quote continues:

Doubtless it does not, because of ignorance of the theater of future wars.
I have evolved a system of signs, and on a gray background of such maps they
would make the color for show if I clearly marked the houses of my friends
and girlfriends, the assembly halls of various collectives, from the "debating
chambers" of the Youth Movement to the gathering places of Communist
youth, the hotel and brothel rooms that I knew for one night, the decisive
benches in the Tiergarten, the ways to different schools and the graves that
I saw filled, the sites of prestigious cafés whose long-forgotten names daily
crossed our lips, the tennis courts where empty apartment blocks stand today,
and the halls emblazoned with gold and stucco that the terrors of dancing
classes made almost the equal of gymnasiums. (Benjamin, "Berlin Chronicle,"
596–97)

60. The primary Greek military formation was the blocklike formation known
as the phalanx. It was composed of heavy infantrymen or hoplites armed with

a shield on their left arm and a spear in the right, arranged in a mass eight men across and four to eight men deep. One consequence of the formation is that in combat a straight march was impossible. The formation inevitably swerved to the right as each soldier leaned toward his companion's shield for protection. As I move across the memory landscape around the Big House, I swerve. It's not a straight line or an even mapping. Pieces of me, fragments of memories, are locked together in a formation like a phalanx. I keep leaning against the swerve to feel the sharp pain of loss.

61. When Tyree was a kid I told him the story about the Big Lake. From his room on the second floor he could see it through the pine trees on the ridge overlooking the creek a quarter mile away. When we played in the backyard we were still high enough to see the lip of the lake's shore. But my memory may be playing tricks on me. In the story the surface of the lake turns to glass when Tyree's feet touch the surface. He walks toward the center. A witch approaches from the trees in the spillway. The icelike glass turns back to water under her feet. Thousands of green frogs come from nowhere and emerge from the mud and swarm the witch. In an instant she is eaten and the frogs vanish back into the water. The water is murky with mud stirred up from the bottom. At the center the water is clear and impossibly deep. The lake in actuality is no more than fifteen feet at best. At the bottom Tyree sees a castle. Tyree reaches down, finds a doorknob in the water that opens the door to the castle. This is the kind of thing Patrik looked for in rotting flesh and fat. Tyree pauses. Then he opens the door and walks into the castle. The castle is fitted to him. There are his lost toys. His dog that was shot is running in the hallway. He can see his own bedroom in the Big House in a mirror. It was a favorite for Tyree. It was put together from various pieces, a Russian folk tale, my own childhood memories, and Jesus and Peter on the water. Freud chooses an architectural metaphor for the way memories cover the past. He calls them screen memories, borrowed from the elaborate dressing screens that were part of middle-class households in the late nineteenth century, pointing as well to the new cinema screens of the twentieth.

62.

Beauty Is the Beast

These two shows have afforded their audience the rare opportunity to see two sides of a coin at the same time, and it turns out to be a trick coin—both sides are the same. This should come as a relief to those worried about the state of art: all is well. The machine is still cranking out artists like the $20 bills they emulate. In such a process, technique is replicable, not content. It's no surprise, then, that the two shows showcase technical virtuosity rather than the content of involvement. Though several pieces are the exception—Walter Dunderville's "Dust in your eyes are crocus, geraniums and ash," Jill Schultz's

"Christmas lights," Karen Adams's "Lone mountain night II," Anita Butler's "Moon road," and Deborah Cinnater's "Wanton withdrawal"—only Patrik Keim's work as a whole stands out. Thematically, his work is more ambitious. It stresses the personal involvement with structure inside and outside himself. His work is in contrast to a narcissistic self-absorption: we are in the absence of themes larger than the artists themselves, the artists consume themselves in exquisite pastels for the new bourgeois cathedral, the gallery. Like ghosts, these artists haunt us with images rather than revolutionize us with the real. The problem lies in the definition of art being promulgated. It's not so facile as what pleases the eye; rather, it goes deeper so as to flavor the mind itself with its own deliciousness. Within this look is a political-cultural hegemony constructed out of the individual's fragmented existence. By acquiescing to its power, we concrete in the status quo in exchange for a sweet flavor without substance. Despite the flaws in Keim's work (a certain disdain for technique and a tendency toward self-indulgence), it does not acquiesce; it is a grappling with structure that holds out the possibility of a revolutionary transformation of the artist himself as well as his audience. His work teaches the subversive look and the artificiality of the present as he artfully deconstructs society's artifacts like the mind, the school, utopia, or order, a state of moving. It's difficult to remember this when confronted with the beautiful images the artists present us. But they are images manufactured out of our alienation, a fact that must be remembered. (Shelton, "Beauty")

63. After the publication of *Dreamworlds of Alabama* I tried two times to give a talk at the local university from which I had graduated. It's free, I told them. There's no need for money. I just want to come home. Two times I was told there was no interest. Each time I knew whose voice it was. These were men I had known from a long time ago. One had written a strong review of the book and used it to get a merit raise. He described me as "a brave man." For over a year I was listed as a notable citizen of the town on *Wikipedia*. My name had a hyperlink that, clicked on, took the reader to another man's biography. His name was also Allen Shelton. He was a North Carolina banjo player and he was dead. Now my name has been erased, edited out. This report will make it worse. Patrik's choice to return here will be seen as a curse and not a blessing. It'll be my fault. The Hunter Gracchus deliberately avoided showing up anywhere near his home or in Kafka's neighborhood. The Scriptures are closemouthed about Lazarus's homecoming. It's probable he was seen as a blasphemy in his hometown and was compelled to travel. His transformation wasn't a good miracle. Maybe it was seen as an oblique prophecy of the fall of Jerusalem and its return as a spiritual city outside of any empire, Jewish or not. Patrik's return to rural Alabama is a dangerous prophecy as well. For many he would be a creature that slipped out of hell, the first sign of an invasion different from the grass carp, the kudzu, the coyotes,

the armadillos, and meth. Patrik was queer. Patrik shouldn't have been chosen. He was promiscuous. He was a disgusting artist. He despised his father. But God chose him to break the surface in his coffin and no one else. That I would be the chronicler of this event makes me just as guilty. The professors at the college knew this, as did the editor on *Wikipedia*. For that reason no one waits for me in Alabama. I'm a real orphan. Mom and Dad are dead. I've been gone too long. Thanksgivings come and go. The last Thanksgiving I spent in Alabama was the first after the death of my mother. On Thanksgiving Day there was nowhere for me to go. I was left alone at my brother's house. Tyree went off with his mother for fried turkey. My brothers went to their in-laws'. I watched TV on a leather couch. That night I went alone to my father's house for dinner. It was me, him, and his new girlfriend. There were pecans in the mixed green salad. I watched the two of them get tipsy. My father was more genial than normal. There were only a few comments about my long hair and why I was wasting my life. My ex-girlfriend was serving her new boyfriend dinner across the country. I had helped with the recipes earlier that day.

64. Ulysses S. Grant's autobiography is a prodigious act of memory. The six-hundred-page manuscript was written in a year. He was dying of cancer. In the last part of the writing he was taking cocaine for the pain. He was under tremendous financial pressure. His childhood is virtually nonexistent in the book. The one momentous event is when he bought a horse. He participated in the Mexican-American War, which in his book acts as the introduction to the core of his life, the Civil War. He sees in the desert all the significant actors for the next stage. The manuscript is about the Civil War. He begins and ends his life with the war. His memory for the landscape, movements, and personalities is remarkable. He seems to remember everything, like Borges's character Ireneo Funes. But Grant isn't incapacitated by his recollections. He acts. The meeting with General Robert E. Lee is told in exquisite detail. Grant in his rough and dirty coat secures the surrender of the Confederate Army. His own book is a map waiting for Grant or someone like him to appear in this world again.

65. This small passage particularly concerned Staci Newmahr. She's a classic sociological ethnographer who notably doesn't like to mix what she describes as argument with fictional stories. That she had gotten this far in my account is a testimony to our relationship rather than the veracity of my report. She pointed out I still had two working hands and neither was a prosthetic. Her biggest concern was, how did I cut my hand off so quickly with a pocketknife? "It's not possible." I thought that was a legitimate concern, so I added the phrase "My hand cut like it was baloney." I didn't like the simile. It seemed foreign to Alabama even though I would watch old men slice big hunks of it like it was butter at the Rabbittown general store. It was kept next to the hard cheese. I tried Spam, a composite I grew up with. That had the advantage of actually suggesting the different ele-

ments that were pressed together into a single story. Why Spam? she asked. The answer didn't make Staci feel any better since it pointed back to fiction. She may have actually become more concerned with the account. I told her the passage was kind of like a dream sequence. That reassured her. All of it was baloney. I used fat.

66. This account is based on two different recollections. An ancient Christian definition of evil is nothingness. This nothingness is not synonymous with the void in Genesis out of which God created the universe. It is deeper. This made no sense to me until I read a Russian fairy tale. A man is running from a witch in the woods. She's going to eat him. He sees an ax stuck in a tree trunk. He grabs it. The ax won't move and his hand is stuck to the handle. Quickly he makes a decision. He cuts his hand off with his knife. Thereafter, when asked to define evil, he would point to the quivering emptiness just past his stump: "That is evil," he would say. This is the first account. In the second, I was walking to the same waterfall. On my left on the trail was a creek and the north side of a hill covered in mountain laurel, a small tree that grows only in shade. The brush was thick, but I could hear something in the water. Then as I stopped, I heard it get out of the water. I peered through the brush. I made out a large shape. I called out. There was no response. I pulled out my knife and yelled, "Hello." There was movement and something on two legs ran up the slope under the cover of the mountain laurel. It was dark colored. It wasn't a deer. Maybe it was a black bear. I was shaking. I wasn't alone in the woods after all.

67.

Lost in a Boreal Forest

I saw a thin man carrying a suitcase throughout the forest, walking with a strange gait. He was constantly muttering parts of an eerie sonnet to himself. I decided to try also, me mimicking both his words and his step. After our paths cross[ed], the thin man turned and spit at my feet, prompting me to stop.

I returned to the forest again, this time with my own suitcase, but my new acquaintance was no longer there. (I suppose that he is now the topic of some obscure Institute symposium.) I missed seeing him—no one turned and spit at my feet, no one prompted me to stop.

I am still wandering amongst the simple chaos of that forest, with my suitcase in hand. I'm beginning to ask myself: how will I know to stop my muttering, and when will I stop this curd-stepping? I am now a thin man, tripping a dotted-line path with a strange gait. I am now a madman, talking to a suitcase about death. (Keim, "Lost")

68. "In the fields with which we are concerned, knowledge comes only in lightning flashes. The text is the long roll of thunder coming after" (Benjamin, *Arcades*, 456).

69.

One of the twelve, Thomas, called the Twin, was not within when Jesus came. So the other disciples said to him: We have seen the Lord. But he said to them: Unless I see the holes from the nails, and put my finger into the holes from the nails, and put my hand into his side, I will not believe. And eight days later the disciples were in the house once again, and Thomas was with them. Jesus came, though the doors were locked, and stood in their midst and said: Peace be with you. Then he said to Thomas: Put your finger here, and examine my hands, and take your hand and put it into my side, and be not an unbeliever but a believer. Thomas answered and said to him: My Lord and my God. (John 20:24–28, Richmond Lattimore's translation)

70. Patrik treated the Bible as a thing to be attacked, which oddly connected to what I've been told many times by believers. The Bible isn't a book. It's a sword for the believer. I'm inclined to accept that now. For my grandmother Mary Pullen and her garden club and her gray-haired church friend who was my favorite Sunday school teacher, it was a love relationship even if it had the head of an ax. It was a feeling and talking ax, something like a minotaur in a different kind of labyrinth in which the beloved has the body of a man and a head of steel. Patrik's artistic strategy was to pierce the sacred and then document the resulting fluids as they dried. He was more fascinated with knives than with axes in this parody of a sex act. The sacred for Patrik was his remembrance of his childhood home, his father, and the male body. He left the Bible alone. In his mind it was already a thing. It was something different for me. I'm not an especially religious man, though some would quibble with that. I've read the Bible. I used to be quite proficient in what Southern Baptists call sword drill: I could whip to any book and verse in the Bible called out. That was years ago. I still have several Bibles. I used to preach to the Pentecostals from a black lamb-leather New Jerusalem translation. It was a Catholic Bible and many were worried. At a church retreat in Panama City, Florida, I did a teaching from a translation of the New Testament by Richmond Lattimore, the Greek scholar who translated the *Iliad* and the *Odyssey*. The cover had a close-up of a putrefying corpse's face. The eyes were open. The cheeks were purple. He was looking for Jesus. The rawness of the translation caused confusion. As I read the familiar passage of Jesus walking on the sea's surface, stripped of the King James English, hands went into the air grabbing for Jesus as if they, like Peter, were sinking. Several began speaking in tongues. There was a liquidness to the sound that slowly covered their mouths as if they were now underwater.

71. There had been a property dispute on the eastern side of Crooked Mountain between two men. Each was short and crazy. One had lain in wait in the trees along the road for the other to drive by. He had a shotgun. The second man came down the road in his Ford truck. The first slipped out of the woods, leveled the

shotgun, and fired. The windshield was blasted out but the driver was unharmed. The driver aimed the Ford at the shooter standing on the side of the road and floored it. The shooter's shotgun pointed impotently at the driver as he went over the cab of the truck. Years later the driver was murdered. His body was found floating in the lake at the highest elevation in Alabama. In death he had the grace and buoyancy he had lacked as a man in life.

72. At different junctions in *Capital* there are hints at the existence of a world behind the world, not a spiritual world but the further reaches of the capitalist system. For all the mathematical formulas and physical inventories Marx invokes, there is a dark fairy-tale quality to capital. Marx approached the early stages of his massive work as if he were a physicist. He imagines the capitalist world that was unfolding before his eyes in the middle of the nineteenth century as composed of innumerable interlocked molecular units. His genius was to discover that the basic unit is the commodity. It's a simple but brilliant move. Aristotle came very close in the ancient world, but he was unable to take the final steps. Marx points out that Aristotle's imagination couldn't escape from the gravity of the slave economy that dominated Athens. Marx was unfettered by this particular handicap. As a boy, it is reported he made his sisters make mud pies for him. As an adult, the death of his mother and the redistribution of the family's estate didn't add an iota to his height or bank account. He was left out of the will. Marx begins with the most basic and concrete piece of the already immense capitalist world. He grabs hold of the commodity. A coat, a bar of gold, iron, a bushel of wheat, or lace collars are part of an interlocked but fluid surface of circulating commodities. In the opening pages of *Capital*, Marx introduces the formula "20 yards of linen = 1 coat." The formula seems simple but the coat and the linen inside it are as complex and mysterious as mythical cities. The formula initiates Marx's critical division of the commodity into use and exchange values. He then finds the absorption of humanness in the commodity. Each commodity holds a reservoir of humanness, which Marx described as commodity fetishization. The human becomes objectlike and the commodity becomes humanlike. By the end of the same chapter this molecular world has turned darkly mystical. Marx has become a theologian or an analytical necromancer as he recognizes the more sinister side of his molecular unit, the commodity. The transition is spaced across a long chapter, which hides just how uncanny the original formula occurring in the first pages really is. By the time he introduces the concept of commodity fetishization in the final section, the formula is played out, having appeared over twenty-three times as a marker on a labyrinth wall. There is a spinning, vertiginous quality to Marx's descent into the seemingly simple commodity that threatens to overwhelm him. Hence the marks of the commodity on the labyrinth wall of the commodity. The formula is a reassurance and a reorientation. The text grows more and more surreal as iron is introduced, then bushels of wheat, and glittering gold. All these

commodities are balanced on the coat in the formula (which may be the same coat Marx pawned to pay his household bills). The historian Edmund Wilson reports this singular occurrence and then flatly states that without his coat, Marx stayed at home (*To the Finland Station*, 216). In Marx's account, commodities are dormant like sleeping vampires until they rise up like the dancing table in the final section of "The Commodity" to stalk family members like some kind of predatory insect. The movement of the table spells out a critical story. Even the most solid aspects of everyday life slide into an unseen place. The dining-room table in Marx's London flat was weighed down with stuff. Wilson reports this as well.

73. A police agent's report on the Marx household while they were living in Soho in 1853 states:

> [Marx] lives in one of the worst, therefore one of the cheapest neighborhoods in London. He occupies two rooms. The room looking out on the street is the parlor, and the bedroom is at the back. There's not one clean or decent piece of furniture in either room, but everything is broken, tattered and torn, with thick dust over everything and the greatest untidiness everywhere. In the middle of the parlor there is a large old-fashioned table covered with oil cloth. On that there are manuscripts, books and newspapers, as well as the children's toys, odds and ends from his wife's sewing basket, cups with broken rims, dirty spoons, knives and forks, lamps, an ink pot, tumblers, some Dutch clay pipes, tobacco ashes—all in a pile on the same table. (quoted in Wilson, *To the Finland Station*, 215)

The weight of objects was a caution to check the table's predatory desires and to cloud its wooden brain. Marx makes it clear that commodities live on humanness, not spirits. In *Capital*, the coat's vampiric effect on an individual isn't described. Marx saves the demons for the domestic interiors dominated by the grotesque wooden table. The coat stays asleep inside Marx's incantational formulas. Marx himself may have been afraid to be wrapped up inside a haunted overcoat, too much like his own coffin, or he may have recognized that the family scene is where the demonic fully blooms. The Russian writer Gogol was one of the first to recognize this. His short story "The Overcoat," written in St. Petersburg in the 1840s, has an improvised dead bureaucrat haunting the city to recover his lost coat, whose theft detonated his death. This netherworld isn't supernatural but a supermaterial shadow existing just past the normal range, the far extension of a system that acts like a superorganism. The police agent continues his report on the world inside Marx's apartment:

> When you go into Marx's room, smoke and tobacco fumes make your eyes water to such an extent that for the first moment you seem to be groping about in a cavern, until you get used to it and manage to pick up certain objects in the haze. Everything is dirty and covered with dust, and sitting down is quite

a dangerous business. Here is a chair with only three legs, then another, which happens to be whole, on which the children are playing at cooking. That is the one that is offered to the visitor, but the children's cooking is not removed, and if you sit down, you risk a pair of trousers. But all these things do not in the least embarrass Marx or his wife. You are received in the most friendly way and cordially offered pipes, tobacco and whatever else there may happen to be. Eventually a clever and interesting conversation arises which makes amends for all the domestic deficiencies, so that you find the discomfort bearable. You actually get used to the company, and find it interesting and original. (quoted in Wilson, *To the Finland Station*, 215–16)

74. It was also the creek that filled A.C.'s lake system, which at its peak numbered two small lakes, the Big Lake, and one lake with a hole in its bottom that held water through the winter and spring rains before emptying into the underground.

75. It could be because of the weight of Proust's influence on Benjamin's thin volume that Benjamin avoids anything remotely similar to Marcel's madeleine. It is a telling omission. It cuts away the sensuous sides of the commodity. Marx structures the length of *Capital* around three notable moments involving food. Early on is the table in "The Fetishism of the Commodity and Its Secret" that begins to evolve its grotesque ideas and dance. Marx's stalking table emerges out of the coequality of commodities that opens the book (twenty yards of linen = one coat; a half-ton of iron = two ounces of gold) and forms a virtual metropolis of objects confronting one another in a surrealist moment. Marx saw reservoirs of humanness sunk like lakes deep inside the commodity, but until the table, he chose not to emphasize the specific weight of humanness and memories. Instead it's an abstract city where commodities encounter each other in the same fashion as Simmel conceived interaction in Berlin in 1903: it's a gray exchange dominated by calculation. The table threatens to explode in a Proustian moment if only Marx sets a family down to supper. Deeper in *Capital*, Marx analyzes a loaf of bread, its degraded ingredients, the grueling hours of its construction, and the extreme temperatures associated with its baking. For all his attention to detail, no concrete description of a city emerges in *Capital*. The factory cities are folded into the soft bread dough. The bread stands in for Manchester. In another move, Marx provides an x-ray of dinner at the level of carbon and nitrogen consumption. One step further and dinner is indistinguishable from the diner, another ratio of nitrogen and carbon in a surrealist city.

76. Leiris, quoted in Bataille, *College*, 30–31. Compare this to an almost identical passage earlier in the essay where the sacred is linked with the formation of masculinity:

Thinking back on my childhood, I remember first a few idols, temples and, in a more general way, sacred places. First were several objects belonging to my father, symbols of his power and authority. His top hat with a flat brim that he hung on the coat rack at night when he came home from the office. His revolver, a Smith & Wesson with its small barrel, dangerous like all firearms and even more attractive for being nickel plated. This instrument he usually kept in the desk drawer or in his bedside table, and it was the attribute par excellence of the one who, among other jobs, had the responsibility of defending the home and protecting it from burglars. His money box where we put gold pieces, a sort of miniature safe that was for a long time the exclusive property of the provider, and that, until we each received one like it was a communion present, seemed to my brothers and me the mark of manhood. (25)

77. What Leiris would have made of this new geography is contained in his autobiographical excavation titled *Manhood*. Hardly a conventional gentleman or even nominally masculine, Leiris is fierce in his exploration of this thing he calls manhood. Manhood is a shell, a complete mask encasing the body. This is reminiscent of Patrik's shelling of himself and work. It is a part of the sacred world of violence and sacrifice. Leiris's outline of what was sacred to him in the College of Sociology address traced the shape of his father as a network of simulated photographs of objects associated with him. How else could he have done it? The memoir itself is tight, almost claustrophobic, in his account of details that make up the new geography. It is a mirage of smallness. The tight spaces, like a Communion wafer, open up into worlds the size of the oceans. The coffin craft would have to be abandoned. Patrik's body would have to be greased with rancid fat, like his hero Joseph Beuys, to squeeze through the portals. Or he could be rendered and poured over the landscape, inadvertently outlining the underworld's Achilles' heel in what was left uncovered.

78. Michel Leiris opens his autobiographical account *Manhood* with this frank assessment of himself:

My head is rather large for my body; my legs are a little short for the length of my torso, my shoulders too narrow in relation to my hips. I walk with the upper part of my body bent forward; I have a tendency, when sitting, to hunch my back; my chest is not very broad and I'm not at all muscular. I like to dress with the greatest possible elegance; it is due to the defects I've just described in my physique and to my financial means, which, without my being able to call them poor, are rather limited, I usually consider myself profoundly inelegant; I loathe unexpectedly catching sight of myself in a mirror, for unless I have prepared myself for the confrontation, I seem humiliatingly to myself each time. (Leiris, *Manhood*, 3–4)

One thing that is noticeable in Leiris's opening is how beautifully it is fashioned and the care he lavishes in describing his grotesqueries. It is a beautiful portrait filled with particularities. His assessment goes on for several paragraphs just like this. However stunted and gnomelike he was physically, however perverse he was, the craftsmanship through which he re-creates himself in script is wondrous. Patrik shared none of these physical deformities. Men and women desired him. What he lacked was Leiris's commitment to craft and beauty. He wasn't concerned with delicate touches. He preferred hammer blows.

Curriculum vitae

I am living in a state of precise ambiguity: walking a fine tightrope (a level of an enlightening, inquisitive, and educational existence).

My childhood allowed no sense of base or roots; our family was transplanted eight times coast-to-coast with my dictatorial father as he climbed the over-achieving executive's ladder of success to the ultimate climax of the coronary death two years ago. However, a strong sense of self-worth and independence was implanted to compensate for the constant environmental uprooting. In addition, self-taught actualization and resourcefulness was created to deal with the space of constant confusion, where many questions remained unanswered and unanswerable: precisely ambiguous.

The corporate transfers also afforded me the opportunity to travel and experience much of the United States: living in Tennessee, Texas, Louisiana, California, Iowa, New Jersey, and Georgia, and sightseeing in most of the states in between. Definitely influenced by the combination of residence, from New York City's suburban life to Cassville, Georgia, rural world dwelling, my scriptural environments draw upon that plethora of allegorical information: faces, voices, colors, seasons, physical surroundings, aromas, foods, ethnic cultures, regionality. And working summer jobs since the age of thirteen gave me the financial capacity to spend the summer in Europe several years ago. The effect of such a sojourn is immeasurable: precisely ambiguous.

Considering that the last nineteen years of my life have been involved in the institutionalized public school system, it too must be credited with influencing who Patrik Keim is today. After so many years of education, I have thus far concluded that life itself is the true application of that education; yet life, too, is that which presents the need for further education, questioning, and searching: once again, precisely ambiguous.

Louis Armstrong was once asked, "What is Jazz?" and he replied, "If you have to ask, you'll never know." So, too, I feel about art—a sensibility to see and feel and therefore "know." Life is art, art as life: a beer glass sitting on the edge of the table constantly aware of the presence of the darkness below, harboring the hardness of the cement floor: a fine tightrope. A tightrope between control and release, discovering truth and delving into confusion. A personal precise honesty that confronts universal ambiguity: in and out exiting existence.

This is how he opened his MFA thesis. He too is frank. But Patrik himself is out of the focus of the piece. It's a list of where he has lived and a description of a life that is undoubtedly his and simultaneously empty of Patrik at any stage of his life. It is autobiographical without a biography. Only the vaguest traces of him are there as a child. There is no hint of him as a teenager coming to grips with being gay. He describes himself as working summers to save for his escape to Europe. The portrait of Patrik on the opposite page as a young dandy looks over his empty life. It's a state of precise ambiguity.

79. Grandfather Marshall was Patrik's actual grandfather. This is what Patrik wrote. "One grandfather died planting grass seed (heart attack); the other, a math professor, smashed by a train while reading a geometry text on the railroad tracks." My grandfather Eli Landers was ushered into his death by bee stings. He kept a hive in the backyard. There was an accident. My grandmother used to tell me the story. She was never clear as to what happened. But he was stung by a swarm of angry bees. My other grandfather, A.C., had nearly thirty hives on the farm. He ran a small honey business on the side. The only notable accident with bees for A.C. occurred with a single bee. A.C. had large ears. The bee alit on the edge of his ear like it was a large flesh-colored flower and crawled inside. A.C. sat down and waited. The noise inside his head must've resembled an ocean, though A.C. had never seen any seas. It took several minutes, but the bee emerged covered in orange wax and flew away. A.C. died in a hospital from his own will to leave.

80. *Objet d'Art* (September 1983) was the first installation in his thesis. There is no narrative introduction or commentary. The piece just appears, followed by the other installations in a relentless but silent temporal order. I have no memory of this piece. I'm not sure I actually saw it. I have the plastic-seeming photograph Patrik took for his own documentation. The piece could stay together for a matter of days before smaller pieces would begin to desert through the door or be abducted. What was left was dumped in a landfill. The photograph is a color three-by-four taken from approximately seven paces away. There are no supplemental close-ups or descriptions. An inventory of pieces is absent. It looks like a chance assemblage in a dump. I see a hanging coat, a white plastic bucket, an orange stool, a three-legged wooden stool painted to resemble a psychedelic highway cone, some kind of platform printed in the same psychedelic stripes, a box bound in layers of electrical tape, a heavy highway cone standing solemnly. It's all placed on a floor covering like a canvas tarp in a bare room in some kind of gallery and lit like it was art. It's the earliest of Patrik's larger-scale installations. There is so much color tugging at the viewer's eyes, it's a retinal attack. It's Patrik's version of the water lilies. In his history, the Impressionists focused on the city dumps rather than the gardens. The next installation is *Mind over Matter* (February 1984). This installation seems familiar. Again there is no other documentation than a cheap three-by-four print. In this photograph it's clear it's in a gallery. You see

the framing wall and then larger windows above the wall. It's nighttime. Whether Patrik intended to project the gallery as a prison can't be ascertained. But my eye continually escapes into the night sky. It's a far more austere installation than the first one. Instead of a jumble there are space and distance. The center is dominated by what seems to be a clothesline constructed from crucifixes covered in vines. Seven rectangular boxes hang like towels, sheets, or bodies. There are six chairs scattered around facing in different directions with their legs balanced on bricks encased by wire. There are two stools likewise positioned. There is nothing remarkable about the installation on its own. With Patrik's biography it seems to sink back into tragedy. Here is a portrait of the suburban life he hated.

And yet Patrik used Clinique shave cream. He kept a tube in his medicine cabinet and talked to me at length about how wondrous it was. I used Edge Gel. He insisted I try Clinique. He watched me shave. He commented on its moisturizing effects and how much closer you could shave without irritation. Afterward he offered me Clinique aftershave lotion. A relatively poor man, he shaved luxuriously.

81. Most of Patrik's works lingered inside buildings, but in *Feast or Famine* (May 1984) Patrik moved his work outside. There are trees in leaf in the immediate background. A small lake can be seen. A larger tent is set up for crowds in the right corner. The installation is set discreetly on the grass. What it is supposed to be is completely unidentifiable. It's a blot on the landscape. Out of a pile of stuff, candy-striped poles stick up randomly at various heights from three to ten feet. There is a second photo included in Patrik's documentation. The close-up shows a thin red mattress on top of smaller poles stuck unevenly in the ground and then a jumble of plastic milk jugs painted black and white running underneath like a species of gallon-sized beetles.

82. The first photograph in *Sucking the Heads of Ab-Average Crawfish* (October 1984) is unreadable. The image is a wreck. There's some sort of structure in the foreground constructed out of a tangle of interconnected black and white poles and latticework. Two red and white spears run through it. Behind it is a wall constructed in the same way. The close-up is no help in clarifying. It's a jungle. The lighting blazes. At night, though, the piece comes alive. The same rhythmic garbage glows with the darkness around it. Now the wreckage looks like a demented version of an insect colony. Patrik has exploited the soft lighting in the gallery to create something eerily beautiful like the inside of his nervous system. A small plain table is turned into an altar piled high with orange and white sticks. It's a tangle in the hair of the fire to come. I see no crawfish.

Patrik was uncomfortable outside. He was built for the art scene. His hands were soft. His skin was white. He was sensitive to bug bites. He didn't own a pair of shoes that would allow him to venture very far past mowed lawns. Consequently he brought the wild indoors. Patrik never saw crawfish in a creek. He saw their shells in a restaurant's dumpster, the aftermath of a massacre. This work is a part of his Holocaust series, which never materialized on the surface as a definable project but continually poked like a snake trapped between fat and skin trying to come out.

83. *Translucent Lid* (February 1985) appeared nearly a year later. There are two simple photographs. In the top image a single light bulb hangs from the ceiling on an industrial-orange work cord. It's a large bulb and provides the only light in the room. Patrik didn't use flash. The walls are bare. There seem to be paper sacks stuffed with flat newspapers stacked in front of a low blocky table, with another box on top. Its surface is bathed in a white light. No other details are recognizable in this image. The second image shows the area in the bright light. It's a twisted beef tongue laid on broken glass.

84. Within a month, Patrik had completed *48 Hours of Bliss* (March 1985). Patrik documented the show with a Polaroid. It's the only incident in his thesis where he used this kind of representation. The two photos are warm. The lighting is soft. A reddish darkness fills the frame and covers any details. The top recording shows a line of folding chairs stacked against the wall. In the top center is a yellow spot of light around an extremely low-hung painting. The painting is a shape, nothing more. The second recording brings the viewer up close. The painting is still unreadable. The yellow spot of light is extinguished. A light shines on a 1960s-style two-tier coffee table on which a lamp and magazines might have been stacked. On it is a cheap turntable with a record. *Order of a State, moving* (March 1985) was installed while *48 Hours of Bliss* was still up. I saw the show. But my memory is sketchy, in part because here Patrik's work looked exactly like the deserted interiors of sharecropper houses that I had seen so many times before. What I do remember clearly is shown in close-up. It's a low table with a small lamp turned on: it's blocking a door propped up against the wall. The table surface is covered in matches stuck in wads of clay. Beneath the table on an oval throw rug are two dingy turntables with records. In a jumble by the door is a pile of large white numbers. The image is collapsing into color. It's a wreck. Crates with eggshells and an upside-down mantle are pushed against the wall. Sheets of paper are strewn across the floor. Alive in the moment, Patrik's installations were powerful, much like stumbling into a rubbish heap in a garden. They radiated rot. Their normal size was gigantic. It was so much garbage that it couldn't be dismissed as a miniature world. It was a wave slowly forming in the gallery.

85. The installation that takes up the most space in the thesis is *Asylum, Asylum: E Pluribus Unum; Body and Blood* (April 1985). Patrik was physically a part of this installation. There are four pages of photographs and a double copy of Patrik's week-long work journal from the show. The first photograph shows a roughly constructed easel and an upturned cardboard box set in the frame. In the back is a shoddily constructed wall with "have I believed in God and father" in drippy white paint. The line is repeated in four layers. The next photo shows

Patrik sitting at a wooden desk. He's writing. Behind him are a clock and time-cards. It's 10:59. In the foreground on a coffee table are three turntables with records. Presumably they're playing since the arm is down on each. He clocked in at eight every morning. Took lunch at twelve and sat at a high wooden desk. His head was shaved. He wore purple pajamas from one to five p.m., Monday through Friday. On the left side of the page is a copy of his handwritten journal. On the right appears a typed version of the same journal. In the third entry of the first day I appear. On the opposite page Patrik has struck through certain lines with a black marker, forming the black bar slashes that marked the appearance of violence and the sacred in his work. Here they are partially disguised as random censorship. I appear on the typed page like this: "Allen Shelton sits on the chair next to me stuffing biscuit in his mouth . . . " On the handwritten page the full quote reads: "Allen Shelton sits on the chair next to me stuffing biscuit in his mouth . . . he's now inside my gut wrenches with the animal of *Herzog* . . . Shelton taps on the guard desk and gives a great nod—such a man of expression."

A poetic rant wraps around the mazelike structure. The writing drips. The lines are caught in a current. Nothing is straight. His writing is an EKG. The last images are in the interior. Two white mattresses are stacked on top of each other in a crushed missionary position. Each is crusted with gobs of white paint. Splatters surround the bed. Above the bed, where a mirror might be, is a thicket of interwoven sticks—pubic and a holocaust at the same time. A single light bulb is dangled on an extension cord from the ceiling. There are a bloody pillow and a meat cleaver buried in the mattress.

86. The show was exhausting for Patrik. He was fixed in space. His ass sweated. One of the rules he set was no communication during work hours. This took a toll. Patrik writes, "People tend to accept my performance." And then, "She doesn't get anything out of it without talking to me—it's my fault?" There's another photo of Patrik manning the piece. He is staring straight ahead. He's wearing matching slippers. He's painted a Doric column on brown paper stuck on the wall. The column is holding up a line of strung-together timecards in a variation of his familiar slash mark. "Allen's seriousness makes me heed Linda's arrival . . ."

And then at night the strain was clearly visible. "Linda's grandfather has died and this is 'his requiem.' Life has a tendency to be a bit morose, but if not, then the living is casual. That edge can become an enclosed treadmill with no fear of falling off, grinding away the hours, days, years, without the edge. That darkness and my admittance of its presence obviously has people concerned—Nikki's call, Allen's expression over beer last night, mom's voice on the phone, Mario's inquiry, and why not!" And then this line appears near the end—"perhaps we should wash each other's feet." The last entry is dated "19 April 1985 Friday conclusion": "as last images of hysteria on the streets, silence bellowing the call of annihilation, and 30 minutes are all that we have left. I will die with my cleaver and my hair. Checkout time 29 minutes and counting. Goodbye: Asylum, Asylum."

87. This installation marked the completion of a flurry of activity that saw five installations in four months. Whether Patrik felt academic pressure to compete his MFA or another kind, I can't determine. But I was at this show. The last documented installation in Patrik's thesis is *3 Selections (Wise Blood by Flannery O'Connor)* (June 1985). His major professor's signature is there. It's dated "5/30/85," which is at least a few days before Patrik's defense date. Likely it was up during his defense, a space left in the actual thesis for the final evidence to be glued in. The slashes that often characterized his work are now rendered in blocks of black turned on edge and faced with a double, creating the effect of speed and direction as if a jet, a moth, or a hawk had been mounted. The arrow moves from the right to the center to the left, four feet off the ground. "Paul" is scratched above the arrow on the right. In the center, a huge triangle is suspended. It is so shoddily assembled it looks like it might collapse. In both corners and the center are three wooden triangles stacked with bricks under their legs. They resemble poorly constructed crosses. Any crucifixion would be a horrible comedy. The bottom photograph brings the viewer closer to the triangle. It seems to be flat boards covered in small rectangular images. Some kind of convulsive, ugly rose blooms on the bottom leg of the triangle. Across the front is a clothes rack filled with white wire hangers and what look like clear plastic strips hung from the wire. In the foreground are three buckets overflowing with white powder. A white wooden bench has a yellow note nailed with a spike to its seat. Just in front is a short white stool for a workman. This stool had survived *Mind Over Matter*.

88. *Prerequisite of Oleo* (May 1984) has haunted me ever since I first saw it. Patrik took only four photographs of it. In the first photo an easy chair is seen from the right side. The chair is covered in a dark fabric on which Patrik has painted the top and the center around the arms in white paint that has dribbled down. The effect makes the chair resemble a big cupcake with white frosting. The chair is positioned on what appear to be sheets of corrugated cardboard. On the wall, approximately five paces away, hangs a larger canvas covered with four low lines and a slash running from the top center right to the bottom center left. In the foreground is a red grave mounded up with stumps protruding from it. The second photograph looks over the back of the chair downward toward another grave with white sticks like paralyzed antennas extended into the air. Behind it on the wall is a pole painted white and black draped with white and black streamers hung evenly in a line. On either side is a trio of smaller portraits bound together with stiff or swollen American flags glued to the bottoms like beef tongues. I have these portraits. The third photograph is the view from the left over the chair. Again there is a grave. This time the soil is black. Upside-down stools are protruding through it. The legs stick up. Behind it is another canvas with the same slash

marks as on the right. This time they are orange. The last shot has the cupcake
chair straight on. It stares out aggressively. It's bound in thick rubber inner tubes.
What I remember is slightly different. Patrik laid giant slabs of butter in the seat
of a dingy overstuffed chair. The blocks slowly dissolved into butt-shaped blobs.
The back of a chair was strapped with rubber inner tubes, which seemed to hold
the chair together now without an actual backbone anchored in the fat. Outside
of the antiseptic environment of the museum the chair would have attracted ants,
flies, and burrowing mice. What would have been a metropolis was still. Inside
the controlled temperature of the museum, the butter barely softened, only hinting at the asses that were supposed to materialize. The appearance Patrik hoped
for never arrived. If he had hoped for the ass imprints of angels, he got nothing. The problem with the installation was its controlled frame. In my Alabama
home I had a small piece by a black folk artist that was painted and rubbed with
clay and sugar. This added ants to its landscape, and it had to be locked up in a
glass box.

     89. This compulsion to get inside is a dominant theme throughout Patrik's
work. After his death, the same compulsion was reversed. Now he was threatening to get back across the castle's threshold. The inside in his work appears in
many different forms. It appears in *Utopia: Termite Season* as an invitation to burrow through his conscious and unconscious while the artist, dressed like a white
paper virgin, languishes outside the piece. In *Prerequisite of Oleo* and *Sucking the
Heads of Ab-Average Crawfish*, it appears in the form of verbal clues and in the
sampled poetry of the high school suicide he affixed to a desk. The compulsion
emerges in *Translucent Lid*, in the hunk of beef tongue soaked in Pentecostal imagery. Patrik waits for tongues of fire to burst out of the decaying meat. Here the
castle asserts itself in the raw imagery of the decaying tongue and the overwhelming silence, explicitly emphasizing the unequal relations between the two. Patrik
divulges all, the castle nothing: even in what seem to be apparent responses, it is
the artist's voice, and not the castle's, that is detected. It is a kind of pathetic ven-
triloquism. The artist himself steps into the silence and mimes what he consid-
ers to be the castle's part. While this does not bring the inhabitants of the castle
into clearer focus, it does reveal the nature of its domination. It represents the
hegemony of a history that he did not make of his own choosing. Housed behind
its smooth cerebellumlike walls are the very luxury of his oppression and the
object of his work. This oppressive luxury is expressed in a simple form within
the body of Keim's work. The castle replaces the audience as the object of the
work. In *Oleo*, it is expressed in the dead turning blue in the grave. In *Translucent
Lid* and *Asylum*, it is that Bible-black God, while in *Order of a State*, the past
is laid open like a cadaver to get inside the castle. The mind itself becomes the
object, as well as the scene, of the art in *Utopia* and *Oleo*. All these function in
the role of the castle, as distant and desirous as Duchamp's sister's remembrance

of the black boots floating in the corner by the bed. A consequence of this is that the audience's relationship with the artist is reduced to that of an accomplice to get the artist inside the castle. The audience is simply another found object. It is not the object of Patrik's designs or veneration. Communication with the viewing audience is more akin to a rehearsal of memories, with the artist in the role of the doctor, fitting the viewers into the nexus of the treatment and his own life history, by amputation or grafting or any means possible, rather than by what is conventionally considered communication. The viewer is mere material, an object or a memory to be manipulated and disposed of once the piece is complete. And as with K., what wouldn't be given up to get inside the castle?

There was so much silence around Patrik's work and so much noise around him. His works made me want to talk and write. That might be most easily attributed to my own anxieties rather than others' inabilities to grasp what Patrik was up to. I started going to his shows equipped with a pencil and a notebook. I made specific measurements, pacing off the spatial dimensions of his works. This was my introduction to allegories of space outside my own world. His work shared certain qualities with Benjamin's *Arcades*. It too was suffocating, unreadable, and nonhuman. Benjamin was, I think, attempting to build an automaton on paper with the *Arcades*. The human bits left behind were superfluous. Patrik's art was a different kind of thinking machine. It was a cerebral dumpsite. There were a few complete sentences generated. It seemed more attuned to producing incoherent groans and the low moans that could have been the noise underneath his own suicide. Why I could hear these sounds was never discussed. Patrik liked me. He never corrected my translation of his works. Others saw him as a genius. I didn't share that view. I saw Patrick as a material ventriloquist, skillfully displacing his own horror into found objects and at other times skillfully letting loose the horror trapped inside his collected pieces.

90. In his MFA thesis there are three images of Patrik apart from those of him to be found in one of his last great installations, *Asylum, Asylum*. The first is the most peculiar. He looks like a fraternity pledge on a scavenger hunt. It shows Patrik bent over, collecting something from the ground and stuffing it inside a pack or bag. He's in a train yard. The train runs along the back edge of the photograph. He has on athletic socks and running shoes, shorts, and a tucked-in baggy white T-shirt. It's a photocopy of the original image and darkens his frizzy hair, his shorts, and the ground. The second occupies the entire page. He's dapper. The last shows him with a shaved head and eyebrows, gleaming in a dark tweed jacket and a V-neck T-shirt. It's another photocopy, but this time the effect is to make his torso seem like a block of marble or a shell out of which one hand and his head protrude. In sequence the photos show a transformation not just in style but in the terrain or object of his art, moving from the debris generated by outside things to the debris that is him. His head is never erect. In the first it is

bent so that his face is obscured. In the second and third the head is tilted, cocked sideways in a kind of luxuriant defiance. His image begins and closes the thesis, appearing just beyond and prior to his writing. What would Patrik give up to get inside? He would give everything, including himself. The theme of communication is subservient to another motif—a crime that has been committed in the past. Whether it is Patrik's or K.'s makes no difference since the very objects used in his works cry out for blood. Always and everywhere it is reenacted in different scenarios with the same ending—mute guilt, as in the artist's participation in *Asylum*. The crime is expressed in two principal ways. The first is the repetition of violence throughout his work, particularly in *Oleo*, in the form of the total deconstruction of death, relationships, and the artist himself, and in the three body bags in *Utopia*, the animal fleece in *Order of a State*, the suicide desires in *Utopia* and in *Crawfish*. Those images are not the exception. They are the rule with Patrik's work. *Objet d'Art* betrays a violence toward the whole institution of art. Even the seemingly calmer piece *Mind Over Matter* hints at a conceptual undertow washing away matter itself. Violence is integral in Patrik's work. It speaks of a crime built into K.'s castle stone by stone.

There is a violence in his attitude toward the work itself. After the show it is destroyed, broken back into the rubbish that it was, stripped of its imagery to maintain the superiority of experience over the object. The viewer is left with only his experience. There is no body, only the photograph and the title by which the experience is gauged. This is calculated to extend the guilt of the crime via participation, as the body of the piece exists only as a medium or technology to extend it and disappears completely once the show comes down. Without the body, there is no evidence of the crime. How can the artist be held accountable for the viewer's experience, especially if the artist cannot be held accountable for his own? What hard evidence there is finds itself submerged beneath deliberate ambiguity and philosophical formulations. The titles, and the phrase "precisely ambiguous" itself, are the responses of a prisoner in the dock. They are forced confessions that refuse to implicate. Implicit within them is a smugness that no definite conclusion can be drawn or foundation established since they move— slash, back and forth from dream to waking, from ambiguity to precision, from lies to stripping truths. Another way this can be seen is in the nonspecificity of the titles. There is no straight line drawn from the title to the piece. If one could draw this line, it would more likely resemble the maze that Minos had built, complete with his stepson the Minotaur, rather than the solid relationship between signifier and signified with its instant recognition that this is that and that is this. With the body of the piece broken into pieces and dumped, the title and its connection to the viewer's experience are what persist. What remain are the words and images and vague feelings moving toward articulation. Patrik, like Magritte, asserts the primacy of poetry over visual art. He is a textual poet crossing the gulf between the word and the object. In this sense, the object used functions again only as the medium through which the words are transmitted. To review his work solely at the level of the visual is to reject the weight of his work that exists in the names of things and images beneath the surfaces.

Patrik's work is in direct opposition to Francis Bacon's. Bacon used color to burst the canvas with explosions of the sacred. Patrik's work moved toward black and white, the color of extinguished suburbs and the color of the nostalgia that gripped his father in old photographs. No one remembers me. Even Linda, who wrote the other introductory essay for his MFA thesis, has no recollection of me. How fitting that I would become his historian and barely record any other individual in my record.

91. The dead boy in the Polaroid looks back to the lynching and the racial violence that colored the "Protestant" landscapes at the turn of the twentieth century. This is the same world Weber drew on to make his arguments, but it's a landscape Weber saw through a glass darkly. African Americans don't appear in his essay either as slaves or as free persons. Nor does the labor violence that pock-marked the capitalist economies appear. It's a curious omission. In a theoretical and historical review of the rise and triumph of the spirit of capitalism, Weber avoids any sustained ethnographic accounts of labor, the violence underpinning what Marx called the primitive accumulation of capital, or any of the dark and ugly things associated with the rise of capitalism. Smoke doesn't mar the sky in Weber's account. At the slaughterhouse in Chicago, Weber marvels at the orga-nization. He has paid a boy fifty cents for a tour. He saw the streams of blood. He undoubtedly soiled his shoes and pants. The stench must've been suffocating. But Weber sees something beautiful in the slaughter yard. This episode appears in the margins of his essay, relegated with many other similar passages to the endnotes or outside the text completely.

92. Just before the initial German publication of "The Protestant Ethic," Weber with his wife Mariana came to the United States to present a paper in St. Louis, Missouri. They used the opportunity to visit what for Weber were the key outposts in the Protestant ethic. They saw New York, Buffalo, Cleveland, and Chicago. Turning south out of St. Louis, they visited Tuskegee, Alabama, then Atlanta, and then went north to North Carolina, where Weber had relatives. This is where he observed the full-immersion baptism. Finally they came to Philadel-phia. The Webers visited with W. E. B. Du Bois. The trip solidified his argument in "The Protestant Ethic." Episodic pieces also appear in Marianne's account of the trip, like this one from a working-class district near Buffalo where there was a concentration of German immigrants:

> The very appearance of the little town is an unparalleled contrast to the
> skyscrapers of New York. Nothing but little wooden houses of one or two
> stories along the sidewalk consisting of diagonally placed boards—each with

a veranda, flowers, and a little garden, trees by the road, infinitely friendly
and modest on the outside, tiny on the inside. The houses, like a coat, are
cut to order in large sawmills and factories, then transported here and put
up. Depending on the size all of them naturally have the same distribution
of space and cost $1,000–$3,000 each. The rooms are very small. Six persons
plus tables and chairs filled the largest to the bursting point, and one can
touch the ceilings with one's hand, but the cheerful decor with the beautiful
American hardwood paneling and door frames as well as the single colored
wallpaper makes the rooms very pleasant. The kitchen is always next to the
dining room; the toilet, the wash stand (one for everybody), and the bathtub
are squeezed together in one room. The windows are tiny. The parsonage, not
substantially larger than the other houses, was next to a small wooden church,
which was very cheerfully and cozily furnished (with a kitchen and a "dining
room") (for the frequent congregational festivities). (Marianne Weber, *Max
Weber*, 285)

There was an affective dimension to the Protestant landscape. Weber
chronicled his optimism in the early twentieth century. Patrik worked over its
grotesque nature. The contemporary anthropologist Kathleen Stewart has put together an impressionistic history of the Protestant landscape's current emotional
range in her work *Ordinary Affect*. Here is the world Weber could have called
the Protestant landscape. It appears for an instant before disappearing back into
his text. The new Protestant landscape and the modern world haunt this text.
Weber's world was the same one Patrik's father occupied: the small businessman,
the traveling salesman, the professional. Weber gives tiny, selective views back;
Patrik's attention was riveted on this landscape. He just couldn't see any of the
pretty, decent things here. Weber's own vision was innocent with devastating
consequences. He was an ardent and vocal supporter of the German battleship
expansion in the early 1900s. This was one of the key causes of World War I. The
Germans built heavily armored ships with a limited range. They were not part of
the world fleet but a fleet positioned to take control of the North Sea. With the
outbreak of the war, Weber saw the horror behind the nationalism.

93. At the end of a service at Faith Temple, a young man came up for prayer.
He was just another individual in a long prayer line that stretched across the front
of the church. I was seated in the middle of the church and could see everything
at the front. He was a college student from the local school. The church was a gigantic prefab metal building stuck in the middle of what had been the preacher's
pasture. As pastureland it was poor; as a parking lot it was packed. The congregation was drawn primarily from the working poor in the mill village. There were
very few with any college education. The young man was the beginning of a new
trend. The old Pentecostal experience was being gentrified. He wasn't from the
area, though he was Republican like the others in the congregation. He wore

pressed slacks. He took his position at the beginning of the prayer line. In front of the congregation he expressed his desire to speak in tongues. Immediately he was surrounded by eight deacons, all extending their right hands toward his head for contact, all of them gesturing toward heaven with their left arms and speaking loudly in tongues. This went on for at least two minutes before they all receded in unison as if they were part of an invisible octopus. The preacher brayed out, "Speak in faith!" The student was suddenly paralyzed. He stood very still and silent. The congregation was entirely focused on him. Suddenly he began to speak: "*Goo goo. Who goo goo.*" It was a miracle. There was a collective roar. The young man was a music or theater major. He *goo-goo*ed louder with his arms over his head. He had manifested one of the gifts of the Holy Ghost. The original Pentecost, recorded in the book of Acts, moved a bit differently. I doubt whether Patrik knew this account or ever witnessed speaking in tongues. He was drawn to the juxtaposition of the glistening glass against the cushy sounds of the New Christy Minstrels. Then again, his family would have congregated in a similar church. There were faith temples everywhere under different names like the Living Word or the Church of the Faithful, all in thin metal buildings along the highways or in abandoned theaters. Patrik's tongue was aimed back at his own family history, but it nevertheless captures the degradation of Pentecost into a bland, fatty experience that encased God's fire in a rotting tongue. The young man was not speaking in tongues. It was not a manifestation of the Holy Ghost. It was a desperation for that fire that ended in blandness and, for Patrik, a soft dick and pressed slacks. In the background of that service, an American flag hung limply on a metal staff. Outside in the parking lot there were numerous Alabama and Auburn football vanity plates. Under the parking-lot lights the plates were like colorful plastic flowers on an altar, not unlike Patrik's installation.

94.

In Athens, while Paul was awaiting them, his spirit was exasperated within him as he saw that the city was full of idols. And he would have discussions with the Jews and the worshipers in the synagogue and in the marketplace every day with anyone he happened to meet. And some of the Stoic and Epicurean philosophers encountered him, and some of them said: What might this vagabond be trying to tell us? And others said: He seems to be an announcer of foreign divinities because he brought the gospel of Jesus and the resurrection. So they took him in hand and let him up to the Areopagus, saying: Can we discover what is this new teaching of which you are telling us? You are bringing something new to our ears. So we wish to learn what this means. All the Athenians and their visitors from abroad spent their time on nothing except saying or hearing something novel.

Then Paul, standing on the middle of the Areopagus, said: Gentlemen of Athens, I perceive that you are in every way more God-fearing than others; for as I went about and observed your sanctuaries I even found an altar inscribed: To the Unknown God. (Acts 17:16–31, Richmond Lattimore's translation)

95. Next to Pearl's house was a wooded lot. My mother's Boston terrier was buried there. The grave was marked by a pile of rocks next to a young water oak. Inside there was a portrait of the dog my aunt had painted. The woods were overgrown with secondary growth and cavelike structures woven out of honeysuckle and brush. I would crawl into these hideaways and read. At school I'd been sent to the principal because I wouldn't recite the Pledge of Allegiance. I told my teacher I couldn't support a country that broke as many treaties as it did with the Indians. I was seven. I identified with Crazy Horse, Geronimo, King Philip, and Little Turtle. My father the Marine captain was informed of my act. He wasn't proud. He pointed to the wooded lot: "The Indians were like a rabbit in those woods. They didn't own the land. Don't be stupid. It was ours." At that moment I wished with all my might I was a red Indian.

"If one were only an Indian, instantly alert, and on a racing horse, leaning against the wind, kept on quivering jerkily over the quivering ground, until one shed one's spurs, for there needed no spurs, threw away the reins, for there needed no reins, and hardly saw that the land before one was smoothly shorn heath when the horse's neck and head would be already gone" (Kafka, "Wish," 390).

96. On the figure of Matt is the shadow of an actual sociological fieldworker. That shadow passed me by. He's making a recording, letting people talk. His own presence is minimal. He had no training in field methods. His degree was in psychology. When he does speak up on the tape, he often confesses an ignorance of the situation, which pulls out a more detailed elucidation. He makes occasional judgments during the course of the recording, but these are short in duration. As a figure he is hidden. There is no description given in the text. He was tall. He had dark thinning hair. He cleaned offices for a living. He was an aspiring artist and musician. We had been very close, like brothers. He produced in this recording the first mapping of A.C., the farm, and this particular dreamworld.

97. *Berlin Childhood around 1900* is constructed like a set of black-and-white descriptions organized around a vivid image or sentiment. Benjamin pioneered this method in his surrealist text *One-Way Street*. Here the effect was cakelike, as if each piece were dissolving in a pile of red ants. The writing is haunted by the image of Benjamin himself, who flits in and out of his own descriptions without ever materializing. It's a history of a childhood without a child. Instead there is what Benjamin refers to in a note on a scrap of paper as an empty "I" in a gray world:

There is something that Proust has in common with Kafka and who knows whether this can be found anywhere else. It's a matter of how they use "I." When Proust in his *Remembrance of Time Past* and Kafka in his diaries used "I" for both of them it is equally transparent, glassy. Its chambers have no local coloring; every reader can occupy it today and move out tomorrow. You can survey them and get to know them without having to be in the least attached to them. In these authors the subject adopts the protecting covering of the planet, which will turn gray in the coming catastrophes. (Benjamin, *Walter Benjamin's Archive*, 41)

98. Benjamin, "News," 85–86.

99. This essay is considered one of his finest and was profoundly influential in marking off a sociology devoted entirely to cities. For a short time it seemed likely he would be hired by the University of Chicago. In the 1920s after his death, he was the most widely cited sociologist in the United States. Robert Park at Chicago was deeply influenced by his works. Simmel wasn't hired. Who was is forgotten. His works fell into obscurity in the ensuing decades as a different kind of sociology rose to dominance in American universities. Unlike his colleague Max Weber, he didn't expand and harden the arguments in his essay into a book-length manuscript. Weber republishes his 1906 essay "The Protestant Ethic and the Spirit of Capitalism" in 1920 as a book by the same title that became so successful over time that it virtually erased the formative essay. Simmel's chances for employment in the United States might have been improved with a book-length manuscript strategically translated, as Weber's was, by the rising American star Talcott Parsons. More importantly, he could have recast himself and the essay in line with the American popular imagination. Simmel was shot in the street with a small-caliber pistol by a tenant who owed him money. He didn't stand him down but turned and ran. He was shot in the back as he fled. Unexpectedly, he provided a gloss on how hard the protective shield was. Retold, the account could have had Simmel like a cowboy or a stalwart citizen, a muckraking journalist, wresting the gun away from a cheap gangster. Instead Simmel, a Jew in Junker Germany, was shot by a desperate tenant, ur-man of the fascists to come.

100. In a recent work, *What Color Is the Sacred?*, the anthropologist Michael Taussig activates the elementary relationship between color and the marking of the sacred by quoting from Michel Leiris's 1938 lecture: "If one of the most 'sacred' aims that man can set for himself is to acquire as exact and intense an understanding of himself is possible, it seems desirable that each one, scrutinizing his memories with the greatest possible honesty, examine whether he can discover there some sign permitting him to discern the *color* for him of the very notion of sacred" (quoted in Taussig, *What Color*, 191). Taussig weaves a history of color, personal vignettes, and three writers—Walter Benjamin, Marcel Proust, and William Burroughs—who were all obsessed with the tactility of color. He moves from the explosion of color in the nineteenth century through coal tar dyes to its connection to the mystification of power in the twentieth century. Another theorist working on color is Lesley Stern. Her new work is centered on the history of her garden and its pornographic delights of colors, textures, and

tastes. I have visited her garden and marveled at the skunk wall she constructed. She did a color critique of an early draft of this manuscript. It was too dominated by Patrik, she said. No other colors take hold. I didn't know how to respond. It's about Patrik, I feebly replied. Yes, but it isn't altogether. There are too many dark reds and browns, too much blood. She was right. It needed more color even if that meant coming up close to his face on the floor after his suicide and focusing entirely on the color of his eyes.

101. "As Karl Rossmann, a poor boy of sixteen who had been packed off to America by his parents because a servant girl had seduced him and got herself a child by him, stood on the liner slowly entering the harbor of New York, a sudden burst of sunshine seemed to illuminate the Statue of Liberty, so that he saw it in a new light, although he had sighted it long before. The arm with her sword rose up as if newly stretched aloft, and around the figure blew the free winds of heaven" (Kafka, *Amerika*, 3).

102.

Before the emperor's seat stood a tree, made of bronze gilded over, whose branches were filled with birds, also made of gilded bronze, which utter different cries, each according to its varying species. The throne itself was so marvelously fashioned that at one moment it seemed a low structure, and at another it rose high into the air. It was of immense size and was guarded by lions, made either of bronze or of wood covered over with gold, who beat the ground with their tails and gave a dreadful roar with open mouths and quivering tongue. Leaning upon the shoulders of two eunuchs I was brought into the emperor's presence. At my approach the lions began to roar and the birds to cry out, each according to its kind; but I was neither terrified nor surprised, for I had previously made enquiry about these things, from people who were well acquainted with them. So after I had three times made obeisance to the emperor with my face upon the ground, I lifted my head, and behold! The man whom I just before had seen sitting on a moderately elevated seat had now changed his raiment and was sitting on the level of the ceiling. How it was done I could not imagine, unless perhaps he was lifted up by some sort of device as we use for raising timbers of a wine press. On that occasion he did not address me personally, since, even if he had wished to do so, the wide distance between us would have rendered conversation unseemly, but by the intermediary of the secretary he enquired about my master's doings and asked after my his health. I made a fitting reply and then, at a nod from the interpreter, left his presence and retired to my lodging. (Liutprand of Cremona, ambassador of Otto I, quoted in Canetti, *Crowds*, 401)

103. Kafka provides schematic diagrams of this layered landscape and its anxieties in his animal stories, particularly "The Burrow," and in the mazelike pathways of *Amerika* and *The Trial*. The mole narrator of "The Burrow" constructs a

labyrinth and is in turn pursued by a smaller network of labyrinths shadowing his own: every tunnel he imagines as an escape route is haunted by the tiny noises of mice burrowing capillary tunnels around his own. Karl's trip through the ship is repeated at several points in the novel. Early on, he is in a mansion in the suburbs of New York. It's night. The electric lights are not working. Karl wanders through the hallways against the wall. Space and time have become dreamlike but simultaneously concrete and anxiously stretched. These two worlds, the animal and human, share the same labyrinth, much as the Minotaur and Theseus did. But they meet only in Kafka's "The Metamorphosis." Here Kafka's Gregor slips from the human to the nonhuman, overlapping the human and animal mazes within the confines of a single short story. Kafka doesn't repeat the move. It was singular. For both Theseus and the Minotaur the labyrinth is a space bequeathed to them by their fathers.

Behind the walls and between the first and second floors we had cellulose blown in, which together with the cottonseed hulls, dirt-dauber nests, and an occasional snake skin added to our insulation. The advantage of cellulose was how easy it was to install in a preexisting home. A hole was drilled in the exterior siding, a hose attached, and it was blown in. It can also breathe, dispensing moisture over time. The cellulose accelerated the rot in the house as the wet clumps dried more and more slowly, turning moldy—creating a friendlier environment for termites. Powderpost beetles had at various times invaded the floor joists underneath. The interior walls bulged, swollen with cellulose.

104.

When we look at the plants and bushes clothing an entangled bank, we are tempted to attribute their proportional numbers and kinds to what we call chance. But how false a view is this! Everyone has heard that when an American forest is cut down, a very different vegetation springs up; it has been observed that the trees now growing on the ancient Indian mounds, in the Southern United States, display the same beautiful diversity and proportion of kinds as in the surrounding virgin forests. What a struggle between the several kinds of trees must have gone on during long centuries, each annually scattering its seeds by the thousand; what war between insect and insect— between insects, snails, and other animals with birds and beasts of prey—all striving to increase, and all feeding on each other or on the trees or their seeds and seedlings, or on the other plants which first clothed the ground and thus checked the growth of the trees! Throw up a handful of feathers, and all fall to the ground according to definite laws; but how simple is this problem compared to the action and reaction of the innumerable plants and animals which have determined, in the course of centuries, the proportional numbers and kinds of trees now growing on the old Indian ruins! (Darwin, *On the Origin*, 125–26)

105. "The city is, rather, a state of mind, a body of customs and traditions, and all the organized attitudes and sentiments that inhere in these customs and are transmitted with this tradition. The city is not, in other words, merely a physical mechanism and an artificial construction. It is involved in the vital processes of the people who compose it; it is a product of nature, and particularly of human nature" (Park, "City," 1).

106.

As they were thus talking, a dog that had been lying asleep raised his head and pricked up his ears. This was Argos, whom Ulysses had bred before setting out for Troy, but he had never had any work out of him. In the old days he used to be taken out by the young men when they went hunting wild goats, or deer, or hares, but now that his master was gone he was lying neglected on the heaps of mule and cow dung that lay in front of the stable doors till the men should come and draw it away to manure the great close; and he was full of fleas. As soon as he saw Ulysses standing there, he dropped his ears and wagged his tail, but he could not get close up to his master. When Ulysses saw the dog on the other side of the yard, he dashed a tear from his eyes without Eumaeus seeing it, and said:

"Eumaeus, what a noble hound that is over yonder on the manure heap: his build is splendid; is he as fine a fellow as he looks, or is he only one of those dogs that come begging about a table, and are kept merely for show?"

"This hound," answered Eumaeus, "belonged to him who has died in a far country. If he were what he was when Ulysses left for Troy, he would soon show you what he could do. There was not a wild beast in the forest that could get away from him when he was once on its tracks. But now he has fallen on evil times, for his master is dead and gone, and the women take no care of him. Servants never do their work when their master's hand is no longer over them, for Jove takes half the goodness out of a man when he makes a slave of him."

As he spoke he went inside the buildings to the cloister where the suitors were, but Argos died as soon as he had recognized his master. (Homer, *Odyssey*, 117)

107. A Berlin psychoanalyst collected her Jewish patients' dreams during the rise of the Nazis in the 1930s. There were recurring sex dreams involving Hitler from her female patients. The book is aptly called *The Third Reich of Dreams*. The work shows just how deeply soaked into the person the Nazi regime was. Benjamin's memories of his childhood in Berlin are drenched in the same fluids. He captures Berlin at the moment before it slips into the trajectory that would lead to World War I and the subsequent rise of the Nazis. Whereas Benjamin's grandmother's apartment was dense, my grandmother Pearl's house was wide

open. The house was built from the Sears and Roebuck plan with a long hallway running down the center of the house from the front door to the back. On either side was a sequence of rooms arranged in compartments. Just off the living room, behind French doors, was Eli's study. The doors were always closed. There was a piano stuck in the corner. There must've been a desk, though I can't remember it. What I do remember are the drawers I went through to get his old fountain pens that I used to play with. I thought they looked like submarines. It was a small room. The door to the side porch went out its back. This door was seldom if ever used. No one sat on this porch anymore. I treated it as a castle and climbed up from the yard. The most prominent occupant of this room was a large Expressionist portrait of my great-aunt Tallulah that my aunt Jeffy painted. The painting was haunted. My brothers were wary of it and knew something wasn't right with it. They avoided it. My old girlfriend Patsy Lou saw something emerging from the painting one night. She was terrified of Aunt Tallulah. My grandmother thought nothing of it. When I moved into the house to help take care of Pearl, the portrait was moved out of Eli's study into my bedroom. One night when Pearl was away and I was alone, I was apprehensive. I double-checked the outside doors. I kept a heightened vigilance behind the noise of the TV. I reasoned with myself that if the painting was a door to another world, it was a world in which my dead relations wandered. Why would they hurt me? Aunt Tallulah and I slowly developed a relationship. She stared unblinkingly at me as I slept in the bed that had been Pearl and Eli's. Benjamin describes a similar atmosphere in *One-Way Street* in the passage titled "Manorially Furnished Ten-Room Apartment." He has cut out the supernatural and the Proustian nostalgia. He describes relationships terribly. They are outcrops of an architectural landscape. In his account, the apartment is crowded with large heavy furniture. Sofas, dressers, and cabinets block any avenues of escape from the murderer Benjamin places in their midst. It's the Victorian interior of what Darwin called the tangled bank with new kinds of predators and prey. Benjamin refrains from describing the murderer on top of a heavily corseted woman, gutting her. He leaves the horror implicit in the maze-like description of the apartment. No dead stare out of his furniture. The passage finds its double years later in his most delicate book, the pretty and nostalgic *Berlin Childhood*. Here the murderer is even more deeply hidden in the tangled bank. Benjamin describes his grandmother's apartment in almost identical imagery, inadvertently chronicling the rise of the Nazis in material dreams involving furniture and space.

108. There were three phones in the house: this one in the kitchen, another on my grandfather's desk in the TV room, and the last one in Mary Pullen's bedroom. In *Berlin Childhood around 1900* Benjamin devotes a section to the telephone, which was still a primitive thing: "heavy as dumbbells," he writes (49). The telephone was relegated to the hallway. Houses hadn't yet accommodated

themselves to this new technology. It was still an outsider or a visitor. The ring was startling. It was something that reminded Benjamin as a child, and as a writer, of death. I remember A.C. stretched out in his green swivel chair at his desk. It was the middle of the afternoon. He was talking on the phone to Governor George Wallace. It was long distance. Wallace was calling from his hotel in Maryland, trying to convince A.C. to endorse his candidacy for president. A.C. refused. Two hours later, Wallace was shot. In 1970 A.C. had run as an independent candidate for governor. He gained approximately 8 percent of the vote, enough to piss Wallace's supporters off. As the conversation was happening, I sat in the rocking chair in front of the TV reading the newspaper. A.C. didn't consider the need for privacy. The phone was a transparent thing. While I have trouble dialing my girlfriend's number, I can still without thinking call A.C.'s phone. Benjamin doesn't say whether, after so many years away from home, he could still call that phone in the hallway.

109. In the kitchen of the Big House was a photograph I took of my grandfather A.C. several years before his decline. He's in his early eighties. The temperature is below twenty degrees. The lake he loved but never swam in is covered with sheets of ice near the shore. He has on a ridiculous helmet of a hat with giant batlike earflaps. It's even black. It's a hat made for Montana or Moscow in the winter. But it's the coat that grabs my attention. It's a great green army coat cut above the knees. It must've been longer originally. The scarlike hem still shows the scissors' touch. It's thick, so thick the green wool could still be an animal and A.C. something it's digesting slowly. But he's smiling. There's a steel bucket's handle under one arm. The other arm is attached to his walking stick, which he used to cut weeds, cross fences, and pop bulls. A.C. had no attachment to this coat. It's likely it was one of his sons' from their military careers. If it were my father's, it might've been in China. He wore it and his Elmer Fudd hat only when the temperature dipped way down. Nothing A.C. wore was designed to do what he did with it. In his pockets were baling twine, shelled corn, and dust from the ground feed. He stuffed anything he came in contact with into the pockets. A.C. never used deodorant. But what difference would it have made? Bull snot, afterbirth, formula, blood soaked him. The jacket was never cleaned. It was stored in an aluminum closet with a Marine field jacket, a giant milk bottle, formula, a honeybee suit that was an old suit jacket, black rubber jacket, and pants. There was no outside air or ventilation in this closet. The window across from it was never opened. An infrathin colony of A.C.'s pieces intensified over the years in the coffin-sized enclosure.

110. "But the hands of one man were right at K.'s throat, while the other thrust the knife into his heart and turned it there twice. With failing sight K. saw how the men drew near his face, leaning cheek-to-cheek to observe the verdict. 'Like a dog!' he said; it seemed as though the shame was to outlive him." (Kafka, *Trial*,

231). Still there is no color in Kafka's last entry. The gray city has sucked the color from the blood.

111.

Incendiary bombs and canisters of phosphorus set fire to fifteen of the Zoo buildings. The antelope house and the enclosure for the beasts of prey, the administration building in the director's villa were entirely destroyed, while the monkey house, the quarantine building, the main restaurant in the elephants' Indian temple were left in ruins or badly damaged. A third of the animals died—there were still two thousand left, although many have been evacuated. Deer and monkeys escaped; birds flew away through the broken glass roofs. "There were rumors," writes Heinroth, "that lions on the loose were prowling around the nearby Kaiser Wilhelm Memorial Church, but in fact they lay charred and suffocated in their cages." Next day the ornamental three-story aquarium building and the thirty-meter crocodile hall were also destroyed, along with the artificial jungle. The great reptiles, writhing in pain, writes Heck, now lay beneath chunks of concrete, earth, broken glass, fallen palms and tree trunks, in water a foot deep, or crawled down the visitors' staircase, while the firelight of the dying city of Berlin shone red through a gate knocked off its hinges in the background. The elephants who had perished in the ruins of their sleeping quarters had to be cut up where they lay over the next few days, and Heck describes men crawling around inside the rib cages of the huge pachyderms and burrowing through mountains of entrails. (Sebald, *On the Natural History*, 91–92)

112. "'Sir,' said an older gentleman who was a commercial travel for Undertakers' Hardware (iron tombstone lettering), with whom I spent some time in Oklahoma, 'as far as I'm concerned, everyone can believe what he likes, if I discover that the client doesn't go to church, then I wouldn't trust him to pay me fifty cents: Why pay me, if he doesn't believe in anything?'" (Weber, "Churches," 205).

113.

I personally first fully became aware of this one cold October Sunday, in the foothills of the Blue Ridge Mountains of North Carolina, as I witnessed a service of Believers' Baptism. About ten persons, both men and women, fully dressed, stepped one after another into the icy water of the mountain stream, where the reverend, all in black, was standing up to his waist in water. After a lengthy expression of commitment, they bent their knees, leaning back on his arm until their faces were submerged in the water, and reemerged sputtering and shivering, whereupon they were congratulated by the farmers, crowds of whom had turned up on horseback or in wagons, and were speedily driven home—although some of them lived several hours' journey away. It was faith that preserved them from catching cold, they said. I had been taken there

from his farm by one of my cousins, who watched the process while disre-
spectfully spitting over his shoulder (in keeping with his German origins, he
had no church affiliation!). (ibid., 207)

114. "Even today it's perfectly normal for a land speculator, wishing to see his
sites occupied, to build a 'church,' that is, a wooden shed with a tower, looking for all the world like something out of a box of toys, and to employ a young
graduate just out of seminary run by some denomination or other for $500 as its
pastor. He will come to an agreement, spoken or unspoken, that his position will
be a life-long post provided only he can soon succeed in 'preaching the building
sites full.' And usually he does succeed" (ibid., 204–5).

115. I sent money to Debbie every month for the mortgage and Tyree's
school. Now it's the storage company that waits for my checks. I haven't been
good at preserving my relationships. Once I left Alabama and hit the road,
relationships were streamlined. I was built for speed. But my things from the
Big House wait half-asleep curled up on the concrete floor of the storage shed
for me to come and get them. I won't give them up. The thought that I'll have
a farm again or a cabin in the woods tantalizes me. It isn't unreachable. Even in
Buffalo the woods aren't far away. So why should I get rid of my tools? I'll need
the grubbing mattock to dig up the stump where the tomatoes will go. The iron
tamping bar would give me leverage on the stump's roots. The tangle of thorns
around it would require my bush ax. But these images don't wait for me in the
future as much as they are behind me and will never catch up. They are part of a
younger Allen world where Patrik was still alive and my muscles were still green.
My shoulder aches even as I write this. I'm old. But if I don't move to the woods I
don't have enough closet space in my apartment. My suits would fit nicely in the
pine wardrobe, but could I get it up the narrow stairs? I want to see my girlfriend
on the red velvet loveseat. She has reddish hair. I've priced a moving truck and
storage. I could put one of the big tables in my school office. A rocking chair
would have to be upholstered, but the living-room set would be complete again.
Where would I put the massive dresser my mother gave me that was a great-
aunt's? It was the only piece that made it out of a former dispersal to me. The
pineapple-topped four-post bed I slept on until I left my mother's home and was
eventually Tyree's is irreplaceable, but where would I set it up again? The dog,
Red Cloud, slept on this bed. The workmanship is beautiful. Tyree has no sentimentality around it. I don't have the room for a museum despite its retail value.
With its existence, even stacked against the wall in the shed, there is the hope that
my childhood with my mother and her kin will come back from the dead. It's the
things that will pull the dead back across the threshold. An angel will visit. A Joan
of Arc will be called out of these things in storage and the world will be restored.
More likely it would be Attila the Hun, the scourge of God, who would come and

this empire of memory would vanish back into the woods and fields. It was Pearl who told me stories about Attila. I loved them then and, despite their prophecy, love them now.

It's futile. I'm not strong enough to lift the cast-iron woodstove up two flights of stairs by myself. My restoration fantasies are what the California writer Joan Didion describes as magical thinking. She couldn't empty her dead husband's closet because what would he wear when he came back? She doesn't mention what happened to the table he dropped dead on during supper. It was probably magnificent. Didion makes a good point. The empire of things isn't set in the past, the present, or the future but in all of these simultaneously and in one's own desire to be a certain person. A potlatch, where I can give everything away, won't dispel this desire and grief. The objects lie there like a slothful Greek chorus mumbling barely audible liturgies to me. It's depressing how complacent the things have gotten in storage. They scarcely do any work. They've gotten lazy. My memories are evaporating while they are getting fat with dust. My memories are too heavy for them to carry. It's the complete collapse of the Protestant work ethic.

116. Three years later and I had the spade I had been looking for. It had come home. I was very close on that day. Like the seven-foot coffin, the spade is one more piece of hard evidence that can't be denied. The story of its return verifies my story. My ex-wife called my cousin Joseph. A black walnut tree was down by the creek. Did he want the wood? He did. In the adjoining pasture, the renter kept a burro that Joseph would feed carrots to. The animal was braying in a small overgrown lot nearby. It had gotten tangled in some wire. Joseph freed the animal. Off to the edges, half buried in the mud and leaves, he saw the thick handle of an English spade. He dug it up. The handle was rotten and the blade encrusted with rust. It was certainly mine. "You must've left it here by accident." I hadn't. Someone else had. I had always assumed the spade had been stolen along with others of my tools and sold at the flea market on Sand Mountain. But here it was evidence of some other crime. Joseph mailed what was left of the tool to me in Buffalo. The apostle Thomas believed first in the wound, then in the risen Christ. This hard fact is just one of the wounds that can be verified around Patrik's return.

117. In the blizzard of 1993 eighteen inches of snow fell. The temperature dropped below 10 degrees at night. The power was knocked out. The water pipes in the Big House froze. But that didn't matter. The county water lines had frozen at multiple points. The Jotul had been disconnected. The house was hooked up to central air and heat. Without power, the house froze solid. I let the dogs in to stay warm. My parents' house was a quarter-mile away. They had a big fireplace in the kitchen. Debbie was afraid of the snow. She couldn't push through the drifts. I first carried Tyree in my arms to my mother's house. I came back and

carried Debbie on my back. At night I stayed in the Big House with the dogs. I
ate the leftover Chinese food in the refrigerator. No traffic was moving over the
mountain. Everything was still. I know Tyree doesn't remember me carrying him
through the snow. It's very likely Debbie has forgotten. She was already in a different memory world in which my part was shrinking down to a monthly check. I
remember the weight of her on my back and how difficult it was to push through
the snow even over my footprints left from ferrying Tyree. I've lost her weight.
Tyree has grown up. I think Patrick's dead weight became a substitute for this lost
world, something to balance its loss. But over the years even he wasn't enough to
carry.

I heard a story about the same storm from a fellow Alabamian who has left
the South. The teller drove the next day from Birmingham to Atlanta on Interstate 20. The sun was shining. Only a few cars were on the road. I'm still confused
as to how the trip was possible. Interstate 20 is only twelve miles south of the
Big House. Here the road had eighteen inches of snow on top of it. How it was
plowed I can't imagine. The county had no snowplows or salt. What strikes me is
the movement. In her story there is lightness; the landscape is lonely and beautiful. It's edged with poetry. My world was frozen, heavy, and absent of poetry.
At my desk in the Big House, with the inside temperature just below freezing, I
wrote this desperate job application:

> I'm writing this bundled up in as many layers as I can wear and still move.
> I'm wrapped up in the wool blanket, wearing the only gloves I own—a pair
> of brown gardening gloves with a finger missing. My dog chewed the finger
> off. It's probably twenty-five degrees inside. Outside, the greatest storm of the
> century is knocking my house for a loop. The weatherman on the battery-
> operated radio makes me feel almost privileged to be here, shivering in the
> dark, without power. "This is the storm of the century," he hums, like the
> wind shredding the tin on my barn roof. The worst of it is I'm bored to death.
> There's only so much sleep and staring into space that I can take before I crave
> watching TV. I feel like a stroke victim—cold and numb. The wind is gusting
> up to fifty miles an hour. I can feel it. I live in a house built in 1834. It has its
> own respiratory system. I can see the curtains wheezing. My dogs have taken
> over the kitchen. My wife and son have taken over the big bed. That leaves
> me with either a wicker-backed sofa or where I'm stuck now, at my desk. This
> was desperation. Reading was impossible. I couldn't turn the pages with my
> gloves on. I read too fast to take the gloves on and off and those slow, medita-
> tive books I've been putting off reading—I'm putting off reading. I think they
> make me colder. So why did I listen to my wife and unhook the woodstove?
> It made sense at the time. I could move in some more books. We hadn't used
> it in years. Now it's the storm of the century and I'm freezing. So I'm writing.
> My toes are cold. I look like a character in *A Christmas Carol*. Amazingly, the

ink isn't freezing in my fountain pen. It must be cold in the North Carolina mountains. Do you have a branch campus in Florida? Unless it's the Keys, it might be cold there though. I just remembered the weatherman with his right arm sending arrows streaking through Florida before the cable went out. My house is set off in the country. The nearest house is a half mile away and I'm related to them. The nearest hamburger is seven miles over the mountain. The nearest house right now with running water and power is twenty-six miles down the road, but that changes by the hour. The closest may be in Florida by now. (Shelton, "Job Application")

This job application might as well of have been my last love letter to this world and my first to the place where I am still going. I didn't get the job.

118. Herodotus, who first recorded the existence of the land behind the North Wind in his *Histories*, stumbled upon another secret. In Egypt the priests reported to him that the famous beauty Helen of Troy was never in Troy. She had been in Egypt the entire time. For Herodotus, who apparently doesn't doubt the veracity of Homer's account but rather the Trojans' myopic position on the return of Helen, this clarifies everything. How could they, even with all the slaughter and the prophecies of their own fall, give back what wasn't there:

> The Egyptians' priests [told me that Helen stayed in Egypt throughout the war], and I myself believe their story. I reasoned thus: if Helen had actually been in Troy, then the Trojans would have certainly given her back to the Greeks, whether Paris agreed to it or not. For neither Priam nor his kinsman could have been so insane as to risk their own lives and their children and their whole civility merely so that Paris could live with Helen. Even in the first years of the war, they would have realized this and returned her. After all, many Trojans were killed in every battle with the Greeks, and Priam himself was losing two or three or even more of his sons in every battle, if the poets are to be believed. And if Priam himself had been married to Helen, I think that he would have returned her to the Greeks in order to put an end to these calamities. Paris was not even heir to the throne; if he had been, things might have been in his hands, since Priam was old. But Hector, who was his elder brother and a far better man, was first in line and heir to the kingdom on Priam's death. And it couldn't have been in his interest to support his brother's wrongdoing, especially when it brought such calamities on himself and the rest of the Trojans. So it's clear that Helen could have been in Troy and therefore they couldn't give her back, and this is what they told the Greeks, but the Greeks wouldn't believe them. (Herodotus, quoted in Mitchell, introduction, xxv–xxvi)

This ended the matter for Herodotus. He never attempted to find the ruins of the city or the Greek encampment, though he does record several other instances of the city. The Persian king sacrificed offerings on the hill overlooking the former city before embarking on his expedition to conquer Greece. If he had tried to find the ruins of the city, he would have discovered that it was already too far underground to recover and that Homer's epic city existed now as a story traveling endlessly through the Mediterranean like Odysseus trying to come home. The city wouldn't reappear till 1873, when the German Heinrich Schliemann brought it back to the surface. In this history Troy wasn't just sacked; it sank into the mud. But after years of retelling his account, even Odysseus, who unlocked the city with his wooden horse, needed Troy to be as visible as his own journeys were heroic. And he was right. His own person as an old man was evidence of the ruins of the city slipping underground. Sunk into his grave, he was even more like Troy. Troy continued to exist for centuries as an underground city with Odysseus forever tethered to it.

119. Patrik had picked the suitcase up at a Goodwill store, but it was amazing how quickly the hard surfaces mimicked him. They took on the same color of all his belongings—a washed-out brown with black straps that looked disturbingly like they had been dyed with an elderly vaccine. Patrik lived under the sign of decay, and all of his work carried the same ruined surface and prophecy. The important relic for Patrik was the true cross riddled with worm tunnels, alternately spongy and crumbling, lying in the back of a cathedral in a dusty room that smelled of rat droppings. I've lived with the suitcase for longer than Patrik did.

120. If the inside of Patrik's coffin had been painted, the lid would be colored like the night sky but without stars. The sides would be painted two different atmospheres based on his body's horizons. Below, it would be the color of a dark sea with hints of gray, whitecaps, and a black shiny body sliding beneath the surface. Above the body line, the sky seems to open up. Or is it shutting down like a window? In another version, the inside looks like a steamer trunk's exterior with postcards, insignias, and placards posted across every square inch. On closer examination, each image was made by Patrik before he left. His coffin's interior now has the same claustrophobic feel as his life. If he had a choice, Patrik would choose nothing but the grain of the wood, so much like the sea itself, to travel in as a dead man.

121. After the miracle of the loaves and fishes Jesus sent the disciples on ahead. They would meet at the other side of the Sea of Galilee. They embarked on a fishing boat. Several had been fishermen before following Jesus. A storm came up. The waves were rolling. During the fourth watch of the night Jesus came walking toward them on the surface of the water. Those who saw him thought he was a ghost: on whether the ghost of Jesus or someone else, the Scriptures are silent. Peter called out, "If it is you, Lord, call me." He gestured for Peter to meet him on the water. Peter climbed out of the boat and onto the dark water. Peter's faith held him for a moment before he wavered and he began to sink underneath

the waves. Jesus reached for his hand and steadied him (Matthew 14:22–33). In the gospel account there are no obvious sea monsters. There is no indication that the boat's mast and the cross Jesus would be crucified on may have been made from the same kind of wood. This was the monster beneath the waves. Both Jesus and Peter were to be crucified: Jesus on a hill and Peter upside down. At the last moments before Simon Peter's death, would the dizziness and vertigo from hanging upside down and looking up at the sky recall for him the rolling of the waves and the same dark sky that he saw sinking beneath the water as he was drowning on dry land?

122. Marx never got this far in his recorded writing. The threat of seeing his dead son may have been too much for him. Marx might have found the connection between his childhood home and the world of the dead to be the animating force inside his famous coat that opens *Capital*. The weave of that coat betrays a network of fibers beyond linen or wool. The world in which Marx details how value infiltrates the commodity is the world behind the North Wind. Here the dead and memory wrap around each other like honeysuckle vines.

123.

> To articulate the past historically does not mean to recognize it "the way it really was" (Ranke). It means to seize hold of a memory as it flashes up at a moment of danger. Historical materialism wishes to retain that image of the past which unexpectedly appears to a man singled out by history at a moment of danger. The danger affects both the content of the tradition and its receivers. The same threat hangs over both: that of becoming a tool of the ruling classes. In every era the attempt must be made anew to wrest tradition away from a conformism that is about to overpower it. The Messiah comes not only as the redeemer, he comes as the subduer of the Antichrist. Only that historian will have the gift of fanning the spark of hope in the past who is firmly convinced that *even the dead* will not be safe from the enemy if he wins. And this enemy has not ceased to be victorious. (Benjamin, "Theses," 255)

124. The suitcase in the story of Benjamin's last days has a buoyancy. It floats. At one moment it is extraordinarily heavy. Benjamin is a Hercules lugging it up the mountains. "It is the most important thing," he repeats. Then miraculously it is a small briefcase holding a sheaf of papers. And Benjamin is as heavy as lead, a grossly out-of-shape teddy bear lost in the woods. There is definitely weight here. It is as if the commentators were looking for the solid blocks that dragged Benjamin down. On the trek over the mountains he was on all fours, lapping water out of a puddle like a dog. Benjamin was already folding up. The weight of the suitcase was already there in the small tragedies that marked his life. That his suicide took so long is the perplexing issue, though the moment and the place he chose were perfect: just as he was emerging onto the shoreline, in sight of the sea, and

an inn jammed with Stalin's and Hitler's agents. After the long wait in Marseille, the delay at the crossing seems out of proportion. And his death was likewise out of proportion. He took enough morphine to kill a team of horses or the whole party that he crossed with, or more probably, the angel receding inside him. I can't see Patrik's death as perfect, only expected and devastating. With Benjamin I have the luxury. He's just a character in the book. Patrik was my friend.

125. One possible explanation for Walter Benjamin's famous suicide at the Spanish border is hinted at in this passage from "Theses on the Philosophy of History," which seems to be the last bit of writing he produced before his end. Benjamin worried about the disastrous effects of the fascist victory in the netherworlds. The evidence he had seemed to indicate they were already there and destroying that world. His famous Angel of History is being blown into the future by the storm unleashed by Stuka dive bombers and Panzer tanks. It's a small blessing of God the fascists didn't have heavy bombers. But would Benjamin have seen the end of Dresden and other German cities under the firestorms created by the British and American bombers as any different? And what the Soviet Army lacked in the air it made up for in face-to-face brutality and mechanical engineering. At the end of the war, nine thousand German civilians fleeing the advancing Russians on a passenger liner were sent to the bottom of the North Sea by a Russian torpedo. The storm blows into the netherworlds as well. The dead could be extinguished. The crowds behind the North Wind would vanish.

126. One of the most important moments in the German sociologist Max Weber's career happened twenty-five years after his death when his wife, first cousin, and biographer Marianne destroyed the history of his nervous breakdown. Max had worked relentlessly on the document until his death in 1920. Only Marianne had read the draft. Its erasure covered over a possible future in which Weber wrote the first great autoethnography in sociology. Instead she eased Max's account back underground as the American army was approaching at the end of World War II. She was afraid the Nazis would use the manuscript to discredit his work. Another explanation is that Max's coverage of his illness competed with her own history, in which she appears in the third person like an omnipotent angel. What did come from Max's breakdown was the 1905 essay "The Protestant Ethic and the Spirit of Capitalism." In 1919 he revised the essay into a book. This time the footnotes were longer than the original text, mimicking the nervous conditions that inspired the book. It was Harvard professor Talcott Parsons's translation of this version that solidified Weber's reputation in the United States and established him as a founding father of sociology. With Marianne's blessing Parsons replaces Weber's own imagery in the famous phrase titling this essay. He changes "steel casing" to "iron cage," invoking the Puritan John Bunyan's "man in the iron cage," an account about an imprisoned professor eerily like Weber himself (*Pilgrim's Progress*, 34). It's a brilliant substitution that draws Weber away

from comparisons to his contemporary Franz Kafka, whose Gregor suffered his own nervous breakdown encased in an exoskeleton. Once more pieces are added to Weber's cloak—a clinging wool coat, alligator shoes, a goddess's corset, a pair of red spectacles—the casing hardens up. The cloak becomes heavier and indistinguishable from the person. It proliferates into a network of commodities anchored deep inside the person, forming a new Achilles. Weber might have seen this in his destroyed manuscript (only Marianne knew), but Walter Benjamin, at the edge of Weber's circle, saw something similar: a nervous post-Protestant ethic emerging in modern capitalism. In his unfinished *Arcades Project* Benjamin found a prefiguration of the steel casing in the iron and glass structures that formed the nineteenth-century Paris arcades into modernist ruins. The arcades were breeding swamps for rust, commodity fetishization, and encased identities. Benjamin worked on this history until his suicide on the Spanish border, scuttling like a beetle from the Nazis, lugging a heavy suitcase. There, in a small bedroom by the Mediterranean, he pulled the steel casing off himself like a child's blanket as the morphine tablets melted in his stomach. At the end, he was mouthing a secret history of Paris that he told only his lost lover Asja. Goodnight map of Manhattan, goodnight x-ray, goodnight pipe, goodnight glasses, goodnight watch. According to the Spanish authorities, this was all that remained of Benjamin's project—no manuscript, only mnemonic devices that couldn't be turned on, as if they were solid iron.

127. When Tyree was a kid I wore on my blue jean jacket a fifty-year service medal Pearl had received from the Methodist church. Tyree got it in his head that he wanted to wear it on his jacket. I hesitated. Pearl was gone. This was one of the things that I had fixed to her ghost to hold her floating in my world. But I was touched by Tyree's want. Be careful with it, I told him. I pinned it on his jacket. Now we matched. We breezed through the natural history museum. I was very proud. We had a script we followed on our visits. There was a certain speed to our movement. Tyree would point out his favorite animals and say their names. He was four years old. At the end of the circuit were two Egyptian mummies reclining on two pedestals. Tyree would say "Mummy, mummy" like he was calling his mother in the middle of the night to get up. At home he would say, "Daddy, Daddy I want a glass of water." It was my job to get up. I was the easy touch. Debbie kept sleeping. The final exhibit was a stuffed coyote quizzically staring like Hamlet at a skull with the caption "To be or not to be. That is the question." The skull was from an unidentified grave. It was labeled simply Native American. A plaque showed a comparison between the arrival and success of the coyote in the Southeast and the decline and removal—extinction was avoided—of the Native American population from the same area. This exhibit is gone now, though the same diabolical intelligence still lingers in the other exhibits. They lack the theater. But how could they not? The animals were from the collection of a local

businessman who had donated them. Many of them he had killed on his expeditions around the world. Africa was a favorite destination. In the lobby I realized the medal was missing from Tyree's jacket. It was probably my fault. I hadn't pinned it properly. We retraced our steps through the museum three times. It was a tiny gold thing. There were no other visitors who could've found it. We were alone. I was devastated. It was as if my kite string had been cut and now Pearl was disappearing. When we got home Tyree went to his room. He came out with a piece of paper on which he had drawn the lost medal. "Here it is, Daddy." There it was. I cried. He had written "I love you daddy" in animal-like shapes at the bottom. I preferred the loss of the medal to having it. I considered the medal an offering to all those lost in the museum. The slip of paper was so light. It fit easily between the pages of the book.

128. Patrik is never naked in his work. Here Jesus almost is. A slender cloth is draped across his loins. Once again, there is that curious modesty. But the form of faciality in his work would be the erect penis. These were never his except as an imagined body or as an object of desire. They looked like moray eels pinned back and wrapped with leather bands and buckles on display in a laboratory. Their muscularity seems exhausted, as if it is air that filled them and not blood. They resemble withering fruit trees ruthlessly espaliered against a wall on an imaginary grid. Foucault in *Discipline and Punish* reprints an etching of a tree tied to a stake as an example of the panoptic discipline (illus. 10). The dick and Patrik are both pinned to an invisible stake. The viewer can see only the bands and buckles binding them and imagine the feel of the electrical shock treatment that screwed Patrik to the stake coursing through his work. No cross is visible.

129. This story is told in Jonathan Spence's *The Memory Palace of Matteo Ricci*.

130. In 1929, the same year as the great stock market crash, Sigmund Freud published a small book called *Civilization and Its Discontents* about the psychic structure of civilization. Freud's patient is civilization itself. We are unhappy, Freud writes, because civilization makes too many demands on the body's desires. It was an unhappy time. Patrik was unhappy. He was one of civilization's discontents with his Protestant obsession with belts and buckles and erections and his devotion to discipline. Freud opens the book mulling over a letter from an unnamed friend who has taken issue with one of Freud's arguments in another book, *The Future of an Illusion*. The correspondent describes the feeling of eternity, a boundless, oceanic sense of oneness that he saw as the source of religious feelings. Freud can find no such feelings in his own person, but he does trace his friend's oceanic sensations back to their source. There in his distant memory is a white breast bubbling over with milk like a spring coming to life and his friend's mouth fixed to the nipple. It is a wet memory palace flooded with milk and saliva. There is no possible archaeology beyond the soft tissue of the lips and the nipple. For Freud all that remains of the breast is this oceanic sensation. It's from a time

before the articulation of the self; the self is still undifferentiated. His friend as an infant is unable to distinguish his mouth from the nipple or himself from his mother. It's a warm ocean, and the memory of that sea lurks behind his letter like a land behind the North Wind. It's an unstoppable projection by Freud. How could there be memories even before there is a subject to remember them? The world in the saliva is as differentiated as the oceans are. It's just a question of scale. Freud won't see the mouth inside the mouth inside the mouth and the subtle variations in temperature around the nipple. The infrathin world of flesh and its adhesions are a swamp like the one Patrik emerged in. Freud doesn't trace the memory back as if it were a creek winding through the woods. He projects himself back to the supposed source of the memory: a haunting milky breast like a ripe white seed. Freud's picture of a white breast emerging out of a fog of memory has a certain Man Ray–like quality. Isolated from the body's entirety, the breast could be a ripe round seed. It's no longer entirely human in this memory gallery of breast images. How many images of breasts did Freud shuffle through, from his own wife's to Titian portraits, to arrive at the Madonna-like breast at the beginning of the self? If Freud had stopped at another breast in his friend's or his own history, the so-called oceanic sensation would have been completely recon-figured with a vertigo coming from the rolling waves of the sea caressing a siren's breast that lured Odysseus. The breast is a kind of sea monster, a more solid jellyfish on the surface of the body. Not much deeper in the book Freud comes at how this distant memory is possible. It's one of his most powerful similes. It's a dry world and an alien environment for the living breast. It's a whirlpool made of marble sucking everything into its world.

> Now let us, by a flight of imagination, suppose that Rome is not human habitation but a psychical entity with a similarly long and copious past—an entity, that is to say, in which nothing that has once come into existence will have passed away and all the earlier phases of development continue to exist alongside the latest one. This would mean that in Rome the palaces of the Caesars and the Septizonium of Septimius Severus would still be rising to their old height on the Palatine and that the castle of S. Angelo would still be carrying on its battlements the beautiful statues which graced it until the siege by the Goths, and so on. But more than this. And the place occupied by the Palazzo would once more stand—without the Palazzo having to be removed—the Temple of Jupiter Capitolinus; and this not only in its latest shape, as the Romans of the Empire saw it, but also in its earliest one, when it still showed Etruscan forms and was ornamented with terra-cotta antefixes. (Freud, *Civili-zation*, 18)

Freud's marble city is a set of sets trapped inside the walls of Rome. At the center unmentioned is Michelangelo's *Pietà*. The Madonna's breasts are smooth and cold. The dead Jesus is sprawled across her lap. Patrik has slipped inside the monument. He is shorn of his discontents. His belts and buckles have fallen to the side. He lies in the Madonna's arms like a shrunken erection. She is upright. She appears much younger than Patrik, as if they were headed in different directions. The Madonna no longer ages. Patrik is headed toward a kind of extinction. His final exit wasn't into a city but into deep water. The Madonna's lap was the entrance. In the water he abandoned even his coffin and slipped back into the rolling waves. The whitecaps are like frothing milk. The world Patrik wanders in I call Alabama. It resembles Alabama in every aspect except that the underworld isn't Baptist or Mississippian. It's the North Sea through which Alabama is connected to all the oceans of the underworld and northern Europe. This isn't a preference for one worldview or another. It is the one that envelops me.

REFERENCES

Adam's Rib. Directed by George Cukor. DVD. Burbank, CA: Warner Home
Video, 2000 (1949).

"Allen Shelton." *Wikipedia*. Accessed April 4, 2012. http://en.wikipedia.org/
wiki/Allen_Shelton.

The Arabian Nights. Translated by Andrew Lang. London: Longmans, Green,
1898.

As the World Turns: Classic Episodes. DVD. New York: CBS, 2011 (April 2,
1956–September 17, 2010).

Atget, Eugène. *Atget's Paris*. Cologne, Germany: Taschen, 2008.

Augé, Marc. *In the Metro*. Translated by Tom Connolly. Minneapolis: University
of Minnesota Press, 2002.

———. *Non-Places: An Introduction to Supermodernity*. Translated by John
Howe. London: Verso, 1995.

———. *Oblivion*. Translated by Marjolijn de Jager. Minneapolis: University of
Minnesota Press, 2004.

Bach, Johann Sebastian. *Morimur*. Performed by Hillard Ensemble and Christoph
Poppen. CD. ECM, 2001.

The Bar-B-Q Killers. *1980s Athens Band Bar-B-Q Killers at the Celebrity Club*.
YouTube. Live performance video by Mister Richardson. Accessed March 26,
2012. http://www.youtube.com/watch?v=MLRj5B86yzg.

Bataille, Georges. *The College of Sociology, 1937–39*. Translated by Betsy
Wing. Edited by Denis Hollier. Minneapolis: University of Minnesota Press,
1988.

Baudrillard, Jean. "Simulacra and Simulations." In *Jean Baudrillard: Selected Writ-*

ings, translated and edited by Mark Poster, 166–84. Stanford, CA: Stanford University Press, 1998.

Becker, Howard S. *Outsiders: Studies in the Sociology of Deviance*. New York: Free Press, 1997.

Benjamin, Walter. *The Arcades Project*. Edited and translated by Howard Eiland and Kevin McLaughlin. Cambridge, MA: Belknap Press of Harvard University Press, 1999.

———. *Berlin Childhood around 1900*. Translated by Howard Eiland. Cambridge, MA: Harvard University Press, 2006.

———. "A Berlin Chronicle." Translated by Edmund Jephcott. In *Selected Writings*, 2:595–637.

———. *German Men and Women: A Sequence of Letters*. Translated by Edmund Jephcott. In *Selected Writings*, 3:167–235.

———. *Illuminations: Essays and Reflections*. Translated by Harry Zohn. Edited by Hannah Arendt. New York: Schocken, 1968.

———. "The Lisbon Earthquake." Translated by Edmund Jephcott. In *Selected Writings*, 2:536–40.

———. "Manorially Furnished Ten-Room Apartment." Translated by Edmund Jephcott. In *Selected Writings*, 1:446–47.

———. "News of a Death." In *Berlin Childhood*, 85–86.

———. *One-Way Street*. Translated by Edmund Jephcott. In *Selected Writings*, 1:444–88.

———. *Selected Writings*, vol. 1, *1913–1926*. Edited by Marcus Bullock and Michael W. Jennings. Cambridge, MA: Belknap Press of Harvard University Press, 2004.

———. *Selected Writings*, vol. 2, *1927–1934*. Edited by Howard Eiland and Gary Smith. Cambridge, MA: Belknap Press of Harvard University Press, 2005.

———. *Selected Writings*, vol. 3, *1935–1938*. Edited by Howard Eiland and Michael W. Jennings. Cambridge, MA: Belknap Press of Harvard University Press, 2006.

———. *Selected Writings*, vol. 4, *1938–1940*. Edited by Howard Eiland and Michael W. Jennings. Cambridge, MA: Belknap Press of Harvard University Press, 2006.

———. "Some Reflections on Kafka." In *Illuminations*, 141–45.

———. "Theses on the Philosophy of History." In *Illuminations*, 253–64.

———. "Victory Column." In *Berlin Childhood*, 44–48.

———. *Walter Benjamin's Archive: Images, Texts, Signs*. Translated by Esther Leslie. Edited by Ursula Marx, Gudrun Schwartz, Michael Schwartz, and Erdmut Wizisla. London: Verso, 2007.

Beradt, Charlotte, and Bruno Bettelheim. *The Third Reich of Dreams: The Night-*

mares of a Nation, 1933–1939. Translated by Adriane Gottwald. Chicago: University of Chicago Press, 1968.

Beuys, Joseph. Art of the 20th Century: Joseph Beuys. Accessed April 4, 2012. http://www.all-art.org/art_20th_century/beuys1.html.

Bierce, Ambrose. "An Occurrence at Owl Creek Bridge." In *The Complete Short Stories of Ambrose Bierce*, edited by Ernest Jerome Hopkins, 305–11. Lincoln: University of Nebraska Press, 1970.

Blanton, Anderson. *Until the Stones Cry Out*. Chapel Hill: University of North Carolina Press, forthcoming.

Blue Velvet. Directed by David Lynch. DVD. Los Angeles: MGM, 2002 (1986).

Borges, Jorge Luis. "Funes, the Memorious." In *Ficciones*, translated by Anthony Bonner, edited by Anthony Kerrigan, 107–16. New York: Grove, 1962.

———. "Partial Enchantments of the Quixote." In *Other Inquisitions: 1937–1952*, translated by Ruth Simms, 43–46. Austin: University of Texas Press, 1984.

Braudel, Fernand. *The Wheels of Commerce*. Translated by Sian Reynolds. Berkeley: University of California Press, 1982.

Breton, André. *Nadja*. Translated by Richard Howard. New York: Grove, 1960.

Buck-Morss, Susan. *The Dialectics of Seeing: Walter Benjamin and the Arcades Project*. Cambridge, MA: MIT Press, 1989.

Bunyan, John. *The Pilgrim's Progress*. Boston: Houghton Mifflin, 1896.

Calvino, Italo. *The Castle of Crossed Destinies*. Translated by William Weaver. New York: Harvest/HBJ Books, 1976.

Canetti, Elias. *Crowds and Power*. Translated by Carol Stewart. New York: Farrar, Straus and Giroux, 1962.

Casablanca. Directed by Michael Curtiz. DVD. Burbank, CA: Warner Home Video, 2010 (1942).

Cornell, Joseph. *Joseph Cornell: Navigating the Imagination*. With an essay by Lynda Roscoe Hartigan. New Haven, CT: Yale University Press, 2007.

Coronado, Francisco Vázquez de. *The Journey of Coronado*. Translated by George Parker Winship. Amazon Digital Services, 2011.

Crapanzano, Vincent. *Tuhami*. Chicago: University of Chicago Press, 1980.

Dante Alighieri. *The Divine Comedy 1: Inferno, Part 1, Text*. Translated by Charles S. Singleton. Bollingen Series. Princeton, NJ: Princeton University Press, 1990.

Darwin, Charles. *On the Origin of Species*. New York: Penguin Classics, 1985.

Deleuze, Gilles, and Felix Guattari. *A Thousand Plateaus: Capitalism and Schizophrenia*. Translated by Brian Massumi. Minneapolis: University of Minnesota Press, 1987.

Dickens, Charles. *A Christmas Carol: A Facsimile of the Manuscript in the Pierpoint Morgan Library*. New York: Dover, 1971.

Didion, Joan. *The Year of Magical Thinking*. New York: Vintage International, 2005.

Duchamp, Marcel. *Étant donnés*. Edited by Michael R. Taylor. New Haven, CT: Yale University Press, 2009.

Durkheim, Emile. *The Elementary Forms of the Religious Life*. Translated by Karen Fields. New York: Free Press, 1995.

"*Dynastinae*" [rhinoceros beetle]. *Wikipedia*. Accessed April 4, 2012. http://en.wikipedia.org/wiki/Dynastinae.

Eno, Brian. *Before and after Science*. LP. Island, 1978.

———. *Discreet Music*. LP. Obscure, 1975.

Euripides. *The Trojan Women*, translated by Richmond Lattimore. In *Euripides III*, vol. 2 of *Greek Tragedies*, edited by David Grene and Richmond Lattimore, 243–95. Chicago: University of Chicago Press, 1960.

Faust, Drew. *The Republic of Suffering*. New York: Alfred A. Knopf, 2008.

Foucault, Michel. *Discipline and Punish*. Translated by Alan Sheridan. New York: Vintage Books, 1979.

Frazer, James. *The Golden Bough*. Abridged ed. New York: Macmillan, 1951.

Freud, Sigmund. *Civilization and Its Discontents*. Translated by James Strachey. New York: W. W. Norton, 1961.

———. *The Future of an Illusion*. Translated by James Strachey. New York: W. W. Norton, 1962.

———. *The Psychopathology of Everyday Life*. Translated by Anthea Bell. New York: Penguin, 2002.

———. "The Uncanny." In *The Uncanny*, translated by David McLintock, 121–59. New York: Penguin, 2003.

Gibran, Kahlil. *The Prophet*. New York: Alfred A. Knopf, 1923.

Gogol, Nikolai. "The Overcoat." In *Diary of a Madman, The Government Inspector, and Selected Stories*, translated by Ronald Wilks, 140–73. New York: Penguin, 1972.

Grant, Ulysses S. *Personal Memoirs*. New York: Penguin, 1999.

Grimm, Jacob, and Wilhelm Grimm. *Grimm's Fairy Tales*. Illustrated by Arthur Rackham. London: William Heinemann, 1925.

Haraway, Donna. *When Species Meet*. Minneapolis: University of Minnesota Press, 2008.

H.D. *Tribute to Freud*, vol. 4. New York: New Directions Books, 1956.

Herodotus. *The Histories*. Translated by Andrea Purvis. Edited by Robert Strassler. New York: Pantheon, 2007.

Hoffmann, E. T. A. "The Sandman." In *Tales of E. T. A. Hoffmann*, edited and translated by Leonard J. Kent and Elizabeth C. Knight, 93–125. Chicago: University of Chicago Press, 1969.

Holldobler, Bert, and E. O. Wilson. *The Superorganism: The Beauty, Elegance, and Strangeness of Insect Societies*. New York: W. W. Norton, 2009.

Homer. *The Iliad*. Translated by Stephen Mitchell. New York: Free Press, 2012.

———. *The Odyssey*. Translated by Samuel Butler. Calyton, DE: Prestwick House, 2006.

House, Son. "Death Letter Blues." *Father of the Delta Blues: The Complete 1965 Sessions*. CD. Sony, 1992.

Jøtul. "Experience the spirit of Jøtul." Accessed March 23, 2012. http://www.jotul.com/en-US/wwwjotulus/.

Journey to the Center of the Earth. Directed by Henry Levin. Film. Los Angeles: Twentieth Century Fox, 1960.

Jowett, John Henry. *The Whole Armor of God*. N.p.: Nabu, 2010.

Joyce, James. *Ulysses*. New York: Penguin, 2000.

Kafka, Franz. *Amerika*. Translated by Willa Muir and Edwin Muir. New York: Schocken, 1974.

———. "The Burrow." Translated by Willa Muir and Edwin Muir. In *Franz Kafka: The Complete Stories*, 339–59.

———. *The Castle*. Translated by Mark Harman. New York: Schocken, 1998.

———. *Franz Kafka: The Complete Stories*. Edited by Nahum N. Glatzer. New York: Schocken, 1946.

———. "The Hunter Gracchus: A Fragment." Translated by Tania and James Stern. In *Franz Kafka: The Complete Stories*, 231–34.

———. "The Metamorphosis." Translated by Willa Muir and Edwin Muir. In *Franz Kafka: The Complete Stories*, 89–139.

———. *The Trial: A New Translation Based on the Restored Text*. Translated by Breon Mitchell. New York: Schocken, 1999.

———. "The Wish to Be a Red Indian." Translated by Willa Muir and Edwin Muir. In *Franz Kafka: The Complete Stories*, 390.

Keim, Patrik. "Dog Eat Dog." Unpublished.

———. "Manifesto." *Art Papers* 22 (March–April 1988).

———. "Lost in a Boreal Forest." Unpublished.

King Crimson. *In the Court of the Crimson King*. LP. Atlantic, 1969.

Kracauer, Siegfried. *The Mass Ornament: Weimar Essays*. Translated by Thomas Levin. Cambridge, MA: Harvard University Press, 1995.

Kraftwerk website. Accessed April 4, 2012. http://www.kraftwerk.com.

Kröller-Müller Museum website. Accessed April 4, 2012. http://www.kmm.nl.

Kukoda, John. "Bridgestone MB1: Fat Tires Meet Drop Bars" (review of Bridgestone's MB1 bicycle). http://www.sheldonbrown.com/bridgestone/pdfs/bstoneMB11987.pdf.

Küng, Hans. *Does God Exist? An Answer for Today*. Translated by Edward Quinn. New York: Vintage, 1981.

Lattimore, Richmond. *The New Testament*. New York: North Point, 1997.

Leiris, Michel. *Manhood: A Journey from Childhood into the Fierce Order of Virility*. Translated by Richard Howard. San Francisco: North Point, 1984.

Lévi-Strauss, Claude. *Tristes tropiques*. Translated by John and Doreen Weightman. New York: Penguin, 1992.

Lewis, Jerry Lee. *Definitive Collection*. CD. Hip-O Records, 2005.

Lindbergh, Charles. *The Spirit of St. Louis*. New York: Scribner, 2003.

MacDonald, George. *At the Back of the North Wind*. Philadelphia: David McKay, 1919.

Marx, Karl. *Capital*. Translated by Ben Fowkes. New York: Vintage Books, 1977.

Mauss, Marcel. *The Gift*. Translated by W. D. Halls. New York: W. W. Norton, 1990.

McPartland, Marian. *Piano Jazz*. National Public Radio (June 4, 1978–November 10, 2011).

Melville, Herman. *Moby-Dick*. New York: Penguin, 1988.

Michelangelo. *Pietà*. Image at website of Chapel of the Pietà, St. Peter's Basilica, Rome. Accessed April 4, 2012. http://saintpetersbasilica.org/Altars/Pieta/Pieta.htm.

Mills, C. Wright. *The Sociological Imagination*. New York: Oxford University Press, 1959.

Mitchell, Stephen. Introduction to *The Iliad* by Homer, xv–lv.

Montgomery, Lucy Maude. *Anne of Green Gables*. New York: Farrar, Straus and Giroux, 1935.

Narratives of the career of Hernando de Soto in the conquest of Florida, as told by a knight of Elvas, and in a relation by Luys Hernández de Biedma, factor of the expedition. 2 vols. Translated by Buckingham Smith. Edited by Edward Gaylor Bourne. Ann Arbor: University of Michigan Library, 1922.

Naugahyde. "A Nauga Story." Naugahyde website. Accessed April 4, 2012. http://www.naugahyde.com/history.html.

Newmahr, Staci. *Playing on the Edge: Sadomasochism, Risk, and Intimacy*. Bloomington: Indiana University Press, 2011.

Nietzsche, Friedrich. *The Birth of Tragedy*. Translated by Walter Kaufmann. New York: Random House, 1967.

Osborne, Thomas. Review of Siegfried Kracauer's *The Mass Ornament*. *Times Literary Supplement*, June 14, 1996.

Park, Robert. "The City: Suggestions for the Investigation of Human Behavior in the Urban Environment." In Robert Park and Ernest W. Burgess, *The City*, 1–46. Chicago: University of Chicago Press, 1925.

Poe, Edgar Allan. "The Fall of the House of Usher." In *Selected Writings*, 138–57.

———. "The Murders in the Rue Morgue." In *Selected Writings*, 189–224.

———. "The Purloined Letter." In *Selected Writings*, 330–49.

———. *Selected Writings: Poems, Tales, Essays and Reviews*. Edited by David Galloway. New York: Penguin, 1968.

Proust, Marcel. *The Way by Swann's*. Translated by Lydia Davis. New York: Penguin, 2002.

Pylon. *Chomp*. LP. Db, 1983.

Rank. Otto. *Der Doppelgänger: Eine psychoanalytische Studie*. Vienna: Internationaler Psychoanalytischer Verlag, 1925.

Rashomon. Directed by Akira Kurosawa. DVD. New York: Criterion, 2002 (1950).

REM. *Murmur*. LP. IRS Records, 1983.

"Ripper Letters." Casebook: Jack the Ripper. Accessed March 14, 2012, http://www.casebook.org/ripper_letters.

Rulfo, Juan. *Pedro Páramo*. Translated by Margaret Peden. New York: Grove, 1994.

Schliemann, Heinrich. *Troy and Its Remains: A Narrative of Researches and Discoveries Made on the Site of Ilium, and in the Trojan Plain*. Edited by Phillip Smith. London: John Murray, 1875.

Schwitters, Kurt. "Kurt Schwitters—Ursonate." YouTube. Accessed April 4, 2012. http://www.youtube.com/watch?v=6X7E2i0KMqM&feature=related.

Sebald, W. G. *On the Natural History of Destruction*. Translated by Anthea Bell. New York: Modern Library, 2004.

———. *Vertigo*. Translated by Michael Hulse. New York: New Directions, 1999.

Shelton, Allen. "Beauty Is the Beast: The Politics of Art. A Review of the Scholarship Exhibit in the MFA Show." Unpublished manuscript.

———. "Curriculum vitae." Unpublished manuscript.

———. *Dreamworlds of Alabama*. Minneapolis: University of Minnesota Press, 2007.

———. "Job application." Unpublished manuscript.

Simmel, Georg. "The Mental Life of the Metropolis." In *On Individuality and Social Forms: Selected Writings*, edited by Donald N. Levine, 324–39. Chicago: University of Chicago Press, 1971.

Spence, Jonathan. *The Memory Palace of Matteo Ricci*. New York: Penguin, 1984.

Stach, Reiner. *Kafka: The Decisive Years*. Translated by Shelley Frisch. New York: Harcourt, 2005.

Stern, Lesley. "The Great Grid." In *Edible Estates: Attack on the Front Lawn*, edited by Fritz Haeg, 36–39. New York: Metropolis Books, 2008.

Stewart, Kathleen. *Ordinary Affect*. Durham, NC: Duke University Press, 2007.

Sullivan, John. *Pulphead*. New York: Farrar, Straus and Giroux, 2011.

Sussman, Henry. Academic biography. http://www.complit.buffalo.edu/faculty/sussman.shtml.

———. *Idylls of the Wanderer: Outside in Literature and Theory*. New York: Fordham University Press, 2007.

Talking Heads. "This Must Be the Place." *Speaking in Tongues*. LP. Warner Brothers, 1983.

Taussig, Michael. *Shamanism, Colonialism, and the Wild Man: A Study in Terror and Healing*. Chicago: University of Chicago Press, 1987.

———. *What Color Is the Sacred?* Chicago: University of Chicago Press, 2009.

Taylor, Frederick Winslow. *The Principles of Scientific Management*. N.p.: Create Space, 2011.

———. *Shop Management*. N.p.: BiblioBazaar, 2007.

Tracy, Spencer, and Katharine Hepburn. See *Adam's Rib*.

Verne, Jules. *Around the World in Eighty Days*. New York: Bantam Books, 1984.

———. *Journey to the Center of the Earth*. New York: Penguin, 1965.

Virgil. *The Aeneid*. Translated by Robert Fagles. New York: Penguin, 2006.

Weber, Marianne. *Max Weber: A Biography*. Translated and edited by Harry Zohn. New York: John Wiley and Sons, 1975.

Weber, Max. "'Churches' and 'Sects' in North America: An Ecclesiastical and Sociopolitical Sketch." In *"The Protestant Ethic" and Other Writings*, 203–20.

———. *"The Protestant Ethic" and Other Writings*. Edited and translated by Peter Baehr and Gordon C. Wells. New York: Penguin, 2002.

———. "The Protestant Ethic and the 'Spirit' of Capitalism." In *"The Protestant Ethic" and Other Writings*, 1–202.

Wheeler, William Morton. "The Ant Colony as an Organism." *Journal of Morphology* 22, no. 2 (1911): 307–25.

———. *The Social Insects: Their Origin and Evolution*. New York: Harcourt Brace, 1928.

White's Gap Baptist Church. "Equipping Our Churches for Kingdom Work." Calhoun Baptist Association website. Accessed April 4, 2012. http://cbasbc .org/churches/whitesgap.html.

Wilde, Oscar. *The Picture of Dorian Gray: Authoritative Texts, Backgrounds, Reviews and Reactions, Criticism*. Norton Critical Edition. New York: W. W. Norton, 1988.

Wilson, Edmund. *To the Finland Station*. New York: New York Review of Books, 2003.

Xenophon. *Anabasis: Seven Books*. Translated and edited by William Rainey Harper and James Wallace. New York: American Book, 1921.

Yourcenar, Marguerite. *Mishima: A Vision of the Void*. Translated by Alberto Manguel. Chicago: University of Chicago Press, 2001.

Žižek, Slavoj. 1992. *Looking Awry: An Introduction to Jacques Lacan through Popular Culture*. Cambridge, MA: MIT Press.

INDEX